"Just because I'm a good cop, doesn't mean I'm not a bad boy."

"Ohhh," Rachel moaned. "I think you're on the verge of making *me* a bad *girl*."

"Good," Mike whispered. Then he kissed her again and she forgot the rest of the world existed, though when he reached for the button on her jeans, it brought home exactly what was about to happen here. She pulled back and said, "I want to be clear, though—this doesn't mean I like you."

His answer came just as raspy. "Good—it doesn't mean I like you, either. Now shut up and kiss me."

———————

By Toni Blake

SUGAR CREEK
ONE RECKLESS SUMMER
LETTERS TO A SECRET LOVER
TEMPT ME TONIGHT
SWEPT AWAY

Coming Soon

WHISPER FALLS

TONI BLAKE

SUGAR CREEK

AVON

An Imprint of HarperCollinsPublishers

This is a work of fiction. Names, characters, places, and incidents are products of the author's imagination or are used fictitiously and are not to be construed as real. Any resemblance to actual events, locales, organizations, or persons, living or dead, is entirely coincidental.

AVON BOOKS
An Imprint of HarperCollins*Publishers*
10 East 53rd Street
New York, New York 10022-5299

Copyright © 2010 by Toni Herzog
ISBN 978-0-06-176579-7
www.avonromance.com

First Avon Books paperback printing: June 2010

Avon Trademark Reg. U.S. Pat. Off. and in Other Countries, Marca Registrada, Hecho en U.S.A.
HarperCollins® is a registered trademark of HarperCollins Publishers.

Printed in the U.S.A.

10 9 8 7 6 5 4 3 2 1

This book is dedicated, with fond memories,
to my late grandmother,
Mary Irene Hargis Blevins
(1922-1992)

Acknowledgments

My thanks go to Renee Norris, for her early brainstorming, along with her thorough critique and helpful suggestions, as well as to Lindsey Faber, for listening so patiently to all my story concerns, and for all the wonderful ways she gets the word out about my books! Also to Manda Collins, who is always on brainstorming alert! I'd be lost without you guys!

I offer my utmost appreciation to my editor, May Chen, for her very helpful story suggestions, and for always being so fun to hang out with.

Thanks also to Lindsey Bohrer and Staff Lieutenant James Hamilton of the Ohio State Highway Patrol, for answering my questions about some specific law-enforcement procedures.

And finally, a big thank-you to all the wonderful folks at Avon Books, as well as to my agents, Meg Rulcy and Christina Hogrebe, for all their ongoing support.

What's in a name? That which we call a rose
By any other name would smell as sweet.

William Shakespeare, *Romeo & Juliet*

One

Rachel Farris came speeding down the dusky two-lane highway toward Destiny just as fast as she'd left town almost fifteen years ago. Flooring it on a straight stretch, she turned up the radio, trying to let the Rolling Stones drown out her thoughts. But Mick's gravelly voice, reminding her that you can't always get what you want, had just the opposite effect.

One day life was great, near perfect, and you thought you had it all figured out—and then the next: *massive implosion*!

Well, okay, it hadn't imploded just yet, but signs of imminent collapse were everywhere lately.

It was bad enough she was headed back to her hometown of Destiny, Ohio, a place she'd never planned to return. But the timing couldn't have been worse.

Her grandma, Edna, was lonely again, thus claiming

she needed help with the fall apple harvest—and Rachel's number had come up. Fair enough. Family came first. Yet life would have been easier if this hadn't happened right when Conrad/Phelps, the small but prestigious Chicago ad firm where Rachel had worked since college, was about to downsize. And right after her boss had warned her they'd soon be eliminating one of only two account director positions, putting her career in serious jeopardy.

Given that Pamela Tremaine, the other director, had been with the company less than three years, Rachel should have felt totally confident she'd be the one to stay—if her team hadn't just lost the firm's largest account. And it didn't help that Pamela was ridiculously young, and ridiculously pleasant, and beloved by everyone who came into contact with her. So Edna's call had left Rachel feeling duty bound to take a leave of absence at a time when she could least afford it.

Yep, the potential for implosion was getting serious—a thought which made her press her Manolo Blahnik clad foot a little deeper onto the gas pedal as she took a slight curve, her BMW hugging the road. The sooner she got to Destiny, after all, the sooner she could leave. That was how Rachel operated—quickly and with purpose; get in, get out. If she applied the same work ethic with Edna as she did on the job, she'd be back in the windy city trying to salvage her career in no time. And after nearly seven hours behind the wheel, she was more than ready to reach the Farris Family Apple Orchard.

It was just as the Destiny city limits sign went flying past in a blur that a blast of evening sun cut between the rolling hills up ahead, blinding her. Yikes—suddenly she couldn't see a thing, so she reached for the glove box in search of sunglasses, and the car swerved a little.

That's when the swirl of blue lights reflected in her rearview mirror and the *whir, whir, whir* of a siren split the air.

Oh, damn. Just what she needed. *Not.*

As she pulled to the side of the road—which, in Destiny, was just a narrow shoulder of gravel that crunched beneath her tires—she took a deep, calming breath and prepared to face some paunchy, overeager Deputy Dawg type who was all excited to catch a speeder. This was probably the highlight of his day. But that didn't mean she couldn't talk her way out of it. Being convincing and persuasive was what she did for a living, after all.

She dug for her license and registration—without coming across her sunglasses, darn it—then turned down the radio and lowered the window, only to have a thick wave of hot August air burst in to override the effects of her A/C. Blegh.

When she looked up, the sinking sun still glared directly in her face, forcing her to lower her eyes. She saw dots and felt disoriented as the cop approached.

"What's the hurry?" he snapped in a deep, rather *mean* voice.

Sheesh—can we tone it down a little, Barney Fife? She squinted, attempting to see him alongside the painfully bright beams of sunlight, and when that failed, she settled for trying to read his badge. "I'm sorry—I didn't realize I was speeding," she fibbed in her best polite-yet-confident tone. "But I'm afraid my frail, ailing grandmother is expecting me and I don't want her to worry. I'd call to let her know I'm on my way, but I can't get a signal here . . ." She narrowed her eyes on the badge further, still trying to make it out. ". . . Officer Romeo."

"That's *Romo*," he corrected her stiffly.

And Rachel's jaw dropped. Oh no. He was a Romo? A freaking *Romo*? The Farris and Romo families were long-time enemies, and even if most of the Farrises had left Destiny, she knew the bad blood remained.

And then, as if to add insult to injury, he said, "License and registration, ma'am"—and she instantly wanted to slug him. Since when had she become a ma'am? She was only thirty-two, for heaven's sake! *I bet Pamela doesn't get called ma'am.* As her chest tightened, she handed the paperwork over and waited for a reaction.

"Figures," he muttered under his breath. Ah, there it was.

"What's that?" she asked anyway, playing dumb.

"You're a Farris," he informed her, like she might not know. Then he shifted his weight to one side until his broad shoulders blocked out the sun—finally allowing her to see him.

The first thing she noticed was the way he scowled at her from behind typical mirrored cop sunglasses.

And the second was . . . oh dear. Oh *my*. Her throat went dry.

He was no Deputy Dawg—and a far cry from Barney Fife. In fact, he was . . . a cop *god*. With thick, dark hair and olive skin, a day's growth of stubble covering his strong jaw, and shoulders that filled out his beige uniform quite nicely, he was . . . shockingly hot. Even behind mirrored sunglasses. And in Destiny, of all places! How was that possible?

But then she recalled her friend Amy—who still lived here—mentioning some sexy-as-sin Romo being a town policeman. Her heart beat faster than before and she suddenly had to work to control her breathing.

Even while he snarled at her.

But wait—stop. Get hold of yourself.

Sure, he's hot—but he's a Romo. And a mean, growly one at that.

He proved her point by glancing back down to grouse, "Out-of-state license."

"That would be because I live out of state," she heard herself reply dryly. She didn't normally talk back to cops, but apparently she just couldn't take this attitude from a Romo lying down.

Not that she would *mind* lying down with him. If he were a little nicer. And not a Romo, of course. But he *was*—and her unwitting attraction to him was making her all the more irate.

Her remark earned another handsome scowl, to which he added, "Edna's not frail or ailing, by the way. So your excuse doesn't fly."

Oops. Clearly, he knew the town well enough to know Edna was the only Farris left who might have a granddaughter coming to see her. "Well, that's not how *she* tells it," she argued. "All I know is that she summoned me to help with the apple harvest, so that's what I'm doing—if you'll kindly let me go on my way."

To her surprise, he lowered his chin, appearing suspicious. "You don't look like much of an orchard worker."

Who asked you? She bit her tongue for once, though, and tried to regain her composure. In fact, it suddenly hit her that all her powers of persuasion had pretty much gone out the window somewhere along the way. So she gave her head a confident tilt, and in her smoothest voice replied, "My skill set might surprise you." And . . . hmm, was that being confident—or flirting?

"And no way I'm letting you off that easy," he added.

Okay, didn't matter whether it was confidence or flirtation since, either way, it hadn't worked. So now *she* scowled at *him*. "Come on, Romo, cut me a break."

When his dark eyebrows rose behind those sunglasses, she realized what she'd just said—but again, she couldn't let him . . . *win*. Since, that quickly, that's what it felt like with this guy—a matter of winning or losing. Farris vs. Romo. She couldn't let him get the best of her without at least fighting back.

"I've got news for you, *Farris*," he practically growled. "Maybe you can argue your way out of tickets up in Chicago, but not in Destiny. You were going twenty over the limit."

Whoops. Twenty? Really? Still . . . "Can I be honest with you?" It was time for a new tactic.

"All right," he said dryly, sounding doubtful already.

But that didn't stop her from gazing up into that sexy cop-god face and saying, with true sincerity, "When such a low speed limit is posted on such a wide open stretch of highway, I don't actually know how a person can be expected to *go* so slow. I'm sure you know what I mean— it's nearly impossible."

And when he peered down on her, his expression softening a bit, she suspected he was beginning to understand her point—and she found herself wishing she could see his eyes. Were they as gorgeous as the rest of him? What color were they? Brown, maybe? That's when he said to her in a completely patronizing tone, "Let me explain it to you, Farris. You *ease. Off. The gas.*"

Okay, he was hot as hell—but still a jerk. So she forgot all about his eyes and said, "Romos always *were* smart-asses."

"Farrises," he announced, "*set the bar* for being smart-asses. Not to mention the fact that they have a long history of not abiding by the law."

All right, that might be true, but she still rolled her eyes in an exaggerated manner and tried to look deeply insulted. "Can you just give me my ticket now, so I can get to Edna's before she has a heart attack or something?"

Mike Romo seldom stood around arguing with traffic offenders, but something about this woman had gotten under his skin, quick. Maybe the fact that she was a city girl to the bone, made obvious not only by her arrogant attitude, but by the stylish haircut that didn't quite reach her shoulders, the trendy dark jeans she wore, and the sleek-looking scarf hanging loose around her neck. Or maybe it was because she was extremely attractive— blonde, slender, the works—and had probably thought that would get her off the hook. Or . . . maybe it was just because most people didn't have the nerve to back-talk him when openly breaking the law.

"I *could* arrest you, you know," he informed her—mainly because her lack of regard for authority pissed him off. Yet as he heard his own words, something low in his gut warmed and he realized he could think of plenty of things to do to her that would be a lot more pleasant than arrest.

Hell. Where had *that* come from? She was a speeder, not some babe in a bar, and he *never* had those kinds of thoughts when on the job. So when she blinked her shock—saying, "*Seriously*? You *could*?"—he got back to business.

"*Twenty over*, Farris. Plus swerving. Together, they border on reckless driving."

She gasped at the accusation. "I was in complete control of the car at all times!"

He simply gave his head an *are-you-kidding-me?* tilt. "That would be great if the law stated you could drive like a maniac as long as you control the vehicle, but the law doesn't state that. And besides, you were fishtailing all over the road." Narrowing his brow further, he leaned closer to her window—and that's when a soft, feminine scent of some sort struck him. Which he felt in his groin, damn it. But he was still pissed and needed to make sure she knew it. "Frankly, I don't get the idea you're taking this infraction very seriously."

"*Infraction*?" she repeated like he was crazy. "Look, what's the big deal here? It's not like I murdered anybody. I'm from Chicago. We drive fast. We'd get run over otherwise."

Was she serious? "Well, you're not in Chicago anymore, Farris, so get used to it."

As Mike scribbled out key information on the little clipboard he held, he tried to wrap his brain around this. Around her. Or maybe around the way his body was reacting to her. His head—it was in the right place, damn irritated by her attitude. But his body . . . shit, his body was tightening in all the wrong areas at the moment. He couldn't make sense of it, and he didn't like it.

When he shoved the ticket at her along with her license and registration, she took a look and let out yet another gasp. "This is for a hundred and fifty dollars!"

"Uh, *yeah*."

Then her voice dropped and she suddenly sounded a little meeker. "Well, the last time I was pulled over in Destiny, it was more like . . . thirty."

Thirty? His eyebrows shot back up, in disbelief this time. "When was *that*?"

She appeared to be thinking back, the little spot between her brows scrunching. "When I was seventeen."

Figured. He just shook his head. And wondered, as a life-long Destiny resident, how he'd not known this girl when she was seventeen. She seemed . . . memorable. "Well, I see you still haven't learned. But times change, and we don't tolerate speeding here anymore. You speed, you pay."

She simply looked disgusted, and maybe a little beaten—although it was hard to feel very sorry for her when she rolled her eyes at him again. "Whatever you say, Officer Romeo."

The words made his jaw tighten. "It's not too late for me to haul you to jail, you know."

And he'd been sure that would change her tune—so he couldn't have been more shocked when she simply stared up at him in blatant, blue-eyed defiance, as if just daring him to do it.

When he leaned back toward her window, he wasn't sure if it was because he wanted to take one last stab at intimidating her—or because he was following some animal urge to get closer to her. "Let me give you a little advice, Farris," he said gruffly. "Learn some respect for the law. And *slow down*."

Then he turned to go back to his car—but stopped to glower down at her one last time, adding wryly, "Welcome to Destiny."

The next day, Rachel pulled her car to the curb along Destiny's town square, in front of Amy's bookstore, Under the Covers. Both Amy and their other lifelong best friend, Tessa, worked there, and as soon as Rachel saw how cute the old refurbished building looked from the outside, she felt guilty for not having seen it sooner. Just as her family always brought Edna up to Chicago for Christmas and other holidays, Rachel always made her friends trek north to see her, too, instead of ever coming home. But as she stepped onto the sidewalk, she reminded herself that the girls *loved* their annual fall trip to the city. And Tessa had even sounded a little disappointed on the phone when Rachel had explained *she* was coming *here* this year instead.

A charming bell tinkled overhead as she pushed through the door, yet she still called out, "Knock, knock. Anybody home?"

"Rachel!" Amy screeched, bursting from between two tall bookshelves, arms extended and strawberry blonde curls bouncing—but before they could hug, a humongous cat leaped from somewhere high above, landing on the floor between them and forcing Rachel to squeal and step back.

"What the *hell*?" she asked, glaring at the cat.

Amy just shook her head. "Sorry. That's Shakespeare. He's kind of a pain in the butt. He's always jumping down from the upper shelves and making a nuisance of himself. Nearly scared the wits out of old Mrs. Lampton one day—she may never come back. I really need to find him a home."

"I'll say," Rachel agreed as the cat wove annoyingly between her legs. "You made him sound much more appealing on the phone."

She shrugged. "Well, you know I have a soft spot for all felines."

Amy had a soft spot for *lots* of things: books, people, Destiny, you name it. And, of course, cats—even stray ones like Shakespeare. Rachel had often wished she were so easily pleased in life as Amy.

"Are you sure Mr. Knightley wouldn't like having a friend at home?" Rachel suggested.

Yet Amy drew back in horror. "God, no. He'd disown me." Mr. Knightley was Amy's own beloved cat, and according to Tessa, Amy had an unhealthy attachment to him. Which Rachel was starting to believe. "Maybe Edna could use a nice cat at the orchard?" Amy asked.

Rachel tilted her head. "Could be. I'll check."

Just then, Tessa emerged from another set of shelves, looking as dainty and pretty as ever, her hazel eyes going wide. "Rach, you're here!"

And finally hugs were traded, and Rachel couldn't deny that this would be *one* nice aspect of her return to Destiny. She looked forward to Tessa and Amy's visit every autumn, and this one—though much different than usual—would be extended. And it was probably high time she saw what *their* lives were like now that they were all older—even if she *would* miss dragging them up and down the Miracle Mile.

"Let's have a seat," Amy said, motioning to a friendly grouping of overstuffed easy chairs by the door, so Rachel and Tessa sat down while Amy poured coffee into big, brightly colored mugs from the pot she kept brewing.

"So, how's Edna?" Tessa asked as Amy passed her a large cup, then settled into another chair.

Rachel rolled her eyes. "Fit as a fiddle, of course. Until I reminded her that her knees were supposed to be hurting, and she grabbed onto the nearest piece of furniture for support. But that's Edna. All I can do is indulge her, spend time with her, and help with the apples for a couple of weeks to make her happy." It had become a semi-annual occurrence the last few years—Edna claimed some illness or injury in order to make one of her children or grandchildren come visit for a while. And because they all loved the ornery old woman, they tolerated it. Although the thought reminded Rachel again what bad timing this was.

"Why do you call her Edna instead of Grandma?" Amy asked, squinting lightly. "I've always wondered that."

Rachel shook her head. "I don't know. All the grand-kids just always have, since we were little. A Farris family tradition, I guess. Or maybe we just all tend to be smart-asses, " she added with a laugh. Then she remembered using the same word to describe the Romos last night. The pot calling the kettle black, she supposed, as he'd pretty much pointed out—but Officer Romeo had been asking for it.

Amy smiled, looking giddy. "I'm so happy you're here—this is going to be great!"

Yet Rachel gave her head a pointed tilt, gladly letting Amy yank her thoughts off her encounter with Mr. You-Speed-You-Pay. "Don't get too attached to me, Ames. The minute I feel I've done my duty and can make a safe get-away, I'm outta here."

The words instantly replaced Amy's smile with a frown.

"Sorry, but there's trouble in Ad Land, girls," Rachel informed them, applying the little moniker they'd always used for her job at Conrad/Phelps.

As she told the whole horrid story about suddenly being in competition with Pamela Tremaine—"who I trained and mentored, I might add"—her stomach churned. Now that she was actually in Destiny, it was starting to hit her in a whole new brutal way that she really might not have a job to go back to. "My bosses always claimed I had 'the magic' when it came to getting and keeping clients, but I guess I haven't been pulling enough rabbits out of my hat lately. And I could probably get another job, but times are tight in advertising, so I might come off as over-qualified for whatever's out there. And besides, I've been at Conrad/Phelps for over ten years—a third of my life."

Amy leaned over to give her another small hug without spilling any coffee, while Tessa looked truly pained for her—and if Rachel had been the kind of girl who cried, she might have started tearing up a little. After all, she'd left Destiny with a plan, a goal, a dream, and she'd achieved it *all*. She'd built the life she wanted—from nothing. To think of losing it was devastating.

"Do you have some money socked away, in case you need it?" Tessa asked.

Rachel nodded, both hands wrapped around the big coffee cup she held. "I'd be fine for a while—but it's more the . . . far reaching implications that worry me."

The truth was, she was well paid and enjoyed spending what she earned—on travel, a nice condo on Lakeshore Drive, and yes, she squandered more money on shoes than most people would consider sane—but she didn't spend it *all*. Far from it. And it had been more than a desire for jet-setting in Jimmy Choos that had pushed her to climb the corporate ladder—she had other financial issues no one knew about.

Fortunately, though, her friends didn't ask what implications she was referring to, probably assuming it was a general worry about her future. And it wasn't that she *meant* to keep secrets from them, but . . . well, she didn't even like *thinking* about this stuff, so she certainly saw no reason to *talk* about it.

"And if that's not enough," she went on, "I got a speeding ticket last night coming into town. From that Romo guy, of all people." But why on earth was she bringing *him* up? *It's probably just money concerns, one leading to another in your mind, that's all.* Not to mention how disconcerted by her own behavior she'd been. Somehow, her normal, cool confidence had completely abandoned her.

Given how glum she surely sounded, it surprised her when Amy's eyes lit up. "Was I not right? Is he not hot?" She totally ignored the speeding ticket part of the equation, along with Rachel's grimace.

And even as her skin tingled at the memory, Rachel found herself loath to admit she found *anything* about him appealing. "I suppose. But good God, the guy's an ass."

"Amen to that," Tessa agreed, long tawny locks framing her face. "You're not the first person to get pulled over by him to think he was a jerk. My Aunt Alice, for one."

Amy sent Tessa a chiding look. "How many times do I have to remind you that your Aunt Alice drives like a lunatic?" Then she glanced back to Rachel and tried to smooth it over even more. "He's not that bad. He's had a rough past, you know."

This perked up Rachel's ears. "No, I *don't* know. What was so rough in his past?"

"Oh, come on—you remember. What happened back when we were kids."

But Rachel remained in the dark, so she freed one hand from her mug and made a rolling motion, encouraging Amy to keep going. "I've been gone since high school—I need more to go on."

Just then, Shakespeare—who Rachel had nearly forgotten about—bounded heftily up into her lap. "Dear God," she snapped, drawing back slightly. "This is a freaking *enormous* cat." She suspected the pushy tabby weighed a good fifteen pounds.

"*Shakespeare*," Amy scolded. "*Bad kitty.*" Then she lifted her gaze to Rachel. "He's not usually that rude. He must like you."

"Lucky me," she said. Then tried to get back on topic. "So, about Officer Romo."

"Mike," Amy clarified for her.

She hadn't noticed his first name last night, too wrapped up in discovering his last. "Okay—Mike," she said, if that would get Amy talking.

And then Amy got a familiar look in her eye—one that made all her friends recoil on a regular basis. "You know what would get your mind off your troubles? A little romance with Mike Romo."

Oh brother! Rachel rolled her eyes and tried to budge the cat from her lap—but he wasn't moving. "You've *got* to be joking." Because yeah, the mere thought of Officer Romeo might make her flutter in all the right places, but it was an impossibility—for *numerous* reasons.

"Need I remind you how good-looking he is?" Amy prodded.

"Need *I* remind *you* that he's a louse, and a creep, *and* a Romo? Who gave me a hundred-and-fifty-dollar speeding ticket?"

Both girls hissed in their breath at the amount. "Ouch," Tessa said.

"Ouch is right. That could cost me a heating bill, or groceries. Or . . . a pair of shoes. If they were on sale anyway."

"Well, if you're not into Mike Romo," Amy said, back to being her perky, habitually matchmaking self that fast, "what about Logan?" Logan Whitaker had been Amy's neighbor growing up and he was like a brother to her.

"What about him?" Rachel asked.

Now Tessa rolled *her* eyes. "She tries to fix *everyone* up with Logan. Me included."

Poor Tessa. And poor Logan, too, having to deal with Amy in Cupid mode. Rachel narrowed her gaze on Amy. "Why? Is there something wrong with him?"

"God, no—there's definitely something *right* with him."

"It's true, he's utterly hot," Tessa added, clearly knowing Rachel trusted her opinion of guys more than she did romantic, idealistic Amy's. "But there just wasn't any chemistry between us. And he's probably a commitment-phobe or something—he never dates anyone for long."

"Maybe he's one of those guys who gets bored when the chase is over," Rachel suggested.

Yet Amy only responded with a shrug. "I'd just like to see him find a nice girl and settle down, you know?"

Absently scratching the big fat cat on her lap behind his ears, Rachel lowered her chin. "Then you're barking up the wrong tree, sister, since you know *I'm* not the settling down type." She was a committed career girl to the core.

"Maybe that's why I thought you'd like Mike," Amy said. "He's not into settling down, either."

Hmm. "Not that I care," she pointed out, "but how do you know that about him?"

Amy leaned forward in her chair, as if ready to tell a secret. She was as pure as the driven snow, but she did enjoy her Destiny gossip. "Well, from what Logan says, Mike's with a different girl every weekend, over in Crestview."

"I see," Rachel said, instantly annoyed at the notion Officer Romeo was a womanizer in addition to being a jerk. "He seemed like such a straight arrow. Who'd have thought?"

"And he's Logan's best friend, so that means Mike can't be *all* bad," Amy added.

"Or maybe Logan just . . . feels sorry for him or something. Because of that rough past you mentioned." Rachel lowered her coffee cup to a side table and bent over the cat, ready to draw Amy back to her original tale—but then she sat up straighter, wondering aloud, "Wait—why don't I remember him?"

"He was a few years ahead of us in school," Tessa replied.

"Ah." Made sense. "And I thought one Romo was as bad as any other, so they mostly all ran together in my mind. But back to whatever happened to him—"

And that's when the bell on the door jingled brusquely and all three girls looked up to see none other than Mike Romo himself suddenly towering over them in all his tall, hot, masculine, uniformed glory.

Oh boy. Speak of the devil. The words lingered on the tip of Rachel's tongue, but she held them back—she had no intention of letting him know they'd been talking about him. Still, just like last night, the mere sight of him affected her. Physically. Which was disappointing. She'd been hoping she'd overreacted—that maybe it had been the result of being so tired, or of having the sun in her eyes the whole time. Yet somehow he looked even *better* than last night. Maybe because she could really see him now—no sun, no glare. Nothing to keep her from feasting her eyes on just how sexy he really was. Jerk or not.

"There's a car blocking the fire hydrant outside," he barked toward all of them, just as gruff as the previous evening—and only then did his eyes drop to *her.* "I *thought* that Beamer looked familiar. Out breaking more laws, Farris?"

"Officer Romeo to the rescue," she muttered under her breath.

But apparently not low enough to keep him from hearing. "Aching for another ticket? If not, move your car."

Oh, relax, Fife. And quit talking about aching—since she *was*, but for something far more pleasurable than another ticket. "All right, all right, Romo—keep your pants on. I'll be out in a minute."

He gave her a funny look—and she realized with horror that she'd made a remark about his pants, which could indicate she was thinking about what was in them—but then he went back to being his usual crusty self. "No, not in a minute. *Now.* Unless you want that ticket."

"Sheesh," she said, peering up at him. "So much for small town hospitality." Then she heaved Shakespeare to the floor, murmuring, "Silly cat," as she pushed to her feet and whisked past Mike Romo.

Only she passed too close, in order not to trip over the cat—and accidentally brushed up against him. Her arm touched his, and—oh dear—her breast grazed his biceps, too. And a hot, sizzling sensation rippled through her whole body as she made her way out the door. *Holy God, what was* that*?*

Well, okay, it was a feeling you got when you came into contact with a sexually attractive man, that was all. It was a hormonal thing—even if she didn't like knowing some small town Romo could produce that kind of response in her. But it meant nothing. It was time she got that through her head and Mike Romo off her mind. Since the two of them clearly disliked each other, even without a nasty family feud hanging over them to make it official.

Yet as she headed toward the curb, she sensed him catching the door behind her and following her out. And she became aware that he'd smelled . . . kind of manly. In a different way than men in Chicago smelled. Sort of musky. And rugged.

Oh, stop it, for heaven's sake. The man smells like sweat, that's all. It's August.

But when had the smell of sweat started . . . turning her on?

And as she made her way around her car, noting the police cruiser parked in front of it, she found herself wondering if he might be watching her—her body, her ass.

When she reached the driver's side door, she gave him a cutting look over the roof of her 325i. "Um, aren't *you* illegally parked, too?"

Although she hadn't been trying to make a joke, Officer Romeo appeared, for the first time, as if he might actually crack a smile. But then he didn't. "Cops can park wherever necessary in order to uphold the law."

"Of course they can," she murmured. Then said,

"Where am *I* supposed to park, Romeo? Since I'd like to come back and see my friends, if you don't mind."

He pointed. "There's an open spot on the other side of the square."

"Fine," she snipped, then got in, started the car, and pulled out, careful not to nip his bumper. God, he probably *would* put her in jail *then*.

As she maneuvered her car into in the empty spot, she wondered when on earth Destiny had started having enough traffic to run low on parking. And as she got out, she realized Romeo had circled the square in his cruiser and was pulling up beside her. What *now*? Was he going to criticize her parking in some way? Or . . . was it possible he just wanted to watch her some more when she walked back across the grassy square? Not that she was *positive* he'd been watching in the first place—but she thought so.

And without quite planning it, she found herself sauntering toward him, even leaning down into his open window. "Is that good enough, Romeo? Did I get inside the lines? Am I close enough to the curb? Am I walking too fast, or too slow? Is there any other way you can harass me? Anything more you want me to do?" Then it hit her—good Lord, was she trying to flash him her cleavage? Surely not.

Like back in front of the bookstore, she almost thought he would smile—yet, again, he didn't. "Yeah. You can tell Edna I said hi."

Thoroughly surprised, Rachel raised her eyebrows. "As if she'd want a hello from a Romo." That's when she realized his eyes had that bedroom quality to them. *Crap— why did I have to notice that?* Something about looking directly into them had just turned her knees to putty.

"Actually, Edna and I get along just fine," he claimed. "In fact, she's the most reasonable Farris I ever met."

Hmm. Was that supposed to hurt her feelings? Well,

he'd have to try harder than that. "Afraid you'll have to tell her yourself, because I'm pretty sure you'll be off my mind as soon as you're no longer in my face." *Or would that be in my cleavage?*

"You wish," he mumbled as she turned to go. Or at least that was what it sounded like.

So she spun on her heel. "*What?*" Was he really that arrogant? Even if she *was* putty, she couldn't stand conceited men.

And *now*, of all times, he grinned. Just a little. In an infuriatingly cocky way that made his eyes sparkle. "Nothing, Farris. Just keep walking."

And, oh my—they *were* brown. His eyes. Kind of a rich, chocolaty color that made her stomach feel a little hollow. And—oh God—*that* was why he looked even better to her than he had last night. She could see his eyes now. His warm, sexy, bedroom eyes.

Meeting his gaze one last time, just daring him to say another word, she finally turned back around and did what he said—walked across the Destiny town square toward the bookstore. But she was pretty sure she felt him watching her with every step. And it made her body tingle like crazy.

Uh-oh. This was bad. Really bad.

His gorgeousness hadn't been a figment of her imagination.

And a mean, bossy, small-town cop was *so* not her type.

And, worst of all, he was a Romo.

Damn him for that.

What sadness lengthens Romeo's hours?

William Shakespeare, *Romeo & Juliet*

Two

Mike Romo sat in his cruiser, just off Meadowview Highway near the Destiny city limits, the car partially camouflaged by a copse of small cedars, his radar gun at the ready. He knew people thought he was a hard-ass when it came to speeding—probably thought he was an overzealous cop bent on meeting some kind of monthly quota. But Mike wasn't motivated by bringing citation money into the town coffers—he was driven by one sole purpose: keeping people in Destiny safe.

Maybe that made him some kind of stick-in-the-mud, but he didn't care. And if each ticket he wrote did anything to make someone drive—or live—a little more cautiously . . . well, then it helped him sleep at night.

Just then, Willie Hargis's old red pickup came ambling up the road—Willie was an elderly man who took his time at whatever he was doing, driving included, and Mike liked him for that. Willie even lifted his hand in a wave as the truck went past, accustomed to seeing Mike monitor this stretch of highway, and Mike returned the gesture.

As for Rachel Farris, she was at the opposite end of the spectrum. She clearly had no respect for the law, and people like *her* made it harder for *him* to keep people safe.

And he'd been ready to forget all about her, including his bizarre reaction to her—since he was usually much more in command of his own lust, especially on the job—until, damn it, she'd had to block that fire hydrant today.

And before he'd quite known what was happening, she'd been brushing past him, leaving behind that seductive scent again—something light, fruity maybe—and putting all his senses on alert. After which she'd accidentally touched his arm—with her breast. Damn—soft. Nice. And since when did fruit smell *seductive*?

He'd unwittingly started noticing other things about her, too. Like that even today, in town, she hadn't dressed like most women in Destiny, who were fond of floral skirts and soft colors. She'd seemed more . . . sexy, again in dark jeans, with strappy high-heeled shoes and a stylish top that had hugged her long, lean curves. And he'd gotten a closer look at some of those curves when she'd bent down into his window.

Up to then, he really *had* shoved her out of his mind—mostly. But now . . . hell, what was the deal?

After all, she was the exact opposite of everything he liked in a person: self-righteous, entitled, argumentative, and reckless to boot. Plus it was clear she considered Destiny below her—she didn't even have to say it, he could see it in her eyes. So . . . maybe it just pissed him off to be having such a primitive reaction to her. *Me Tarzan, you Jane.* That wasn't him. Usually.

Not that he planned to respond to his urges. Even if, in an off moment, he'd *almost* flirted with her. Nope, he'd keep his Tarzan-like impulses to himself.

She just had too much going against her. Besides everything else, it bugged the hell out of him when she called him Officer Romeo. And sexy as hell or not, the girl was a Farris on top of it all.

Mike didn't make a habit of judging people by their families—but a lifetime of observation had shown him that most Farrises were cut from the same cloth: often in some kind of scrape, either financial or legal, and generally out for themselves. He considered it good riddance that most of them had moved away.

And he wasn't sure what had originally started the feud between the two families, but he *did* know the Farris Family Apple Orchard had once belonged to his grandfather, who'd emigrated from Italy, and that his family had always felt it should be rightfully theirs. Of course, Edna had always refused to sell, which had angered Mike as a boy—but as time had passed he'd tried to let that go, coming to know and like Edna, despite her quirks.

Just then, he realized—maybe he *did* remember Rachel Farris at seventeen. Judging from the birth date on her license, he'd been doing his police training in Chillicothe around that time, but he'd never been away from Destiny for long—and hadn't there been some cute, rambunctious little Farris girl flitting about town in those days? A cheerleader, if he remembered. And he had the vague sense that she'd driven fast even then— back before he'd had the ability to do anything about it. He suspected she was the same then as now—probably the only difference being that she'd grown from a cute, reckless, over-confident girl in a cheerleading skirt into an attractive, reckless, over-confident woman in jeans that hugged her ass real nice.

But Rachel Farris's *jeans* and Rachel Farris's *genes* were two different things—and he could admire one without admiring the other. He could think she was attractive without acting on it. And besides, if he wanted a woman, he was capable of getting one whose last name wasn't Farris.

He knew he wasn't exactly charming, but despite that, all he usually had to do was buy a girl a drink and she was his for the night. Logan had started calling him the Italian Stallion, claiming it was all in *his* genes. And maybe it was. Everyone always claimed that his late grandfather, Giovanni Romo, had had a way with the ladies, too.

It was just then that Mike caught sight of a vehicle rounding the bend in the distance so fast the car was a blur—an electric shade of purple, but that was all he could tell as he lifted the radar gun and aimed it out the open window. The speeding car blew past in a streak of color —at ninety-two miles per hour! *Shit.* Now *that* he could haul somebody's ass to jail for.

The only problem might be catching the son of a bitch.

But Mike tore out of his spot just off the road, throwing up mud and grass as he pressed the gas pedal to the floor, committed to trying. He fishtailed but straightened it out, then switched on his lights and siren.

As the car had *whoosh*ed past, he'd identified it as a late model Mustang—which meant catching the bastard would be difficult at best. He didn't know the car, had never seen it around—but this guy made Rachel Farris look like a Sunday driver.

Mike drove as fast as possible under the conditions, thinking the guy might be slowed down by curves or—God forbid—other vehicles. And he tried to keep an eye toward the roadside—it wouldn't take much at that speed for the asshole to make a wrong move and go skidding off the pavement into a tree or a ravine—but going ninety, it was hard to concentrate on more much than the road itself.

He drove that way for nearly ten minutes down the country highway, never catching even a glimpse of the Mustang—before he accepted the fact that he wasn't going to. *Damn it.*

Slowing his cruiser, he banged his palm on the steering wheel and cursed. What the *hell* was that idiot thinking, driving that fast on a twisting two-lane highway?

Finally, he located a spot to pull off and turn back— he'd gone well beyond the Destiny city limits, past his own house and out into farm country. It was rural here, but there were plenty of roads crisscrossing each other every few miles—so the Mustang could be headed anywhere now.

Once back in town, he drove toward the police station, every muscle in his body still tensed. It was the first time anyone had ever even *tried* to outrun him, and though he knew it wasn't his fault the guy had gotten away, the Mustang had put him in a rotten mood. Pulling up in front of the station, he slammed his door shut with too much force.

"Whoa, dude, who pissed *you* off?"

He glanced up to see Logan Whitaker, the person who knew him best in the world. And the truth was, he didn't particularly like *anyone* knowing all the things about him that Logan did, but it couldn't be helped—it was the price you paid for lifelong friendship. A fireman, Logan sat outside the firehouse next door in a DFD tee and blue jeans—apparently just soaking up the sunny day and looking far too chipper for Mike at the moment. "Some son-of-a-bitch Mustang just blew by me on the Meadowview going ninety-fucking-two," he growled.

Logan drew back slightly in his folding chair. "Damn. You catch him?"

Mike raised his eyebrows. "Do I look like I caught him?"

"Oh." Logan left it at that, since he knew how Mike felt about speeders, and reckless people in general.

Pushing through the door into the station, Mike was glad to see things mostly quiet, empty—only Chief Tolliver sat at his desk doing paperwork, and he lifted his hand in absent greeting, raising his eyes only briefly. "Mike," he murmured.

"Walter," Mike returned—then planted himself at his own desk, where he signed on to his computer to contact the Ohio State Highway Patrol with what little information he had about the car. Who knew what they'd find in the master Bureau of Motor Vehicles database without even a partial on the plate, but on the other hand, how many purple Mustangs could there be in the area?

Half an hour later, it turned out the answer was none. No purple Mustangs anywhere nearby. But there were a considerable number of hits statewide, and when he ran an inquiry through the Law Enforcement Automated Data System, he found out a purple Mustang had been stolen from a Cleveland suburb a couple of weeks ago. Hmm. He'd lay odds he'd just chased that same car up the Meadowview.

Maybe he was assuming too much, but his cop's gut instincts had told him almost instantly there was something more at work here than just a wild joyride. Something . . . worrisome. Shit.

Taking a deep breath, Mike e-mailed the jurisdiction where the stolen Mustang was registered, to let them know of the possible sighting. And upon closing the database, he leaned back in his chair with a sigh, glad the chief was too immersed in work across the room to notice his mood.

Then he caught a glimpse of the picture of Anna he still kept on his desk. It had been taken one Easter—she stood in the yard wearing a lacy white dress.

Somehow, at a moment like this, the very sight of her, looking so happy and carefree, so innocent, stole his breath. She'd had no idea, no idea at all what was coming. None of them had.

And he thought, as he did at some point every single day, of all the bad things happening in the world that he was powerless to stop. He kept trying—he tried with everything in him—but he just couldn't ever fix it all.

Where are you, Anna? Where the hell are you?

Despite himself, even after all this time, he never quit wondering.

Rachel turned left at the quaint wooden sign that read Farris Family Apple Orchard and drove across the little stone bridge crossing Sugar Creek. Sunbeams broke through the billowing trees to dapple the ground with light and remind Rachel of time spent here as a little girl. Edna's house had been the gathering place for the Farris clan back then—Sunday dinners, holidays, it had all taken place at the orchard. A fleeting memory of hide-and-go-seek with her cousins made her envision crouching behind tree trunks, or slipping into the cheerful red barn that had just come into view. She stopped the car far short of the barn, though, parking alongside Edna's little Toyota pickup and the circa 1940 fruit truck that she suspected hadn't hauled anything anywhere in at least twenty years.

Edna's little white house with gingerbread trim was the kind everyone entered through the back screen door more than the front one—so that's what she did now, letting it slam behind her as she called out, "Hey Edna, I'm home!"

No answer. But no biggie. She might be napping. Or for all Rachel knew, Edna was out picking a few ripening apples on her not-really-so-bad knees—she'd promised to bake an apple pie, since Rachel *loved* Edna's pies.

Moving through the kitchen to what Edna still called the parlor, Rachel realized the house was filled with furniture from the first half of the last century: an antique sofa and chair, small end tables with spindle legs, a huge wooden radio from the thirties, an old upright piano adorned with old photos atop a white doily. Little had changed since

Rachel had last been here almost fifteen years ago. Except that Edna had gotten older. Which made her a little sad when she looked at the framed pictures on the piano of Edna in younger days—and of *all* of them, all her family, in earlier times.

For some reason, all those pictures together—Edna in her youth, then Rachel's parents as teenagers, and then Rachel herself, with other cousins, as a small child— made her chest tighten. *How swiftly fly the years.* Maybe it was easier not to focus on that aspect of life in the city, where days were brisk, busy. Here, though, from Amy's refurbished storefront to that old truck outside, from early twentieth century farmhouses to the pictures spread across Edna's piano, it was hard not to be aware of the way time passed, of the way each person's time was . . . limited. Life didn't go on forever. For anyone.

"Fleetin', ain't it?" Edna said.

And Rachel flinched—then turned, scolding Edna with her eyes for sneaking up behind her. "What's that?" she asked.

"Life. It flits by faster than you'd expect."

Edna was like that sometimes—she could read your mind just from the look on your face. Rachel had sort of forgotten that.

"Look at *you*," Edna went on. "All grown up and with your big city job. And it feels like just yesterday I bounced ya on my knee and wiped chocolate off your face and fed ya Coke over crushed ice when you were sick."

"I never really got that," Rachel admitted thoughtfully. "The Coke-over-crushed-ice thing. What is that supposed to do for you?"

"Settles your stomach. Everybody knows that. It's been a family home remedy long as I can remember. "

"Hmm," Rachel mused. "Not to burst your bubble, Edna, but . . . even though Coke settles my stomach, I don't think the crushed ice adds anything."

Edna shrugged. "Do you still eat a bowl of it when ya get sick?"

With just a hint of hesitation, Rachel nodded. "Not because I think I'm getting anything extra from the crushed ice, but it's . . . well, just what I do when I'm sick."

"There ya go. If ya do it, you must get somethin' out of it."

"Comfort, I guess," Rachel admitted. "Because you always said it would make me feel better."

"Comfort's enough," Edna said. "In fact, I can't think of much better to leave a grandchild with. And when I'm dead and gone, you'll still have that."

Rachel made a face. "Shut up—it's not like you're going anywhere anytime soon." Then she turned back to the piano, focusing on a photo of Edna taken in the fifties, out by the creek. She wore a short-sleeved sweater with a white lace collar and a dark skirt. "You were really pretty," Rachel said.

"Took after my mother," Edna replied immodestly, motioning to an even older picture, on the wall—from the thirties—of Rachel's great-grandmother, who was, indeed, just as lovely, even in what Rachel saw as a long, shapeless dress and flat hair pulled tight behind her head. "And good thing, too, because looks and charm was about all a girl in Destiny could hope for back then. I'm glad times have changed."

Which reminded Rachel of something that *hadn't* changed, or apparently not much—the Farris/Romo feud. "By the way, I didn't get a chance to tell you last night, but I got pulled over by Mike Romo on my way into town."

Rachel waited for Edna to fly into a fit over "those damn Romos" as she'd done on a regular basis in Rachel's youth—so she couldn't have been more stunned when Edna smiled and said, "Ah. Mike's a decent fella. Caught ya speedin', huh? He's a stickler—you'll really have to slow it down while you're here."

Rachel just stared at her grandmother, her mouth hanging open. "What the hell is *this*? Since when do you have anything nice to say about a Romo?"

She shrugged again, tilting her gray head. "Like I said, times have changed. Oh, I still don't have much nice to say about *most* of 'em, but Mike's a good egg. Not much of a talker, at least not to most folks, but he does a lotta good around here."

"Huh," Rachel said blankly, still trying to get over it. "He told me you and he got along, but I didn't believe him. And . . . well, he still has plenty bad to say about the Farrises, just so you know."

"Never claimed he was a saint."

"He said we'd never had any respect for the law—and that we were smart-asses." She neglected to mention that she'd actually *started* the name-calling.

Yet Edna just cracked a smile, clearly amused. "Sounds like he's got us pegged."

And Rachel rolled her eyes in disbelief. "Where's your family loyalty gone? This isn't the Edna I know."

"Maybe the better question is—where's my *family* gone? Once you're by yourself . . . well, maybe it stops feelin' like there's much to be loyal to. Or maybe I just got old and tired of bein' rambunctious. Easier to just get along with folks. That's somethin' I wish I'd figured out sooner in life."

Rachel just stared, planting her hands on her hips. "Who *are* you? And what have you done with my grandmother?"

"I don't see what the big to-do is. We *are* all smart-asses—except maybe for your cousin Elaine, but that's just 'cause she's not very bright. Takes some brains to be a good smart-ass. And your uncle Dave *did* have some shady real estate dealin's years ago when he was runnin' short on cash, and your great aunt Liddie was practically famous around here for writin' bad checks back in the seventies—recession and all, you know. And your cousin Robby—"

"Stop." Rachel held up a hand. "I already know all this and don't like being reminded."

Yet Edna just shook her head. "We are what we are, darlin'. Don't mean all of us are that way, but nobody's perfect, either."

And what was it the Farrises were? Bad with money. Most of them anyway. For Rachel, *that* was the resounding theme that ran through every branch of her family tree. Some relatives, like Dave and Liddie and Robby, let it show, way too much—while others, like her parents, appeared comfortable on the surface, yet mostly squandered everything they made. So, for her, it wasn't about being perfect or not—it was about being responsible. About choosing smart, prudent paths in life.

And that was one reason Rachel felt so pressured to hold on to her good job—this was what she hadn't wanted to think about in Under the Covers today. From a personal standpoint, her career success defined her; it was a huge part of her identity and what made her feel good about herself and her life. But it was also vital from a practical standpoint, too. The fact was, she'd had to give her parents money on occasion, and her older brother, Noah, as well. Sometimes it was doctor bills, other times car payments. And sooner or later, she feared they'd require her help in *bigger* ways. Her parents, her brother, Edna— what if the time came when one or more of them ended up dangerously broke? Where would rescue come from if not her?

Fortunately, Edna didn't seem to notice Rachel's lack of reply—instead, she headed into the kitchen and said, "Think I'll whip up that pie, and maybe fry us some chicken for supper. How's that sound?" she asked, her voice filled with cheer.

"Great," Rachel said, and it truly did. Another good thing about being back in Destiny: Edna's cooking. There was nothing like it in Chicago. So she let it draw her mind from her lifelong worries. "But, uh . . . how are your knees today?"

Edna gritted her teeth and took on a tortured look. "Painin' me pretty bad, but I'll hold up. Can ya hand me my cane?"

"Another round?"

Mike looked up to the bartender at the Dew Drop Inn, Anita Garey, a saucy forty-something woman who he'd quickly grown to like and respect since her arrival in Destiny more than a year ago. Usually, Mike and Logan headed to Crestview, the next town over, on a Saturday night, but the Dew Drop had gotten a lot nicer since Anita bought the place.

"Sure," Mike said, and she uncapped three bottles of beer—one for him, one for Logan, and one for the brunette hanging on Mike's shoulder. It was just like he'd been thinking earlier—he'd bought her a beer and now she wouldn't leave him alone.

Not that he knew why he was so glum about that—she was an attractive girl, even if a little giggly for his taste. And she wasn't shy, and that usually worked out fine for the kind of hookup he preferred—quick, easy, no muss, no fuss.

But he still hadn't managed to get over his bad mood from earlier, which went a lot deeper than a reckless driver in a potentially stolen Mustang. Like so many nights, thoughts of Anna—and questions without answers—lingered on the edge of his mind.

He knew he should let go of it, knew he should have let it go *years* ago—but he just didn't know how you let go of something *that* awful. And every so often, some little thing set him off, took his thoughts in that horrible direction, and he wasn't able to shake it for a while. Today, it had been a guy in a Mustang.

"To an adventurous night ahead," the brunette said,

and Mike realized she was toasting. So he clinked the neck of his bottle against hers, then turned to do the same with Logan, who sat on the other side of him at the bar—only to see Logan raise his eyebrows knowingly. Mike could easily read his look. *The Italian Stallion strikes again.*

"So, Tracy," Logan leaned around him to ask, "you live around here?"

Hmm, she must have said her name was Tracy—Mike had missed that. And he guessed Logan was doing the social part *for* him since *he* wasn't making much effort.

"Over in Crestview," she said, giggling—at what, he had no idea. "I manage the Full Exposure Tanning Salon, next door to Bleachers—I think I've seen you guys there."

Well, that explained a couple of things. Like why she was unnaturally tan, and why she looked a little familiar. Bleachers was a sports bar they frequented.

"Yeah, Mike and I get over there pretty often, especially once football season rolls around. *Don't we, Mike*?"

Feeling Logan's pointed stare, he drew his gaze absently from his beer bottle upward, to the girl. "Um, yeah."

Then he heard Logan's sigh. "You'll have to excuse him. He had a rough day on the job."

"Oooh, did you catch some dangerous criminal?" the brunette asked.

And that's when it hit him—girls liked him because he was a cop. Even in a tiny little town like Destiny. Why had it taken so long to figure that out? Well, maybe because he didn't exactly see himself as the hero type. "Uh, no—nothing like that," he answered.

"What then?" Tracy asked.

And now it was *his* turn to sigh. He didn't want to be rude, but . . . "I'd rather not talk about it. In fact, it would probably only make my mood worse."

"Well, we wouldn't want to do *that*," she said, giggling some more. "What do you want to talk about?"

In response, he just looked to Logan—since his buddy seemed a lot more into this conversation than he was anyway.

And Logan let loose the grin that chicks always went gaga over and said, "Why don't you tell us . . . all about tanning. Everything there is to know."

Mike shot him a sideways glance, knowing full well this was Logan's way of torturing him and trying to make him laugh at the same time. And Tracy merrily launched into a long, painfully detailed lecture about tanning beds and settings and various skin types, giggling all the way. It wasn't long before Mike wanted to gouge his eardrums out—but instead, he just took a long swig from his bottle, hoping to feel a little more amused by it all. Damn, why'd he buy the girl a beer in the first place? He hardly even knew—habit, maybe—but now he just plain regretted it.

After all, it was pretty bad when your wingman had to take over for you. But that's how it was with him and Logan. They had each other's backs, always, without ever even discussing it. Logan had been there when all the bad shit had happened, back when Mike had been only twelve, Logan ten. That was probably why Logan tolerated him. And it was why Mike would put his life on the line for Logan in a heartbeat.

"So if you guys ever want a tanning package, I could get you a discount," he heard the girl still glued to his shoulder saying. He vaguely wished he could have his arm back so he could reach for some peanuts without having to set down his beer. "Although, *you*," she went on, mooning at Mike, "have such gorgeous coloring that you'd never need a tan. Are you Italian or something?"

He looked up. "Uh, yeah—half anyway."

"But I, on the other hand, am a dog?" Logan asked, teasing, flirting.

"No, silly, you're a total hottie, too. And you've got a nice tan going already. But the bed would even you up around the edges, you know? Hey, do you guys have any change? I want to play something on the jukebox."

Since Logan started digging in his pockets for quarters, Mike let him. And when his buddy had supplied the girl with coins and she went gliding across the floor to select a song, Logan said, "How about *her*?"

Mike barely glanced up, more interested in peanuts than Tracy now that his arm was free. "How about her?" he asked absently.

"For your grandma's party?"

Mike turned to Logan with a look of disbelief. "Are you kidding? No way in hell." Because Mike's family had recently started giving him a hard time about being thirty-five and unmarried, and because Mike's parents were coming to town soon for his grandmother's birthday party, Logan had suggested Mike bring a date to shut them all up and at least make it appear he was trying to remedy the situation. Even though he wasn't. Because in *his* mind, there was no situation to remedy. He'd told Logan he had no intention of giving anybody the idea he was even *thinking* about marriage—since he just didn't see that in the cards for himself—but every time he was around a girl lately, Logan brought it up anyway.

Now, Logan just shrugged. "Look at it this way. They meet *her* and they might prefer you stay a bachelor."

Mike couldn't deny the idea held some merit. But not enough for him to torture himself with a whole party's worth of tanning talk. "I'll take my chances alone, thanks. And I'll thank *you* to butt out."

That's when Tracy returned, latching back onto Mike's arm. So much for the damn peanuts.

Just then, the door opened across the room and Mike glanced up to see three women walk in—and one of them was Rachel Farris. He had no idea what made him look— there were plenty of patrons coming and going every few minutes; people shot pool at the tables in the corner, and music and talk filled the bar. But something drew his attention, and when he saw her, every muscle in his body tightened. Including the one between his legs.

Damn, she knew how to make a simple pair of blue jeans look good. And the rest of her was easy to look at, as well. As usual, she appeared city-chic and confident, and the hot pink top she wore hugged her breasts and brought out the blue in her eyes. Shit, something about this woman messed with his radar like a fuzzbuster— despite all his resolve, she had a way of getting past his defenses merely on sight.

That's when he realized he was staring at her.

And that she was staring back.

And that there was a girl attached to his side.

Did Farris look annoyed by that? Maybe.

Not that it mattered. He still had no intention of hooking up with someone like her. And if he was staring, well, could be he'd finally started feeling his beer.

So he drew his eyes back down, pushed the bottle away since he was driving, and decided maybe the tanning bed queen wasn't so bad. God knew she was a lot friendlier than Rachel Farris, and there was a lot to be said for friendly when a man was getting a hard-on.

"I'm gonna go find the little girls' room," his babe-for-the-night said.

He nodded absently, then watched as Rachel Farris and her friends—the same from the bookstore, Amy and Tessa—took a table near the jukebox.

Logan gave him a nudge. "Dude, not that I want to criticize your technique, but it's bad form to undress a woman with your eyes when there's already another woman hanging on your shoulder."

Hell, he was looking at her again—so he turned around to face the bar. "The last thing I was doing is undressing Rachel Farris with my eyes," he lied.

Logan raised his eyebrows. "Oh, that's Rachel? Amy

mentioned she was coming home for a while. Damn, she grew up nice."

"Nice to look at, maybe—that's about it."

Logan tilted his dark blond head accusingly. "What's wrong with her—did she speed or something?"

Yep, Logan knew him too well. "Sixty-five in a forty-five," he replied, tipping his bottle for another drink.

And Logan just chuckled. "Shit, bud—doesn't take much to get on your bad side."

"She's got a smart mouth, too, and she's reckless as hell—and as far as I can tell, she thinks she's too good for this town and everybody in it." With that, he set his beer aside again, remembering he hadn't meant to drink any more. "I don't think much of her."

"Except that she's nice to look at. And you were *so* undressing her with your eyes. Practically having sex with her on the bar."

Mike drew back and flashed a doubtful expression. "With a Farris? Not likely."

Logan just let out another light laugh, lifting his beer to his mouth.

And Mike looked at her again.

He didn't mean to.

But once his eyes went there, it was hard to pull them away.

What devil art thou, that dost torment me thus?

William Shakespeare, *Romeo & Juliet*

Three

Rachel tried like hell to focus on her conversation with Tessa and Amy, especially since she was the one talking, but Officer Romeo was ogling her. More specifically, he was making the juncture of her thighs tingle with his gaze.

So she just kept talking, trying to distract herself from the sensation, and from those eyes. "Anyway, then I handed Edna her cane and she got this happy look on her face and said how nice it was to have me here. And the truth is, as worried as I am about my job, in that moment, making Edna happy kind of . . . made it all worthwhile."

"See," Amy said, smiling. "Being in Destiny isn't so bad."

Whereas Tessa just slanted Rachel a look of disbelief. "And ya think ya know somebody."

"I can be nice," Rachel insisted. Then she gave her head a playful tilt, realizing she kind of *dug* having Mike Romo's eyes on her—in a way she felt at her very core, like it or not. She found herself wanting to look gorgeous and like she was having a fabulous time.

"Yes, but not usually when you're being duped," Tessa pointed out, drawing Rachel's thoughts back to Edna.

"True," Rachel agreed. "But there's a part of me that's starting to wonder . . . if maybe Edna's actually telling the truth. Maybe her knees really *do* hurt."

"Why do you think that?" Tessa asked, looking surprised.

And Rachel hesitated, weighing it. "I'm not sure. It's just . . . something in her eyes." Even if she was loathe to admit that—since it might just mean she was the only Farris gullible enough to believe Edna's tall tales, and Rachel liked to think she was far too sharp for something like that. Besides, maybe she was wrong—maybe Edna just had her feeling sentimental or something. So she changed the subject. "Um, where's Sue Ann? You said she'd be here."

Amy let out a sigh. "Sophie got sick."

"Bummer," Rachel said. Sue Ann was another old friend, one she hadn't seen since high school. But she knew from having other mom friends that a sick kid trumped a night out.

"Jenny and Mick might stop by, though," Tessa added.

According to Tessa and Amy, another girlfriend from their youth had come home last year and ended up marrying one of the baddest bad boys the town had ever known, Mick Brody. "I still can't get over that—Jenny with a Brody." Jenny had been a fellow cheerleader for the Destiny Bulldogs and the ultimate good girl, never letting Rachel lead her into trouble no matter how hard she'd tried.

"Sometimes opposites attract," Amy said.

Then Tessa leaned closer, lowering her voice. "And from what Sue Ann lets slip, Jenny says the sex is amazing."

Rachel popped a peanut in her mouth from the bowl on the table just as their drinks arrived. "Sue Ann's still got a big mouth, huh? Well, tell me this—how does Mick

Brody *look*? Because . . . I never said anything, but in high school I secretly thought he was hot."

Both her friends erupted into loud laughter and Rachel wasn't sure why, until Amy said, "Us, too! And Jenny and Sue Ann, too!"

"And he still is," Tessa assured her.

"So, what's her dad think about all this?" Jenny was Police Chief Tolliver's only child and he'd always been over-protective.

"Well, in the beginning," Amy said, reaching for her amaretto sour, "there was lots of sneaking around and secret-keeping. But it eventually worked out—because Chief Tolliver couldn't be too judgmental of Mick after *he* started dating Anita Garey."

"Who's Anita Garey?"

Tessa answered over her glass of white wine. "The woman behind the bar talking to Mike Romo."

"Whoa," Rachel said when she looked. The lady barkeep was built and not afraid to show it, wearing a sparkly, low-cut top. "Edna was right—times *do* change."

Of course, her glance toward the bar had also informed her Officer Romeo was still staring at her. And despite herself, she was glad she'd bothered to change clothes before coming out—she wore a silky, slinky top that showed off *her* shape nicely, too. She only hoped he didn't think she'd been looking at him, since she hadn't.

"So," she said, focusing squarely on her friends—and *not* on the hot cop, "you never told me what happened to Mike Romo. His tragic past and all that."

As Rachel took the first sip of her margarita, Amy looked aghast. "Well, I'm not going to do it *here*, with him right across the *room*. I wouldn't want anyone hearing and telling him we're gossiping about him. It's just bad form."

"Yes," Tessa said, "it's much nicer when we gossip about him behind his back."

Amy made a face, and despite herself, Rachel supposed she was right—even as she continued to tingle under the table.

And that tingling was beginning to become a concern—at the moment, a bigger concern than whatever had happened in Mike Romo's past. Because a reaction to a guy's attention was one thing, but this particular sensation was on the verge of becoming . . . nagging. Sheesh.

Stop it, stop it, stop it. You cannot keep having the hots for a mean, nasty Romo.

Then, as Amy chatted about how she and Logan were working the concession stand at some ballgame next Wednesday night, Rachel ventured a subtle look back across the room at Officer Romeo, and thought—*Oh, hell. Who am I kidding? I seriously have the hots for a mean, nasty Romo.*

But she'd just have to keep trying to ignore it, that was all.

And how does a girl ignore her lust for a guy? Find another one to lust for! It seemed the perfect solution—and suddenly spurred her to announce, "I just thought of a bright spot if I get fired!"

"You can stay in Destiny?" Amy suggested.

Rachel scowled. "Bite your tongue. I love you girls, but small town life is not for me." Then she perked up again. "No, the bright spot is that there's always been a mild flirtation between me and my very debonair boss, Chase Alexander, and if I'm no longer employed by him, we can finally explore that. And frankly, I could use some good sex right about now."

At which Tessa laughed and Amy pursed her lips. "*Rachel*," she scolded.

And Tessa said, "Ignore her. All that Jane Austen has brainwashed her into thinking women must remain prim and proper at all times." All their lives, Amy had been a huge Jane Austen devotee.

"Well, thank God this is the twenty-first century," Rachel muttered, "since I've never been very good at prim and proper." *And if you knew what I was feeling right now, because of Mike Romo's eyes, you'd know just how prim and proper I'm not.*

Just then, the chick who'd been hanging on Romo came back and resumed the same position—which kind of brought Rachel down. She'd thought *Yuck and good riddance* when she'd first seen them together, but when the girl had disappeared, she'd decided maybe it had been only a momentary flirtation. And now that she'd admitted to herself, straight out, that she was attracted to him, it made her heart pinch up a little. *Think of Chase, think of Chase.* Chase really *was* handsome. And much better suited to her than any small town guy like Mike Romo could *ever* be. And she really *had* always been attracted to him.

But then—the clinker. The clingy girl with Romo giggled and said, loud enough to be heard across the room between songs on the jukebox, "I bet I know a way to cheer you up," and then she whispered in his ear.

Although it was pretty easy to figure out what she was offering. Especially when she and Mike stood up from their bar stools a minute later.

Oh Lord. They were leaving together. To go have sex. For some reason, it hit Rachel like a brick. Her gut clenched and she prayed her emotions weren't as apparent to everyone else as they always were to Edna.

Amy motioned in the direction of Mike and his "date"—as if they weren't already being completely obvious and noticeable. "Guess it's true. And apparently not just in Crestview."

"Who cares?" Rachel said, then bent over her margarita for long, cool drink. She'd just decided it was a good time to get drunk. So she wouldn't have to think about what Officer Romeo was doing with his too-tan girlfriend.

Which was a ridiculous worry anyway. *You barely know him! And he's been nothing but mean to you! So who cares what he does with who? Not me. No way, no how.* She punctuated the thought with another lengthy sip.

Just then, the guy who'd been with Mike at the bar picked up his beer bottle to head their way, and Rachel was sure they were about to be hit on until he looked down at Amy and said, "Hey, Freckles, what's up?"

And then she knew it was Logan—since she also knew that was his lifelong nickname for Amy. And wow, they were right—he'd grown into a very good looking guy. Greetings were passed all around, as well as re-introductions between him and Rachel, and he pulled up a chair, turned it around backward, and took a seat.

Rachel was on her seventh or eighth big sip of margarita, just starting to make small talk with Logan—when the bar door suddenly jerked open and everyone looked up to see Mike Romo come storming back in.

Storming . . . toward *her*!

As he brusquely approached, she instinctively drew back, peering up at him. What the *hell*?

"Farris, you've blocked my damn truck in! I've never met a Farris who drives less responsibly than you!"

Was he seriously *that* upset about *this*? "Turn it down a notch, Officer Romeo," she said.

And Logan said, "Romeo?"

"She doesn't read very well, either," Romo griped.

And as usual—though he might be sizzling hot in his faded jeans and casual blue button-down shirt, even hotter than when in uniform—he was really pissing her off. "Not with the sun glaring in my eyes, no." She glanced from him to Logan. "I couldn't read his stupid badge when he gave me an outrageous ticket the other day."

"Keep it up, Farris," Romo growled, "and I'll show you outrageous."

"I'd like to see you try." And she wasn't even sure what

she meant by that, or what he'd meant either, but she was just arguing now, because it was better than lusting and being jealous.

"Are you gonna move your car, or do I need to have it towed?"

"Damn, bud," Logan said, "give the girl a chance to find her keys."

"Thank you, Logan," she said emphatically, reaching for her purse and digging inside. "It's hard to believe you're friends with Officer Snotty here."

"He's had a bad day," Logan said.

"Don't make excuses for me, dude."

"Whatever," Logan replied, throwing up his hands, then pushing to his feet. "I'm gonna shoot some pool. You girls wanna join me?"

Amy hopped up and Tessa went, too, which left Rachel with Mike Romo and the keys that seemed to have sunk to some secret, hidden corner of her purse. Next to her, he stood looking irritated, fists clenched at his sides, and she wondered what the hell he was so upset about. Sheesh.

"Got 'em," she finally said, and hoped she hadn't sounded *too* relieved. As if she was worried about keeping him waiting. She kind of *was*, because he seemed so angry, but she'd be damned if she'd let him know that.

Marching outside, she sensed the heat of his body just inches away behind her—and appreciated the fresh evening air, because she'd smelled that musky, masculine scent again when they were inside. Maybe it wasn't just sweat. Whatever it was, it had just increased everything she was suffering—she'd just become very aware of her own breasts; in fact, they ached with desire. Oh brother. This sucked.

Approaching her car, she realized Mike's truck was the big pickup in front of it—the tan girl leaning against the bumper in a ridiculously short skirt tipped her off.

"Just so you know," she said to Romo, "I didn't realize

the parking lot actually *ended* in front of your truck—I thought I was making a second row of cars and that you'd be able to pull out in front and circle around."

"Whatever, Farris," he snarled.

And as was usually the case, she kind of wanted to slug him, but instead she just went to her car, her insides burning up as she watched Mike load the tan girl into the passenger side of his truck. *This is so stupid. How can I be jealous? The guy's an incredible asshole, no matter what Edna and Amy say.*

Still, as she started the car and backed it up in the gravel lot, she endured the physical pang of wanting to be the one in that truck, the one he was about to start kissing, touching. How did Mike Romo kiss? Probably not softly—probably really intensely and passionately. And she thought she could get into that, darn it.

Pulling the BMW into another spot she hoped wouldn't block anyone, she got out, clicked the lock button on her keychain—and was surprised to see Mike still in the parking lot, standing by his driver's side door. It was too late to choose another path between other cars without looking like she was afraid to face him, so she resolved to simply trudge past—until he grabbed onto her arm.

Oh God. More tingling. Not only where he was touching her, but shooting up her arm and out into her breasts, too.

She peered up at his face and nearly melted because of how close they stood, their bodies almost touching. Every part of her pulsed.

"Listen, Farris—what Logan said, he was right. I've had a shitty day."

She blinked, not sure how to respond. "Is that your way of apologizing?"

He appeared irritated again, uncertain. She'd never met a man who could look so damn *sexy* being irritated. "Just explaining," he replied, clearly too proud to simply say he was sorry.

In no mood to cut him any slack, she responded coldly. "Well, you should get going. Your girlfriend is starting to look impatient."

"She's not my girlfriend."

Oh, that *makes it better. Like I'm so relieved to hear she's just a one-nighter.* "Whatever," she said, then yanked her arm away and started marching back toward the Dew Drop Inn.

"Rachel! Is that you?" The voice came from her right and she looked up to find an older-but-still-just-as-pretty Jenny Tolliver headed her way, smiling brightly, arms open for a hug. Rachel was thrilled to see her girlhood friend and smiled back, glad for the hug, and glad for Mike Romo to see she had better things to do than mope over him and his soon-to-be lover.

But even as she hugged Jenny and said all the appropriate things, even as she was introduced to Mick Brody—who was indeed as hot as promised—she felt as if she wasn't really there, as if she was just watching it happen to someone else.

Because all she could really think about was how tightly her stomach still clenched—all because Mike Romo was taking some other girl home tonight.

It made no sense.

And it hurt like hell.

Edna and Rachel both stood on easel ladders beneath a Gala apple tree. Edna had suggested Rachel wear some of her work clothes, so both were clad in oversize cotton smocks and straw hats, and Rachel prayed no one would see her this way. She'd brought some old tops to wear, but Edna had insisted they were too nice for apple picking.

"Now, do you remember how to pick 'em from when you were little?" Edna asked, demonstrating on a ripe apple. "Grip, roll your hand upward, and twist." The apple popped free and Edna lowered it into the basket hanging from her ladder.

Rachel looked at all the apples covering the tree, then thought about all the trees filling the meadow along Sugar Creek. "Are you telling me that in this day and age there's no better, more modern way of picking apples? No handy dandy machine or a tool that picks twenty at a time or something?"

"That's what I'm tellin' ya. At least not at the Farris Family Apple Orchard. We do things the old-fashioned way here."

"Because we *like* the old-fashioned way? Or because we just don't know about any other ways?" Rachel asked, curious.

But Edna just shook her head. "You and machines. I like to keep things simple—you know that." Indeed she did. Rachel had once gotten Edna a computer for Christmas, mainly for e-mail and Internet access, but Edna had wanted nothing to do with it. And every time Rachel checked her Blackberry, trying to keep up with events at Conrad/Phelps, Edna scolded her and had even hidden it for a while yesterday.

"Not that I'm, uh, anxious to get back to the city or anything," Rachel said as she found a ripe apple and proceeded with the grab, twist, and pull method, "but can you refresh my memory on exactly how long the harvest will take?"

"Well, I usually hire a few hands, but this year money's a little tight, so I only have one high school boy, Betty Cahill's son, comin' to help in the afternoons and on weekends, startin' tomorrow. That—plus the fact that I'm not movin' as quick as usual these days," she added, "is sorta why I called on *you*."

Ugh. Rachel didn't like hearing Edna was low on money—although it didn't surprise her, given that the orchard was a seasonal business. And again, she remained unsure whether or not Edna was faking the whole knee thing. She'd been certain of it when she'd gotten Edna's call, and just as certain when she'd arrived. But maybe Edna *was* moving slower than usual. And climbing up and down ladders all day was pretty hard work.

"Anyway," Edna went on, "the harvest has to be done by the apple festival, the first weekend of October."

Rachel had gone on plucking apples, but at this, she stopped and looked up. "Apple festival? What apple festival?"

And Edna blinked, as if it were a silly question. "Why, the annual Destiny Apple Festival. It's a big deal around here—I can't believe you don't know about it. Takes place right on the town square—we got apple pie eatin' contests, bakin' contests, bobbin' for apples, caramel apples, apple butter, apple cider, apple sauce, you name it. People come from miles around."

Rachel was still dumbfounded—because there'd been no apple festival when *she* lived here. "How on earth did this apple festival start? And when?"

"Well, it was *my* idea, of course." Edna's tone implied Rachel should have known that. "Suggested to the town council about ten years back that Destiny needed a fall event and that an apple festival was as good as any. Frankly, between me and you, the festival is what keeps me in business. Sure, I get folks who come to pick a bushel or two on weekends, but this orchard provides every apple used in every pie or fritter or dumplin' at the festival—without it, the Farris Family Apple Orchard would be history."

Rachel barely knew which fact to contemplate first. That she had to hand it to Edna for creating her own festival to keep the business solvent? Or that—dear God—Edna expected her to stay until October!

A few words Chase had imparted before she left suddenly rang in her ears. *Take the time you need with your grandma, but don't stay* too *long, if you know what I mean.* It was actually his higher-ups who held Rachel's fate in their hands, and Chase had given the advice kindly, from concern—but it hit her so hard now that she got a little dizzy. She had to grab onto the ladder with both hands to steady herself.

"Good Lord, darlin'—you all right?"

Still holding on tight, Rachel began to feel less woozy. "Yeah, fine," she lied. "Just lost my balance a little."

Of course, she could just *tell* Edna—the whole thing, about her job, and that she'd expected to be leaving in a couple of weeks, as opposed to *six*, and surely Edna would understand. And even if spending didn't sound like the wisest move right now given that she had a fifty-fifty chance of soon being unemployed, she *could* just *pay* for the usual hired hands. After all, it wouldn't be the first time she'd bailed out a loved one with a check.

"Well, you be careful," Edna said. "Wouldn't wanna lose my apple pickin' partner." Then she sighed, her face taking on a sadder, more confiding expression. "Ya know, darlin', I don't like admittin' this sorta thing, but . . . reckon I've missed havin' the family around me here in the orchard over the years. Once upon a time, the whole place was so full—you kids runnin' ever' which way— and now it's empty. It gets a little lonely sometimes," she concluded.

And Rachel's stomach dropped.

The fact was, if Rachel laid it on the line about her job right now, Edna would likely say, "Why the hell didn't ya say so in the first place?" and demand she go start packing her bags this instant. But . . . the very idea of Edna being *lonely*—really and truly *lonely*—ripped at Rachel's soul.

She wasn't sure why—because her family had *always* assumed Edna's calls for help had to do with her being lonely. But somehow *this*—hearing Edna say it—made it real, and a little heartbreaking, in a way Rachel hadn't felt before. And the fact that Edna had actually acknowledged it . . . well, from confident, no-nonsense Edna, it was a confession of epic proportions.

So to leave Edna *now*, for *any* reason, would feel like . . . abandoning her. Emotionally. Not that Edna usually seemed fragile in any way—far from it.

Except for what she'd just said.

And . . . except for that moment Rachel had told Tessa and Amy about, when Edna had smiled and said how nice it was to have her here. Something in that simple smile had looked . . . almost girlish, childlike. Something in it had touched her far more deeply than she'd thought matter-of-fact Edna could.

And suddenly Rachel understood why. Stubborn, ornery Edna wasn't always so tough.

Rachel let out a breath. She knew she couldn't leave— not now, and not even in a couple of weeks. Her job was extremely important—but at this strikingly candid moment, Edna was *more* important. And if Edna needed her until the apple festival, well . . . she'd have to stay until the apple festival. Her heart demanded it.

Her heart. Sheesh. She'd not expected her *heart* to get involved when she'd come here just a few days ago. But already, something here—whether it was Edna, or her friends, or the town itself—was softening her. Just a little.

Which was a pretty big revelation—no one who knew Rachel would ever call her soft, or sweet. But she just tried to steady herself, push all those thoughts from her mind, and come back to the matters at hand: picking apples and spending time with her grandmother. And wrapping her head around the idea that this was her life until October.

The weather remained warm, but the apple trees provided enough shade that, along with a breeze sifting through the trees, the day was comfortable. And the work was punctuated with the occasional buzz of a passing bumble bee and the fluttering bits of color provided by butterflies in the wildflowers that lined the creek. And when Rachel stopped to soak all that in . . . well, to her surprise, it was almost enough to make her forget all *about* her job. For a little while, anyway.

"Times change in Destiny," Rachel mused to Edna without warning, "but they don't really change *here*, do they? I mean *right* here, in the orchard. I guess nothing much has changed about these trees, or picking the apples, from when I was little. Or maybe even since you came here."

She looked over in time to catch a another uncharacteristically wistful expression crossing Edna's wrinkled face. "Maybe that's why I like this time of year so much. It's a lotta work, and a rush to make sure the apples all get harvested, but you're right—standin' on this ladder . . . well, if I didn't know better, I could close my eyes and believe it was the first time I ever picked apples here next to Sugar Creek."

Rachel watched as Edna did that then—closed her eyes, one hand on the ladder, the other pulling on the apple she already had in her grasp. Another happy, girlish look overtook her and Rachel wondered what she was remembering.

When Edna opened her eyes, Rachel asked, "When was it, your first year here?"

"Nineteen fifty-eight. I was eighteen years old. And so in love."

Wow. In Rachel's whole life, she'd never heard Edna talk about being in love. It shook her a bit. Perhaps because . . . well, *she'd* never been in love. And Edna had known what it felt like at eighteen? Although Rachel had never aspired to all that traditional love-and-marriage stuff, for some reason, it almost made her a little envious.

"With Grandpa Farris," Rachel chimed in, feeling wistful herself now.

So when Edna said, "No, with Giovanni Romo," Rachel nearly fell off her ladder.

She turned her head. Stared. "Wait. Who?"

Edna tossed her a sly glance. "You heard me."

Rachel barely knew what to say. Edna had never mentioned any man but her late husband, Edward Farris, who'd died when Rachel was fifteen. But as she caught her breath, she had a feeling this was a good time to ask, "Um, how exactly did our feud with the Romo family start?"

Edna resumed picking apples and said, "You never heard this story, huh?"

"No. By the time I was old enough to wonder, I'd moved away. And I once asked Mom, but she didn't really know, either."

"Well, let me start by sayin'—it wasn't entirely my fault. But the Romos never quite saw it that way."

"Let's try here."

Edna's older brother, Dell, pointed at the silver mailbox sitting on a wooden post at the end of a pretty little lane. Staring back through the trees, she could see the path led across a creek to a little white house. They'd walked at least a mile since their truck had broken down and this was the first home they'd come to, so it seemed the obvious place to look for some help.

Her other brother, Wally, spit on the ground, then stuck his thumbs in his suspenders to hitch up his overalls, before he said, "Destiny my ass."

"Don't cuss, Wally," Edna scolded him, but his scowl told her it was the wrong time for scolding. And she couldn't blame him. They were all in bad moods for lots of good reasons.

The three of them had driven the old family truck up from Kentucky looking for work. It was that or send the boys to the coal mines now that they were of age, and

Daddy wouldn't hear of that. But there were five more children at home and not enough money to keep everybody fed come winter—let alone get shoes for school. So they'd decided Dell, twenty-one, and Wally, nineteen, ought to strike out for Ohio and see if anybody needed farm hands. Edna had decided to come, too, claiming she could hoe a row or dig up taters or shuck corn as good as any boy—and besides, she'd never been more than twenty miles from the farm. So it had seemed like an adventure. And when they'd passed by a sign telling them they were in a place called Destiny, well, it had felt a little magical. "Here," she'd said. "Here's where we'll find what we're lookin' for."

That had been about two minutes before the truck sputtered and died. And about an hour after the last time they'd been turned down for work. They'd stopped at farms and in towns, at produce stands and even churches, all the way from the Ohio River north, with no luck. "Told ya we shoulda gone to Cincinnati," Wally said as they crossed the bridge on foot. "We coulda got work there for sure."

"Mama didn't want us in the city," Edna reminded him.

"Well, Mama ain't the one tryin' to put food on the table right now, is she?" he snapped, and Edna ignored him, peering down at the pretty stream below, at the water rolling gently over the stones, washing them clean. It was a peaceful sight, and frankly, she could use a little peace after Lord knew how many hours in a truck with Wally.

The bridge led to what Edna thought was the prettiest little farm she'd ever seen. The white house had fancy carved trim all around the front porch and gable, and the drive led farther back to a bright red barn. A small grove of apple trees set across the lane, and behind the house was a huge garden—she even saw some grapevines along a fencerow. The moo of a cow told her there must be a pasture full of cattle, maybe behind the barn where she couldn't see. And looked like somebody had been busy loading fresh hay into the barn, getting ready for winter—just like she and her brothers were trying to do. "Well, ain't this nice," she said.

When neither of her brothers replied, she could figure out why easily enough: envy. Any of them would be plum lucky to ever end up with a place this nice, and things weren't looking too promising for any of her family these days.

Dell marched up onto the porch and knocked while she and Wally stood back, waiting. But no one came to the door.

"Son of a bitch," Wally muttered, then threw his hat down on the narrow front walk. Edna didn't bother scolding him this time. When she'd seen this place, she'd been filled with hope, but now she realized that was silly. Nothing had gone right on this trip so far—why had she expected their luck to suddenly change?

Silently, the three trudged toward the lane, headed back to the road—when they all looked up to see what had to be the fanciest car on God's green earth crossing the bridge toward them. It was long and sleek and turquoise. "Damn," Dell murmured, eyes wide.

"What kinda car is that?" Edna asked. Dell knew about cars—Mr. Dills at the drugstore in town sometimes let him have the car magazines from the rack in back if they sat there a long time without selling.

"That, sis, is a Cadillac," he said, still in awe as it neared them. "An Eldorado Biarritz. First one I ever seen outside of pictures. Look at them fins."

But by now Edna was too busy studying the fella inside the convertible to worry about the car's fins. The man appeared dark and handsome in a beige suit and matching hat, and to Edna's way of thinking, he was just as nice to look at as the Cadillac.

He didn't seem alarmed to see three strangers standing in his yard—instead he just smiled and waved as if he knew them, the picture of confidence as he drove past to park behind the house.

Edna's knees nearly knocked beneath her skirt as he approached.

"Buongiorno," he said. "How can I help you?"

And then she nearly swooned. He had some kind of foreign accent she'd never heard before, except maybe in the movies.

Dell explained, hat in hand, their run of bad luck—the broken-down truck and that they were looking for work. "Anything you got, we'd be willin' to take. Me and Wally here are good field hands, and Edna, too—and she can cook and clean a blue streak. Makes the best apple pie you ever had—even better than our mama's, and that's sayin' a lot."

Edna had no idea why she was suddenly so nervous— except that she'd never been in the presence of such a handsome, well-dressed man before. And in this moment, it felt like he held their fate in his hands.

"As luck would have it," he said, "I am alone here, keeping the place up myself. I had two hired men, but they quit a week ago for factory jobs in Columbus. I could use some help."

Dell looked like he might drop to his knees in gratitude, and it was all Edna could do to hold back tears. Wally, always the tough one, stepped up to negotiate wages, but they all knew they'd accept whatever the handsome man offered. Turned out, though, he was willing to pay a fair price, and even said they could sleep in a spare room in his home, all with a genuine smile on his face. As Edna listened to the exchange, she found herself caught up in the way he talked.

"Mister," Edna stepped up to ask once the arrangements had been made, "mind if I ask where you're from?"

He smiled at her curiosity and her heart flip-flopped in her chest. "I come from a small fishing village called Vernazza, on the Italian coast."

The Italian coast? Heavens above. One day Edna hadn't traveled out of the county where she'd been born, and a few short days later she was working for a man who'd come from the other side of the world. She tried to hide her excitement, but suspected it showed in her eyes. The man just laughed, though, and it somehow put her at ease, made her feel less backward than she probably should in her mama's old hand-me-down dress and shoes.

"So, this pie. Is it as wonderful as your brother promises? Or was that just to tempt me into hiring you?" He winked, his eyes sparkling, and—goodness gracious—Edna felt that wink in the very crux of her thighs. It was all she could do not to collapse.

"Well, if I do say so myself, it's about the most delicious thing you could eat in the whole world." Although, after she spoke, she felt a little less certain. Her world, after all, had just grown—by leaps and bounds. So she added, "At least in Rowan County, Kentucky—which is where we come from. I can't really speak for Italy, of course."

The man who'd just saved them continued to smile at her. "Well, we shall soon see. There are apple trees right over there." He pointed. "When the apples ripen, you can bake me one of these delicious pies."

"You won't be disappointed," Dell said, still perfectly confident. Then he added, "You said you was alone here? So then . . . you don't got a wife or nothin'?"

The man shook his head. "Oh, no—no wife for me. Not yet."

Dell nodded and Wally grinned, and Edna wondered why—until she figured it out. They thought the handsome man liked her. That way.

Could it be? Surely not. She was so . . . country. And

he was so sophisticated. Even if he was a farmer just like them, well . . . they truly came from different worlds.

So she was sure her brothers were being way too optimistic as she asked, "What's your name, mister?"

"Giovanni Romo," he said, drawing the syllables out with his exotic accent.

Edna repeated it in her mind, to make sure she remembered. Giovanni Romo. It was the most wonderful name she'd ever heard.

"Time for lunch," Edna announced, beginning to back down her ladder.

"Wait," Rachel said. "You've just barely gotten started and I'm not even hungry yet." She was still stunned by the notion of her grandmother once being in love with a Romo, and she was dying to hear the rest of the story.

"Well, I *am* hungry. And it's a good story. One I only tell once in a blue moon, by the way. So if ya don't mind, I think I'll just stretch it out, take my time. Do it in . . . what did they used to call it in magazines? Installments," she said. "Yep, we'll do it in installments."

"What if I *do* mind?" Rachel said, peering down at her. Edna was on the ground now, so Rachel backed carefully down, as well.

"Too bad," Edna said pointedly.

So Rachel just rolled her eyes, then followed Edna into the house. "No perks for the free help, I see," she muttered under her breath, letting the old screen door slam behind her. Rachel still couldn't believe it—Edna and a Romo?

As Edna set about washing her hands, then grabbing a fresh loaf of bread baked in the bread machine Rachel had gotten her one Christmas, she said, "Speakin' of the Romos, though, there's somethin' I reckon you oughta know."

She said this like it was nothing, but Rachel instantly

•

knew it was *something*. Something big. Especially with the way Edna's story had begun. "What's that?" she asked, lathering up her own hands.

Edna moved around behind her, gathering lunchmeat and cheese from the fridge. "Mike Romo wants to buy the orchard from me."

Everything in Rachel froze solid as she turned off the faucet. *"What?"* It felt like . . . like Mike Romo had just tried to rob her house or something, like he'd invaded her personal space in an unforgivable way. It was one thing to be mean and nasty to *her*, but another to try to take her grandma's beloved home and business.

"Now, nothin' new about a Romo offerin' on the place—one or t'other of 'em's been tryin' to get the orchard nigh on fifty years now. But what's different about this time is . . . I'm thinkin' about sellin' it to him."

In response to Rachel's dropped jaw and outraged expression, Edna said, "Now simmer down, girl. I'm thinkin' about sellin' it to him—*eventually*. In a few years, when I just plain can't run the place anymore."

Rachel blinked, her mouth still hanging open. She couldn't believe Edna, of all Romo haters, would consider such a thing. Even with the new revelation that she'd once had a thing for Mike's grandfather. And besides . . . "What on earth does *he* want with an orchard? Isn't he busy enough terrorizing the citizens of Destiny at every turn?"

Edna worked on the sandwiches, not looking at Rachel as she replied. "Says he wants it in case he decides to retire from the department at some point. And that he'd enjoy runnin' the place. He came to me a few months back with the proposition—said he'd already started savin' towards it and that I could even stay here in the house 'til I die."

Rachel felt her eyes bolt open wider. "He's killing you off in the bargain?"

Now Edna looked up. "Believe or not, even *I'm* gonna die one of these days."

Maybe so, but . . . well, Rachel *really* didn't like think-ing about that.

"I thought it was a right generous offer. Knowin' I'd have my little home 'til the end does a lot to put my mind at ease about the whole idea."

Rachel remained livid, though, and still in utter dis-belief. "Since when do you want to sell this place to a Romo?"

"It's simple," Edna said, placing two ripe apples along-side the sandwiches she'd just set on plates. "My whole life, I figured one of my children or grandchildren would want to take over the orchard when I'm gone. But it's lookin' like that ain't gonna happen. Now, I don't make a big deal over it, but the fact is, when I pass on, I'd much rather know the orchard'll live on and be cared for by a Romo than not live on at all."

Of course, the words did exactly what they were de-signed to do—make Rachel feel guilty. On behalf of her whole selfish family. For not being here. For not helping more. For not caring about the family business. "Okay, I get that," she admitted. "But still, a *Romo*? Of anyone in the world, you'd pick a Romo to keep the place going?"

Edna shrugged. "Is a Romo my first choice? Nope. But a Romo's what I got to choose from. And like I said, Mike's a good enough fella—and he's better than *no* choice." She poured two glasses of iced tea, adding, "If you or one of your cousins suddenly decide you wanna run an orchard, you let me know. Otherwise, I'd be a fool not to consider Mike's offer."

Heading into the old-fashioned dining room complete with blue flowered wallpaper, they sat down at the antique table and ate silently for a few minutes, and as Rachel bit into her Gala apple she turned it all over in her mind. Fi-nally she said, "Are you making this whole thing up about Mike Romo? Inventing some elaborate scheme to try to trick me into saving the family business?" She shook a potato chip at her grandmother across the table. "Because I gotta tell ya, Edna, you're seriously on the wrong track with that. I won't do it. I can't. I'm willing to help you out here for a few weeks, but I'm not an outdoorsy kind of girl and things like that don't change."

"*You're* tellin' *me*," Edna said. "You're about the slowest apple picker I've come across. Not that I don't appreciate the help, and I'm sure you'll get better with practice, but . . . nope, Rachel Marie Farris, this ain't a trick. I know that somehow or other I turned out a bunch of city-dwellin' offspring—and I'm just finally startin' to accept it and make plans accordin'ly."

"Well . . . good," Rachel said, adding, "I *think*." Since Edna had somehow made being city dwelling sound like a highly undesirable trait. "Good that you . . . get that, I mean. But I still can't believe you'd ever sell the orchard to a Romo."

Particularly the one that still made her skin tingle every time she thought about him, damn it.

Thus from my lips, by yours, my sin is purged.

William Shakespeare, *Romeo and Juliet*

Four

Rachel drove along a ribbon of dark, winding road, headed to Tessa's place for "snack night," a tradition from their girlhood. In high school, she, Tessa, and Amy had gotten together once every couple of weeks, each forgoing dinner and providing a snack of their choice to share over girl talk. They always recreated snack night at least once on their annual visits, and now that Edna had dropped the apple festival bomb, looked like they might be able to get *several* snack nights in while Rachel was here. Tonight, she'd come bearing Edna's pie.

As the road dipped deeper into a dark valley, though, she couldn't get her mind off the day, so chock-full of revelations. Like that she now had until *October* to work on her apple-picking skills! And that Edna had some sort of history with Mike Romo's grandfather! And the kicker—Mike Romo was trying to get the orchard from Edna.

Just thinking about that incensed her.

Maybe it shouldn't—because everything Edna said made sense. It was better *someone* keep the place going than no one. But she couldn't help thinking of Romo like some vulture waiting for just the right time—now that Edna was getting older and in need of help, bad knees or not—to swoop in and convince her this was what she wanted. When it really wasn't. Because Edna *couldn't* really want to sell to the Romo family. She'd spent Rachel's whole life denouncing their evil ways. So if she sold to Mike Romo, it would be a move of desperation.

Which *did* make her feel guilty—even though she knew she shouldn't. There were *plenty* of Farrises to take the blame, after all—she wasn't the only one who had left. And why should *anyone* feel obligated to take on a business that didn't inspire them? Besides, Rachel was busy with a career that would provide Edna financial support when she needed it. She was only one woman; she could only do so much.

And she *had* gotten a bit of *good* news today. An e-mail on her Blackberry informing her that her team had won a new account for an organic skincare line—she'd been courting the Natural Girl people for a few months, and though it wouldn't make up for the recent loss of the massive K&K account, it was still a nice feather in her cap right now. In fact, she would have been in a downright celebratory mood . . . if not for everything else on her mind.

As she swung the car around an *S* curve winding through the tree-shrouded valley, she appreciated the way the BMW hugged the road—but good God, where on earth did Tessa live? The log cabin out on Whisper Falls Road had sounded quaint and rustic, but now it seemed more . . . dangerous and spooky. Tessa, of all people, wanted to live out *here*? She knew Tessa had gone through some big changes in the last couple of years, yet now that Rachel saw the drive Tessa made just to get home at night—yikes. She was waiting for a headless horseman to go riding by any minute.

And that was when the glow of blue lights illuminated her rear window.

Rachel instantly began muttering a long string of curse words. *Unbelievable! He'd gotten her again?*

It never even occurred to her that it might be some other Destiny cop—and it wasn't. Because Mike Romo was apparently the only one out prowling the rural roads looking for lawbreakers like her.

"Are you stalking me?" she said when he shone a big, stupid flashlight in her eyes.

"No, I'm ticketing you. You're going fifty-five in a thirty-five."

"Are you serious?"

"Yep, that's what I clocked you at."

"No—I mean are you serious about giving me another ticket? Before I've even had a chance to recover from the last one?"

She could see his pointed look even in the dark. "You seem recovered enough to me. Since it didn't slow you down any." She could also see that—oh, crap—his eyes were just as gorgeous as usual, even in the dark.

"You know, Officer Romeo," she said as he finally pulled the flashlight away to write out the ticket, "you have a lousy way of making someone feel welcome in this silly little town."

"It's not my job to make you feel welcome," he said without glancing up from his work. "In fact, the sooner you leave, the sooner I can quit writing out all these tickets. My fingers are starting to get tired."

She rolled her eyes in response—and just in case he didn't see, she let out a large harrumph, too.

And then she noticed, as she always did, how ridiculously broad his shoulders were. And how good-looking he was. He hadn't shaved in days, and she found herself wanting to touch the dark stubble on his jaw. And suffering that familiar fluttering sensation in her panties again.

And then—yuck—she remembered that the last time she'd seen the big lug he'd been taking Miss Tan Chick home to bed. A thought which made her stomach hurt, just as it had then. Ridiculous that she still felt the gnawing ache, but she did.

"And another thing," she said, suddenly remembering. "You leave my grandmother alone. Because I know what you're up to."

He looked down at her over his clipboard, completely unfazed. "Oh? What's that?"

As she met those dark bedroom eyes, his face illuminated in the glow of the flashlight, she struggled not to let them affect her. "You're trying to steal her orchard and I won't allow it."

"No, Farris—you've got it wrong, as usual. I'm trying to *buy* her orchard, fair and square. And if she decides to sell it to me, there's nothing you can do to stop it."

Oh yeah? Well . . . "Maybe I'll take it over myself," she boasted. She didn't mean it, of course, but it was something to say.

And at this, he cracked up. Mike Romo. Who'd barely even smiled the entire time she'd known him. He leaned his head back, laughing out loud, looking completely overcome with the hilarity of it all. "That's a good one, Farris. You tell Edna that one? I bet it'd give *her* a good laugh, too."

She blinked, fuming. "What's so funny about it?"

He gave his head a short, definite shake. "You're not cut out for farm work. And I'm surprised you're here in Destiny at all, now that I've gotten a good look at you."

She bit her lip. Despite the blatant insult, something in his last words made her feel a bit warm. "Like the look you took at the Dew Drop Inn the other night? Because from what I saw, you couldn't take your eyes off me, Romeo."

He shrugged, straightforward as ever. "Never said the package wasn't nice. But what's inside it isn't somebody who could run an orchard. And stop calling me Romeo, Farris."

"Well, guess what—you're right. I *don't* want to run Edna's orchard. I'm too busy with my *own* career, thank you very much."

"Race car driver?" he shot back. Oh boy, he was suddenly Mr. Funny tonight.

"I'm an executive account director at a prestigious ad agency," she announced, purposely sounding superior and hoping he was impressed, whether or not he let it show. "But that doesn't mean I'll stand by and let you wheedle her out of what she's worked to build her whole life, so I suggest you leave her alone."

"Or what?"

"Or you'll have the whole Farris clan to deal with."

"I'm shaking in my shoes," he said dryly. "And you keep tossing around words like steal and wheedle, but we suspect *Edna* is the one who stole that land from my grandfather back in the fifties. So the way I see it, I'm only getting back what was supposed to be mine to begin with—and, frankly, I'm being pretty damn nice about it."

He was leaning down now, closer, and she was noticing his mouth . . . his skin . . . his dark eyelashes, for heaven's sake. And she was thinking again about kissing him. It was that darn rugged smell of his, damn it.

"Do you know the story—what happened?" she asked, but her voice came out softer than intended. "Between Edna and your grandfather?"

"Not exactly," he admitted. "He never would talk about it. But I know he felt cheated. And he went to his grave wishing he could have left that farm to my dad."

"Well, I don't know the story, either," she said, sounding stronger to herself now, "but it's the *Farris* Family Apple Orchard, and I'll be damned if the name Romo goes up on that sign."

His only reply? To tear off the ticket and pass it to her through the window.

As she took it, their hands brushed. And—dear God—

she felt it *everywhere*. Like . . . some sort of mini-orgasm or something! She couldn't help peering up at him as she drew in her breath.

"What?" he asked.

"Nothing," she lied. But his eyes said he knew. And she figured hers were pretty much saying it all, too. *I just tingled wildly between my legs over our hands touching.* God, this was horrible.

So she yanked her eyes from his and glanced down at his dark, jagged writing. And it actually managed to take her mind off her physical reaction. "Holy crap—another hundred and fifty?"

"Twenty over, Farris."

"I'm surprised you're not threatening to take me to jail again."

"Don't tempt me."

As usual, she rolled her eyes—a gesture that was beginning to feel overdone with him, but it was all she had. "You're only doing this because I'm a Farris."

"No, I'm doing this because you're a reckless driver. The fact that you're a Farris is just a perk."

She let out a belligerent sigh—still out of punchy comebacks—and said, "Am I free to go, Officer?"

"As long as you quit speeding on my roads."

"Consider me motivated, Romeo. Whatever it takes to quit running into you."

As Rachel drove away, she couldn't deny the fact that her palms were sweaty. And her heart still beat too hard. And it had nothing to do with being pulled over.

She really disliked him. She disliked everything he stood for: thinking that badge gave him the right to bully people, being angry and arrogant all the time, and now trying to cajole Edna out of the orchard. Plus—again—he was a Romo.

But none of that, it seemed, was quite enough to keep her from wanting to rip his clothes off.

"Not that that will *ever* happen. *Ever*," she told herself. Even if he did think her "package" was nice.

Oh God, since when was she attracted to men who called her a "package"?

She'd known from the start that coming back to Destiny was a bad idea, and with each passing day she was beginning to fear it was an even worse one than she'd realized.

"How on earth," Rachel asked across Tessa's kitchen table, nibbling on one of Amy's caramel brownies, "did I not know there was an apple festival?"

"Don't ask *me*," Amy said. "It's a Destiny tradition now—everyone loves it."

"And it's in *October*! I have to stay 'til *October*!" When she was standing in the orchard with Edna, Chicago seemed a world away and it was easier than expected to shove her worries aside—but now she felt a little panicky. "I debated phoning Chase and telling him, but I decided it's better not to call the length of my absence to anyone's attention."

"Like they won't notice?" Tessa asked, forking a bite of apple pie into her mouth.

And she made a darn good point. But . . . "Who knows—maybe they won't. Maybe getting the Natural Girl account will make it seem . . . like I'm working from afar." Or—maybe the new client wouldn't count for as much as she hoped. Maybe it was dumb to stay just because Edna was lonely.

"Oh, and get this," she said then. She'd regaled them with the tale of tonight's ticket already, but . . . "Mike Romo wants to buy the orchard from Edna!"

Both girls' eyes flew wide, and it pleased her to see they were just as surprised as she was.

"Mike Romo, running an orchard?" Tessa balked. "He doesn't have the temperament for something so . . . calm."

"My thoughts exactly," Rachel said with an emphatic nod.

"The orchard *was* in his family once, though, you know," Amy countered.

"Yeah, yeah," Rachel replied, swiping a dismissive hand down through the air. "But that's ancient history." And she almost started to tell them what she'd found out about Edna having a fling or something with Mike Romo's grandfather—but then she held her tongue, because maybe it was a private story. After all, no one in either family seemed to know the details, and Edna had said she didn't talk about it often. So, as much as Rachel wanted to share it with her friends, she kept it to herself.

In fact, it seemed like a good time to change the subject. There was too much Romo talk lately anyway. And if it kept up, she might admit that he got her all hot and bothered. And if she said it out loud, that would make it feel a lot more *real*, and *unavoidable*. "So, what's going on in *your* lives, girls? Ever since I got here, all we've talked about is me. Do either of you have anything fun going on?"

Tessa shook her head. "No big plans in my immediate future other than the bookstore and some yardwork. And I might—out of desperation—put an ad in the *Crestview Tribune*." Tessa was trying to get her interior design business off the ground, working from home, but she'd had no customers yet—there just weren't many people willing to pay someone to decorate their houses in a small town like Destiny.

It broke Rachel's heart that her friend had been forced to give up a budding career in Cincinnati after developing a chronic but frustratingly undiagnosed digestive condition, suffering flare-ups too often to keep her job. And Tessa's younger brother was on his second tour in Afghanistan, which kept her under even *more* stress. Growing up, Tessa had always been Rachel's comrade-in-arms in wanting to leave Destiny, so she couldn't imagine all Tessa had endured before making the decision to return. Now, she tried her best to smile. "You'll get some business once word gets out."

They commiserated on Tessa's career woes a few minutes more, all scarfing down some of the pumpkin bread Tessa had made, until Amy said, "Well, like I told you the other night, my only extra plans this week are working the concession stand with Logan at the donkey ball game at the high school on Wednesday."

Oh Lord. Rachel hadn't caught the "donkey" detail when they'd discussed this at the Dew Drop Inn. "People here still play donkey ball? Tell me it's not true," she pleaded, recalling the odd tradition from her youth: coaches, teachers, and other well-known people in the community played a game of basketball—while riding donkeys. Just one more reason why Destiny wasn't her personal cup of tea.

"Of course it's true. There's a game every fall to benefit the athletics program."

"And you have to do this *why*?" Rachel asked. She could only imagine the smells involved—even from outside the gym at the concession stand.

"Well, the fire department volunteered to take tickets and run concessions, and they ended up short a few people, so Logan asked me to help."

Rachel nodded. She could relate to being called on for help these days—although she thought Amy sounded far too delighted about working in the vicinity of a herd of donkeys. "Doesn't the gym floor get messed up? From hooves and . . . you know, droppings?"

"Nice topic while we're eating, Rach," Tessa scolded, reaching for a brownie.

"Well, I'm not the one who brought up donkeys and I always wondered about this. *I* got yelled at for walking on the gym floor in heels, but ten donkeys can go trotting around on it all night?"

Amy just laughed. "They put down a protective covering."

"Okay, no more donkey talk," Tessa insisted, and Rachel agreed.

"Tell us more about your boss," Amy suggested, cutting a slice of Edna's pie. "I mean, you never mentioned before about the flirtation, in all these years."

Much better topic, Rachel thought cheerfully, happy to launch into it. "Well, it seemed completely unfeasible. But yeah, he's extremely handsome, wears Armani, drives a Jag, and is to die for in every way."

And he *was*, so she kept right on talking about Chase for a long while—even if, for some insane reason, she kept seeing Mike Romo's belligerent face in her mind the whole time.

Rachel had come in from picking apples with sore shoulders and sore thighs, needing a hot shower—but at Edna's, she had to settle for a hot bath in the old clawfoot tub. It was doing the trick, though—the steaming soak eased some of her aches, and she was starting to feel like her old self again.

As she drained the tub a few minutes later and slipped into a plush, hot pink robe, she heard the phone ring, just before Edna's voice echoed through the bathroom door. "For you, darlin'. It's Amy."

Rachel opened the door to take the old corded receiver. "Hey," she said easily.

But Amy sounded stressed. "I need a huge favor."

Uh-oh. "What?"

"Can you fill in for me at the concession stand tonight? At the donkey ball game?"

Oh brother, that was tonight? And she was being asked to *go* there? "Why?"

"I hate to ask, Rachel, but it's book club night."

Book club and donkey ball, all on the same Wednesday

night—how would the people of Destiny choose? But she kept that thought to herself. "What about Tessa? I thought she was hosting the book club in your place."

"That's just it," Amy said. "She's not feeling well. I think it's been coming on for days and finally hit her hard."

And Rachel's heart dropped. Despite all she knew about Tessa's condition, she'd never been around during a flare-up, and she suddenly felt guilty for always being so far away when her friend was in need. "How bad *is* she? Should one of us go see her?"

"No. She doesn't like company when she's sick—and if she needs anyone, she calls her mom. Anyway, can you work the concession stand for me? You hung out with Logan the other night—he's a nice guy, and he'll really appreciate the help."

Hell. How could she say no? Tessa was sick, for God's sake. And her friends never asked her for anything. "Of course. I'll be there." *Donkeys be damned.* "What time?"

Rachel dressed quickly in dark jeans, a fitted white long-sleeved blouse, and her red Gucci peek-toe pumps. And after a quick chicken salad sandwich, courtesy of Edna, she was out the door and on her way to a place she'd never expected to see again: Destiny High School.

She actually had a lot of good memories there—she'd been a cheerleader, active in clubs, and she'd made good grades. But she'd also often been bored, already longing for a life someplace bigger and busier, and that had frequently led her into trouble, too. Nothing serious—just some class cutting, a bit of sneaking around, and she'd once been caught making out with Russell Jamison in the janitor's closet.

Turning out onto the highway that led into town, she accelerated—yet then she slowed down. In case Officer

Romeo was lurking somewhere. Other than her brain, that is. She hadn't seen him since that last ticket he'd bestowed on her, but she gave a little shiver, unable to believe how often the guy penetrated her thoughts.

Well, she was about to spend the evening with the hot cop's best friend, so she hoped Romo's name wouldn't come up. She just wanted to do her duty behind the counter, try not to inhale too much *eau de donkey*, then head home and get a decent night's sleep. To her surprise, she was slowly getting a little better at apple picking, and she and Edna had been up and out at the Gala trees just after sunrise the last few days. Soon all the Galas would be harvested and they'd move on to the ripening Honeycrisps and McIntoshes.

Parking in front of her old school felt downright weird, and the place seemed much smaller than she remembered. It was still light out, so she kept her head low while trudging toward the gym entrance, hoping no one recognized her. Despite herself, she did have fond memories of many people in Destiny, but she just wasn't in the mood for reminiscing. She'd been on edge ever since getting to town and between her career worries, the extended stay, and Mike Romo, her stress level had gone from bad to worse. She found a sense of calm in working with Edna up in the trees—but it seemed that whenever she was anywhere else, all she could do was fret and worry. So in that way, the long days in the orchard felt almost pleasant at times.

Reaching the line of doors stretching across the gym's lobby, she explained to a guy in a black-and-yellow DFD T-shirt that she was here to work concessions and he ushered her in.

She remembered the snack stand from her years here—a small room with painted cinder block walls like the rest of the school, it was situated just outside the gym, with a large window on one side that opened into the lobby. A metal partition was pulled down and shut with padlocks when the stand wasn't in use.

Although the partition was already up and the lights on inside, she didn't see anyone through the window as she approached and figured she must have beat Logan here. Walking around to the open door, she stepped inside and hung her red pashmina on a hook behind it. Then rounded a cinder block corner—to see Mike Romo standing in front of her.

She reacted the same as if she'd just discovered some grotesquely spoiled food in her refrigerator—she drew in her breath, crinkled her nose, and looked on him with pure horror. When their eyes met, she uttered the only word that came to mind. "Shit." Then, "You have *got* to be kidding me."

He appeared to be just as stunned and surly. "Is this some bad joke?"

"Amy couldn't come," she said curtly.

He replied in an equally irritated tone. "Neither could Logan."

After which Rachel simply stood there for a moment, her mouth still gaping. Finally, she gave her head a short shake, concluding, "I don't think I can do this—put up with you for two or three hours, or however long people plan to ride around on donkeys in there." She pointed over her shoulder. The idea of grabbing her pashmina and getting the hell out of there was all too tempting.

"Nice attitude, Farris," Romo snapped. "Because, believe me, I don't want to work with you, either, but I'm not the kind of guy to leave a friend hanging."

"Neither am I," she bit off through clenched teeth. "I was leaving *you* hanging."

"*Sounds* like something a Farris would do."

Oooh, low blow.

And she really *couldn't* walk out after that. She'd look like a bad person and prove him right.

So she took a deep breath and told herself to act like an adult here. "Fine, Romeo, I'll stay if you want me so much. And don't think I don't get that you're trying to use reverse psychology on me. I'll just be damned before I give you one more bad thing to say about a Farris."

"I wish to *hell* you'd quit calling me Romeo," he grumbled.

"Good to know—Romeo. *I* wish to hell you'd quit giving me tickets, but we can't always get what we want, can we?" Just as the Stones had reminded her on her way into town. And boy, was it ever turning out to be true.

At that moment, a woman with wildly out-of-date big hair came dashing into the concession stand wearing a red-and-white Destiny Bulldogs sweatshirt. "Hi, I'm Madge—do you two have everything you need?" Before either of them could utter a word, she answered her own question by looking around, pointing, and counting things off out loud. "Change drawer, candy bars, snack chips, drink cups—and if any of the fountain drink canisters run out, just come and find me at the athletic boosters table in the gym. Looks like you're all set."

She started to rush right back out, but Rachel stopped her with, "Wait!"

The big-haired woman looked up.

"Will you be back for the money after the game—or do we need to lock it up somewhere?"

The woman leaned her head back with an oh-silly-me smile and actually grabbed Rachel's hand to give it a squeeze. "Glad you asked—I almost forgot." Then she leaned forward, as if confiding in her. "It's a little crazy trying to herd a dozen donkeys around the gym, let me tell ya."

"Of course," Rachel said in understanding, as if she'd done it many times herself.

"I'm gonna have my hands full of donkeys afterward, so if you two could just count up the proceeds less the twenty dollars of change provided, write down the total, and leave it here, that would be just dandy. There's a calculator, notepad, money drawer, and a little leather zipper bag with change right over there"—she pointed to some metal shelves in one corner—"and the door will lock automatically when you leave, so it'll be perfectly safe." Then her eyebrows shot up. "Oh, and that's another thing!" She sounded almost alarmed.

"What?" Romo asked.

"You need to leave the door to this room standing open at all times until you leave, because it locks from both the inside and out."

"*That's* weird," Rachel mused aloud.

"*That's* a quirk of a fifty-year-old building with its original doors," she informed them. "If it gets locked, you'd have to climb over the counter and track down Elmer, the custodian. So keep it open 'til you go. Now, is there anything else? 'Cause if not, I've got a dozen donkeys calling my name."

"We've got it," Romo assured her, and she was off, like a bolt of heavily hairsprayed lightning.

Forgetting for a moment how much she disliked Mike Romo, Rachel turned to him and said, "A dozen? Aren't there only ten players in basketball?"

He looked at her and shrugged. "In case a couple of the donkeys foul out?"

But she refused to smile. Because it was just then that she got over the flurried visit from Big Hair and remembered very clearly who she was being forced to work with.

Just then, their first customer arrived, a little red-haired kid who wanted Skittles and a small Coke. Since Rachel was standing closest to the fountain drink machine and Romo was by the candy and chips, she said, "I can do drinks if you can do the rest."

"That'll work, Farris," he said—and it was a good

thing they'd agreed so easily, since after that they doled out snacks and soft drinks nearly nonstop for the next fifteen minutes. Rachel couldn't believe a donkey ball game drew such a big crowd—but then again, there wasn't a lot of entertainment in Destiny.

At a break in the action, Rachel located the calculator and set it up where Mike could punch in numbers to add up larger orders. And when she stooped to plug it in under the counter, then turned to find herself face-to-face with the bulge behind his zipper—she nearly fainted. Holy God.

She should have been horrified by where she suddenly found herself, but instead she was instantly much more . . . fascinated. She hadn't had much chance to notice that part of him before—and noticing it now made her start to sweat. His jeans fit nicely, not too snug, not too loose—but they were a little snug right *there*, which made her bite her lip with . . . oh hell, *longing*. She had to accept that once and for all, she supposed. *You have a weird animal attraction to him—get over it already.*

"You all right down there?"

Crap. She glanced up to see him peering down at her, and the position she found herself in was . . . suggestive, to say the least. So she quickly darted her eyes away, then crawled back under the extended counter to say, "Just looking for a plug." Even though she'd already found it. A good minute or so ago.

She stayed there long enough to let any telltale blush fade, thankful when some little girls came bounding up with an order just as she took her place next to him again. Remaining a little freaked out—by his bulge and her blatant desire for it—she resumed filling cups with ice and soda and wondered exactly how clear it was to Officer Romeo that she'd been checking out the goods. Sheesh.

Fortunately, however, the rush on snacks continued, so there was no time to chitchat. Of course, all the moving around the window area meant they sometimes bumped. Or brushed. That their arms briefly connected and sometimes their hips. And one time, when they ran right smack into each other, Romo planted his palms at her waist and physically moved her to one side.

After which Rachel nearly swooned. Simply from having his hands on her. She'd felt the touch just a little lower than where it had actually been. And she'd tried like hell to hide the fact that she'd just suffered another one of those mini-orgasmic reactions. Yikes. This was bad. This physical attraction was getting . . . well, more and more physical by the moment.

It wasn't until halftime, when the doors opened and the fans came flooding out en masse, that she smelled the scent of donkey for the first time. Yuck. But she said nothing—because Romo would only think her weak and girly. *This is Destiny, not Chicago; they have farm animals here—suck it up.* They spent the next ten minutes vigorously handing out Cokes and Sprites, chips and pretzels, M&M'S and Milky Ways. Whenever she caught up on drinks, she took over calculating totals while Mike accepted the money and made change. And she tried to concentrate on *anything* besides her crazy yearnings.

"Hey, how's the game going?" Mike suddenly asked a pretty, dark-haired teenage girl.

"The faculty's beating the community leaders by four points," she said with a smile. And Rachel was on the verge of being aghast, wondering if he was flirting with a high schooler, when the girl asked, "What are *you* doing here, anyway?"

"Got roped into it by Logan," he answered—then handed her some peanut M&M'S before she even said what she wanted. "On me. Now be good and don't talk to any boys." He concluded by pointing a threatening finger at her.

"Uncle Miiiiiike," the girl said, rolling her eyes. "Knock it off."

He tilted his head. "You know I'm not really your uncle, right? More like your second cousin. And your uncles Tim and Jay get pissed when you kids call me that."

The girl just shrugged. "Uncle's easier. And we like you better than them." And then she was gone.

Hmm. Wow. He had young relatives who actually liked him? She'd just never thought of mean Mike Romo having a relationship—even a teasing, scolding one—with . . . well, much of anyone.

Right before the second half began, Ralph Turley, the school principal, came hurrying in the door behind them, saying, "Don't mind me—just need to grab some towels," which he found on the metal shelves. "Ball got messy," he added on the way out, pulling the door shut behind him.

"Ewwww," Rachel commented when he was gone. "That's one example of why you couldn't *pay* me to play donkey basketball."

And she had no idea why Romeo was looking at her so oddly until he said, "Did he just close that door?"

"Uh-oh," she replied, then rushed up to twist the knob and pull. Sure enough—Big Hair hadn't lied; it was locked tight. "Hell," she muttered.

"No big deal," he said with a short head shake. "I'll send out a search party for Elmer." Then he summoned one of the firemen still manning the doors, asking him to find the janitor.

A few minutes later, a squat old man—about ninety, from the looks of him—arrived at the window. Elmer had been the custodian when Rachel had gone to school here and he'd been old *then*. In fact, he'd been the one to discover her with Russell Jamison in his closet, though she doubted he remembered her.

"Ya cain't shut that door," Elmer told them, pointing at it through the window.

"We know," Mike said. "It was an accident."

"Locks on its own, ya see," Elmer went on.

"Yeah, we know," Mike answered.

"Now I'll have to dig out m'keys and unlock it, and then ya need to keep it open. Cain't shut it," he repeated. "It'll lock up on ya again."

"We understand," Mike told him.

After which Elmer toddled around the corner and could be heard fiddling with what sounded like a very large set of keys, until finally the door opened inward. "Got 'er open," Elmer said. "Don't shut 'er again or we'll be back where we just come from."

"*Got it*," Mike said, finally starting to sound a little testy, but Elmer didn't seem to notice—he just went on his way.

"Just in case you missed that," Rachel said, completely straight-faced as Elmer ambled off down the hall, "that door locks if you shut it."

And to her surprise, Mike Romo smiled. Even laughed a little. And her chest tightened when his eyes sparkled and she saw once again that he wasn't always so awful. Apparently, his little cousin knew something Rachel didn't.

"I don't like admitting this," she told him, "but you and I work pretty well together."

He took a second before replying, "I'd have to agree, Farris. Guess miracles *do* happen."

A moment later, a teenage couple—glued to each other and clearly in the throes of teenage love—ordered a pack of Starburst and two Cokes. And when they walked away, Rachel heard herself say, "So—I hope I didn't hold you and your girlfriend up too long the other night." And—oh Lord—why had she said *that*? *Shut up, already. This is actually going well now and you're going to wreck it.*

Mike tossed her a sideways glance. "I told you, she's not my girlfriend."

"Whatever." Rachel glanced down, pretending to straighten the bills in the money drawer.

Then she felt Romo's eyes on her, and like earlier, grew

a little too warm. "Just so you know," he said, "I took her straight home."

She drew in her breath, her stomach pinching at the reminder, and still refused to lift her gaze. "Look, I don't need the gory details. It was pretty *clear* you were headed straight home."

From her peripheral vision, she saw him tilt his head. "No, I mean I took her home, to *her* home. Then I went home to *my* home. That was it."

Oh. God. It was like he'd lifted a boulder from her chest. "Not that I care what you do . . . but, uh, why?" Finally, Rachel peered up at him, more than a little curious. "Because she didn't look like someone who was hoping to be dropped off at the door."

Mike just shrugged. "Dunno. Wasn't into it. Wasn't into *her*. Was in a bad mood."

"You don't need to remind *me*," she said, recalling his tirade about her parking mistake. "But . . . most guys would be happy to let her *change* their mood. She was certainly willing to try."

"Like I said, just wasn't meant to be. And I just . . . wanted to let you know."

She couldn't prevent a slow grin from sneaking onto her face. "Afraid I'll think you're easy, Romo?"

He grinned back, just slightly, and their eyes met, and his sparkled again. And it was almost as if his gaze had some direct connection to the crux of her thighs, since, again, that's where she felt it.

"Watch it," she teased him, "or you'll just be giving me more ammunition. Next thing you know, you'll be hearing it all over town—all Romos are easy lays."

He laughed, shrugged. "We've had worse said about us. Probably by Farrises."

Which made her giggle. Yet then she caught herself and said, "Stop that. I don't like you and I refuse to have any fun with you."

"Too late, Farris. I think you *already* like me. A little anyway."

She didn't deny it, but she did cast him a sideways glance. "I'm just waiting to see what you do to ruin it."

When the game was over and most of the crowd had gone, Rachel wondered aloud, "How do they get the donkeys out? Through the lobby?"

Mike looked amused as he started putting away the un-bought chips and pretzels. "Nope, they herd 'em through the back, by the locker rooms."

"Oh," she said on a sigh.

He glanced over. "Am I crazy, Farris, or do you actually sound disappointed?"

"Not really. They stink. But I've never been to a donkey ball game, and here I am at one, without even seeing a donkey."

He blinked. "You grew up here and never saw a donkey ball game?"

"Wasn't my thing," she explained.

And then, to her utter surprise, he took her hand and said, "Come on." After which he led her out into the hall, through the lobby, and into the gym.

"There you go," he said. They arrived just as the very last donkey was being led toward the back door on a lead line. And Rachel smiled. She wasn't sure why. At the absurdity of it all? Or because Mike Romo had just indulged her sudden urge to see a donkey? Or . . . because he was still holding her hand and it was making her thighs feel achy and sexy.

"He's bigger than I expected," she mused about the donkey. Then noted that the protective surface had already been rolled up in large sections and was being hauled out as well. The floor looked good as new. "That fake floor makes for easy cleanup."

"Speaking of which, we'd better get to ours."

She nodded, and only then did he finally let go of her hand. And now, damn it, *that* was tingly, too. All the way up her arm. Sheesh. What kind of crazy lust *was* this?

As they passed back through the now empty lobby, Rachel noticed that Elmer must have come along and locked down the metal partition while they were gone, closing the concession stand window. They stepped inside—leaving the door open, of course—and Mike counted the money while Rachel started cleaning. It wasn't a lot, just some soft drink drips on the counter and floor. By the time she finished, thinking the place looked as tidy as when they'd arrived, Mike had a total. A moment later, the money was in the bag, and she zipped it shut as Mike stooped to unplug the calculator—giving her a nice, even if too brief, view of his butt.

After placing the calculator back where she'd found it, Rachel announced, "All right, guess we're done," then walked to the entrance and shut the door to retrieve her pashmina from the hook on the back. She wrapped it around her shoulders, picked up her purse—and turned to see Mike slap his hand against his forehead, looking at her like she was an imbecile.

"What?" she said, confused.

"You just shut the fucking door, Farris."

She gasped slightly as his words shot through her. "Oh. Shit."

"Shit is right." This was a lot different than earlier—the window was locked and the place had emptied.

She widened her eyes on him, beginning to feel a little panicky. "Do you think anyone's still out there?"

In response, he joined her at the door and they both began beating on it and yelling. "Hey! Hey, we're locked in here!" Rachel screamed.

"Anybody out there?" Mike called.

"Help! Get us out of here!"

"Elmer? Dude, if you're still here, come let us out!"

After a minute, they stopped, quieted, and listened. To nothing. Not a sound. They were locked in the concession stand and no one was outside to hear them. On the rare occasion Rachel had actually rushed off without her Blackberry, too.

She dared to glance up at Mike, who stood right next to her—glaring down. He looked ready to kill her. "Why the *hell* did you shut that door?"

She bit her lip. "I wasn't thinking. I just needed to get my pashmina from behind it. It could have happened to anyone."

He simply stood hovering over her, shaking his head in disbelief. "And what the *hell* is a pashmina?"

She motioned at her wrap. "This. It's Persian."

"Looks like a shawl to me," he muttered.

Now it was *her* turn to glare at *him*. "No, your *grandmother* wears a shawl. *This* is a *pashmina*."

"Well, your damn *pashmina* just got us stuck in here. Hope you're happy."

Rachel sighed audibly. He was back to being his jerky self, that fast. "No, as a matter of fact, I'm *not* happy. I'm freaking *miserable*, actually."

"Well, it's your own damn fault," he complained.

And that was *it*. She stared boldly up into those dark brown eyes of his, thoroughly disgusted. She'd had it with his rude behavior. She'd had it with . . . everything. "Look, I didn't want to come here tonight. I did it as a favor for a friend. I don't even want to be in this stupid town, but here I am, trying to help out my grandma. And now I've got *you*, giving me ridiculously expensive tickets and acting like I'm a terrible person every time I see you. Well, I'm not that terrible, Romo. So why don't you just take your attitude and your blame and your self-righteousness and shove it up your—"

"Stop!" he said then, reaching up, closing his hands tight on her upper arms. "Be quiet! Be quiet."

At first, she thought maybe he'd heard something outside and wanted to listen. But that's when she realized he was staring at her lips. And that somewhere during her diatribe his eyes had drifted half shut, while his mouth now fell slightly open. He still had that light, stubbly beard going, and being right next to him like this, she could smell that musky scent again—in fact, it was permeating her senses. He stood so close, just a few inches away. How had she not noticed that until now?

As she'd spoken, her adrenaline had risen, and peering up at him, she heard herself breathing—and *he* suddenly seemed to be breathing pretty heavily, too.

"Maybe we should just do this, get it over with, get it out of our systems," he said.

She blinked up at him. "Do what?"

And then he kissed her—hard.

His mouth sank over hers with such power that she had to lean into him just to keep from collapsing.

"Oh. That," she breathed when the kiss ended.

Then she instinctively kissed him again, pressing her hands to his chest. She was a little shocked—by his actions, by hers—but mostly just . . . pleasured.

"Yeah. That," he said, voice ragged with passion.

After which their mouths came back together, kissing feverishly, and Rachel followed the urge to ease back against his sturdy body, now feeling his kiss . . . everywhere.

Mike pulled her to him and his hands roamed her back, her ass. She felt that big bulge of his hardening against her thigh and hungered for it more than she'd known she could. Part of her couldn't believe she was standing here making out with Mike Romo, but *most* of her couldn't think straight enough to stop. She *had* been aching for him—she couldn't deny that. And maybe he was right, about them getting it out of their systems. As more and more pleasure echoed through her body, it seemed as good a reason as any to barrel full steam ahead.

And then he slowed down. Just a little. He lifted both hands to her face and kissed her more deeply, his tongue snaking between her lips. She met it with her own and surged with moisture below.

Mmm, God, yes. Now *this* was kissing. She couldn't remember the last time a man had kissed her so thoughtfully, so thoroughly. She hadn't imagined it being like this with Mike Romo at all. The harder, more urgent kissing—yeah, that was what she'd expected, and she'd been perfectly turned on by it. But this—this she felt in her chest, in the small of her back; it stretched down her inner thighs.

When he finally ended the kissing, they were both breathing audibly. He drew his hands from her face—one he molded to her hip, and with the other he skimmed his knuckles down over her neck, her chest, just barely grazing her breast. It was that last part that made her flinch, her very womb contracting, as she let out a hot little gasp.

Their eyes met and her lips trembled. Mike let out a small moan in response. Then he eased his palm gently onto her breast, using his thumb to stroke across the tip.

She had to shut her eyes, lean her head back, as she drew air deeply into her lungs. She felt him watching her, seeing her passion, and she didn't mind. Suddenly, something about the way he looked at her made her feel beautiful.

When she didn't object, he lifted his other hand, as well, and began slowly kneading *both* her breasts. It was all she could do to keep standing, the pleasure rushing through her like a river.

Then *her* hands were on *his* face—she never made the conscious decision to touch him there, it just happened— and she was kissing him again, indulging in more slow, deliciously deep kisses that made her feel a little like she was drowning, in him. Finally, she was touching that dark stubble on that strong jaw, running her fingertips over that warm, olive skin. And sinking, sinking, deeper with each passing second.

Until finally he released her breasts from his grasp and began to unbutton her blouse. Wow. She stopped kissing to murmur against his mouth, "So we're gonna do this—here?" Up to now it was just making out, touching. But this changed things.

"Unless you stop me," he said, low, deep.

She didn't *want* to stop, but she couldn't help thinking about consequences. "What if Elmer comes back and opens the door?"

"Not likely. Everybody's gone," he said, his lips but an inch from hers. Her arms twined around his neck now, and he continued undoing her buttons.

"I'm . . . surprised you'd do this, have sex on school premises," she whispered raggedly. "Isn't there some kind of law against that?"

"Not that I know of." Her shirt was entirely unbuttoned now, and he eased his arms around her waist underneath to run his palms over the flesh of her lower back.

She caught her breath, trembled slightly, and bit her lip. "But it still seems . . . you know, *bad*. Naughty."

That's when his hands dropped to her ass, squeezing her tight against the hardness between his legs. "Just because I'm a *good* cop," he said, "doesn't mean I'm not a *bad boy*."

"Ohhh," she moaned as the sensation dug deeper into her, and she heard herself rasp, "I think you're on the verge of making *me* a bad *girl*."

"Good," he whispered. Then he kissed her again, and as he grew still stiffer against her, she followed the urge to show him what a bad girl she could be—she reached down between them to press her hand over the stone-like column in his jeans.

"Jesus God," he muttered, his eyes dropping shut, and she liked feeling that little bit of sexual power over him. He wasn't the only one here with the ability to deliver pleasure.

They kissed some more and Rachel forgot the rest of the world existed, though when Mike reached for the button on her jeans, it brought home for her once more exactly what was about to happen here. She pulled back and said, breathily, "I want to be clear, though—this doesn't mean I like you."

His answer came just as raspy. "Good—it doesn't mean I like you, either. Now shut up and kiss me."

Take all myself.

William Shakespeare, *Romeo & Juliet*

Five

$\mathcal{R}$achel wasn't the sort of woman who went around having sex with every hot guy who crossed her path. With no real aspirations toward marriage, she had, of course, learned to appreciate sex for the pure pleasure of it, and she'd had her share of lovers, but . . . this was the first time she'd ever done it with a guy she barely knew. Or didn't like. Which felt a little weird.

But she couldn't stop. Because it felt too good. And she reminded herself again that he was right. This would get it out of their systems. So that made it okay. And when he parted her blouse, feasted his eyes on her, and moaned at the sight—she nearly melted in his arms, still loving how desirable he made her feel.

Though she wished she'd worn a prettier bra—but she'd gone with plain white, smooth cup, because of the white blouse. And, ugh, she knew she had on plain cotton panties, too, having been in a hurry to go someplace she'd never dreamed anyone would see them. "I usually wear better underwear," she heard herself say.

"I don't care about your underwear, honey," he breathed low and hot against her neck, starting to kiss her there. "I just care about what's under it."

Rachel sucked in her breath and kissed him some more, luxuriating in the feel of his large hands on her body as he started easing down her jeans. Thoughts of stopping seemed long in the past, so she bit her lip, glanced down at the waistband around her thighs, and kicked off her pumps to make things easier before stepping free of the denim.

Losing the heels instantly made her aware of how tall he was, over six feet, almost towering over her now—it was the first time she'd been her real height in his presence. As he pushed the blouse from her shoulders, she reached for the buttons on his shirt, suddenly desperate to see his chest, stomach.

She wasn't disappointed—he had just the right amount of muscle to make her want to run her hands over him, and she let her fingertips play lightly at the smattering of hair on his chest. Then she moved on, downward— to his belt, to the zipper. She liked that he sucked in his breath as she lowered it. She liked the sensation behind her fingers—it felt as if he was about to burst from the jeans whether she undid the zipper or not.

His breath came harder then, more urgent, and she whispered, "Condom?"

"Unh," he said, and she guessed that meant yes when he withdrew his touch to reach in his back pocket, flipping open a well-worn leather wallet.

A second later, he was yanking at her panties, murmuring, "Take these off."

After finally getting her arms free from her blouse, she complied, pushing them down, starting to feel very naked in front of him—in a *sexy* way.

The next thing she knew, he was taking her hand, pulling her with him as he sank to the floor. He sat, his back against the cinderblock wall, and she straddled his lap. Every part of her body pulsed with nervousness and need. But mostly need. So much that she boldly curled both hands into his underwear—typical white from what she could see—and tugged downward. He lifted slightly to help her and his erection came free, making her let out a ragged breath. He was big. And rock hard. Her whole being went liquid with lust.

Still breathing rapidly, he ripped open the foil packet and Rachel didn't hesitate to pluck the condom from it. Her chest contracted as she sheathed him. Oh God, *oh God*. Finally, she would have him. And she knew it hadn't exactly been a long wait, but it felt that way. It felt, strangely, as if she'd been waiting a lifetime for this.

Mike's hands were on her ass then, molding, lifting her, until she was balanced atop him. He didn't push her down, though—he left that part to her. In response, Rachel bit her lower lip, pressed her palms to his chest, then sank slowly, tightly onto him.

They both groaned with the lengthy descent, the deep immersion that seemed to fill her entire body. "Oh God," she gasped, her head falling back as the pleasure encased her.

When she looked at him again, his eyes were barely open—he appeared lost in passion. His hands remained on her hips, caressing, his fingertips digging in lightly, in a way she felt at her very core. It made her begin to move on him, gentle but potent, still adjusting to having him inside.

"Good?" he asked.

She simply gave a nod, let out a breath. *Very* good.

He squeezed her ass then, and began to thrust up into her, still slow, deep.

As Rachel swayed in a grinding, primitive dance that

came not from thought or decision but simply as a physical response, she realized she'd thought for a few minutes there that this part would go faster, harder, be more urgent. But she loved that it was slower, that they were soaking up every nuance of every sensation together. Flattening her palms to his chest again, she leaned in to kiss him some more. Mmm, God, yes, she liked kissing him. She thought he liked kissing her, too—his tongue licked at hers in the same hot, lingering rhythm they'd found below.

As they exchanged more sensual tongue kisses, he found the clasp at the center of her bra and released it. And then his warm hands were easing over her needy breasts, massaging deeply, making them both groan. Her scalp tingled, the sensation skittering all the way down her spine.

When he bent to take one nipple in his mouth, she shuddered as the pleasure echoed through her, arching her back to give him easier access. Oh God, this was just what she needed. Even if she couldn't believe where they were or who she was with. Then she glimpsed the words GO BULLDOGS, painted in red stenciled letters above his head. How surreal. Who'd have dreamed she'd ever find such pleasure within the walls of Destiny High, and mmm, this was phenomenally better than making out in Elmer's broom closet.

She glanced down to watch him—his tongue now twirling around her distended nipple, the sensation shooting straight to the juncture of her thighs—to find him gazing up at her, those chocolaty eyes devouring her soul as much as his mouth devoured her breast.

He shifted to the other then, enrapturing her further. Had sex ever been this good before—this hot, this perfect? Their eyes continued to meet as he suckled her, and it made her move against him with more intensity. *Oh, mmm, yes.* She bit her lip as sweet release gathered within her, like a million heated cells rushing to her very center, and she rode him harder, getting lost in it, starting to moan. "Oh—oh God," she purred as the orgasm hit, hard, like a tidal wave, rocking her body, jolting it almost electrically as she sobbed her ecstasy through the concession stand.

As she rode it out, undulating deeply, breath coming thready, Mike's arms closed tight around her waist, bolstering her, and when she opened her eyes to see him peering intently up at her, it stretched out the climax a few beats longer.

She gazed down at him, a little stunned to realize what she'd just done, was still doing, with Mike Romo. But it didn't make her want to stop—no way. Instead, it made her feel strangely giddy inside, and supremely naughty. She bit her lip again and gave him a sensuous smile. "Is this how you punish all criminals? Because if it is, I might have to break some more laws."

He shook his head, flashing a sexy grin. "No—but it might be how I show you outrageous."

She giggled softly, remembering their yelling match at the Dew Drop Inn. Looking back, now it just seemed like foreplay. "This is pretty outrageous, all right."

Mike had never imagined he'd want to be trapped in a small room with a Farris, but this changed that. And he supposed it had been coming, like a storm, since they'd met. And this would do what he'd told her—get it out of their systems. But he was in no hurry for that at the moment, saw no reason in the world to rush through this, so he planned on taking his time.

He took his time thrusting slowly up into her moist warmth some more. He took his time leaning back in to sensually curl his tongue up over the hard bead of her perfect pink nipple. And then the other. Again. Again. She began to rock her body on his once more, so now he took his time watching the way she moved, undulating like a slow, rhythmic wave. God, she was a sensual woman—going slow like him, not afraid to show him her pleasure even beneath the bright fluorescent lights of the concession stand. Damn, he was already about to explode, and just watching her got him hotter and hotter.

"I loved seeing you come," he said. "I want to make you come *again*."

She sucked in her breath, a pretty little sound that tightened his cock further inside her. Shit, he hoped he could hold it together for as long as he wanted.

"Just keep doing what you're doing," she whispered.

So he did. He drove his erection up into her, slow, thorough. He caressed her breasts, kissed them, licked them. He listened to more hot, sexy sounds echoing from her throat—and then he splayed his hands across her round ass, squeezing in rhythm with her movements.

"Oh God," she said, then, "*oh God!*" Despite that they were both working toward it, he got the idea it caught her off guard, this second orgasm, as it seemed to hit her in a more jagged way, jerking her body, making her breath come in short, tight gasps. He held her tight, taking deep pleasure in her loss of control, soaking in her every hot movement and sound.

And then she collapsed against him, her breasts against his chest, her head on his shoulder, her warm breath on his neck. He held her tight, cradling her against him, sensing what he'd wrung out of her that time. Damn—intense. Enough that he whispered, "You okay?"

He felt her nod, then a moment later, she managed, "Just . . . feel limp. Weak."

He grinned over at her, teased her. "You're not gonna quit on me, are ya?"

Head still resting on his shoulder, she peered up at him, touched her tongue to her upper lip. "No way."

Thank God. Because he wanted more of her. In other ways. In every way.

"Can you stand up?" he asked.

She lifted her head and blinked, looking surprised. "Are . . . we done or something? Because I'm tired, but not *that* tired. And I didn't think you had, you know . . . finished."

He held back his smile this time, but he liked how much she didn't want this to be over yet, either. "Don't worry, honey—we're not even *close* to done. Now stand up."

In response, she eased off him and together they got to their feet. Mike finally shrugged out of his shirt, even though his pants were still on, and he pushed her bra off her shoulders as he gently turned her beautifully naked body around, facing away from him. Then he leaned into her, her back warm against his front, and used his hands to press her palms flat into the painted cinderblock wall.

"Oh," she said softly, sounding more surprised by the position than he might have anticipated.

But he didn't hesitate. He couldn't; he needed to be back inside her. So he gripped her hips and entered her thickly from behind, loving it when she let out a long, low sob.

"Is it okay? Feel good?" he asked near her ear.

"Unh," she said.

"Is that a *good* sound?"

"Uh-huh."

Damn, she couldn't even talk. "You feel it that much?" he asked.

"Uh-huh."

"Good."

And then he began to move in her again, sensing her slickness in spite of the condom, thrusting harder now into her tight warmth—because slow and deep had been good for a while, but now he needed her fast and hard.

He growled his expanding pleasure as she met his every stroke, and soon they were both crying out with each impact. Mike's whole body was taut with the hot bliss of being inside her, his chest tight, his thighs aching, his

heart beating like a drum. He reached around to caress
her breasts, to run his hands over her slender stomach,
to dip one into her moisture. Aw, damn. She was just as
wet as he suspected, and feeling it on his fingertips only
escalated his heat.

He groaned through clenched teeth as he drove into
her soft flesh again and again—until he sensed her legs
giving way and whispered, "I've got you, I've got you,"
his arms closing around her waist as he eased them both
to their knees on the floor.

He resumed moving in her that way—shit, it was hard
to control himself now. And when she leaned back into
him, turning her head to gaze at him, she looked so beautiful—cheeks flushed, lips parted, eyes half shut—that he
had to kiss her. Hard.

Until he was getting weak, too, and simply pressed
his cheek to hers as he continued delivering firm strokes
below, his hands moving slowly over her breasts and
torso.

On the verge of coming, he pulled out, and she gasped.
At first, he couldn't make sense of why he'd done it,
stopped like that, when sweet ecstasy had been only a
few heartbeats away. But when she turned to look at him
again, he understood his actions. He just hadn't gotten
quite enough yet; he'd just wanted more of her.

"Lie down," he said without preamble. "On your
back."

And so she eased down onto the tile beneath them,
propped on her elbows, looking so gorgeous that for a
second he feared he'd explode, right then and there.

"The floor's cold," she told him.

"Sorry," he said, just realizing that part. "Probably
hard, too."

"It's okay," she promised. "Just please come back.
Inside me again."

Christ. The plea nearly buried him. She sounded so

much more . . . tame than the Rachel Farris he'd come to know, but at the same time, still demanding—and for once, he didn't mind.

Parting her bent knees, he moved between them, took another satisfying perusal of her naked body, and pushed his way back in. "Aw, damn," he bit off, growling as her flesh closed around him. So good, so tight. Then he met her gaze. "I'm gonna come soon."

She just gave a short nod, still looking completely impassioned, and he began to move in her. And it was slow again, their bodies pushing and grinding against each other, Mike straining to be deeper and deeper inside her.

It didn't take long before that supreme heat had gathered once more, stretching tight through his groin and aching erection, and he knew he had to let it go, let it happen. "Aw, now," he groaned. And then he did something he *never* did: he came while looking into her eyes.

Rachel lay beneath him on the painfully hard floor thinking, *What the hell was that?*

Because even though she fancied herself a worldly woman and had had her fair share of good sex, she wasn't sure she'd ever had sex like *that* before. It had felt like . . . an invisible force of nature traveling through them, passing between them. Her body had moved of its own volition, her responses coming from somewhere deep inside, a place she'd never encountered before. She'd felt at once weak but powerful. Needy yet commanding. Too, too vulnerable at moments. And it had all felt . . . insanely intimate.

So intimate that, now that they'd rested quietly for a few minutes, recovering, she had no idea what to say.

But he took care of that for her, announcing, "We should get dressed."

Okey doke. She supposed she should have known he wouldn't suddenly be Mr. Tender Guy. He was Mike

Romo, after all. Maybe she'd forgotten that for a moment in the afterglow of the most amazing sex of her life. "Right," she murmured as he rose off her. "Of course." Then she remembered . . . "But, uh, what's the hurry? I mean, I'm not sensing imminent rescue."

Romo was on his feet now, zipping his pants. God, he looked good. Then he replied, "Because I have a cell phone."

Sitting up to hug her knees, she simply rolled her eyes. "And you're just now mentioning this?"

"It just now hit me. I was preoccupied before."

"With?"

He met her gaze briefly, then let his eyes run pointedly over her nakedness.

"Oh, yeah, that," she said. Then tried to shake off the intensity of the encounter, hoping he couldn't see it written all over her face. She'd just indulged in casual sex, and Romo's matter-of-fact attitude reminded her there was no reason to make a big deal of it.

She reached for her bra and eased into her panties as Mike said, "I'll try Logan. He had a funeral visitation for a family friend in Crestview, but he should be back."

Although a minute later, she heard Mike leaving a call-me-when-you-get-this message and waited to see who he'd try next as she finished buttoning her blouse. She'd just slipped on her red pumps when she heard something jingling on the other side of the door—like keys.

She and Mike both froze in place, then he looked down at his bare chest. Rachel scooped up the blue shirt at her feet and flung it at him as the jingling continued. "Anybody in there?" It sounded like Principal Turley.

"Yes! We're locked in!" Rachel yelled—and Mike made a face at her since he was still trying to get his shirt on, but what was she supposed to do, ignore rescue?

Fortunately, by the time the door opened to reveal Ralph Turley standing there with a set of keys nearly as big as

Elmer's, Mike came around the corner with his shirt buttoned, even if his hair was a little messed up.

"Just finished getting the donkeys loaded in the trucks and was passing back through the lobby toward my car when I saw a light under the door. What on earth happened here?"

If you only knew, Rachel thought. And Mike said, "Rachel here shut the door and locked us in." He sounded less judgmental than usual when it came to her, but his tone still left her slightly embarrassed.

Until the principal said, "Well, easy enough to do—we really oughta get this thing fixed one of these days," and Rachel gave Mike a smug nod.

The three of them left together, Rachel feeling a bit like she was in the Twilight Zone. Five minutes earlier she'd been naked under her nemesis, Mike Romo, and now they were chatting with Mr. Turley about concessions and donkeys like they hadn't just had wild sex in numerous positions, like they hadn't just left a used condom wrapped in a napkin in the concession stand wastebasket, like her world hadn't just radically changed.

And it had. Partly because she'd just had sex with a dreaded Romo, something she couldn't have imagined up until now, or at least not until very recently. And partly because—damn, after sex like that . . . would any *other* sex ever seem good? It felt unlikely. Her body still pulsed with memories of the ways he'd moved in her—like an aftershock.

The principal's car was parked near the door, leaving Rachel and Mike to walk to the lot in front of the school on their own in the dark. The night had turned cooler than any so far, the first hints of autumn in the air.

"Just so you know," she said after a few minutes of silence, "I don't usually do this."

"Have sex on school premises? 'Cause you seemed pretty worried about that."

She lifted her gaze to his as they walked. "I was worried about being caught. And no, I meant I don't usually . . . you know, have sex . . . with someone I barely know."

"And don't like," he pointed out.

"Right. I'm no saint and no prude, but . . . well, this was unusual." And it really was. Casual sex wasn't new to her, but she *was* generally pretty discriminating in terms of partners.

"What was the occasion?" he asked.

Crap. Good question. It hung in the air a second too long. "Like you said, getting it out of our systems."

"Is it out now?"

"Completely." Although that was probably a lie.

"Good. Me, too," he replied. And her stomach pinched up.

"This is me," she said, pointing to the BMW near the front of the parking lot. She glimpsed a big, heavy-duty pickup truck farther back, near a light pole, and since it was the only other remaining vehicle, she guessed it was his.

Although she suddenly felt weird, yucky, disappointed—like she didn't want the night to end like this, so coldly. Not that he was being his usual mean self, but . . . she'd never had sex that hadn't ended with at least a *little* warmth, a kiss goodbye, some nice words. *Looks like there's a first time for everything.*

And since it didn't appear that he was even going to respond, the rat, Rachel started to veer off their current path toward her car—so it surprised her when his hand grabbed hers, pulling her back toward him.

Then he leaned down to whisper in her ear. "Just so *you* know, getting something out of my system never felt so good." After which he lifted one hand to cup her jaw and gave her a passionate open-mouthed kiss that stretched on long enough for her to feel it between her legs. Oh my. *That's more like it.*

" 'Night, Farris," he said when the kiss was done.

"Good night. Romeo," she added for good measure.

When Rachel walked into Under the Covers the next day, Amy stood on a chair, stretching a little string of ghost-shaped lights across the ceiling while Tessa arranged some miniature pumpkins and gourds on the counter. Relief rushed through Rachel to see Tessa up and about. "You're here," she said. "Does that mean you're feeling better?"

Tessa tilted her head, her smile a bit wilted but sincere. "Better enough. I don't like letting it get me down for long when I can help it."

Another whoosh of guilt came over Rachel. "I feel bad," she said. "Like I haven't been here for you since you got sick."

Tessa's hazel eyes widened. "How *could* you be? You live in Chicago."

Rachel shook her head. "Still, I should have come long before now. When one of my best friends is going through something like this, I should be there."

"Don't sweat it," Tessa said. "You call me all the time, and we e-mail. It's cool."

"Well, okay, but . . . I just wanted to make sure you know I care."

Tessa flashed a suspicious look. "I don't know what's come over you, but don't worry—I know."

And that's when Rachel nearly tripped and glanced down to see the fat bookstore cat, Shakespeare, weaving a figure eight around her ankles. "This cat is a trouble-maker," she said as Tessa reached out to help her keep her balance.

"I know, I know," Amy replied from atop the chair. "Did you ask Edna about him yet?"

Oops. "No, I forgot. But I will soon—promise."

"So, how'd last night go?" Amy asked, turning back

to her ghost lights. "Did you have fun working with Logan?"

Rachel could only sigh. "No. Because Logan didn't show up."

Amy paused her work to look back down. "You're kidding."

"Nope—apparently he had some last-minute visitation in Crestview. So he sent Mike Romo instead."

Amy winced and Tessa said, "Uh-oh."

"So did you two go at it again?" Amy asked.

Rachel considered the question, then sucked in her breath. "That's one way to put it, I suppose."

Amy lowered her chin, lights still in hand. "What do you mean? What happened?"

"Well, after the ball game, we had sex on the concession stand floor."

Amy's ghost lights dropped from her fingertips, looping around her body and scattering beneath her—as a tiny gourd escaped Tessa's grip to hit Shakespeare on the head. The cat screeched and darted—through the lights and wire on the floor, with enough force to yank Amy off balance. She came stumbling down, but fortunately managed not to land on any of the lights, instead going headfirst into one of the easy chairs near the door. After which she smoothly turned over and plopped her butt on the cushion, staring at Rachel in disbelief.

"Like I said," Rachel told them, "that cat's a menace."

"This wasn't exactly the cat's fault. It's not the one dropping bombshells while I'm up on a rickety chair."

Tessa gaped at Rachel, too. "So—you wanna say that again?"

"Sure, that cat's—"

"No, the part about Mike Romo. Because we *must* have misunderstood."

Rachel let out another short, confessional sigh. "Nope, it's true. I had sex with Officer Romeo."

"Holy crap," Tessa said.

And to Rachel's surprise, as Amy's shock passed, she began looking . . . downright pleased with herself, even with tangled ghost lights strung around her shoulders like a necklace. "And you acted all disgusted when I suggested you two get together. Well, clearly I was right and you decided he's more hot than creepy." Then she clapped her hands together. "Hooray, a fall romance for Rachel!"

Rachel threw up her hands in a stop motion. "Whoa there, Speedy Gonzales—back it up. I said we had sex. But let's be clear—he, uh, wasn't exactly Mr. Romance."

As Tessa dragged Rachel over to the easy chairs and both of them sat down, Tessa said, "Dare I suggest that one might not necessarily *expect* a lot of romance when one does it on the floor of a concession stand with a guy she barely knows?"

Rachel just shrugged. "Agreed. And I'm not complaining, exactly. Which is to say . . ." she bit her lip and tilted her head ". . . there were moments when he was . . . *considerate*. But he could use some serious lessons on post-orgasmic cuddling."

"Again," Tessa pointed out, "floor, concession stand, stranger."

"So there were . . . orgasms," Amy sought to confirm, even though she didn't appear entirely comfortable with the word. Amy liked to fix people up, and she was okay discussing sex in simple terms, but she always seemed embarrassed when it came to talking details.

"Multiple," Rachel informed her.

"Wow."

"Yeah, that part kinda threw me, too. Since that's not my, uh . . . usual way."

"How many?" Tessa asked.

"Just two. But it was more than enough. Any more and I'd have had to be carried out on a stretcher."

As Amy finally got unlooped from her lights, she asked,

"Can we start over please? Like at the beginning. How on earth did this happen?"

So Rachel told the whole story of the mysterious locking door and the pashmina, finishing with, "And then he started kissing me."

"Okay, okay, enough foreplay," Tessa said. "How was he?"

And an uncharacteristic blush warmed Rachel's cheeks. For her, it was kind of like crying—she never cried, and she never blushed. Crap. And it wasn't like they'd never discussed sex before, but she was suddenly acting more like Amy than herself.

"That good?" Tessa asked, clearly fascinated.

So Rachel glanced back and forth between her best friends and told the brutal truth that had been plaguing her since last night. "The best. Ever. In my life."

"Wow, that's saying a lot," Tessa said. "'Cause you've had a lot of sex."

Rachel shot her a look and Tessa held out her hands, palms up. "I'm just sayin'." And Rachel couldn't really argue the point since she *had* lost her virginity before any of her friends—with Russell Jamison, the closet guy—and had indeed possessed a healthy even if fairly selective sexual appetite ever since.

"So what made it the best?" Tessa asked, and Rachel flushed again—and this time Amy did, too. Probably, Rachel guessed, due to the lusty look surely forming on her face.

"I . . . can't really explain," she said. "It was slow and really steamy. And he just . . . knew what to do. With his hands. And with his . . . you know, penis."

All three girls just sat there, apparently thinking this over, and that's when Shakespeare came padding cautiously out from between two bookcases, quietly making his way to Rachel's chair. Without being invited, he bounded up to the empty space beside her and curled into a big fat ball against her thigh.

"So . . ." Tessa finally said, "what now?"

"What do you mean, what now?"

"Are you seeing him again?"

Rachel drew back slightly, sitting up straighter. "Oh—no. It wasn't . . . that kind of thing."

"It was the best sex of your life," Amy reminded her, still a little red-faced.

"True, but as I've tried to explain to you on numerous occasions, sometimes sex is just sex. Just two people indulging in . . . human urges. And we both agreed that this was just something we needed to get out of our systems."

"Like an infection?" Tessa asked, clearly not buying it.

Yet Rachel tried to make her understand. "Okay, so we've had this bizarre attraction to each other since I met him. But since we strongly dislike each other, and we pretty much live in two different worlds, it would be silly to take it any further. We're lucky if we can get along for more than five minutes." She knit her brow then, thinking. "Except for during the sex. We got along *really* well then. Afterward, though, it was pretty much back to the way it was before. So that's all there is to it."

Her friends just looked at her like she was crazy. But then she had to remind herself—this was Destiny, land of picket fences and small town values. It was hard for Amy—and maybe even Tessa now, apparently—to get where she was coming from, about not pursuing this. And it was one more reason why she belonged in Chicago, where people were more . . . forward thinking.

"And even though I feel a little weird about it," she went on, "I'm much calmer than I was before. I think it really worked some stress out of me." And since Rachel wanted to *stay* unstressed, as in not thinking about her job woes or other worries, she decided to change the subject. "So, *finally*, can you tell me what happened to Romo that was so horrible?"

"Well, not *now*," Amy replied, eyes widening. "Sue

Ann and Jenny are due any minute. They both came to book club last night and I invited them to lunch with us today."

"That's great," Rachel said, and she meant it. "But this is getting ridiculous. Come on and spit it out already. Because it was one thing when I was just curious because I hated him, but now I've had sex with him. Sex, Amy! So tell me. Right now."

Amy let out a big, conceding sigh. "Fine, but I'll have to hurry."

"Please do."

"Okay." She leaned forward in her chair, looking as if someone might be eavesdropping even though the three of them were alone. "When Mike was twelve, he and his family were camping at Bear Lake, north of Crestview, in the state park. He was watching his little brother, Lucky, who was ten at the time, and his sister, Anna, who was five, while their parents left to get some supplies or something. And while they were gone, Anna disappeared."

Rachel's heart nearly stopped. "Oh Lord, he's *that* Romo? I *do* remember this story."

"Yeah, I couldn't believe you *didn't*—it was such a big deal when we were kids. I guess we were around nine at the time."

"There were just so many Romos, and I remember Lucky since he was only a year ahead of us, but I had no idea Mike was the other brother in that family. God." Amy was right—at the time, it had been a tragedy felt by the whole community. "My dad even went over there looking for her. He said when it came to something like that, feuds didn't matter."

"My dad and uncle drove to the lake to help, too," Tessa added.

"Right," Amy went on. "There was a huge search of the whole park."

"But they never found her," Rachel recalled.

Amy nodded. "To this day, no one knows what happened to her."

And it was Mike's *sister*! "Lord." It gave her chills.

"Anyway," Amy said, "according to Logan, Mike never got over the guilt. Because he was supposed to be keeping an eye on her when it happened."

"Oh, that's awful." Her stomach wrenched.

"And now . . ."

"Now what?"

"Well, now he's pretty much alone."

But she didn't know what Amy meant. Suddenly *she* was the one leaning forward. "Alone how?"

"Well, Lucky was pretty messed up—he turned out to be a pretty bad kid." Yeah, that's exactly how Rachel remembered Lucky—like a guy you stayed away from, a guy who was always in trouble. "And he left town after high school and never came back—so no one knows what became of him. And after that, Mike's parents moved to Florida. They never got over the loss, and they just couldn't take being here anymore."

Rachel asked what she thought was an obvious question. "Why didn't Mike leave, too?" After all, what did he have to stay for?

Yet Amy shook her head. "Who knows? But . . . that's why I cut the guy some slack for being so angry all the time."

Just then, the little bell above the door jingled and in walked Sue Ann and Jenny. "Rachel Farris, back in Destiny—I thought I'd never see the day!" Sue Ann said, smiling brightly. And just like when she'd run into Jenny at the Dew Drop, Rachel was excited to see her old friends—and in a few minutes, she was sure she'd be immersed in catching up with them and enjoying their lunch. But at that particular moment, she was still reeling, struggling to catch her breath after hearing what had happened to Mike Romo. It was worse than anything she'd imagined.

"Yeah, me neither," she finally managed, rising to greet Sue Ann.

"I can't wait to hear all about your world travels. I hear you went to Italy last year and I'm insanely jealous."

Rachel forced a smile. "I'd rather hear all about *you*. And I'm told there's a little miniature Sue Ann these days"—everyone said Sophie looked just like her—"so I hope you have pictures."

As Amy locked up the bookstore for the hour, Mike Romo's painful past still weighed heavily on Rachel—but she tried to concentrate on her friends and tell herself it didn't matter.

After all, he didn't like her anyway—and vice versa.

They'd had sex one time and gotten it out of their systems. It was over and done now.

But to her surprise, her heart still broke for him.

O Romeo, Romeo, wherefore art thou Romeo?

William Shakespeare, *Romeo & Juliet*

Six

*N*ow that August had given way to September, the orchard was hopping. Rachel would normally have spent the long Labor Day weekend jet-setting to Miami with girlfriends or boating on Lake Michigan with some of her co-workers—Chase owned a cabin cruiser and frequently invited his employees out on the water with him. But on this particular holiday weekend, she was greeting customers who paid to come to the Farris Family Apple Orchard and pick their own apples.

She stood just outside the barn in jeans and a fitted red tee, distributing bushel baskets and directing visitors to the grove of their choice: there were still some ripening Galas left, and the McIntoshes and Honeycrisps were mostly ready for harvest now, too.

"Rachel, can you show the Benson family out to the Honeycrisp grove?" Edna requested. "And when ya come back, you can help me restack all these baskets we just emptied. It's early yet and we'll have lots more customers today."

Frankly, Edna was running her ragged. But she didn't

mind. Mostly because she didn't like to think of Edna juggling all this without her. Yet she also found the work more invigorating at times than she might have expected, too. It was a beautiful blue-sky day, the sun shining brightly overhead, and the scent of apples floated on the breeze. Somewhere a bird sang. And after all the standing on ladders she'd done lately, it actually felt good to do a little walking along one of the paths that led between rows of trees as she showed the Bensons the way. When she saw Brian Cahill—the boy Edna had hired part-time— helping an older couple lift their baskets of McIntoshes onto one of the wagons the orchard provided, she raised her hand in a wave.

She also couldn't deny that talking with people about apples was . . . weirdly relaxing. It was a hell of a lot less stressful than talking with stern men in suits and ties about spending tens of thousands of dollars on advertising. The apple trade was, quite simply, a much kinder and gentler business.

But that's why you make a lot more money in advertising than Edna makes on apples. And money makes the world go 'round. And it keeps roofs over people's heads and food in their mouths.

And maybe the apple business was *too* simple in a way. Because it wasn't enough to keep her mind off Mike Romo. While she wasn't thinking too terribly much about life at Conrad/Phelps, everything she knew about Mike Romo remained front and center in her brain. From the way he kissed to the way he'd moved inside her, making her feel so amazingly . . . full. And connected to him. She didn't like admitting that part to herself, since they'd both agreed it was a one-time thing, but it was hard to have sex *that* intense and not come away feeling . . . a little bit attached.

In a *weird* way, of course. Since she barely knew him and couldn't seem to get along with him outside of a concession stand—and at times not *in* the concession stand.

She even felt a little . . . *unsettled* about not having seen him since then. Not that she knew what she'd do when she did, but the situation had certainly changed from a few days back when she'd been trying to avoid running into him.

Well, as far as a sense of attachment went, she'd just have to shake that off. She wasn't a woman who formed attachments to guys to begin with, so a small town Destiny cop on a power trip was the last guy to be wasting that sort of emotion on. And she'd be leaving soon anyway.

"Here you go," she said to the Bensons, a typical family of four with a friendly yuppie-dad—day-trippers from Columbus. The adolescent brother and sister shared wagon-pulling duty. "This whole section is Honeycrisp and they're good and ripe, particularly the apples on the outer branches. Remember, don't go by color—they should feel crisp and firm in your hand. If you need help or have questions, let us know, and otherwise, have fun."

As she returned to the little red barn, though, she found herself pondering more than just sex with Mike Romo or her shock that it had happened. Learning he was part of the family whose little girl had disappeared when they were all kids had left her dumbfounded. And despite all she disliked about him, hearing he felt responsible for it made her ache every time she thought about it. He'd been only twelve, after all, just a little boy himself. What must a loss like that—and the weight of thinking it was his fault—do to someone?

"Good, just in time to help me check these folks out," Edna said as Rachel rounded the barn's corner. Several families and couples were ready to pay for their apples and leave. So Rachel began tallying up totals and helping Edna run credit cards through—just in time to see another few vehicles cross the bridge, ready to join in.

By six P.M. when the last car departed, Rachel was bushed. And Edna looked tired, too—but she kept right on going, like some kind of Energizer bunny.

"You should call it a day," Rachel told her. "I can tidy things up out here." There wasn't much more to do—stack some baskets, put a few stray wagons in the barn, bring Edna's old portable cash register and ancient credit card press into the house.

"Soon," Edna said, bustling about the barn's entrance.

"After all, you have bad knees, *remember*?" Rachel added, *still* unsure if Edna was faking the knee thing or not.

Neatening the money in the cash drawer, Edna paused and reached down to rub one of them. "They *are* hurtin', now that ya mention it."

Okay, were they or weren't they? And . . . oh hell, did it even matter anymore? "Then go inside and let me finish."

But Edna looked torn between concluding the work and resting. "I reckon they'll last me a little longer—and now that everybody's gone, there's somethin' I wanna show ya."

"What's that?"

"Follow me," she said, so Rachel headed around to the back of the barn with her grandmother—to the old root cellar she'd forgotten about until just now.

"Oh, we used to play here," she said cheerfully, remembering it had made a great "dungeon" during make-believe games with her brother and cousins.

"Used to damage a fair amount of apples is what *I* recall," Edna grumbled.

"It was Robby who used to stomp on them and try to crush them, not the rest of us. He just lied to spread the blame around."

Edna shook her head and muttered, "That Robby—he was a sneaky one," as she bent over the old cellar doors, which lay nearly flat, edged by the tops of stone walls that descended underground.

"Here, Edna, let me," Rachel said since, again, Edna looked worn out and seemed to struggle as she stooped to unlock the faded green wooden doors. Rachel took the key ring Edna held and did the honors, swinging the doors wide open. Then they both went carefully down the rocky steps into the cool darkness below.

"There aren't rats down here, are there?" Rachel asked—she'd never been particularly fond of dark, closed-in spaces underground, even basements.

"I hope not, or our apples'll be in trouble," Edna said, implying it was a needless worry.

"So what are we doing down here?" They'd reached the earthen floor and around them stood lots of mostly empty shelves.

"I don't know if you remember from when you were little about storin' apples, but I been meanin' to give ya a refresher course."

"All right—refresh away."

"Now, apples that need to be stored for any length of time come down here. You see," she said, pointing, "that I already sent Brian down with a few bushels of Galas I'm savin' for the apple festival—the coolness and darkness keeps 'em fresh.

"As the festival gets closer, though, we'll also wanna hold back plenty of apples for the winter, and those we store a little different. See that stack of newspapers?" She pointed again. "I save those up because each apple needs to be wrapped individually in about a quarter sheet. Then we stack 'em on the shelves and use 'em as needed. Mainly we take about a bushel a week up to the General Mercantile—you remember, run by Willie Hoskins?"

"Oh, that's still there?" The old-fashioned store sold only the basics: snacks and soft drinks, some fruits and vegetables, and Grampy Hoskins, as most everyone her age had always called the proprietor, had kept old-time candy dispensers Rachel had thought pretty as a little girl.

"Sure is—and he's my most dependable customer. I also get occasional folks stopping by who might just want enough for a pie or cobbler—so I just trot on down here to get 'em. And, of course, I keep 'em on hand for my own use, too. So we'll need to start wrappin' some when we're not busy pickin' 'em so I'll have me a full cellar to last through next summer."

"So was the cellar here when you first came or did Grandpa Edward build it?" Rachel asked absently as they climbed back to daylight. She'd never wondered before, but she supposed she was growing more curious about the place as an adult, getting more interested in the orchard's past.

"Neither," Edna replied as they each swung one green door shut. "Giovanni Romo and my brothers built this cellar that first summer I was here."

Ah yes—good old Giovanni. "You never did tell me the rest of the story," Rachel hinted as she bent to padlock the handles together. She'd gotten so unwittingly caught up in Giovanni's grandson lately that it had started to slip her mind, but now that she remembered, she wanted to know how Edna's crush on Mike's grandpa had turned out.

When she rose up, she found Edna peering wistfully across the top of the cellar, as if seeing something that wasn't there. Rachel was having a hard time getting used to Edna being wistful about *anything*, but it made her ask, "What are you thinking about?"

"About how good Giovanni looked workin' in the hot sun without a shirt."

Rachel drew back slightly. "*Edna*," she gasped.

But her grandmother just cast a critical look. "You think I'm not human? You think just 'cause I'm old I never had them kinda feelin's?"

Rachel blinked. "Well, no, I'm sure you did, but . . ."

"But what?" Edna asked, hands on her hips.

"I guess . . . I'm just not used to hearing about them. And you *are* my grandma, after all, so it's a little weird."

Edna lowered her chin and spoke matter-of-factly. "Well, I'll tell ya, darlin', if you wanna hear this story, then it'll probably feel a lot weirder to ya before I'm done. Can ya handle it or not?"

Holy crap. "Yes," she said. Because it *was* strange, but she really wanted to know.

"Come on, then. I got some apples in the barn I wanna load up and drive to the Mercantile. I can tell ya while we work."

Edna sat on a blanket in the shade provided by the barn, breaking the green beans she'd picked from the garden this morning into a bowl in her lap—she planned to make them with a cottage ham for supper. But she was having a hard time concentrating on the beans—because her eyes kept being drawn to Giovanni's back, and his arms, too. His olive skin glistened with sweat and rippled with muscles. Every time he spread mortar across one of the flat field rocks he used to build the root cellar, the muscle in his right arm shifted a little, and watching it made her tingle all over. Of course, Dell and Wally worked right alongside him and sweated just as much, but she didn't even notice them—to her, Giovanni was the only one there.

When Giovanni stood up tall, stretching his back, then reached for the handkerchief in his pocket to wipe his brow, she took in his broad chest and noticed the wayward lock of hair that dipped over his forehead.

"Take a break, boys," he told her brothers. "It is too warm to keep working at this now." Indeed, it was high summer—late June—and the temperatures were blistering. Even in the shade, perspiration trickled between Edna's breasts.

"Reckon we could fix the tractor instead, if we had the parts," Dell suggested. "Seein's it's already in the barn, it'd be a damn sight cooler job."

Giovanni nodded. "You are sure you can fix it yourself, Dell?"

"Told ya I could. Just ask Edna."

Her brothers had both learned that Giovanni's soft spot for Edna was often the quickest way from point A to point B, so when Giovanni glanced over, she called to him, "Dell knows all about motors. He's kept plenty of tractors runnin' in his day—our daddy's Farmall, and our neighbor's Allis-Chalmers, and lots more."

Giovanni looked back to Dell. "You can get what you need at the tractor supply in Chillicothe, yes?"

"Sure thing," Dell said.

A few minutes later, they all stood in Giovanni's kitchen. The fellas had cleaned up and put on fresh shirts, and Edna was packing up cheese sandwiches and apples to send with Wally and Dell for the ride. Giovanni opened his wallet and gave Dell money for the parts—then he handed over a set of keys, as well, and said, "Take the Cadillac."

Dell had long since fixed the old family truck using money from their first week's pay, and Giovanni owned an old farm truck, too—so it was a shock to see him offer up the fancy turquoise car Dell admired so much. Edna saw her brother trying not to look too excited as he said, "You sure, Giovanni?"

Giovanni gave a short nod and told him to fill up the tank on the way back, and as she and Giovanni watched her brothers drive away in the shiny car, she knew Dell would be in seventh heaven for the rest of the day.

She smiled over at Giovanni. "That was real nice of you. You know how he fancies that car."

Handsome Giovanni, now in a sleeveless T-shirt and trousers held up by suspenders, simply shrugged and smiled the smile that never failed to turn Edna's heart on end. "He is a good fellow, your brother," he said. "Both of them—even if Wally can be . . . what's the word? . . . hotheaded."

"You want a cheese sandwich, too?" she asked, motioning toward the kitchen, just through the back door.

The tilt of his head somehow felt mischievous. "Make enough for two and we will have a picnic in the orchard."

It wouldn't be the first picnic they'd been on, just the two of them. She and her brothers had been living and working with Giovanni Romo for nearly a month now, and it was clear he'd taken a special liking to her.

But he'd never touched her—never once. And she was burning up inside, hungering for that. She knew it was bad—Brother Trapp at the Trinity Church back home had preached against such things—but it didn't feel bad. Except for the-not-getting-what-she-craved part, that was. All she had to do was look at Giovanni and she melted inside—and not from the June heat. She thought about him all the time, from the moment she woke up until she fell asleep at night. When she got dressed in the morning, she tried to make herself pretty—for him. When she cooked, or cleaned the house, or worked in the garden or the grapevines, she did it all with a mind to please him. She'd never felt so wrapped up in anyone or anything.

As for him never touching her, she wasn't sure what to make of it. Almost every boy she'd spent even a few minutes alone with—behind church after Sunday-evening services, or times she'd end up walking with one of Wally's friends when he was supposed to be keeping an eye on her—had tried to touch her. Seemed to her that touching and kissing was all boys wanted to do, and she'd told them all no. Yet the one boy—well, man—whose touch she longed for wouldn't give it. So maybe Giovanni only saw her as a friend.

Edna put together a basket with sandwiches, apples, some grapes from the vines on the fence, and a couple slices of the apple pie she'd baked yesterday, along with two bottles of Coca-Cola and an opener. She covered it all with a gingham cloth, tucking it in on the sides, as Giovanni grabbed their usual plaid picnic blanket from the closet.

*He led the way through the trees across the lane,
taking them deep into the orchard, picking a spot near
the creek—she couldn't see the water, but she could
hear it gurgling past as they spread the blanket in the
shade of a billowing tree, the apples overhead beginning
to show the first hints of red color. "I love the sound
of the creek," she said. "It makes me feel all peaceful
inside."*

*Giovanni smiled as they settled on the blanket. Edna's
summer skirt fluttered a bit in the breeze, revealing her
knees for a second, and she simply laughed, pushing it
down, but she wondered if Giovanni had noticed.*

*"You told me that once before," he said, stretched out
on his side, propped on one elbow. "About the creek.
That is why I chose this spot."*

*Edna flushed lightly, embarrassed about repeating her-
self. She wanted to seem smart to him. "Guess I just . . .
can't really get over it."*

"Over what?"

"How . . . nice it is here. Not like at home."

*"It is not good at home?" he asked, and she instantly
wanted to smack herself for being so honest—she didn't
want to answer.*

*Yet she couldn't think of anything but the truth. "Well,
times are hard," she explained. "It keeps Mama and
Daddy irritable, strained. And . . ."*

*"Go on," he prodded, reaching into the basket for the
sandwiches and soda pop.*

*She pursed her lips, then let out the rest. "Our house
ain't so nice as yours. And you've seen our old rattletrap
of a truck. And . . . I like all the color here. We got color
at home, of course, but . . . I like the flowers in front of
your house, and the red barn. I guess . . . everything here
just seems brighter to me." She looked into his eyes as
she said that last part, ready to be bolder than usual—
she didn't mind him knowing that when all was said and*

done, it was really him *that made everything seem so bright in her world right now.*

"It pleases me that you are so happy here, Edna," he told her, and another bead of sweat rolled between her breasts. Even in the shade, it was hot, but with Giovanni, she didn't mind it. "I want you to know," he said, "that I have been very happy since you came here, too."

Edna bit her lip, her chest tightening with excitement. "Why's that?" she asked cautiously.

And his answer came smooth as fresh-churned butter, not at all nervous like when she spoke. "I enjoy being with you very much."

She glanced down at her sandwich, not quite able to meet his eyes. "Um, same here. I mean, I . . . I like your company."

"Edna, you are the first person since I left Italy who has made me feel . . . almost as if I am at home again, just in a new place."

She wasn't sure exactly what he meant by that, only that she liked it. "Tell me more," she requested, "about home." She asked him often, and he told her stories of his past, or bits and pieces of information about his family or the village where he'd been born.

"What would you like to know today?" He always made her come up with a particular question to spur his thoughts.

So she bit her lip, thinking. "How long has your family been in Vernazza?" He'd shown her wonderful snapshots of the village that always reminded her all over again that he came from the other side of the globe. And he'd asked the same recently about her family's history, listening as she'd explained that her people had been in the Appalachians as far back as anyone knew. "A hundred and fifty years at least," she'd boasted.

And that had always sounded like a long time to Edna, until he said now, "The Romos have resided in Vernazza

*since medieval times. The name signifies someone who
has gone on a pilgrimage to Rome."*

It left her stunned. *"And you don't mind leavin' it
behind? I mean, that's a mighty long time."*

But Giovanni only shrugged. *"I love Vernazza, but it is
a tiny village, trapped between hills and sea—there are
no opportunities for a man who longs for open land and
wants to build something of his own. If my ancestors saw
fit to travel and find someplace new, why should I not
follow my own course, as well?"*

And in that moment, Edna thought about how fate,
or God, or something, had led her to Destiny. And that
maybe it was all meant to be.

Soon Giovanni was unwrapping the slices of pie, and
teasing her. *"Oh, two for me? That is very generous."*
Since the apples on his trees weren't yet ripe, and Giovanni
hadn't stored any last winter, he'd grown impatient and
bought some at a produce stand for her to use in a pie. Like
everyone, he'd loved it, and this was the third she'd made.

Feeling a little giddy, she reached in the basket for the
deep purple grapes she knew he adored—he'd brought
the vines all the way from Italy to grow here. *"Then I'll
just eat all your grapes,"* she said playfully back.

*"Hmm—perhaps we can bargain. One slice of pie for
half the grapes."*

"Sounds fair enough." She smiled.

"Except . . . you must feed the grapes to me."

Edna met his gaze and something about the demand
made her cheeks flush with extra warmth. *"Feed them to
you?"*

He gave a concise nod. She'd never met a man so sure
of himself, so comfortable in his own skin, and it made
him all the more appealing. *"Pluck one from the bunch,"*
he instructed, *"and put it in my mouth. Like Roman
times,"* he added with a wink.

Edna didn't know much about Roman times, but lean-

ing nearer, she eased one plump grape into Giovanni's lush Italian mouth. His lips closed over it—and around her fingertips, as well. She felt it at the juncture of her thighs, and their eyes met, and she knew he knew. All she felt. Every bit of it.

After a long, hot moment, she slowly began to draw her hand back—surprised when Giovanni caught hold of it and gently pulled her closer, closer, until she was lying down alongside him.

He lifted her hand back to his mouth then—taking her index finger, running the end of it along his moist lower lip. Inside she shuddered but tried to be brave. This was what she'd wanted, yearned for. It wasn't happening exactly like she'd expected, but she should have known Giovanni Romo would make it more exotic, more intoxicating, than any Kentucky farmboy could.

He lowered a soft, sensual kiss to her fingertip—before turning her hand over and kissing the palm. It was all she could do not to shiver, even amid the June heat. Still holding her hand near his mouth, he met her gaze and spoke low. "I suspect, my dear Edna, that you are as delicious as a fresh grape off the vine, or as your sweet apple pie."

Then he kissed her. Not her hand this time, but her lips. And then it was like she'd expected, like she'd imagined lying awake in her bed every night the last few weeks. She felt Giovanni's kisses everywhere, spanning her whole body somehow—both gentle and deep, soft and capturing.

His hands cupped her face, making her feel treasured. Then one skimmed downward, across her breast, over her stomach, caressing her hip through her skirt. Nearby, Sugar Creek still gurgled, and the sun still shone brightly overhead through the thick branches of the apple tree— but Edna knew nothing in her world would ever be the same. Giovanni's kisses, his touches, were the best thing she'd ever experienced.

And so when he began to unbutton her blouse, it never occurred to her to say no. And when he reached under her skirt, sliding his strong hands up her thighs, she hadn't the power to resist.

"I'm kinda nervous," she told him. Because she wasn't even totally sure what would happen next. And this was all going faster than she'd envisioned.

"Do not be nervous, Edna," he whispered between kisses, and then his mouth dropped to her neck and his fingers were stroking between her legs and the pleasure almost paralyzed her. "I only wish to be closer to you."

"I want that, too," she assured him.

Edna shut her eyes as if to close out the overwhelming sensations—the pleasure was almost too much to take. But she felt her body moving against his hand, and she heard her own breath grow labored, heavy, and she knew that, despite her fears, she wanted whatever he chose to give her.

When he drew her underwear down and settled between her parted thighs, she began to tremble. "I'm . . . scared, Giovanni."

His face hovered just above her now—oh Lord, he was handsome—and his warm voice reassured her. "Everything will be all right, Edna. Everything will be all right because I love you."

Oh. Oh my! He loved her! And she knew then his words were true—this would be okay. "I love you, too," she whispered.

Giovanni was patient, his touch gentle, sweeping Edna up in the wonder of it all—when he pulled back to extract something from a pouch in his back pocket. "Wh-what's that?" she asked.

"Shhh," he whispered soothingly. "Just something to protect us."

"Protect us?"

"From having a baby."

Oh. She didn't ask any more. She didn't want to know any more. She just wanted to let Giovanni keep making her feel this good forever. She was almost even relaxed— when the hardness she'd felt between his legs pressed into her, and . . . oh God! It hurt. She cried out, then crushed her eyes shut, trying not to weep.

But then Giovanni was soothing her again, gently brushing her hair back from her face, promising her the difficult part was over, raining kisses across her forehead, and then her mouth. And she realized with startling clarity that they were connected, deeply. She hadn't known what that part would feel like, and it surprised her.

And it was true, the hardest part was past. And then an even better, more shocking part came. He reached between them and touched her again. And she soon felt her whole being exploding into bits, as if she'd left her own body for a few seconds, and when she opened her eyes, Giovanni was smiling down at her, telling her she was beautiful.

When it was over, they lay side by side again on the blanket and Edna knew she'd been right: everything had changed. She knew secrets now that she hadn't before. She'd just become a woman in Giovanni Romo's arms. The mere knowledge took her breath away.

Next to her, Giovanni stroked her cheek, then drew his touch gently across her breasts. How strange it felt to have them bared, out in the open that way. "You make me happy, Edna."

"You make me happy, too," she breathed, overwhelmed.

"Do you think your brothers would approve of me? As your . . . um, what word do you use here? Your beau? Boyfriend?"

Giovanni was hardly a boy—he was well into his twenties, while she was only eighteen—but she didn't bother correcting him because she liked the sound of that so much. "Yes. Yes, I'm sure they would."

"And you would, too, yes?" he asked with a smile.

It felt like bright lights were being turned on all through her body. "Very much."

"Then it is official," he said with the confident manner she so admired. *"You and I, we are . . . um, what would be the word for . . . ?"*

She knew what he meant. Something like going steady. But with a man as sophisticated as Giovanni, that sounded childish to her. So, instead, she said, "In love. You and I are in love."

"Completely," he agreed, gazing down into her eyes.

Holy God. Rachel sat in Edna's truck outside the old General Mercantile, waiting as she finished talking to Grampy, and trying to wrap her head around everything Edna had just told her. Mike Romo's grandfather had been Edna's first lover! At some point before Grandpa Farris had shown up in her life. Even after hearing Edna had been in love with the guy, she somehow hadn't realized things would go this far.

Or, more likely, maybe she just hadn't imagined she'd be hearing about it in such detail. From her grandma!

"Well, what happened *then*?" she'd asked when Edna had finished the tale of her deflowering.

"I think that's enough for today," Edna had said. "Besides, we're here," and she'd pulled the Toyota pickup into a parking space in front of the old wood-façade storefront just off Destiny's town square.

Once Rachel got past her own weird shock, she had to admit that, like before, something about Edna's story had her feeling oddly . . . envious. What must it be like to be that young and in love with a man who adores you? Rachel would never know.

She'd never realized she missed that in her life, that maybe she'd actually *wanted* some romance. From a young age, she'd been all about career and independence, and for her, romance had been mostly about sexual urges and deciding what to do about them and with who. But maybe she *had* missed having all those other emotions.

Of course, it was too late now. And Rachel was a big girl, not one to get sappy. *Soon you'll be back in Chicago, back in the world you know, and you'll stop feeling things so much.* Yep, that would be good. Because ever since she'd come home to Destiny, nothing inside her had quite been the same.

Mike hadn't particularly planned to stop by the orchard, but it was his day off, the sun was shining, and he wasn't in the mood to go home yet after doing some errands. He needed to replace a board on his front porch and clean out a clogged drain, tasks he wasn't particularly looking forward to, so it seemed easy to put them off a little longer. As he passed by Creekside Park, he made the split decision to flip on his turn signal and cross the stone bridge over Sugar Creek toward Edna's house.

He hadn't seen Edna in a while, and he supposed all his run-ins with her granddaughter had the old woman on his mind. It wasn't unusual for him to stop by from time to time—besides wanting to convince her to sell him the orchard, he figured it wasn't a bad idea to check on her occasionally, given that she was an elderly person living alone. Of course, Rachel was with her for the time being. But he still felt overdue for a visit to the place that had once belonged to his grandfather.

Never mind that his groin tightened a little at the thought of Rachel Farris. His stomach contracted, too. And it wasn't the memory of sudden, unstoppable sex that caused the reaction—he'd had that before. And it wasn't the "forbidden Farris" aspect of it, either. It was . . . the sex itself. After all, that had been some *seriously good* sex. When their bodies had come together, the chemistry had felt . . . almost electrical, like some force that had pulsed through his veins, driving him to deepen the connection with her—over, and over, and over.

Shit. He glanced down. He didn't need to have a hard-on when he saw Edna.

And Rachel Farris wasn't the reason he'd come here anyway.

But he guessed seeing her wouldn't be the worst thing in the world. As long as she wasn't speeding or breaking any other laws. And if they could keep from yelling at each other. Since they *had* shared some pretty mind-blowing sex in that concession stand last week, he guessed at least saying hello would be the decent thing to do.

Not that Mike generally worried that much about being decent to women he hooked up with—which, according to his mother, was an unfortunate Romo male trait he'd inherited. According to her, even his usually mild-mannered dad had been "a tomcat" in his teenage years.

Though as he parked his truck and got out . . . hell. Yep, he had a sizable erection now. *Thanks a lot, Farris.* Damn it, even when she wasn't around, she was affecting him.

Well, it was a nice day, and a glance at the house showed Edna wasn't coming out to greet him, so maybe he'd just take a short walk through the orchard and let himself calm down. Maybe he'd think about all the years his family had wanted this land back and felt it should be theirs. Yeah, that should kill a hard-on pretty damn quick.

As he'd told Rachel, he didn't know the details—his grandpa had never wanted to talk about it, right up to his death almost ten years ago. But he could still hear his grandpa's voice, gravelly with regret. *It was mine and it should have been yours. I built the house and the barn and the root cellar with my own hands, I planted the first trees—and it should have been passed down to all of you.*

As the oldest son of Giovanni's oldest son, Mike would have likely inherited the place directly if the Farris family hadn't taken it—so maybe that was why he wanted the orchard now. But mostly, he thought it would make his parents and other relatives happy. And as he'd told Edna, he'd welcome a side income and a business to run for whenever he retired from the force, whether that was in five years or *twenty*-five.

As he meandered through the front grove, then deeper into the orchard as it stretched past the barn, he met his goal—his arousal faded while thinking about all his family had lost. It brought over him a familiar feeling of . . . emptiness. But he quickly pushed that down. Because he'd gotten pretty good at that. Except for when he thought about Anna.

Yet he wasn't going to let his mind go there today—no way. And sometimes he could even control *that*, if he worked really hard at it, if he just turned everything off inside him for a little while.

Besides, it was a good time to focus on better things—next weekend was Grandma Romo's birthday and his parents would be here. While they kept in pretty close touch with him, he only saw them a couple times a year—so this was no time to be thinking depressing thoughts about Anna or the lost Romo family legacy.

Although—damn—it reminded him that his mother *would* give him a hard time about the whole bachelor thing, and not just on the phone now, but in front of the whole extended Romo clan. And shit—once Grandma Romo got her hooks into him, it would be even worse. All she'd need is a little ammunition on the subject from Mike's parents to get her on a roll, too—and probably in Italian.

He felt bad about the situation—although he'd started out with a brother and sister, he'd effectively become an only child somewhere along the way and his parents' only chance to do the grandma-and-grandpa thing. But he didn't feel guilty enough to live his life any other way than how he wanted to live it.

Before Mike knew it, that familiar empty feeling began to threaten again—yet like before, he pushed it aside. Because that was what he did—he had to be tough, not let it touch him anytime he could avoid it. Of course, sometimes things set him off—like that asshole in the Mustang a couple of weeks ago. Something like that, something he couldn't fix or stop or change, was enough to keep him in a bad mood for days. So whenever he *could* take power over anything—including the emptiness—he sure as hell had to.

Just then, he heard a rustling sound in nearby branches—too big to be a bird—and glanced to the right to see a pair of tennis shoes on a ladder. A woven fruit basket hung from the ladder, and as he stepped closer, he caught sight of a large, billowy smock and, up above, a big floppy straw hat.

"Hi, Edna," he said.

Then Edna turned to look down at him. Only it wasn't Edna. It was Rachel Farris—looking like she wanted to die of embarrassment.

Which he could easily understand—since she looked ridiculous.

He couldn't hide his amusement. "That's a pretty good disguise, Farris."

That's when she shifted slightly to scowl at him, lost her balance—and came tumbling to the ground with a hard *thud*. She let out a yowl.

Aw, shit. "Are you all right?" he asked, moving toward her.

She lay on her back in Edna's clothes, glaring up at him. "No, actually, I don't think so. But as soon as I am, Romeo, I'm going to kill you."

Men's eyes were made to look, and let them
gaze.

William Shakespeare, *Romeo and Juliet*

Seven

*O*h, good God. Just what every girl wanted: for a guy
she'd had sex with to mistake her for her grandmother.
Rachel wished she could disappear. No wonder she'd
fallen. It was all his fault. And she couldn't even get up
and stomp away from him—no, she could only lie there
on the hard ground in the McIntosh grove wondering
what she'd done to deserve this.

"Can you sit up?" he asked.

She started to try—when he bent down to take her
hands, helping her.

So he was touching her again. And the mere sensation of his large hands closing around hers rippled up her
arms. That was all she could process, despite the pain
and embarrassment of the hideous situation: *He's touching me again and it feels good.*

"What hurts?" he asked, stooping down beside her.

"My left ankle." It throbbed with a dull but intense ache—
which she felt a lot more now that he *wasn't* touching her.

In response, Mike reached over and jiggled her left shoe back and forth—producing shooting bursts of pain. "Ow!" she screeched, smacking his hand away and flashing a look of disbelief. "I tell you my ankle hurts, so you think it's a good idea to wiggle it?"

"Sorry," he said—yet he went right on acting like he was Doctor Romo or something, now gently lifting her heel and pushing up the leg of her blue jeans. Then he felt around on her ankle for a few seconds, which she discovered she didn't mind quite so much. "Starting to swell," he informed her. "Hopefully you just twisted it and didn't do any serious damage."

"What on earth are you doing here anyway?" she snapped, remembering she was still irritated by the whole situation, even *with* his hands on her.

"I came to see Edna."

"*Why?*" She didn't care if she sounded accusing—she continued to feel very protective of Edna where he was concerned.

But his incredulous expression implied she was making too much of it. "Calm down, Farris. I just dropped by for a visit. I told you we get along. Far better than *you and I* get along, that's for damn sure."

"Well, she's in the house taking a nap," Rachel informed him. "She was tired this morning, so I told her I'd work by myself awhile."

Suddenly, she found him smiling at her . . . oddly. So even though the smile was kind of *sexy*, she said, "What's so funny?"

"Your hat," he told her, still looking amused. "Can you take it off? I don't mean to laugh while you're hurt, but I can't help it."

Fairly outraged, she gasped, then shot him her best death glare. "For your info, Edna insisted I wear this stuff. She thinks my clothes are too nice to pick apples in."

"Yeah, the clothes are awful, too," he said, sweeping

his gaze down over her, "but that doesn't explain the hat."

"She's afraid I'll get a sunburn," Rachel said.

In response, he looked doubtful and clenched his teeth lightly, as if weighing the options. "Um—if I were you, Farris, I think I'd risk the burn."

"Fine," she snipped, then untied the ribbon beneath her chin, again lamenting that Mike Romo had found her looking like some crazed, overgrown version of Little Bo-Peep. She'd feared this very thing, of course, but Edna had promised no one would see her. *Yeah, right—thanks, Edna.* As she slipped Edna's big straw monstrosity off, she hoped like hell she didn't have hat hair.

"Okay, that's better," he said. Then his eyes dropped back to the big, flowery smock. "Mostly. Anyway, guess we better get you inside."

Hmm—*we*? They were a team now? But she decided not to put too much stock in the statement—he was a cop, after all; it was his duty to serve and protect. And besides, as he anchored an arm around her waist to help her to her feet, she was suddenly a little too busy smelling that sexy, musky scent again to analyze it all.

Only—"Mother of God, put me down!" she yelled the second she tried to sink weight onto her ankle.

Mike lowered her hurriedly back to the grass.

"That's not gonna work. I don't think I can walk—at all."

"Shit," he said. "That means I'm gonna have to carry you."

She glowered up at him. "Is that so terrible?"

He gave his head a frank tilt, his face close to hers. "It's not that I mind touching you, Farris, as I think I proved the other night. It's that it's a damn long way."

She sucked in her breath. "Fine then—leave me here."

He rolled his eyes. "Quit being ridiculous."

"Well, then quit complaining. It's not my fault you snuck up on me and then insulted my clothing."

"It's not *my* fault you can't take a joke."

"Oh. So you were joking about thinking I was Edna." This changed everything.

"No, that part was real," he replied, extinguishing her relief. "I was talking about when I said it was a good disguise. *That's* when I was joking. Sort of."

She just blinked at him, getting more irate with each passing second. "So are you carrying me to the house or not? If you're not strong enough," she accused, "you could go to the barn and get one of the wagons. Or . . . I'm sure I could scoot there on my ass eventually."

He simply peered down at her, fists at his hips. "Your ass is too nice to wear it out that way. And screw the wagon— I can carry you." Good, her little jab had worked—she'd known he wouldn't be able to handle the implication he was weak.

And with that, he stooped down and scooped her up into his arms. She automatically looped one wrist around his neck, latching on. And now they were *really* close. The kind of close that had led to sex last week.

She resisted saying anything, though, deciding instead to just enjoy the ride. Since it was kind of nice being pressed up against him again, even with clothes on, even the big, billowy, ugly ones she wore at the moment. And even with her ankle throbbing. She'd just learned something new about herself: Apparently, with the proper stimulation, she was able to lust through pain.

Although it turned out Mike was right—it was a long way to the house, and toward the end of the walk he started breathing heavily, his chest starting to heave, and she hoped like hell they'd make it or she'd end up all the more mortified by this whole event.

So it was a relief when he carried her up the back steps and said, "Can you grab the handle?" She pulled the old screen door open and Mike maneuvered her inside without banging her sore ankle on the door frame.

"Where to?" he asked, sounding impatient now.

"The couch," she said, then directed him through the dining room to the parlor.

"Damn," he muttered, breathless, as he lowered her there.

"Sorry." She was beginning to feel, for the first time, a little sheepish about the fact that he'd had to lug her all that way. And she immediately missed being in his arms.

"No problem, Farris," he said, slightly gruff—but not *too* gruff. Then he glanced down at her. "You mind if we get you out of that sad excuse for a shirt?"

"It's a smock," she pointed out.

"Whatever. It's horrible."

"What do *you* care?"

He shrugged. "I don't know. Just used to seeing you look . . . the way you *usually* look."

"Which is?"

"Uh . . . good."

Hmm. Something inside her warmed. "So you think I usually look good, huh?"

Kneeling down beside Edna's antique sofa, he gave his head a skeptical tilt. "You know damn well you look good, Farris." And then, to her surprise, his bedroom eyes suddenly got a little more bedroomy, and he spoke a bit slower, his voice deeper. "And . . . guess I was just remembering the last time I saw you. You looked *damn* good then."

Oh. My. Rachel bit her lip as a vision filled her head: the two of them writhing on the concession-stand floor together. Now feeling *extremely* sheepish, she whispered, "I was, um, naked."

"Right. And I'm not saying you have to be naked to look good, but *this*"—he reached out to finger the smock—"isn't working." Then he reached up to begin unbuttoning it.

She let him, since she wore a fitted black tank underneath—her original choice this morning before Edna had chimed in, as she had pretty much every day since she and Rachel had started harvesting apples together. She sat up slightly, already propped on couch pillows, and he helped her free of it, tossing it aside. "There, that's better. Now you're the Rachel Farris I've come to know—reckless and belligerent, but at least nice to look at." Then he returned his attention to her ankle, slipping his hand beneath the hem of her jeans to give a gentle squeeze. "Still hurt?"

She nodded. But even so, his touch skittered all the way up her leg.

"Still swelling, too," he told her. Then he set about removing her gym shoes and propping her left foot on a pile of more throw pillows he assembled. He did it as comfortably as if . . . as if he knew her. And even after having had wildly intense sex with him, something about the simple act felt strangely . . . personal. She sure hadn't planned on Mike Romo ever touching her again, after all.

"Does Edna keep ibuprofen in?" he asked, and a moment later, he'd gotten her two Motrin and a glass of water. After that, he went into the kitchen, returning with a dish towel and a bag of frozen peas.

"What the hell?" she asked at the sight of the peas.

He laid the towel across her ankle, placing the freezing cold bag on top. "Instant ice pack," he replied. "Fifteen minutes on, fifteen off—and change it out for a fresh bag after Edna wakes up. She has some frozen broccoli in the freezer, too," he added with a wink.

"Quit being nice to me," she demanded, letting her brow knit, "or I won't recognize you." She really wouldn't know how to function around a truly pleasant, considerate Mike Romo.

"I'm not being nice," he assured her. "I'm being a cop.

We all have a little first aid training." Then, as his hand came to rest on her knee as comfortably as if they were a couple, he glanced around the quiet house . . . and got an undeniably wicked look in his eye. "So—you think Edna's still asleep?"

"Must be." The house was too small for them not to have heard or seen her if she was awake. And Rachel liked having his hand on her knee, but she had no idea why he looked so . . . mischievous.

Until he slid that hand oh-so-slowly up her thigh and said, "That means we'll have to be quiet."

Oh. Good Lord. She sucked in her breath and peered up at him from her pillows. "Quiet?" He wasn't serious?

"While I take you your mind off your ankle," he said, grazing his warm palm a little higher, and making Rachel feel light-headed, even while lying down. The juncture of her thighs began to spasm. Oh God, he was serious.

"It's . . . freezing," she said of her ankle, trying not to feel what she was feeling. Because Edna was in the next room, for heaven's sake. And what had happened to this being a one-time thing?

"That's my point," he said, bending lower, his gaze on her mouth now. "You need a distraction."

"I do?"

"Yep."

Uh-oh. She couldn't do this, couldn't let this happen. Once was . . . an accident. But twice was . . . something more. "Stop," she said.

"Stop what?"

She sucked in her breath. "Whatever exactly it is you're planning on doing."

"Be quiet, Farris, or Edna will hear you."

Mike hadn't really intended to put the moves on her, but hell, by the time he'd gotten her on the couch, his hard-on had reappeared. And he knew he couldn't do what he *really* wanted to do given that Edna was in the house, but he couldn't resist the urge to fool around with Rachel again at least a little. Now that he had her out of that ridiculous get-up, her body looked just as ripe and curvy as he remembered, and the mere sight had sent his mind barreling back to that concession stand.

That part kept surprising him—that he kept thinking about it. Once sex was over, he didn't usually sit around dwelling on it, reliving it. But he'd revisited that concession stand in his mind more than once since it had happened, and right now, their sizzling encounter at Destiny High was all he could think about, all he could feel. It pumped through his veins the same as if they were still there right now, doing it on the floor.

So he didn't hesitate to bend down and kiss her. Slow, deep. Just like their sex had been. He let his mouth play over hers, felt her response between his legs, and obeyed the impulse to ease his tongue between her lips.

She tasted like apple, and it made him smile a little inside—apparently she'd been eating on the job. But he didn't take the time to comment—he was much more interested in following other urges. Like slipping his hand between her thighs.

Aw, damn, she was so soft there—even through her jeans. He used his fingertips to stroke, his palm to mold, and when she began to move against his touch, his gut clenched with heat.

But then she was pushing him away, her hands to his chest, her breath thready as she said, "We can't do this."

"Why not?"

"Well, besides the fact that we don't like each other . . ." She let out an impassioned breath even as she glanced toward Edna's bedroom.

"Shhh," he soothed her, lowering another small, warm kiss to her lush lips. Then promised, "We'll hear if she wakes up."

"What if we don't?" she whispered.

Tired of talking, he only answered by kissing her again.

And yeah, he knew it was risky—it was exactly the kind of reckless thing he might expect *her* to do, now that he examined it. But . . . hell, it was just easier not to think about that as he sank deeper into the warm kiss and resumed massaging between her thighs.

Soon her soft, ragged breathing twined around him the same as if it were her arms and legs, making him almost painfully hard as he deftly unbuttoned her jeans and slid the zipper down.

So it surprised him when she protested yet *again*. "Mike, stop," she breathed.

He simply gazed into her blue eyes, so close to his right now—then leaned near her ear, his mouth almost touching it, to rasp, "I want to show you outrageous again." After which he slid his fingers down into her panties.

And then she didn't ask him to stop anymore.

In fact, she gasped at the touch, her eyes closing in pleasure.

And thank God. Because Mike got so caught up in it, in stroking his fingers through her warm moisture, that he soon felt . . . almost like he would if *she'd* been touching *him* that intimately. His limbs went weak with a lust that gave him the sensation of drowning—but in a good way. Like surrendering. Being swallowed up by something bigger than him.

She moved against his palm in a perfect, sensual rhythm, her eyes still closed, which allowed him to watch her unabashedly. Her pretty cheeks flushed with color and her jaw went slack, her lips parting prettily. Her body undulated like liquid heat, rising to meet his fingers.

Finally, he kissed her some more—he couldn't help it; he needed to have his mouth on her. He kissed her cheek, her lips, her neck—he kissed her breasts through her clothing. He lifted her shirt with his free hand and kissed her pale, slender stomach. And he wanted to kiss her lower—but he knew he couldn't, not here, not now, so he simply went as low as he could, down around her belly button and just below, and he stroked her more deeply still, acutely aware of her wetness.

Suddenly, both her fists clutched at the couch cushion at either side of her body and she let out a soft moan—making him hope like hell Edna was a sound sleeper—and then she thrust at his hand, harder, harder, and he knew she was coming. She was coming gorgeously, powerfully, and he watched her face contort into what looked like agonizing pleasure—before finally relaxing again, appearing replete.

And he felt desperate to yank her jeans down and do some thrusting of his own—but he still couldn't. He'd started this, and he'd just have to suck it up and live with it for now. So instead he simply watched her some more—as he gently extracted his hand, as she finally opened her eyes.

"I should kill you," she said.

Even from her, it caught him off guard. "That's not the response I usually get to something like that."

"You know what I mean," she whispered harshly, reaching to do up her jeans.

"Well, what I *hope* you mean is something more like, 'Thank you, Mike—that was very generous and I forgot all about my twisted ankle.' "

Despite his words, she drew in her breath in a huff. "What I mean is that Edna could have walked in here at any moment."

"But you *did* forget about your ankle," he pointed out.

She shrugged. "Fair enough. And . . ." She seemed to be losing the attitude some, being a little friendlier, like she eventually had in the concession stand. "And that was, um . . . nice." Ah—it appeared the afterglow of orgasm was finally hitting her. *Note to self: Rachel gets nicer after orgasms.*

"That's more like it, Farris," he said.

And to his surprise, she even reached up and drew him back down for another long kiss, a really *hot* kiss, which—shit—felt great but made his dick ache all the more.

And for some odd reason, an idea hit him, and he didn't even stop to think about it—he just said, "I have a thing a week from Saturday."

"A thing," she repeated dryly.

"A family thing. And I need to bring a girl."

With her arms still around his neck, she drew back slightly into the pillows, lowering her chin and narrowing her gaze critically. "Is that your way of asking me on a date?"

He shrugged. Since he hadn't thought this through, he didn't know the answer. "Guess you can call it that if you want."

At this, Rachel released him from her grasp entirely and crossed her arms. "I *don't* want. And . . . I don't think so." She shook her head, as if making the decision final.

He made a face. "Damn, Farris, am I *that* bad?" Because, despite all the negative stuff between them, her refusal surprised him. Since they'd discovered there were *some* ways in which they got along very well.

"Well, you certainly know how to take a girl's mind off her troubles, but . . ." She shook her head against the pillows. "We really can't keep going like this. And it would be too weird to be a Farris at a Romo family event. They might throw food at me or something."

Mike laughed at her theatrics. "Not likely. It's my grandmother's birthday. And don't worry—I'll protect you."

Their eyes met—and for a second, he thought she was considering it. Until she said, "Still . . . no. I know we've managed to put our differences aside long enough to fool around, but other than that, we can barely tolerate each other. And besides, I still don't like you trying to steal the orchard from Edna."

Huh. Fine then. Who cared anyway? And it was probably for the best. He simply shrugged once more and said,
"Your loss."

The words made her eyebrows shoot up. "How so?"

Wasn't it obvious? He let a slow grin unfurl. "I might
have shown you some more outrageous again."

Rachel's face first registered contempt, then took on an
expression that told him maybe that didn't sound like such
a bad idea—when they both heard a soft stirring elsewhere in the little house. "Edna!" she whispered.

"We're good," Mike said softly, trying to calm her back
down. "You're all zipped up."

Which made her bite her lip and look all dreamy again,
like maybe he'd reminded her how recently she'd been
*un*zipped and why. And damn, that didn't help the strain
behind *his* zipper one bit—but he still liked knowing the
mere memory could re-excite her that fast.

As he pushed to his feet, he hoped his erection didn't
show—hell, that was what had started this whole thing
and sent him into the orchard, so it seemed ironic that
he found himself in exactly the same position he'd been
trying to avoid: facing Rachel's grandma while sporting
a stiffy. He simply shook his head. What was the world
coming to when he couldn't rein in his lust any better
than this?

Just then, a door opened somewhere nearby and seconds
later, Edna came toddling into the room. "Oh—Mike. Ya
damn near scared the wits outta me." Then she reached
up to touch her hair. "I just woke up, so I probably look
like Halloween came early."

"Sorry, Edna," he said.

That's when her gaze dropped to Rachel, stretched out
on the couch with her foot propped up under the bag of
peas. "Uh-oh. What happened to *you*?"

"Fell," she said. Then she hiked a thumb in his direction. "*His* fault."

Edna's brow knit, first as she walked over and lifted the peas to study Rachel's ankle, then as she peered toward Mike.

It seemed to Mike like a good time to remind Edna she liked him better than most Romos, so he said, "I just stopped by to check in on you. I know it's harvest season and you've got a couple helpers, but if there's anything else you need, let me know."

Mike watched the wrinkles on Edna's face shift slightly as a small smile unfolded there. "You're sly, Mike," she said, shaking a finger at him. "If I were to take your help, it might just obligate me to you."

He lifted his hands as if in surrender. "No such thing, Edna. I'm just trying to be neighborly and put the feud in the past."

Which caused a loud *harrumph* to rise from the couch. When he glanced down, Rachel's arms were crossed again. "You sure haven't put it in the past with *me*."

He couldn't help giving her a pointed look—part disbelief, part amusement. "Come on now—you and I have been getting along a little better *lately*, haven't we?"

She met his gaze and he knew they were both back to the concession stand again.

"Even just a little while ago," he reminded her. "I thought I was *very* nice to you."

Her eyes narrowed into thin slits as if to say *Shut up*. But he saw heat in that blue gaze, too. "I . . . guess," she finally said.

So he turned back to Edna. "Like I was saying—before I was so rudely interrupted—let me know if you need anything. It's an honest offer, Edna—no strings attached, okay?"

Edna's arms were crossed now, as well, as she eyed him warily—and he began to feel a little ganged up on by Farris women . . . until she finally relaxed her stance to say, "We're doin' okay so far, but I'll keep it in mind. And thanks for stoppin' in—despite what Rachel here thinks, I reckon you mean well."

"I do," he said, then glanced back to the belligerent girl on the couch. "As for you, stay off that ankle. And remember, veggies on, veggies off."

"Whatever." She rolled her eyes.

"I'm pretty sure you mean, 'Thanks, Mike, for nearly breaking your back carrying me in from the orchard,' but that's okay." Then he shifted his gaze back to her grandma. "Take care of yourself and Miss Mean Jeans there, Edna. See ya soon."

Rachel watched as Mike disappeared through the dining room, headed toward the back door. Then she sat up, reached down, and removed her peas—surely fifteen minutes had passed, probably more.

"You two have the hots for each other, don't ya?" Edna asked.

"*What?*" Rachel exploded, outraged. Mainly because she had no idea how Edna could tell. Damned old mind-reading woman. "Are you crazy?"

"No, just observant."

Rachel flashed a look of disbelief, then recrossed her arms. "And just what is it you think you observed?"

"You bein' ornery to a good lookin' fella who was tryin' to take care of ya, for one thing."

Rachel shrugged. "Like I need somebody to take care of me," she grumbled. Then blinked, remembering. "Okay, yes, I did need someone to carry me in the house, but I'm here now, and I have you if I need help, so no big deal."

"Don't sell short a man who'll take care of ya—it might be worth more than ya think."

Rachel didn't know what Edna meant by that, so she simply rolled her eyes and scooched around on the couch to get more comfortable—and tried to forget she'd let Mike Romo put his hand down her pants a few short minutes ago. How had *that* happened?

"My other clue," Edna went on, "was that I don't believe Mike generally wears his jeans that tight. He must have quite a trouser snake for it to make such a big difference in the fit of his jeans."

Rachel's jaw dropped as she stared at her grandmother in utter shock. "Quite a *what*?"

And Edna just looked at her as if she were thick-headed. "A penis, girl, I'm talkin' about his penis. He must have a pretty nice one for it to make his jeans so tight when he's excited. The same was true of his grandpa," she mused, growing instantly more lighthearted. Then she lifted one finger in the air. "Now *that*, I gotta say, is one good thing about the Romos."

A few days later, on a crisp September Saturday, Rachel meandered through Creekside Park with Tessa and Amy. All the girls were casually dressed in jeans and gym shoes. Although Rachel generally reserved such shoes for manual labor or exercise, her friends had convinced her it only made sense.

"We're going to the park, not a fashion show," Tessa had pointed out when she and Amy arrived at Edna's to pick her up.

"And you're just getting over a twisted ankle," Amy reminded her.

Yet she topped the outfit with a comfy soft pink zip-up hoody she seldom wore but which suddenly struck her as cheerful. Since she had to like *something* she was wearing, fashion show or not. She couldn't help it—she considered her clothing a reflection of herself.

"You're not even limping," Amy said with surprise as they crossed the grass, shuffling through the first autumn leaves scattering the ground. Hints of gold and orange tinted the trees billowing above them.

"I'm lucky it healed so quickly," Rachel replied, nodding. "I stayed off it for a couple of days, and since then it's been fine. I even got back out in the orchard with Edna yesterday. Which is important."

"Because the sooner all the apples are picked, the sooner you can leave," Amy said glumly.

"No, Miss Sad Sack," Rachel corrected her, stuffing her hands in the pockets on her hoody. "I'm stuck here until the apple festival anyway, so it's more a matter of . . . making sure Edna doesn't push herself too hard."

"So did you ever figure out if she was faking her ailment?" Tessa asked.

"Not really," Rachel replied. "But either way, she's getting older, and as much as I don't like to see it, she's not as spry as she used to be."

Walking along the split-rail fence that lined this stretch of Sugar Creek, Rachel could hear the water cascading over the rocks below, and it reminded her of Edna's sexual encounter with Giovanni Romo—somewhere just across the creek, in the orchard. It probably seemed to Edna like it had happened just yesterday, and yet look how many years had passed. And though Rachel still didn't know the whole story, it made her a little sad to realize that *whatever* had happened, later in life Edna had ended up by herself. She'd never thought much about that until lately, because her grandmother had always seemed so capable and independent—but who really wanted to end up alone?

Apparently, me. Or that's what her plan in life called for anyway, now that she thought about it. She'd just never seriously looked that far down the path, to old age and what it might be like. The strange insight made her chest tighten slightly.

"So how'd you fall off the ladder anyway?" Amy asked.

Oh. She hadn't told them that part yet. "It was Officer Romeo's fault," she explained as they continued following a paved, twisting path along the creek bank. Then she proceeded to share the whole story, from the embarrassing start to the painful middle to the orgasmic conclusion.

The last of which left poor Amy blushing madly.

"Yeah, I was shocked, too," Rachel said. "That I let it happen. I certainly had no intention of it, and I tried to stop, I really did." Then she bit her lip. "The thing that shocked me even *more*, though, was that he was so . . . selfless. Sexually, I mean."

But next to her, Tessa shook her head. "It wasn't selfless," she insisted. "He just got off on . . . you know, getting you excited. That makes some guys feel all hot and powerful."

Rachel simply lifted her gaze. "I still say I got the better deal."

And they all laughed. And Rachel couldn't deny how nice it was just spending a lazy, breezy Saturday afternoon with her best friends. She'd felt bad leaving Edna with the day-trippers, but she had Brian Cahill with her, and she'd insisted, afraid Rachel would end up rushing around on her ankle.

As for Mike, even if Tessa was right and it was just another power trip for him, it still caught her off guard. He'd struck her as a man who would be all about his own satisfaction when it came to something like sex— yet in the concession stand, and again at Edna's, he'd surprised her. And if he *was* a guy who took pleasure in *her* pleasure—well, she could only see that as a win/ win situation.

A few minutes later, the girls had wandered to an empty playground, settling onto a row of wooden swings. As Rachel gently scraped the toes of her shoes through the sandy dirt beneath her, she remembered: "I didn't tell you guys the rest of the story, about when I fell."

Tessa shoved a windblown lock of brown hair behind one ear. "Good God, there's more?"

"Not about Romo—about Edna," Rachel explained. Then she told them what Edna had said after Mike had left. It was one thing to have Edna regale her with the story of losing her virginity, but . . . "When did she start thinking it's okay to talk about penises with me?" she asked as they departed the play area, strolling through more swirling leaves toward the pretty white gazebo in the center of the park.

Amy pointed out, "*You* talk about penises with *us*. Sometimes." Then she added, "Sometimes more than we'd prefer."

As they settled on the gazebo steps, Rachel shot her a look. "Are you saying you don't want to hear about Mike Romo's penis? Fine—I can cease and desist with all details right now."

But Tessa held up her hands in a stopping motion. "Wait a minute. I, for one, am interested in penises. I haven't seen one in quite a while, after all." Soon after Rachel's return, Tessa had confided that she hadn't had sex in a few years.

"It's this town," Rachel told her, happy to blame Tessa's lack of a love life on Destiny. "You came back here and haven't had sex since then, am I right?"

"True," Tessa conceded. "But you, on the other hand, came back here and had sex in record time."

Hmm. Oh. "Good point." Which firmly negated the Destiny-is-death-to-your-sex-life theory. "But I definitely didn't plan it that way."

Tessa let out a teasing, long-suffering sigh. "Sure, the girl who needs some fun and romance in her life can't get any, while the girl who *always* has lots of fun is getting still more. Figures."

Although Rachel only scrunched her nose in reply. "I'm not sure Mike Romo qualifies as *fun*. Exactly. I'm not sure *what* he qualifies as."

"Sounds pretty fun to me," Tessa replied. "Although . . . what happened to it being a one-time thing?"

"Yeah, I was wondering that, too." Rachel bit her lip.

"But it's definitely over now. He kind of . . . asked me out, and I said no."

And they both glared at her, as if she'd done something heinous.

"What?" she asked, taken aback. "Look, it's bad enough I'm in Destiny, period—no way am I getting involved in some small town affair. It's just . . . not me. And besides, the date was to a family thing, a *Romo* family thing. And it was hardly a romantic invitation. So I turned him down. I mean, I didn't want him to think I actually . . . like him or anything."

Tessa rolled her eyes. "How very sixth grade of you."

"Well, since when *do* we like him?" Rachel argued. "He was mean to your Aunt Alice, remember?"

"Whatever," Tessa said. "So he's mean when he pulls people over. Some things are more important."

"Like sex?"

Tessa just widened her eyes as if to say a resounding *yes*.

Just then, someone yelled, "Hey Freckles—heads up!" And Rachel raised her eyes in time to see Amy leap from where she sat on the steps to catch a football—which sent Rachel and Tessa ducking for cover.

When she decided the danger was over, Rachel looked up to see Logan Whitaker walking toward them in an orange Cincinnati Bengals jersey, complete with tiger stripes on the sleeves. More importantly, behind him came Mike Romo, wearing a Steelers jersey, along with another guy in a red hooded sweatshirt sporting an Ohio State emblem.

As usual, just seeing Mike sent a chill fluttering through her, but she tried to tell herself it was the brisk fall air. As he approached, she sort of found herself wishing she hadn't *just* finished telling Amy and Tessa about what had happened on the couch—she felt like they were thinking about it now. She knew *she* certainly was. The only question remaining: Was Mike thinking about it, too?

"What's up, ladies?" Logan asked with a sexy grin that might actually have made Rachel a little hot for him if she wasn't already struggling with so many bizarre emotions for his best friend.

"Just hanging out," Amy replied. Then she pointed toward the guy in red. "Rachel, you remember Adam Becker, right? From high school?"

Oh, wow, that was Adam? She hadn't realized at first—too busy obsessing over Mike—but the one-time prom king and Bulldogs quarterback looked as handsome now as he had then, even if a little more rugged. "Of course," she said, still seated on the steps with Tessa. "It's nice to see you, Adam."

"You, too, Rachel," he replied with a winning smile. "Welcome back to Destiny—the place has been quiet without you."

She returned the smile, appreciating the comment.

And was she imagining things, or did Romo actually look . . . a little jealous? Hmm . . . Despite herself, she liked the idea of that. And couldn't stop herself from doing something to egg it on a little. "I hear from Amy that you're in landscaping—all that outdoor work must be good for you, since you look great."

Adam grinned, and she thought she saw Mike's chest heave, like he was trying to keep himself in check. "Thanks," Adam said. "You're looking fine yourself."

"*How's that ankle, Farris?*" Officer Romeo cut in, stern as ever.

She casually shifted her gaze to him. "Fine now, thanks."

"Good. I didn't want to hear you complain about it."

Okay, whatever. Maybe he wasn't thinking about the couch. But she still thought he was jealous. Not that she knew why she cared. She'd turned down his stupid invitation, after all, committed to keeping this what it was: a weird sexual thing. But wait, that didn't sound very nice. Okay, a *hot* sexual thing. Which, like she'd told her friends, was over now anyway. Because hot didn't override the fact that he was still a Romo who wanted the Farris Family Apple Orchard. And sex with him, no matter how good, still felt like a strange betrayal of some kind. Not a Romo/Farris kind of betrayal, though, she realized suddenly—but more a betrayal to . . . herself.

Because this wasn't her—this small town life, this small town guy. It just didn't fit with who she'd become. And even if she loved Edna and her friends here, she'd worked hard to leave everything small town about *herself* behind.

Whoa. It was startling to suddenly realize her reasons for stopping things with him had to do with something much deeper inside her than a family feud or all the things she didn't like about him—that it actually had to do with *her.* And it even made her feel a little . . . guilty, for maybe being arrogant, or "too good" for Destiny. But it *wasn't* arrogance, she realized. It was just . . . not wanting to go backward in life.

"What's wrong, Farris? You look sick."

She swallowed, then met Mike's gaze. "Like I said, I'm fine." She'd put a little bite in her voice, to make sure he heard it, and that she *felt* it. She *was* fine. She was stuck in Destiny for a little while, and had maybe let herself start getting a little too involved with life and people here, but she was fine. She'd *be* fine. As soon as the dumb apples were harvested and she could get the hell back to Chicago.

"So what are you guys up to?" Amy asked, bouncing the football in her hand. She'd always been sportier than Rachel and Tessa.

"We were supposed to play some touch with a few guys from Crestview," Logan said, "but they didn't show."

"Touch?" Rachel asked, happy for a distraction from her thoughts.

"*Football*, Farris," Mike said as if anyone would know that. "Touch *football.*"

It was then that Logan looked speculatively toward Rachel, Tessa, and Amy—then to Mike and Adam. "*They* could play with us."

"They're girls," Mike said with all the maturity of an eight-year-old.

Logan shrugged. "They're better than nothing."

"All right, stop with the flattery already," Tessa said, and Logan and Adam laughed. Mike, on the other hand, still appeared to be his usual gruff self—at the moment, Rachel saw no signs of the seductive Mike or the Mike who sometimes teased her and made her laugh. So all the better that their weird, hot—whatever—liaisons were in the past; his unpredictable moods were just one more thing not to like about him.

"All right, so we've got ourselves a game," Adam said. "Three on three."

Rachel glanced at Tessa. "Did we agree to this?"

Yet no one paid any attention to her, and Logan said, "Amy has to be on *my* team."

"Why?" Rachel asked, blinking her suspicion.

"Well, because she's . . ." Logan trailed off, looking like he'd been caught at something.

"Good?" Rachel asked. "Meaning that Tessa and I are rotten?"

Logan laughed and held out his hands. "I never said that."

And Adam piped up to add, "Guess this is your chance to prove yourself."

But it was only when Mike Romo looked her way, drawing Rachel's eyes back to him instantly, that she got that horrible, wonderful fluttery feeling between her thighs again. And it hit even harder when he said, "So, Farris, what do you say? Wanna play?"

Here's much to do with hate, but more with
love.

William Shakespeare, *Romeo & Juliet*

Eight

Play what? But she held her tongue. In case that might
sound flirtatious, or sexual. Since that's suddenly how she
was feeling at the moment. But she *couldn't* feel that way
around him anymore, damn it—she just couldn't. So instead she replied, perhaps too softly, "I don't really know
the rules of the game."

"You'll learn as we go," Mike said, a little less brusquely,
their eyes still locked.

And she had no idea why an exchange about football in
front of all their friends was tightening her chest and turning her stomach to mush, but she simply said, "Okay," in
a voice that sounded far meeker than she liked. And she'd
long since forgotten about flirting with Adam.

As she pushed to her feet, she began to wonder what
she'd gotten herself into—but she followed along with the
rest of the gang to a large open green space nearby, barely
able to focus on the conversation taking place around her.

On the perimeter of her brain, she heard Amy ask Mike why he was a Pittsburgh fan when they lived much closer to Cincinnati. And in her peripheral vision, she saw him toss a derisive glance at Logan and his Bengals jersey before he said, "Simple. Super Bowl victories." Everyone laughed and then Logan started explaining—clearly for Tessa and Rachel's benefit—how the game worked, and indicating where the goal line and boundaries were. Fortunately, Rachel had a cursory knowledge of football— she just hadn't actually played it before—so she was able to get the basics despite her heady state.

Yet even as Logan kept talking, she couldn't help noticing that Mike's black Ben Roethlisberger jersey suited him somehow. Maybe because it made his shoulders look just as broad as they were. And he appeared so comfortable, confident—clearly in his element. Kind of cuddly, too, which struck her as weird, since little about his personality would make anyone think of him that way. And he hadn't shaved in a few days, either. He'd been clean shaven again when she'd seen him at Edna's, but now he was back to being all stubbly and, as before, something about it turned her on.

Wait. Cuddly? You think he's cuddly now? So much for getting him out of her system.

"All right," Mike said, "if Logan's taking Amy, I'll take Adam."

Rachel blinked, drawn back to the game. Wow, he didn't even want her on his team. Not that she cared. She and Tessa, obviously the losers in the crowd, just looked at each other.

Ultimately, she ended up on Logan and Amy's team, and a few minutes later, as they huddled, Logan surprised her by announcing she was their secret weapon.

She made a doubtful face, still wondering how her quiet walk in the park—meant to prevent strain on her ankle— had turned into *this*. "How so?"

"Amy will go out for a pass," Logan began, "and they'll assume I'm going to throw it to her, since she's . . ."

"Good," Rachel supplied, again filling in the blank.

"But I'm really going to hand it off to you," Logan said, "then drop back and fake a pass." He demonstrated the motion, showing her how to stand, and how to attempt hiding the ball once she had it.

"What do I do then?"

"You run like hell."

Hmm. "I'm coming off a twisted ankle," she felt the need to point out.

"Just do your best," he told her, then gave her an encouraging pat on the back.

"Won't the other team tackle me?" She really didn't want to re-injure that ankle.

"No, this is *touch* football," Logan explained. "No tackling. It's like tag. Once they touch you, the play's over." Then he put on his game face and spoke louder, so the other team would hear. "*Are we ready to kick some ass?*"

"Ready!" Amy said, slapping upraised hands against Logan's, clearly a lot more into this than Rachel. But she was willing to try. Since she liked the idea of beating Mike Romo at something. She just hoped she didn't come out of it humiliated again.

As the teams lined up, she ended up across from Tessa, who looked at her and murmured, "This is stupid."

"I know," she muttered back.

Then the play began and Rachel did her best to turn the way Logan had instructed, just in time for him to shove the ball against her stomach. Then came the "run like hell" part and, trying to keep the ball hidden, she took off down the grassy stretch toward the sapling that marked the goal line.

She easily made her way past Tessa—and Adam was across the field guarding Amy, as Logan had planned.

Rachel ran like crazy then, picking up speed as the sapling grew closer.

However, it was as Mike Romo came barreling toward her like a Mack truck that she knew for sure she liked football a lot better when she was on the sidelines with pom-poms. As he tagged her shoulder, she stopped running—only to have him trip over her feet and send them both crashing to the ground.

She landed on her back—with Officer Romeo sprawled on top of her. Fortunately, other than the initial *thud*, nothing on her hurt. *Un*fortunately, Mike didn't seem to be moving—and when she met his gaze . . . *oh*. The way he looked into her eyes, even now, made her surge with moisture, damn it.

His hand molded warmly to her waist. "Did I hurt your ankle?"

"No," she said as he lifted off her slightly—yet still held her pinned to the grass. "But I thought you weren't supposed to tackle me."

"I wasn't. Your feet got in my way."

"Well, maybe you can let me up now." *Instead of looking like you want to rip my clothes off right here in front of everybody.*

"How about that family picnic next weekend?" he said, catching her off guard.

"How about it?" she retorted.

And for the first time that day, his expression changed—the corners of his mouth turning up into not-quite-a-grin. "Come on, change your mind. I need a date."

Oh brother—not this again. She tried to push him off her, her hands to his chest, but he didn't budge. "And you can't get one?"

"I can get plenty."

She didn't doubt it. Sometimes *hot* did make up for a lot. "Then why does it have to be me? Is it bring-a-Farris-for-show-and-tell day?"

This time he came closer to smiling, and those intoxi-cating brown eyes even softened a little. "It's not like that."

Again, she tried to get him off her, wrapping her hand around his arm and pushing. "What's it like?"

He didn't move an inch, instead sounding a bit exas-perated now when he said, "I don't know. I just felt like asking you again, damn it."

"You are a silver-tongued devil, Officer Romeo," she informed him.

That's when he traded in his exasperation for a wicked little grin, arching one eyebrow. "You haven't even *seen* what I can do with my tongue yet, Farris."

It made her gasp—and left her totally without a come-back.

"So is that a yes?"

Oh Lord. She really *couldn't* agree to this—but it seemed the only way to get out from under him. And . . . well, maybe the promise of the tongue thing had intrigued her a little, too.

Yet she still tried to sound very aloof, rolling her eyes as she said, "*Fine.* I'll go if you insist." And then she told a lie. "But it has nothing to do with your tongue."

He kept his hot gaze on her to say, "Well, be nice and maybe you'll find out anyway."

Oh my. She knew this was a bad idea. Yet the tongue thing *was* making it seem a little less bad, and a little more . . . thrilling. "I thought you worked me out of your system," she pointed out. "In the concession stand."

"Guess I'm not quite there yet," he told her—finally be-ginning to get up. When he reached a hand down to her, she saw, with relief, that no one was close enough to have heard their conversation. In fact, it appeared they'd all purposely kept their distance—so Mike went on. "And I don't think you are, either. But I'm sure if we try, we'll get tired of each other pretty soon."

She took his hand and said, "Again, you're a smooth talker."

As he pulled her to her feet, he simply cast a confident look and shrugged. That shrug said it all: *I don't need to be.* And it was beyond her at this point to argue or deny it. The chemistry between them was that strong.

So ridiculously strong that *now* . . . oh Lord, she'd agreed to go to Grandma Romo's birthday party?

The next day found Mike and Logan fishing at a spot just off the road next to Blue Valley Lake. No houses were in view from where they sat and Mike didn't even know who owned this particular land, but they'd been coming here for years.

The weather was chilly, same as yesterday, and Mike set his rod and reel on the ground next to him to zip up his hooded sweatshirt. They'd been sitting on the little embankment above the lake for nearly an hour without even a bite, and Mike was in a sour mood.

"I hate fishing," he said, picking his rod back up. The revelation had just hit him.

"Yeah—me, too," Logan agreed.

Mike looked at his buddy. "Then why do we do it?" For two guys who hated fishing, they fished pretty often.

But the question didn't throw Logan, not even for a second. "Because we fished with my dad."

True enough. Logan's dad had died after a heart attack about five years ago, and he'd been like a second father to Mike. Ron Whitaker had taken them fishing all their lives—but for him and Logan, Mike guessed maybe it had been more about that whole male bonding thing. And the truth was that, as a kid, Mike had been a little afraid of water after losing Anna right next to a lake—one big theory being that she'd wandered in and drowned—but Logan's dad had taken them fishing and swimming enough that it had forced him to get over it. So now, Mike supposed Logan was right and fishing was about remembering time spent with Ron.

"So . . . you laid on top of Rachel Farris a long time yesterday," Logan said out of the blue. Okay, apparently he was done reminiscing about his dad.

"Yeah, guess I did," Mike admitted. But it left him all the more irritated.

"Are you still gonna tell me you don't have a thing for her?"

Mike sighed. He felt tired. "Nope. In fact, I'm taking her to my grandmother's birthday party next weekend."

Logan turned to look at him, jaw dropping. "Shit—really?"

Mike only glanced up briefly, then looked back out over the water, slightly choppy today from the fall breeze. "Yep."

"Well, then you might want to consider being a little nicer to her," Logan pointed out.

Made sense, Mike supposed. The only times Logan had been around the two of them together, Mike had been pretty surly. But, of course, there was a lot Logan didn't know. "Don't worry," he said, reeling in his line just a little, keeping his eyes on the bobber in the water. "I'm plenty nice to her—in my own way."

He felt his friend's sharp gaze. "What's *that* mean?"

"Well, I've given her about three orgasms so far."

Logan's fishing rod dropped from his fingers to the ground below. "When the hell did *this* happen?"

Mike just bent down to retrieve his buddy's fishing pole, shoving it back into his hand. After which he filled Logan in on what he'd missed—how getting locked in the concession stand had led to sex, and how carrying Rachel into the house had led to . . . other creative types of fooling around.

"With Edna in the next room," Logan repeated numbly when Mike was done.

But he played it off. "She was asleep."

And Logan just shook his head. "Man, I don't get you sometimes."

Finally Mike looked back up, narrowing his eyes on his friend. "What's that supposed to mean?"

"Well, don't get me wrong. It's not that I begrudge you having sex in weird places—I myself *like* sex in weird places—but it's not like you."

Huh. Mike didn't want to admit it, but Logan was right. And it wasn't that Mike minded sex in weird places, but just that he wasn't usually that . . . haphazard. He could usually wait to get a girl home into bed. If he was gonna seduce someone, he usually orchestrated it exactly the way he wanted. Only with Rachel . . . "Hell," he finally said, "that woman's been driving me crazy since the moment I met her. I don't know what it is, but . . . when I'm around her, I do things I don't plan to do. And when I see her, I want her. Bad. It's strange, like I don't have any power over what I'm doing."

"No, it's normal," Logan said. "Sometimes. With a girl who really does it for you."

But Mike's brow knit. "It's not normal for *me.*"

Logan nodded in agreement. "Well, yeah, that's what I meant a minute ago. Usually you have to run things exactly the way you want 'em—so it threw me to hear you did it with Rachel in a freaking concession stand. I mean, you're usually so . . . by the book. You plan things out. You're controlling."

Mike slanted him a look. "Controlling? What, are you suddenly Sigmund-fucking-Freud?"

"Just stating the facts," Logan replied, and left it at that. Because it wasn't a new topic of conversation, even if Logan had never used a psycho-babble term like "controlling" before. Logan insisted Mike had had certain issues ever since the day Anna disappeared. He always claimed Mike had been a regular easygoing kid before that, but had right afterward turned into the same my-way-or-the-highway guy he was today.

Mike couldn't decide if that was true, if he agreed—because for him, *everything* had changed after they'd lost Anna. So he couldn't pick out particulars in his own personality—he just knew that before that day, life had been good, and easy, and happy; and after that it had been mostly shit, for a very long while. But he didn't spend much time *caring* whether Logan's theories were true, either—he *was* who he *was*, and he didn't worry about it much.

"So why am I just hearing about all this fooling around with Rachel *now*?" Logan asked.

Mike only gave another shrug, eyes back on his line. "I didn't know you were so interested in my sex life."

"I'm not," Logan said. "But dude—sounds like you at least owe me a beer for not showing up at the concession stand."

After a long day of apple picking, Rachel and Edna sat down to a hearty beef stew Edna had let simmer all day in the Crock-Pot. "An amazin' thing, the Crock-Pot," Edna said. "Back before the Crock-Pot, I'd have lost some pickin' time makin' us a decent supper, but it's a dandy thing to have around come harvest."

Rachel nodded and said, "Mmm-hmm," as she forked a carrot slice into her mouth. She wasn't ignoring Edna purposely, but she'd spent much of the day thinking. About how hard Edna worked here. And that maybe there *were* easier ways, whether or not Edna knew it.

"What's on your mind, girl?" Edna asked, sounding annoyed. " 'Cause I can tell ya got *somethin'* cookin' up there."

Rachel met her grandmother's eyes. "I've been contemplating ways the orchard could make more money."

Edna didn't look the least bit impressed. Closer to bored. "Is that so?"

But Rachel ignored her attitude. Edna was a creature of habit, averse to change, but it seemed important to push her on this. "For one thing, we could build a website. A lot of orchards have them." She knew, because she'd done some Googling on her Blackberry. "You'd get a lot more day-trippers from farther away. And that's not all. You could make it worth their drive by having other weekend activities—hayrides maybe, or evening bonfires with ghost stories. And you could put in a bakery counter and sell pies and caramel apples for people to take home."

Edna just blinked at Rachel across the table, flashing that same blasé expression. "And just how do you think I'm gonna do all this when I can't even get the apples harvested?"

Rachel had been pondering that part, too. Even though it still didn't seem like the wisest time in her life to lay out extra cash, she said, "Maybe I could hire a web designer and someone to manage it. And somebody to orchestrate the activities. I could oversee all that from Chicago." It would be more constructive than hiring extra hands as she'd once considered, and it would keep her directly involved, even if from a distance.

But Edna was already shaking her head. "Nope. No, I'm too old a dog for those kinda new tricks. I'm lucky to keep things runnin' as they are without makin' 'em' busier or more complicated. Now, as you know, my hope was always that one of my progeny would care enough about this place to run it someday, but as you also know, it don't look like that's gonna happen. So the way I see it, all I need to worry about is keepin' the orchard afloat until I'm too completely broken down to do it."

A familiar wave of guilt wafted through Rachel, but at least she was *trying* to get more involved with sustaining the place while Edna was still around to handle the day-to-day operation. And again she reminded herself that she came from a large family and no one else wanted to take over the orchard when Edna was gone, either.

So maybe she just plain shouldn't care anymore. She hadn't cared a few weeks ago, after all. But the idea of having the Farris Family Apple Orchard die—in name anyway—still depressed her; she still didn't want Mike Romo to have it. Even if she *had* agreed to go on a strange sort of date with him—almost against her will. She gave her head a slight shake, still in disbelief. "Are you going to sell it to Mike Romo?"

"Don't know," Edna said as she cut into a large chunk of potato with her fork, but she seemed more thoughtful now, like she'd moved beyond her annoyance to seriously consider the question. "It's hard, 'cause to me, it's a Farris thing. The place has meant a lot to me, and I believe it meant somethin' to your grandpa, who really built the business up before he died. But Mike *does* have some historical claim on it, and at least he wants it, at least he'd keep it thrivin'" Edna paused to take a bite, then looked back across the table at Rachel. "Why do you suddenly care so much anyway?"

Rachel stirred her fork through the remains of her stew, feeling a little adrift at the question. "I'm not sure—the same reason you do, I guess. Family pride." She swallowed then, having said it. In a way, she'd left Destiny to outrun her extended family and their sometimes questionable reputation. But since coming back, she'd felt bound to defend her Farris roots to Mike Romo, and now she continued to worry about the Farris Family Apple Orchard ceasing to exist. "I guess if he gets it," she said, "it'll somehow feel like the Romos won the feud, you know?"

Across the table from her, Edna gave a small nod of agreement. "But I've told ya before—the older I get, the more I see it's just easier to let go of grudges. Part of me sees it as the Romos winnin', but part of me sees it as your grandpa's efforts bein' carried on. And besides," Edna said, her voice softening a bit, "Mike's been through a lot—and I think he . . . wants somethin' to care about. He'd never admit that, but he's lost so much—I think he needs some solid ground to stand on. Both figur'tively and liter'lly."

The notion surprised Rachel in a way . . . but then again, knowing what she knew now about Mike's little sister disappearing and how it had apparently torn his family apart, it didn't surprise her at all. There was more to Mike Romo than the gruff cop who liked writing out tickets so much. Even more to Mike Romo than the guy who was so skilled at pleasuring a woman. Rachel wasn't sure she'd ever see it, but if Edna said it was there, she believed it.

As the visual image of Mike standing on that solid orchard ground permeated her thoughts, she also found it easy to imagine Giovanni Romo there, too. And the more connected she began to feel to her *own* family, the more she could understand why Mike wanted this place so much. "Do you have any pictures of Giovanni?" she asked.

Edna didn't even act as if the question was out of the blue. Instead, a sly sort of smile snuck onto her face. "As a matter of fact, I do. Just one. I kept it hid from your grandpa all those years—he just wouldn't have understood. I loved Edward dearly, but savin' a picture of Giovanni just seemed like . . . part of the scrapbook of my life, a thing I had a right to remember." As Edna rose to her feet, Rachel noticed how slowly she moved at the moment, and it made her heart hurt a little despite Edna's merriment. "Stay right here and I'll see if I can't find it."

Edna returned a minute later, holding a yellowed piece of paper in her hand, folded in half, wrapped around a black-and-white snapshot. Remembering the picture was likely over fifty years old, Rachel took it carefully from Edna's fingers—and saw a strikingly handsome man who bore a remarkable resemblance to his grandson. She couldn't hold in her gasp.

"What is it?" Edna asked.

"He looks like Mike."

Edna peered down at the picture now, too. "Hmm—he does, don't he? Reckon I never realized how much. But now you can see why I was head over heels."

Indeed she could. He was lankier than Mike, probably from all that farm work, and of course his hair and clothing reflected the time, but yeah—if Rachel had been around in 1958, she'd have been swooning over Giovanni as badly as she seemed to swoon for Mike.

"So," Rachel said, eyes still on the photo, "you never told me what happened with Giovanni—I mean the rest of it."

Edna looked at herself in the mirror in the pretty new dress Giovanni had given her. He'd not bought it for any particular reason, but just because she was his little fiore, *he'd told her, explaining that the word meant "flower" in Italian. She smiled at herself in the glass, biting her lower lip.* I am his little flower.

At first, she'd worried over having given her virginity to Giovanni so quickly. She couldn't imagine the shame she'd feel if her parents knew, not to mention the folks at the Trinity Church—but it had been so easy, so impossible to say no. Just like it had every time they'd been together since. When she subtracted everyone but her and Giovanni from the equation, it felt perfect. She'd been right about Destiny being a magical place—she'd found more than she'd ever hoped for here.

When a knock came on the back door, she smoothed down the front of her dress and went to answer. It was Eddie, a boy who'd recently come to work on the farm along with Wally and Dell. These days, Edna mostly took care of the house chores—cooking, cleaning, laundry—

and Giovanni had needed another hand. Eddie stood on the back stoop, tall and thin, hat in hand, his pale brown hair looking lighter beneath the sun. "Howdy, Miss Edna," he said with his usual friendly smile.

She returned it. "Afternoon, Eddie." Eddie lived on the other side of town with his parents and siblings, and he struck her as a sweet country boy, the sort she might notice at home—or if she didn't have the most handsome man in the world already in love with her. But as it was, even though he was a few years older than her, that's exactly what Eddie seemed like: a boy.

"Was hopin' you could tell me if Wally and Dell's off in that back field workin' today." His eyes twinkled a little when he spoke.

"I reckon they are," she said.

"Sorry I'm late—m' truck broke down."

"Well, I can surely understand that. Don't worry about it—it was our own broken down truck that led me and my brothers here."

Though it seemed like so long ago now, when she thought about it. So much in her life had changed. She was wearing the first new dress she'd ever owned and she was Giovanni Romo's girl.

"Well, you have a nice afternoon," Eddie said, turning to go—but Edna couldn't help feeling charitable toward him.

"Eddie, you wanna piece of apple pie to keep ya company on the walk?" She'd just been slicing some up, fixing a picnic basket for her and Giovanni.

Eddie's grin widened. "Why, I'd march across a bed of nails for a piece of your pie, Miss Edna."

As Edna stood at the screen door watching Eddie depart with a big slice of pie a moment later, Giovanni's palms closed warmly over her shoulders from behind. "Giving my pie away to another man, my little fiore?" he whispered teasingly in her ear.

"It's not another man, silly—it's just Eddie," she said, turning into his embrace.

Giovanni nodded, looking pleased. "That is good. I could not bear to have you look at another man, my Edna. I cannot help but feel, well . . . possessive where you are concerned," he concluded, his gaze glittering hotly on her.

Despite herself, she liked Giovanni's jealousy. "The same goes for me, with you," she informed him. "And if I ever see you look at another girl, I'll give away all your pie."

Giovanni just laughed, then drew back slightly, his expression playful yet full of torment. "Can I help it if the girls at the theater in town flirt with me when you are not looking? Am I to blame when the bakery lady smiles and winks at me?"

The very images put Edna's stomach in knots, so she planted her fists at her hips. "They'd better not. And you'd better not like it if they do!" To which Giovanni simply raised his dark eyebrows, still taunting her, and she realized . . . "You're teasin' me. You're bein' cruel and teasin' me."

Giovanni let out another full-bodied laugh and pulled Edna back into his arms. "Do not worry, my little fiore. *You will always be my number one."*

An hour later, the two of them rested on a blanket at their favorite spot in the orchard, where they'd first kissed—and more. It was a beautiful late summer day— the sun shone down clear and bright, but a pleasantly cool breeze wafted through the branches above, where the apples were becoming a vivid red. Edna lay back on the blanket, her arms stretched over her head. "I love this place," she said dreamily. "More than I knew I could love any *place." Not that she'd been many places to love, but to Edna, the orchard seemed like heaven on earth.*

Giovanni peered down at her, his eyes heavy lidded,

same as when he wanted her. She thought he would lean down to kiss her then, so it shocked the heck out of her when he instead said, "Marry me, my fiore."

Edna drew in her breath. She'd yearned for this moment with all she was—but she'd never imagined it could happen so soon, so suddenly. "Yes! Yes, I'll marry you, Giovanni!"

As Giovanni's face filled with joy, he scooped her into his arms, lifting her, crushing her in his embrace. "You make me so happy," he breathed in her ear. Then, pulling back, still smiling, he turned more practical. "I had intended to wait, to travel to Kentucky—I wanted to ask your father for your hand, do this the proper way. But you look so beautiful today . . . the words, they just came out."

Sitting up now, Edna curled her fingers into the front of his shirt. "That's sweet, but I'm glad you didn't wait. Mama and Daddy will love you." Then she shut her eyes and simply drank in the warmth of the day, the scent of the air, the wonder of the moment. She was going to be Mrs. Giovanni Romo. "I can't wait to tell Dell and Wally. And, well, maybe me and you could drive down home this weekend."

"That sounds like a magnificent idea, fiore. *I cannot wait to meet the rest of your family. And . . ." He leaned close, that seductive look in his eyes again. "I cannot wait to make you mine in every way."*

Edna didn't even worry about the boys coming upon them as Giovanni began to kiss her, to lay her back on the blanket, soon pushing up her dress. They were far away—the rest of the world *was far away. And* her *world was perfect.*

Late that afternoon, she and Giovanni returned to the house, laughing, hand in hand. "I should go to the field, work with the others," he said, adding with a lighthearted smile, "Such happy news gives me extra energy."

But Edna argued, pouting. "Oh, not today. Take the rest of the day just to be with me."

That's when a blue pickup came rumbling across the bridge, throwing up a light cloud of dust as it drew to a squeaky halt. Edna and Giovanni both watched as Harvey Miller from the bank in town hopped out in a hurry, to press an envelope into Giovanni's hand. "This just came for ya from the Western Union."

"A telegram?" Edna asked. She'd never seen one before, but she knew people sent them when they had something urgent to say.

Giovanni ripped it open as Edna peeked around his shoulder to see.

LA SPEZIA ITALY 646PM AUG 8 1958

GIOVANNI ROMO
RT 1 DESTINY OH USA

MOTHER ILL STOP RECOVERY DOUBTFUL STOP ASKING
FOR YOU TO COME HOME

> YOUR BROTHER BENITO

Edna gasped, then watched as Giovanni's olive complexion turned ashen. "Oh Giovanni, I'm sorry," she said, squeezing his arm.

Five minutes later, Edna watched him pack his suitcase, feeling, she suspected, nearly as desolate as he did. "I hate that you have to leave now," she told him. She didn't mean to whine, especially under the circumstances, but she couldn't hold it in.

"Do not worry—I will be back soon," he said without looking up from his work.

"Take me with you," she said. "Take me to Italy. I should be by your side while you go through this."

In reply, Giovanni stopped packing and turned to face

her, cupping her cheek in his palm. "I would love to take you, fiore, but you have no passport."

She felt deflated, as if the air had just been sucked out of her body. "Oh." And despite the warmth of the day, all of it pouring in through the open windows, Edna wrapped her arms around herself, feeling suddenly cold and alone. "What if you don't come back?"

She knew she shouldn't be plaguing him like this, after him getting such painful news, but she couldn't help it. One moment they were getting engaged, and the next he was leaving? She hadn't found much in life to love this deeply, and she couldn't help but fear this was the end of her newfound happiness, that it would all be taken from her now.

Giovanni gazed down into her eyes. "Of course I will come back, fiore. Everything I own is here. And my love is here, too. And if my mother passes," he added sadly, "well . . . maybe my brothers and sisters will finally come to America with me. I have long wanted them to."

He reached out, grabbing her hand, squeezing gently. "Someday I will take you to Italy and you will fall in love with it. For now, though, you must care for the farm—you and the boys. There is money in my bureau, and I will wire more." With that, he turned back to his suitcase, packing more clothes inside.

Despite all he said, though, Edna couldn't shake off her fears. She felt abandoned already. She knew it was irrational, she knew he had no choice in the matter—but a sense of doom weighed on her. Sinking into an easy chair in the corner of Giovanni's bedroom, she hugged herself tighter.

It was only after he closed his suitcase, buckling it shut, that he turned to see her despair. He knelt down before her and peered into her eyes. "Edna, what can I do? How can I make this better?"

She felt childish. This wasn't like her, and she could

scarcely explain it herself, let alone to Giovanni. Surely it wasn't because of the way he'd teased her about other girls. His proposal had blotted all that out, yet . . . well, she hated the idea of him being so far away when she suddenly felt jealous. "I know you got enough to worry about already," she said softly. "I just have . . . a bad feelin' about this. This has been . . . my magic summer, in my magic place. And I'm afraid once you leave me here that you'll never really be mine again." And then she burst into tears. She hated crying—hated it—and she seldom did it. But right now, she couldn't rein in her silly emotions—she couldn't make sense of anything.

Easing beneath her on the chair, Giovanni pulled her into his lap and hugged her until her tears abated, wiping the last few away himself. "Of course I will be yours. Did I not promise you are always my number one girl? You are only reacting this way because so much has happened today, because it is happening so fast." He rested his forehead against hers, and she simply soaked up the moment, and his warmth.

Then he pulled back and used one bent finger to lift her chin. "In my family, there is a tradition," he told her. "When a man proposes to a woman, he gives her an engagement gift, something dear to him, as a promise that his love is true. Since I had no plan to propose today and do not even yet have a ring, I also have no gift prepared— but I think I know the perfect thing."

He sounded so hopeful, Edna sat up straighter, her mood lifting slightly at the distraction. "What is it?"

"You tell me every day how you love the farm, yes? Well then, this will be my gift to you."

She blinked. "The farm?" She didn't point out that once they married, the farm would be half hers anyway— because it truly seemed like such a significant gesture, from the heart. She'd learned that he'd built the place with his own bare hands over the past five years.

He nodded. "You will keep it safe until I return—and then it will be ours together, always."

And the strange truth was, his promise made her feel better. It was one thing to leave your fiancée on your land; it was another to give it to her before you went. And it wasn't that she'd doubted him, but somehow this made his love feel all the more real and his return all the more certain.

"Look," he said, lifting them both to their feet, then finding a pen. "I will even make it official." Grabbing up the telegram, he turned it over on his suitcase and began to write on the back. A few minutes later, he pressed the piece of paper into her hand and she opened it, peering down.

I, Giovanni Romo, hereby give my dear little fiore, Edna, my farm in Destiny. As a promise of my true and faithful love for her. As a promise that I will soon make her my bride.

It was dated and signed. And she knew the little note wasn't legal—it was scrawled haphazardly on the back of a telegram, for heaven's sake—but it made his promise feel even more tangible, gave her something to hold onto while he was away. She lifted her gaze to his and when their eyes locked, she trusted, she believed. Giovanni would return home to her. And this truly was her home now. Hers and his.

Just then, a knock came on the back door and a male voice echoed through the house. "Hello? Y'all in here?"

"Come in, Eddie," Giovanni called, his gaze still on Edna's. "In fact, come back here, to my room."

And when Eddie walked in, looking a little perplexed, Giovanni said to Edna, "Look, we even have a witness. Sign this, Eddie."

Soon after, Giovanni hugged and kissed her and held

her tight for a long, bittersweet moment—and then she watched as he got in his Cadillac, waved goodbye, and disappeared across Sugar Creek.

"That's it, isn't it?" Rachel asked, pointing to the old slip of paper that had been folded around Giovanni's picture. It was still in Edna's grasp. "That's the telegram."

"Sure as shootin'," Edna said. They'd long since poured iced tea, grabbed a couple of apples to snack on, and moved to the sofa, so now Edna lowered the piece of paper to the flowered cushion upon which she sat and shoved it toward Rachel.

Rachel picked it up and read first the front, then the handwritten promise from Giovanni. It would have been evocative enough without having just heard Edna tell the story, but now . . . well, she'd never felt so close to her grandmother, as if she were holding Edna's heart in her hands.

Finally, she looked back up, ready for more. "What then?"

"That's it," Edna said.

Rachel leaned toward her. "*It?*"

"For today."

Oh brother. Rachel could only glare, crossing her arms over her chest. "You are infuriating, old woman."

But Edna just laughed, and it came as no surprise that she *liked* being infuriating.

Another glance down at Edna's one-time lover again reminded Rachel of her *own* lover, even if that seemed an odd label to put on Mike Romo. "I guess I may as well tell you . . ." she began. Because she *had* to tell her. Mike would be picking her up here, after all. And she wouldn't want to lie to Edna about this anyway—even just by omission.

"Tell me what?" Edna asked when she didn't finish.

Shame dripped from Rachel's voice as she admitted her

transgression. "I've agreed to go with Mike Romo to his grandmother's birthday party this weekend."

Edna simply looked at her, and Rachel couldn't read her expression, but she could guess at her emotions well enough. For a Farris to celebrate with the Romo clan was unthinkable—and if Giovanni was Mike's grandpa, then Grandma Romo had to be . . . the woman Giovanni had somehow ended up with instead of Edna.

"It's hard to explain why," Rachel rushed on when Edna didn't reply, "but basically, he had me trapped to the ground in a game of football and refused to let me up unless I agreed. So I had no other choice."

Slowly then, Edna's eyes turned sly. "I *knew* you two had the hots for each other."

Rachel offered up her usual eye roll in response. "Whatever. He's attractive, I suppose." She left out the part about him being so attractive that she'd already had sex with him. So attractive that it seemed to override all her sense and logic when he touched her. Then she added, "I hope this doesn't upset you."

Edna gave her head a thoughtful tilt, and finally replied, "Actually, I think I'm glad. I'll be proud for all those Romos to see how smart and pretty and funny my granddaughter turned out."

Rachel couldn't have been more stunned—because Edna was a lot of things, but openly emotional wasn't usually one of them. Except for lately, Rachel remembered once more. Apparently Mike Romo wasn't the only one with some hidden layers.

"You just be sure to hold your head high and show 'em how wonderful you are," Edna went on.

And Rachel simply said, "Stop it, Edna, you're making me blush," then threw an apple stem at her.

Give me my sin again.

William Shakespeare, *Romeo & Juliet*

Nine

$\mathcal{O}$n Saturday afternoon, Rachel stood in front of the mirror in Edna's spare bedroom looking at herself in a new dress. That's when she realized. The mirror, the dress—this was just like Edna fifty years ago, with Giovanni. Maybe she was putting too much thought into this.

And then it hit her—hard. She *had* put some thought into this. She'd actually gone out and bought something new to wear. What had gotten into her?

Oh God. Are you losing part of yourself here? With Mike? With this town?

Maybe it was all of Edna's reminiscing about Giovanni—maybe something about it was permeating her thoughts, her soul. Or maybe she wanted to make a nice impression on the Romo family for Edna's sake. Because it had seemed totally natural when she'd gotten the bright idea to buy a dress for the occasion. The shopping, the selection she'd made, it had all seemed completely normal to her—until this very moment.

Still staring at her reflection, she let out a long breath. *This will be okay. It's a pretty dress—you'll wear it again . . . somewhere.* Even though it wasn't her usual style. But mostly, it reminded her: *You can't let this thing with Mike go on. You agreed to go to this party with him, but that's it. No more sex. You can't let yourself get any more enmeshed in this man or this town—or you won't even recognize yourself anymore.*

Just then, she heard Edna gasp from the next room, and walked out to see her grandmother holding back a ruffled curtain to peek out the window. Rather than waste time asking what was so gasp-worthy, Rachel joined her to peer out herself. Then *she* gasped, too. Mike Romo had just pulled up in a big, long, turquoise convertible with fins.

"God above," Edna said, pressing a hand to her heart.

Rachel couldn't believe it. "That's Giovanni's car, isn't it?"

Edna nodded as they both kept staring. "I'd heard Mike ended up with it, but I sure didn't know it was in such mint condition. That car looks just as good as it did the first time I rode in it."

As Mike got out and slammed the door, Rachel yanked the curtain from Edna's grasp and let it fall. "Don't let him see us looking, for heaven's sake."

But Edna just laughed. "It's a nice car—why wouldn't we look?" Then she gave her head a mischievous, teasing sort of tilt. "And I hear he only brings it out for special occasions."

"Shut up," Rachel said, grabbing up her purse and sweater. "There's nothing special going on between me and Mike Romo."

When a light knock came on the not-often-used front door, she whisked it open to find Mike in blue jeans and a white button-down shirt with the sleeves rolled up. As always, he looked good enough to jump on, sending a familiar prickling sensation down her spine.

"Jesus," he murmured, looking her over.

"What?" she said, glancing down at her dress, sleeve-less and feminine, in a bold flowered print. It had looked fine in the mirror a minute ago.

"Nothing—I just thought you'd be in jeans, like usual."

She blinked, suddenly nervous. "Should I be? I can change. I wasn't sure."

But Officer Romeo shook his head. "No, it's perfect. You look gorgeous."

And Rachel nearly fainted. What was *with* him? And what was with *her*? Since when did he say such nice things to her? And since when did she let it make her feel so overcome?

"Hi, Edna," Mike called over top of Rachel's head—and yikes, since Edna was still in the room, she *would* think something special was going on now.

"Howdy, Mike. You two kids have a good time," she said.

"We will," he told her then he took Rachel's hand and led her from the house and out to the Cadillac. Like they were . . . a regular couple or something. On a regular date. She'd known this would be weird.

"Cool car," she said, trying to act normal as he opened the door for her.

"It belonged to my grandfather. It's a 1957 limited edition Eldorado Biarritz Cadillac."

She was tempted to say she knew that already, but held her tongue.

"It's a nice day, and I figured my dad's family would enjoy seeing it."

Like many cars from that era, it was a boat—the front seat seemed a mile wide, especially when Mike walked around and got behind the wheel. Three or four more people could have sat comfortably between them.

"So the dress is good?" she asked—or more like *yelled*

across the wide seat to be heard. It was mostly to make conversation—but despite herself, she liked when he gave her another thorough perusal.

"Like I said, perfect," he called back to her.

"I didn't have anything like this with me, so I bought it at the Daisy Dress Shop in town." It had seemed like the right thing for a Destiny soiree, like something Jenny or Sue Ann would wear—but it was still hitting her hard all of a sudden that she *wasn't* Jenny or Sue Ann, *so why am I dressing like them?*

As they crossed the bridge and turned out onto the highway, he said, "You don't have to sit all the way over there, you know."

So she sent him a sideways glance. "Where should I sit?"

Taking his eyes off the road for a few seconds, he arched one brow to cast a playfully wolfish look, while he patted the seat right next to him.

Hmm. So Romo wanted her closer. Two seconds after they got in the car. One thing she could say for Officer Romeo—he wasn't shy. Even as all her limbs went a little melty at the suggestion, she tried to resist. "Wouldn't that be sort of high-schoolish?"

"Who cares? Right now it feels like you're in the next county."

"Fine," she said, scooching over bit by bit. It wasn't sex, after all—it was just sitting beside him. "But next thing I know, you'll be wanting me to wear your class ring on a chain around my neck."

He replied with an arrogant grin. "Not likely, Farris."

Now that she was closer to him, growing aware of his familiar rugged scent and watching his hands on the old steering wheel—turquoise to match the car—he quit talking. He leaned across her knee to turn up the radio, fitted with an iPod adaptor—and Smokey Robinson's "Cruisin' " filled the car. And within moments, it suddenly seemed . . . well, as if Smokey knew exactly what she was starting to feel being practically *pressed up against* Mike now. Oh boy.

She'd heard this song her whole life, but she'd never realized until this minute how darn *sexy* it was. Of course, the fact that Mike Romo had just bent his torso warmly across her lap might have done something to make her a little more aware.

And as the old Cadillac smoothly hugged the road— well within the speed limit, of course—Smokey crooned about getting closer to every part of each other's bodies, and Rachel began to feel even *more* melty, the lyrics seeming to seep into her skin while her thigh came into light contact with Mike's. And then—oh my—Smokey cleverly dropped in the word *release*. She bit her lip, because she felt that word right between her legs, and stretching lushly up into her breasts. Yep, this song was about way more than driving. And unfortunately, sitting next to Mike was apparently about more than just sitting next to Mike, too.

She drew in her breath and wanted to look at him—but didn't let herself.

God, what was it *about* this guy? Why wasn't she thinking about Chase, like she'd promised herself she would back when this started? That resolution had lasted all of two seconds. And now, here she was, close enough to Mike to kiss him—and wanting to, that fast.

At the same time, though, she realized she also enjoyed . . . just being in the car with him, riding in a convertible on a beautiful fall day with the warmth of the sun on her face. The truth was, when she'd agreed to go to this party, she'd been so wrapped up in the weirdness of attending a Romo family function and the revelation that being with Mike made her feel like she didn't know herself anymore that she hadn't contemplated what this part would be like. The getting there. The being-on-a-date-with-Mike-

Romo. And to her surprise, so far, she liked it, damn it. And from what she could tell, so did some of her more sensitive body parts.

As the music continued, sort of making her want to lie down and make out with him somewhere, she kept watching his strong hands on the wheel. Strong, *good* hands. She knew from recent experience that he had *very* good hands. Then she dropped her gaze and enjoyed the way the denim stretched across his thigh. She liked feeling the simple "maleness" of him so near. Uh-oh—this was bad.

Finally, wondering if he was suffering similar sensual tugs, she stole a sideways glance at his handsome face.

"What?" he asked.

Crap—she'd been caught. Clearly, she was no good at being sneaky. She fudged a reply. "I was just wondering why it's such a big deal for you to bring someone to this thing. Since you practically forced me, I mean." For some reason, she still felt compelled to make it clear that he'd wanted this way more than she had.

"It's for my parents' sake, and the rest of my family."

Oh. Swell. Not exactly, "I have to have you, Rachel!" *Way to kill my lust, Romo.*

But wait, no, this was good. If it was purely for practical purposes, that made it a lot less . . . like a date. It was more like . . . one friend doing a favor for another. Or something.

"This'll keep them from hounding me," he went on. "They worry that I'm some lonely bachelor who's never gonna settle down."

"Are you?" she asked, lifting her gaze back to his face. He was unshaven again and it made her stomach flinch.

"Lonely?" He slanted her a *get-serious* look. "Hardly. The rest of it, though? Pretty much."

Hmm, so Amy was right about him not being the settling-down type. "Good," she said quickly.

"Good?"

Because I wouldn't want you to think that bothers me. And I have no idea why it does, just a little—she wasn't that type, either, after all. But since she couldn't tell him any of that, she smoothly covered with, "That way I know I don't have to worry about you falling in love with me."

Next to her, he let out a hardy laugh. "Don't worry, Farris, you're safe. I don't fall in love."

"*Finally*," she replied, "something we have in common." Despite the odd emotions she'd just been experiencing, it was the truth, and in a way it was a relief to find out they were completely like-minded on that.

Mike, however, just cast a doubtful look in her direction. "*All* women fall in love."

She returned the cynical expression, making certain he read it loud and clear. "Not this one. There's too much else to do. Like build my career."

"And pick apples with Edna," he pointed out.

So maybe the apple-picking thing didn't mesh with the tough career girl image she was selling. Still, the tough career girl was the *real* her. Wasn't it? She wasn't *really* losing herself here, was she?

Stunned that she was even asking herself that question, she tried to shrug it off. "Well, you know how it is with family. Sometimes they need your help—and you give it."

His next glance down at her was more gentle. "You sound almost human, Farris."

And something low in her belly fluttered. Just because he was being nice to her? Or because somehow it all made her feel too . . . soft inside?

Well, enough with the softness. "Watch it, Romeo," she said, "or you'll start falling for me—hard."

"Falling for you, no," he said conclusively—then he raised one eyebrow. "Getting hard, though . . . maybe. You look too good in that dress."

Oh. My. Yep, Officer Romeo never hesitated, but this one caught her off guard more than usual, and she lifted her gaze to his to see that, *oh yeah*, he was feeling it, too. The whole seductive Smokey/Cruisin' vibe. His look, and his words, moved all through her like something warm and liquid. Her lust had just been revived.

Just keep in control here. It's a practical date between friends, that's all. Keep it that way, Smokey or no Smokey.

Mike grew a little stiffer behind his zipper just from the expression on Rachel's face, the way she sometimes managed to go from tough chick to sweet-and-sexy in a heartbeat. But as usual with her, he barely knew what was going on. It was bad enough he'd asked her to his grandma's party—much worse that she was getting him hot. Again. This fast. Less than ten minutes after putting her in the car. What the hell was happening to him?

They were outside town now, on one of the many twisting two-lane roads that crisscrossed the area, and Mike found himself slowing down—and drinking her in a little more, with his eyes. Her warm, pink lips appeared a little pouty at the moment, like they needed to be kissed, and her gaze shone bluer, brighter than usual, beneath the sun. He'd never noticed those little flecks of light in her eyes before.

He was probably looking at her like he wanted to devour her, but when it came to Rachel, he'd quickly learned he wasn't very good at putting the animal back in the cage— or Tarzan back in the trees. He still didn't get it—but he couldn't seem to fight it, either.

Just then, her expression changed again—to something wary. "This isn't . . . some act of rebellion, is it? Bringing a Farris to the party to punish your family in some way?"

He lowered his chin. "Don't be dumb. I told you before, I'm trying to get them off my back—not upset them."

"But then why bring *me*? I mean, from what I hear, you can get any girl you want. And given my last name, I'm not exactly the obvious choice."

Mike shrugged. "Maybe if I'm going to take a date to a family party, I want her to have half a brain. Not all the girls I know fit that description."

She appeared blasé. "That I don't doubt. And I happen to have a *whole* brain, for your information." But then her expression edged back into sexy territory, where he liked it most. "Is that the *only* reason, though?" she asked, biting her lower lip in a way that drove him crazy. "Or is it . . . because you don't quite have me out of your system yet?"

At this, he blew out a long breath. Apparently, she was going to make him say it, straight out. "All right then, Farris—sure. The fact that I might want to get with you again could have something to do with me inviting you." Then he shook his head and redirected his attention to the road unfurling before them. "Damn—most girls would be happy to hear they were appreciated for their minds and not just their bodies. But not you." He didn't get that about her, yet it reminded him once more that she really *was* a city girl, through and through—with a whole different way of looking at life.

"I like to be appreciated for both, thank you."

"Fine—you are. I can't wait to get under your dress. Happy now?"

"Well, not exactly." She suddenly looked a little unsettled. "Because we, uh, can't have any more sex."

His jaw dropped as he stared down at her. Before his eyes narrowed. He spoke slowly. "Then why the hell are you . . . ?"

"What?"

"Looking at me all hot and sexy, and baiting me, making me say I want you?" He arched an accusing brow at her. "You're a lot of things, Farris, but you're not a tease."

In response, she actually looked a little surprised—maybe at herself. "You're right, I'm not. But . . ." Then she let out a huff. "It's like this, Romo. I came back here

to pick apples and spend time with Edna—not get mired
in some small town affair that'll have every tongue on
the town square wagging. Once was . . . well, okay, it was
undeniably hot. And what happened on the couch was . . .
distraction or something, like you said. But that's where
it has to end. I escaped this place once and never looked
back. Now that I'm here . . . well, I'm just doing my time
until I can leave again."

Huh. Well, Mike could read between the lines easily
enough. When all was said and done, she still thought
she was too good for Destiny and the people in it. Maybe
somewhere along the way, maybe at the park that day,
he'd thought he'd seen that changing. But clearly he'd
been wrong. "Just one question, Farris. If you're so ready
for this to be over, then why are you *still* sitting there
looking all sexy and wanting?"

"I'm not!" she claimed, clearly trying to appear
incensed—but the sexy, wanting part still shone through.
"And I don't. Feel that way, I mean."

"Liar," he said softly, eyes back on the road.

"Not," she argued quietly, simply.

And Mike let it go. But he didn't believe her for a
second. And it pissed him off. All of it.

Hell, there for a minute or two he'd truly thought . . .
well, that there might be something between them. Something . . . real. And something even . . . kind of dangerous for him, because he didn't let himself care for people
easily.

So maybe it was best to find out Rachel was still . . .
Rachel. Still looking down her nose at this town—and
was she even looking down on him a little, too? He
didn't want to believe that last part, so he decided, for the
moment, to give her the benefit of the doubt on that one.

Yet as Mike drove on . . . aw hell. Despite himself,
he was actually getting harder. In his pants. Was it possible that arguing with Rachel Farris had actually in-

creased his erection? Shit—what was *that* about? From the start, nothing about his reaction to this woman had made sense.

In fact, he was beginning to feel tense now, impatient. Not just in a lusty way, but . . . maybe he wanted to prove she was lying, that she still wanted *him* as much as *he* wanted *her*. His chest burned with anticipation, and his hands felt itchy—like they should be doing something besides driving. So without much thought, he indulged the urge to lower one to her leg, through her dress.

He waited for her to object, or push it away, but instead, she just drew in her breath, audibly—and it gave him some encouragement.

Enough that he didn't hesitate to reach down, find her knee beneath the flowered fabric, and slide his palm higher, halfway up her smooth thigh.

"Jesus, Romo, what are you doing?" She sounded breathy, at once defiant and excited—par for the course with Rachel.

He didn't bother answering, but her question did bring up some realistic concerns. The concession stand had been one thing. He'd thought they were completely alone there. And they hadn't been out in the bright light of day. And there hadn't been a party full of people expecting them just a couple of miles farther down the road.

But he'd reached that point—quickly—where his cock was overriding his brain. Which never happened to him. Except with Rachel. Before *her*, he'd indulged his sexual needs frequently—yet also with some *sense*, some common reverence. Right now, though, his needs felt *insistent*. Like they had to be met. And he knew, in his gut, she wouldn't have the strength to say no.

Although part of him hated this—hated feeling he'd abandoned his better judgment, hated that he was looking past how arrogant and superior she could be. At a moment like this, he felt like he had no control at all. Because he was stroking her inner thigh with his fingertips, turning her breath thready next to him, and his erection felt impossibly huge, like it would burst his zipper.

And then he was . . . homing in on Carl Dobbins' barn up ahead, to one side of the road, the big doors wide open today—but there was no sign of anyone in the surrounding hay fields other than a few grazing cows, and no trucks or tractors or other signs of people around.

And then he was putting on his turn signal.

And pulling off onto the dirt wagon trail.

And . . . easing the Caddy right into the barn.

And he was hating himself for his weakness. But it was a hate laced with the most wild, intense need he'd ever suffered. He couldn't get the car into park fast enough.

"Wh-what are you doing?" she murmured again.

She sounded understandably confused, and when he looked down at her, now in the shade with bits of shadow playing about her face, for some reason, he saw something new in her eyes, something he'd never seen before. Vulnerability. And he realized he was right, there *was* more to her—even if she didn't know he could see it.

"Proving you won't turn me down," he said, the urgency hitting him full force now that the decision had been made. "'Cause I gotta have you, honey."

And with that, he reached under the wide front seat to move it back slightly, then reached for her, planting his hands on her hips and lifting her over into his lap until she was straddling him, just like in the concession stand.

She sucked in her breath at the contact, and their eyes met, and it was that easy—she wasn't saying no.

"Um, Mike . . ." she murmured instead. Her voice came all feathery and soft, like always when she was aroused—but she was looking around the barn. Fresh hay billowed from the lofts above, the pungent sweet scent permeating the air, and empty stalls and farm implements surrounded them on the earthen floor. Without the sun, the air was slightly cooler, but that was good since he was already too hot. "Isn't this illegal or something?"

Christ—she had to pick *now* to start worrying about the law? He lowered his hands to her ass, pressing her very center against his raging hard-on. They both let out long, low moans at the connection, and as a fresh heat stretched all through him, he growled an answer. "Yes, damn it. It's trespassing."

"Oh," she murmured, her breath going beautifully ragged as they began to move together, grinding.

Heat spread outward from his groin, and it felt so good he went a little lightheaded. Then a hot groan echoed from his throat as he massaged her round bottom and began nibbling at her breast through her dress and bra.

"You're . . . actually breaking the law?" she asked, still all breathy and sexy. She obviously understood that he just didn't do that. Until now.

"Looks that way," he said, not wanting to be reminded. He couldn't think clearly—right now he just needed to feel her where she was warm and wet.

Gathering the dress in his fists until he got underneath, he found lace—and let his fingers drift over it, between her legs. Her head dropped back in pleasure, and she purred, "Ohhhh," fueling him all the more. As if he needed to be fueled.

Using his other hand, he curled his fingers around the lace and pulled it aside, then slid his touch right back where it had just been. Only now he found what he'd been seeking. Warmth. Moisture. *Awww* . . .

"Just . . . when you think . . . you know somebody . . ." she murmured, moving against his fingertips.

Christ—she was still talking about this?

He quit being so irritated, though, when she finally reached down to start working at his jeans. A few seconds later, his erection sprung free, into her hand, and she

peered down at it, looking as completely enraptured as he
wanted her to be.

"I just have to ask . . ." she began then in a whisper.

Damn it, what now? Yet then she squeezed, beginning
to massage him in her fist, in the same rhythm he used to
stroke between her legs, and he couldn't hold in his groan.
God, yes.

"Since when you do break the law?" she rasped. "What
the hell's gotten into you, Officer Romeo?"

Jesus—they had to discuss it *now? Really?*

"*You, damn it*," he bit off sharply, meeting her gaze.
"For God's sake, woman, you make me crazy."

Then he positioned her the way he wanted her, pressed
her hips firmly downward, and suffered an almost brutal
pleasure as she sheathed his painfully hard cock. The
deep groan echoing through the barn came all the way
from his gut.

Pure bliss was his. *Finally.* Not that it had been so long
since he'd been like this with her—a couple of weeks ago.
But it felt a hell of a lot longer.

Sweet sounds of utter abandon erupted from her lips,
as well, which drew his eyes there again, and made him
kiss her. She kissed him back, and he pressed his tongue
into her mouth.

A powerful pleasure swirled through Mike's body as
he thrust up into her, pleased that he'd finally shut her up.
Even when they stopped kissing, she didn't resume talking, but simply gazed down at him, her eyes brimming
with heat.

Yeah, this was more like it. No more talk about law-
breaking or not having sex, no more clothes between
their bodies. At least not where it counted the most. He
molded her breasts in his hands even though he couldn't
get to them completely, and when he felt her nipples
through the layers of fabric, he leaned in to bite gently.
"Ohhhh . . ." she moaned, and the sensual sound permeated him.

Within moments, Mike forgot all about where they were or where they were supposed to be going. There was only Rachel's soft flesh, taking him to heaven. There was only Rachel herself, driving him as crazy as ever—if it wasn't with her smart mouth, it was with her perfect body. Damn, seemed he couldn't find a moment's peace with this woman one way or the other. But he must not have minded too much, or he wouldn't be here with her right now.

Soon, Rachel's sobs of pleasure grew more urgent, and then quick, choppy—and Mike knew she would come soon. And hell, he loved that. In a way he'd never loved it with a woman before. It just excited him more, moved him more, than he could even make sense of.

He never planned to whisper to her, but it just came out. "I want to make you come, honey. I want to make you come *so* hard."

"Ohhhh," she moaned wildly again, arching against him—and then, "Oh, oh, God—yes." After which he witnessed her toppling over the edge of ecstasy, her head falling back once more, her moans actually quieter now but more guttural, coming from someplace deep.

He tried his damnedest not to explode until she was done—he didn't want to decrease her pleasure in any way—but he was on the edge, too. This was different than in the concession stand—when he'd retained at least a *little* control over the sex itself, when he'd been able to go slowly, make her come twice. This was . . . this was eating him alive.

"Oh, Mike, that was nice," she practically purred, smiling gently, suddenly the sweet, sexy Rachel he'd seen only glimpses of.

But damn it, he couldn't savor it. Because—"Shit, honey, I can't stop," he managed between clenched teeth. And then . . . it was as if the old metaphor of fireworks was real. As he pumped up into her, he shut his eyes and saw different colors, the pleasure pummeling him, owning him, forcing his erection deep into her warmth again and again, almost of its own volition.

When it was done, he felt more spent than ever in his life. Police academy had been easier on his body than this. He simply slumped back into the seat with Rachel still atop him. He wasn't one of those guys who usually fell asleep after sex, but he suddenly understood the urge since it threatened now—a sexual exhaustion so complete he'd never experienced anything like it.

A moment later, Rachel's warm breath came on his ear. "Mike?"

He had just enough strength to muster a response. "Hmm?"

"Okay, just checking. There for a minute I was afraid maybe I killed you."

Her typical arrogant humor—which matched his own, he supposed—was enough to bring him back to life, squeeze a grin from him. Then he opened his eyes. "You're damn good, Farris," he said teasingly, "but not *that* good."

Wow. She'd tried. She really had. She'd tried her damnedest to get back that part of herself she feared she was losing here—but now she was afraid she'd just lost it a little more. His mere touch had simply been too powerful.

"So, what now?" she asked, seated beside him again in the car, her underwear back in place.

"Uh, we go to Grandma Romo's party," he said, zipping up.

She blinked. "Just like that?"

"Just like what?"

"Well, aren't you going to give me a hard time, shove it down my throat about how easy I gave in right after I told you we couldn't do that?" She wouldn't even blame him, in fact. Resistance had been beyond futile.

Yet when Mike lifted his gaze to meet hers, she was

surprised at how calm, even somber, he looked. "No," he said quietly. "But it would be nice if I knew you didn't . . . think you're maybe a little too good for me."

She pulled in her breath. Oh God, he thought *that* was the problem? "Mike, no." And sure, maybe in the beginning she'd thought he was some blowhard, small time cop, even if he *was* sexy as hell—but now she couldn't deny that he was smart, and funny, and . . . well, maybe she even thought he was pretty darn strong, knowing what he'd gone through in his youth. And yeah, she'd had plenty of moments when she'd looked down on Destiny—but never him. She grabbed his hand, shook her head. "I swear. It's not that."

"Then what is it?"

How could she explain? She let out a breath—and tried. "It's this place, this town." She shook her head helplessly. "It's making me a little crazy."

Mike let out a sigh. "I need more to go on, Rachel."

So she bit her lip and tried harder, reached deeper into the truth, even though it was difficult to let herself confide in him so unexpectedly. "I . . . really did see leaving here after high school as an escape. And I've worked hard to build a life I'm proud of in Chicago." She struggled to find more words, more explanation, and finally she came back to what she'd realized at the park last weekend. "Somehow, being back here just makes me feel . . . like I'm going backward in life. Does that make any sense?"

"Not much," he said, still unsmiling, his eyes seeming to probe hers. "Unless . . . you're afraid something might happen to make you end up staying here."

At which she gasped. It was an absurd thought. "No. No—there's nothing that could."

An expression she couldn't read passed briefly over his face—before he tilted his head toward hers. "Then can I give you some advice?"

Advice from Mike Romo. Would wonders never cease? "Okay."

"Quit taking it all so seriously, for God's sake." Then his gaze locked on hers again. "And stop denying you're into me. It's silly. Now let's go have some birthday cake, okay?"

When Grandma Romo's house came into view down the country road, Mike could see that cars already filled the yard. Every Romo in the county and beyond was here—all of Mike's aunts and uncles and cousins. And, of course, his mom and dad.

As he found a spot to squeeze in the Caddy, he also squeezed Rachel's knee. "You ready for this, Farris?"

She glanced over at him. "I might be more ready if my name weren't Farris."

He gave her a smile. Things had gotten a little intense back in the barn—during the sex, and after it as well, but it was time to move on. "Forget about that today. Your job here isn't to be a Farris—it's to get my parents off my back about settling down."

"As always, Romo, you really know how to romance a girl."

He lifted one eyebrow. "You never strike me as a girl who *wants* romance."

"True enough," she agreed, and for some reason, the response disappointed him a little. That quick, the sweet, vulnerable Rachel was gone. But he truly *had* come to like this version of her as well—her confidence, her wry wit—so he pushed aside any hint of emotion he felt and prepared for the onslaught of hellos and introductions.

It started with a bunch of kids—his cousin's children, the ones his own children would've been playing with if he had any, and who were probably already reminding his mother of that with their very presence. "Hey, Uncle Mike!" "Wow, look at Uncle Mike's car," they called, just the way sixteen-year-old Kristen had addressed him at the donkey ball game, even though he wasn't really their uncle.

Mike explained to the younger kids that they were actually looking at late Grandpa Romo's car, from when he first came to America back in the fifties, and then he introduced Rachel. Not one of them batted an eye at her last name being Farris, which told Mike the old feud hadn't made its way down to the youngest generation of Romos.

Some weird sense of protection compelled him to take Rachel's hand as he led her up into the yard where the adults milled about, chatting and snacking, and where Grandma Romo sat under a shady maple tree in a white wicker chair, near a table piled with presents. Fortunately, Mike's mom had offered to add his name to theirs—and Mike figured just bringing a girl to the event was gift enough. Although he feared his grandma might not feel the same way once she found out who he'd brought.

He headed toward his parents upon spotting them near Grandma Romo. They'd left Destiny and moved to Florida well over ten years ago, but to Mike, it still felt strange. In most families, the kid grew up and moved away. In his, it had happened the other way around. And whenever he saw them, particularly his mom, he still read in her face everything she never said. *I'm smiling, but I still miss her. I'm better than I used to be, but it still hurts.*

That's when she looked up, her face brightening at the sight of him. "Mike!" she called, hopping up from a lawn chair near his grandmother to give him a tight hug he felt all the way to his bones. Still fit and trim for her age, his mother looked good wearing what he thought of as the official female uniform in Destiny: a pretty, flowery dress.

It was funny—when he'd met Rachel, he'd liked that she didn't fit that typical Destiny mold. But today he liked that she *did*. Or maybe that she could. Or maybe that she *had*, that she'd cared enough about today to want to. He hadn't meant to act so blown away when he'd first seen her—but he hadn't expected her to look so beautiful. And already, she fit in here, without having yet uttered a word, since this was how Destiny ladies generally dressed—like life was a garden party. Yet at the same time she *stood out*— because, again, she appeared so pretty and self-assured.

"Mom, this is Rachel. Rachel, my mother, Nancy."

And as Rachel greeted her, all confidence, his mother appeared . . . way too overjoyed. But then, that was the plan, wasn't it? The whole point of bringing Rachel? And for the first time it occurred to him that, shit, Logan's little "bring a date" plan here could backfire if everyone assumed this was something serious.

In fact, before he could stop it, his mother was pulling Rachel by the arm, away from him and into a circle of people, including his dad and Grandma Romo, to say, "Everyone, this is Mike's girlfriend, Rachel."

Girlfriend? Aw, hell. He just closed his eyes and shook his head, preparing to swoop in and fix things. Now he remembered why he didn't bring dates to Romo parties— and why it was better to be harassed about it than to let his family jump to conclusions, especially his mother. Even if it *was* nice to see her suddenly looking so . . . well, *sincerely* happy. Not the fake happy he could see through so easily. Nope, his mom was thrilled to the tips of her toes that he'd shown up with a girl.

"A pleasure to meet you, Rachel," Grandma Romo said, still sporting a thick Italian accent even after all these years. "Are you from Destiny? What's your last name, dear? We Romos know everyone in Destiny."

At this, Mike thought Rachel would at least freeze up a little, maybe glance his way for help. But she shocked the hell out of him by putting on a friendly smile and speaking as boldly as if the Romo/Farris feud didn't exist. "Yes, I grew up in Destiny, but now I live in Chicago. I'm home for a visit with my grandmother—Edna Farris.

My parents, Dean and Carol Farris, live in Chicago now, too—but were born and raised here."

Now *Mike* froze, waiting to see what happened. And for a long moment, no one said anything, just sat or stood looking at Rachel, wide-eyed. Rachel, though, remained totally calm and cool, as if nothing awkward was taking place.

Finally, it was Mike's mom who moved things along. "I think I went to school with your mother, Rachel. Carol Harney was her name then, right?"

Rachel turned back to her with a big smile. "That's right."

And the next thing Mike knew, conversation resumed— people went back to talking among themselves, and some with Rachel, even acting fairly normal and polite. One of his aunts complimented her dress, and then a big discussion about the Daisy Dress Shop started and Mike realized Rachel didn't even need him around to move comfortably among his family.

He still wasn't sure what had driven him to bring her to the party, why he'd fought for that so hard, but he suddenly couldn't help thinking he'd made a good choice. And the fact was, as he continued hanging back, watching her, he felt . . . weirdly proud to be with her.

Just then his dad slapped him on the back. "A Farris, huh?" he said, laughing.

Mike just nodded, glad his dad was more amused than mad, given that, as Giovanni's oldest son, he would have inherited the orchard.

His dad looked a little *less* amused, though, when he asked, "Did you give any thought to how your grandma might feel about that?"

Mike replied honestly. "Not really. Because Rachel doesn't have anything to do with whatever happened back then, and neither do I. I figure I should be able to bring who I want to a party."

Mike's father shrugged. "That's true, I suppose." Then he even elbowed Mike in the ribs. "And I guess I don't blame you—that girl's a looker."

As the party wore on, Mike barely saw Rachel—she was too busy off talking to other women. And occasionally, one of his cousins or an uncle would come up and say something like, "Dating a Farris, huh?" or "I can't believe you brought a Farris girl here," but their tone said everything he needed to hear: They might not like that she was a Farris, but they were clearly impressed and had ended up looking beyond her name.

Of course, as he watched her, he noticed she was nicer to his family than she generally was to *him*.

And he couldn't quit pondering the question that plagued him: What was it about Rachel Farris that made him so crazy?

As he sat beneath a tree eating a piece of birthday cake, listening to his uncles reminisce about Giovanni's Cadillac, Mike ticked off some logical reasons. One—he wasn't used to being with a woman so mouthy. Two—he wasn't used to a woman who turned him down for dates. Three—he wasn't used to a woman who wanted the sex part without any romance, even though that would usually be fine with him. And . . . mainly, he decided, he wasn't used to wanting to be with someone whose life, whose world, seemed so very different from his.

Except, was all that enough to explain it? Or did he need to revisit that moment—the one where he'd thought he might have the capacity to . . . care about her? Mike didn't open himself up to people—he didn't *let himself* care. His parents, his grandma, Logan, and some of his relatives—that completed the list of people he seriously cared about in this world. Because caring was . . . risky. He'd learned that early in life. So was it even remotely possible he'd let himself start caring about Rachel Farris?

Nah. Not that fast. He gave his head a brisk shake. And

not with a girl who'd made it so clear she didn't want anything from him except maybe an occasional orgasm.

Still, his post-sex lethargy in the car earlier forced him
to ask . . . did that mean this was the first time he'd been
totally, completely consumed by sex? The first time he'd
ever been *that* into it? He loved sex, so . . . was that even
possible? But how else could he explain the reaction? And
what about Rachel made him so crazy that . . . goddamn
it, he'd forgotten to use a condom.

That was a first.

And worse than breaking a law, in Mike's opinion.
"Shit," he muttered.

Conversation around him halted and every cousin and
uncle in the group stared at him.

"Sorry," he groused. "Just . . . remembered something I
forgot to do." Which was putting it mildly.

Wow, what a day. Rachel slid into the big turquoise car,
almost overwhelmed.

Not only had Mike had his way with her in a barn after
she'd vowed not to let it happen—but he'd actually broken
the law to do it! Somehow, from him, that had seemed the
ultimate compliment.

Of course, then she'd been forced to get all serious with
him, trying to explain her crazy emotions, which had sort
of sucked.

But then she'd spent the afternoon charming the entire
Romo clan, which had gone shockingly well. Even
Grandma Romo had started being nice by the time it was
over.

As Mike stretched his arm across the back of the seat,
looking over his shoulder to back the huge car from its
spot in the yard, Rachel didn't hesitate to scoot over next
to him again. She instantly wanted to be near him and,
for a change, decided not to stop herself or question the
move. She was in too good a mood and felt too proud

of herself. And maybe she should follow Mike's advice and quit taking this thing with him so seriously, quit succumbing to that "being sucked back into Destiny" feeling whenever she was close to him.

"Well, I can't deny it, Farris," Mike said, pulling out onto the road, "that was impressive. I had no idea you could be that nice to people you expect not to like you."

She smiled up at him—again, too pleased to be sarcastic or curt right now. "I just thought of it like my job, like walking into a boardroom full of corporate bigwigs I have to win over. Although, frankly, I was impressed with me, too. Since I *was* nervous."

"Really? It didn't show."

"More thanks to my job," she told him.

Mike focused on the road, but she sensed him hesitating—until he finally said, "Well . . . thanks. For being nice to my family."

The sincerity in his voice touched Rachel in a way she couldn't have anticipated. And it also made her wonder—had he really thought she'd be mean to them? Did she come off *that* awful? Maybe she did. "I *am* nice," she said, realizing that maybe he didn't actually know that.

Next to her, he nodded. "Sometimes. And more to other people than to me."

Okay, she supposed she couldn't argue with that. He'd seen more of her bad side than her good. "But I can say the same thing about you."

To her surprise, he gave another short nod, eyes still on the road yet looking almost contrite. "Logan told me I should be nicer to you." Then he peered down at her. "So, why *are* we always so . . . not nice to each other?"

But Rachel didn't think it was such a mystery. "We have *lots* of reasons not to be nice. The speeding tickets you gave me, for instance."

He nodded again lightly. "And you not respecting the law."

"And you trying to buy Edna's orchard away."

"And the whole family feud thing, which we've been fed our whole lives."

She shrugged. "When you look at it like that, it's amazing we even managed to call a truce long enough to have sex."

He chuckled softly in response, so she laughed a little, too. Then bit her lip as another reason she was always mean to him struck her. *Because the way I feel when I'm with you scares me to death.*

It hadn't scared her at first—back then, it had just confused her, annoyed her, caught her off guard. But since then, things had changed—she thought about him too often and wanted him too much. *Lord, no wonder I keep telling myself I have to stop this. He makes me feel more than I should at a time when I'm totally out of my element.* Five minutes after deciding to take his advice, she realized it was impossible.

That's when she heard Ben Harper's gravelly voice echoing low from Mike's iPod-rigged radio, singing "Gold to Me"—so she let the bluesy, sexy rhythm grab hold of her, distract her from it all.

But then she winced. Because . . . maybe being with Mike Romo just made *every* song seem sexy. Damn it.

"What is it?" he asked. "Why do you look weird?"

She flashed a slightly insulted expression, then got over it and said, "It's nothing—I just like this song."

He nodded solemnly. "Me, too."

And together they listened quietly as Mike drove, and the soft breeze and late-day sunshine washed over them, leaving her a little more relaxed. Enough that she found herself subtly pressing her thigh up against his a little more—not a decision, just something that happened on its own.

In response, Mike glanced down at her, and . . . mmm, got that steamy look in his gorgeous brown eyes just

before he lowered the tiniest kiss to her lips—which vibrated all through her. Oh my.

Yet . . . she felt more than just desire at the moment—it
was mixed up with something else. Curiosity? Compassion? The day had made her think about all Mike had
gone through with his family.

"Your mom and dad seem nice," she said, aware that
her voice came out softer than usual—the effect of his
tender kiss just now. Maybe she wanted him to know it
hadn't all just been wanting to make a good impression—
she'd actually *liked* his family. And maybe she needed to
say it out loud because it was such a switch in her own
personal thinking.

"And they're even Romos," he teased her with a grin.

"I'm trying to put that in the past," she confessed.

"Wow," Mike said. "Just when you think you've got
somebody figured out, they do an about-face on you."

He'd done a few about-faces on her recently, as well,
but instead of mentioning that, she asked something that
mattered to her more. Now that she was actually starting
to think he might have feelings. "Is it strange . . . to have
your parents live so far away?"

Rather than answer the question, though, he said, "Lots
of people live far away from their parents."

"Yeah, but it's usually . . . their choice."

He still didn't answer—just said, "I could have moved
to Florida when they did, I guess."

"Why didn't you?"

He shook his head. "Didn't want to. My life was here.
I'd just graduated from the academy and gotten hired by
Chief Tolliver. I didn't see any reason to go." Then he
refocused on the road and his next words came out a little
quieter. "But I understand why they left."

And when he glanced down at her, she sensed him
wondering if she knew. About his family's history. She
had no idea what to say, if she should bring it up or not.
Though finally she did—even if her words sounded weak

to her own ears. "I . . . remember about your sister. I'm sorry that happened."

He simply drew in a breath and nodded, looking ahead, gripping the steering wheel a little tighter. And for a long moment, she thought he wouldn't reply—until he told her, "My younger brother left home, too, when he was eighteen. That was over fifteen years ago now, and we don't know if he's dead or alive."

She swallowed, hard. She hadn't even thought of that as a possibility, that Mike's missing brother could actually be dead, but she guessed after so many years . . . well, it wasn't an unreasonable thought. "God, Mike, I can't imagine how difficult that is." She touched his leg. "I'm really sorry."

He just gave his head a short shake, eyes still on the winding country road. "That's why Mom and Dad had to leave. Too many bad memories—they wanted to start over."

"But you didn't," she pointed out. She didn't mean to pry, yet . . . she remained curious to understand what held him in Destiny when everyone he loved had gone somewhere else.

He responded simply with another head shake—no words.

"It must be hard having your whole family gone," she went on, unable to keep from prodding, wishing he'd tell her more.

But to her surprise, Mike let out a laugh—and she glanced up to see him wearing a jovial expression again, that fast. "What are you talking about, Farris? I've got relatives coming out my ears. They barely give me a minute's peace." He went on to tell her how Grandma Romo was always calling him to fix things at her house, and how his cousins were constantly inviting him to birthday parties for their five million kids. "Nope, afraid I've got way more family here than my fair share."

It lightened the mood and left Rachel feeling a little

relieved for him—and even led her to talk about her own extended family, about how scattered they were now compared to when she'd lived here. She explained that many of them still got together on holidays, though, and admitted that, "Well . . . seeing some of them a couple of times a year is enough for me."

He looked down at her, clearly intrigued, amused. "And yet you defend the family name like we're two gangs in a turf war."

"Aren't we?" she asked, reminding him of the turf at stake. "The orchard."

"I've got an idea—let's not go there right now. Since, just between me and you, I kind of like this being-nice-to-each-other thing."

She shrugged. All her confusion over him aside, she did, too. "Fair enough."

Only then his expression soured.

"What?" she asked. "I said fair enough—I'm not gonna start a fight or anything."

He grimaced down at her. "It's not that. I just remembered something I need to tell you. Something that might yank you right out of nice mode, quicker than orchard talk."

Rachel let out a weary sigh. "Oh brother. What is it, Romo?"

"We forgot to use a condom earlier."

Oops. She bit her lip, then murmured, "I *knew* something had felt extra good about that."

She'd realized they hadn't used one, but had just sort of forgotten they should have. "Yeah," he admitted regretfully.

Fortunately, she could put his mind at ease. "Well, Officer Romeo, I'm willing to bet you're the kind of guy who *never* forgets a condom—am I right?"

He nodded. "You *were* right. Until today."

She slanted a playful glance upward. "Whereas I'm the

kind of girl who, unfortunately, *does* sometimes forget a condom."

"Typically reckless," he muttered beneath his breath.

And she said, "Hey, what happened to being nice?"

The tone of his voice told her he was struggling to stay pleasant. "I'm *trying*—but I just found out my life might be in danger."

Rachel let out an irritated breath. "No, Romo," she said as if talking to an impatient child, "if you'd let me finish I could tell you that your life is *not* in danger. Because any time I have forgotten a condom, I've promptly had myself checked out—and I have a clean bill of health. So . . . not so reckless after all, hmm?" she concluded with a brisk nod.

"Still reckless," he insisted. "Just sensible enough to find out if you have to pay for the recklessness after the fact."

Rachel rolled her eyes. "Nonetheless, you're safe with me. And before you ask the next question, no worries— I'm on the pill. That's why I can forget the condom occasionally . . . if it's somebody I trust."

Slowing the car a bit, he lowered his chin and met her gaze. "Are you officially saying you trust me, Farris?"

"In some ways," she confessed, surprised it was the truth. "In *that* way."

Just then, Mike flipped on the turn signal and, without warning, took a right down a little dirt lane that cut between two fenced fields.

As the vintage car bounced along through the dust, Rachel just gaped at him. "You're not searching for another barn, are you? Because that was fun, but I'm not a machine, you know."

Mike turned to her with a big, sexy grin, clearly entertained by her protests. "No, Farris, I'm not looking for a barn."

"What, then?"

That's when he brought the Cadillac to a halt and

Rachel lifted her gaze to see . . . the last thing she could have anticipated. Donkeys.

"What the *hell*?" she asked, confused. A whole herd of brown donkeys stood in the pasture to the right of the car, some grazing on short green grass, others looking up in response to the Caddy's approach.

"You wanted to see donkeys after the donkey ball game," he reminded her. "Well, here they are. The actual ones from the game, in fact. I happen to know they belong to Hank Speers and live in this field."

"Oh," she said. Then she smiled, realizing Mike Romo had just done something she'd once thought impossible— he'd done something kind of . . . *sweet*. For her.

The truth was, she hadn't given a thought to donkeys since that night. But she really *had* been curious to see one up close right before she'd accidentally locked the two of them in that concession stand. So it felt kind of fun—in a silly, indulgent sort of way—to get a good look at them now.

Together, she and Mike got out of the car and approached the barbed-wire fence where a dark brown donkey stood with his head sticking over the top strand. "Is it . . . safe to pet it?" Rachel asked.

Mike shrugged. "I'm not a donkey expert, but I think so."

So she ran her fingers down over the donkey's long face, petting and scratching the same as she might a dog—just a really big one in this particular case. The donkey closed his eyes for a moment, making her think he liked it. "If I'd known, I could have brought some apples for them."

Mike stooped down and plucked up a handful of grass, much longer on the outside of the fence than on the inside, where the animals had already eaten it down to the ground. "Here," he said, pressing the soft green blades into Rachel's palm.

"He won't take my hand off?" She raised her eyebrows.

"Just hold it open, flat," Mike instructed, "so he can't nip your fingers."

"I thought you weren't a donkey expert."

"Grandma and Grandpa Romo had horses when I was a kid. Same general principle."

So Rachel took Mike's word for it and held her palm to the donkey's mouth, unduly pleased when he ate the grass, snuffling and snorting a bit. "I never thought I'd say this about a donkey, but . . . he's kind of cute."

Mike looked at the donkey and said, "Don't listen to her. She thinks you stink. She told me so at the ball game."

After a smirking grin at her date, Rachel redirected her attention to the donkey, as well, peering directly into his big, black eyes as she reached out to pet him a little more. "Oh, you're not so bad," she told him.

Then she looked up at Mike, and admitted, "You're not so bad, either. Sometimes."

If love be blind, love cannot hit the mark.

William Shakespeare, *Romeo & Juliet*

Ten

$\mathcal{U}$pon returning to the orchard, Rachel could smell something good cooking in the kitchen, the aroma wafting through the open windows. As Mike walked her to the door, she made a spontaneous decision. "It's almost dinnertime . . . if you want to stay. Edna's the best cook I've ever known and I think I smell her trademark chicken and dumplings."

"Thanks," he said, "but I've got a late shift tonight, so I need to get home and grab a few hours sleep first."

She nodded, smiled, and acted like it was nothing— even as it stunned her how disappointed she was that the date was ending. How had things changed so quickly here?

As they stepped up onto the porch, Rachel turned to face him and Mike took both her hands in his. Leaning her back against the house, he bent near her ear and said in a completely sexy, raspy voice, "Thanks for today."

She looked up at him, feeling the same way she had for

a while now. Weakened in his presence. Softened inside. And like she couldn't quite get enough of him. "Did you mean for . . . the sex? Or the stuff with your family?"

His slow grin moved all through her. "I meant for everything, honey," he replied, then bent to lower his mouth over hers.

Rachel's stomach contracted as his kiss consumed her; she looped her arms around his neck, pressing her body into his. Mmm, God, his kisses turned her inside out—she thought she could enjoy just standing here kissing him like this all night long. When he began to harden against her thigh, the small of her back ached and she wanted him again—and decided she probably should have been *asking, begging* for him to look for another barn on the way home.

When finally the kissing stopped, it left her breathless, and still wishing he'd stay for dinner. She bit her lip and peered up into those bedroom eyes, thinking he was about to ask her out again.

His sexy gaze drifted over her lips and then back upward, the mere look getting her hotter and hotter inside—until finally he said, "See ya, Farris." Then turned around and walked away.

Whoa. Rachel sagged back against the house—to keep from collapsing onto the porch.

See ya? That was it?

After all they'd shared today?

And—oh God, please don't let this have anything to do with what he'd said about her thinking she was too good. Because she really, really didn't and was mortified by the very notion.

But . . . wait a minute. Since when did she *care* about dating Mike Romo anyway?

She didn't.

And still, she felt a bit numb, deflated, as she stepped through the front door.

"I'm in the kitchen," Edna called. "So scoot your butt in here and tell me all about the Romos."

Rachel could have used a minute to recover from the barrage of emotions, but since Edna beckoned, she went. She slipped into a chair at Edna's old Formica kitchen table.

"Well?" Edna turned from the stove to ask.

Still dazed, Rachel lifted her eyes to her grandmother for the first time since coming into the room. "They're nice," she said simply, glumly.

Edna snapped her fingers and stomped one foot, clearly annoyed. "Damn it, I was hopin' they'd be mean as a bunch of cats in a bag. But reckon it don't surprise me none." Then Edna pursed her lips, emphasizing the wrinkles around her mouth. "And what about Carlotta?"

Grandma Romo. Who had been Giovanni's wife. "She wasn't friendly at first, especially when I introduced myself as your granddaughter—but even *she* eventually got nicer. I wouldn't say she's the warm-and-fuzzy type or anything, but . . ."

"But neither am I," Edna finished, still sounding a little let down.

"Maybe I should have lied," Rachel suggested, "and told you they were all a bunch of jerks."

Yet Edna shook her head. "No, I can take the truth, and it's better that way. Suppose maybe it just shores up my feelin's about Mike—that he's a good sort and all."

But at this, Rachel could only grumble under her breath, the words *bastard* and *ass* sneaking out.

She looked up in time to see Edna's gaze narrow on her. "Does this mean the two of you didn't hit it off?"

Rachel shook her head emphatically. "No, just the opposite. Before it was done, we got along better than ever."

With a dish towel in one hand, Edna planted her fists on her hips. "Then what's the problem, darlin'?"

Rachel blinked, hesitating. She couldn't tell Edna

the real truth—how mystified she was by her emotions surrounding him, how much it scared her, how foreign it seemed compared to the rest of her life. So she kept it simple—since this part was upsetting, too. "I thought he'd ask me on another date—and he didn't. In fact, when he left, he just said, 'See ya.' Can you believe that? 'See ya.'"

In response, Edna drew in her breath, looking put out on Rachel's behalf. "Damn Romo men," she muttered. "I like Mike, but I reckon some things run in the family."

Rachel widened her eyes on her grandma. "Does this mean Giovanni didn't come back for you?" Of course, she knew he *had* come back to Destiny, so she added, "Or something?"

Edna raked a hand down through the air. "That's for another day. Right now, we'll have us some chicken and dumplin's and see if it don't make ya feel better."

To Rachel's surprise, it sounded possible. She'd loved Edna's chicken and dumplings as a girl, and the very thought of them made her feel somehow a little safer, or loved, or something. Like the world was normal, as it should be. She guessed this was the definition of comfort food.

And how odd that Edna's food in Edna's house comforted her while so much else in Destiny made her want to go running away. There *were* good things here—she couldn't deny she'd found them. She just . . . didn't want to *keep* finding them. Understanding who she was and what she valued in life had been a lot easier when she'd held the whole town in disdain.

Rachel got to her feet and dished up servings onto two plates, straight from the pot, while Edna poured sweet tea and carved into a loaf of fresh bread from the bread machine. "Not that I really care about seeing him again," Rachel claimed as they moved about the kitchen.

"Sounds like ya care."

"Well, I don't," she insisted. Because she had to start thinking straight here. This morning she'd been ready to call it quits with him. And she wasn't the sort of woman who got all hung up on a guy—*any* guy. So what difference did it make if she never saw him again? What difference did it make what he thought of her, or what they'd done or talked about today?

A moment later, she and Edna settled at the dining room table, across from each other, and Rachel dug in—anxious to let the food soothe her irritation.

"So if ya don't care, then why do you still look so upset?" Edna asked matter-of-factly before shoveling a small dumpling into her mouth.

"Ego, I suppose," Rachel replied. It sounded like a good enough answer. "Because I can't imagine what *else* it would be."

"Maybe you're afraid you'll miss the sex," Edna said—and Rachel dropped her fork. Fortunately, it landed on her plate without making a mess or splashing anything on her dress.

"For God's sake, Edna. Just who on earth do you think you're talking to here?"

But Edna just rolled her eyes. "You think I don't know sex is involved in this, darlin'? You think I don't know that a full-grown woman who never has a boyfriend as far as I can tell isn't hookin' up with the fellas she meets?"

Hooking up? Good God, where was Edna getting this stuff? Had she been watching MTV or something? "Look," Rachel said, having retrieved her fork to point it at Edna as she spoke, "it's bad enough that *you* now tell *me* all about your sex life—I'm not telling you about mine. You're my grandma—it's not natural."

Edna's expression said she thought Rachel was being ridiculous. "Fine—make a big to-do over it, act like it don't make the world go 'round if ya want." She took a bite of buttered bread, then added, "But for what it's worth, I don't *really* think that's why you're all in a dither. I think you're all in a dither 'cause you like him."

Rachel gasped. "Of course I don't! At least not in the way *you* mean."

And Edna just gave her a look—almost like she felt sorry for her. "Darlin', why would that be so awful? Surely not 'cause he's a Romo—I been tryin' to make it clear that the more time passes, the less important that old feud is."

Rachel nibbled on her lower lip, taken aback by what appeared to be pity on Edna's face, and still trying to figure it all out. And in that moment, she realized what a stupid reaction she'd had to the simple suggestion that she might care for a man. Yet she heard herself continue to insist, "No, it's not the Romo thing, but . . . I'm really not that into him. I don't know him well enough to be that into him, for heaven's sake. And we have nothing in common." Sex notwithstanding.

Edna just cast her another disparaging glance and said, "Ya know what they say. Youth is wasted on the young."

"Trust me, Edna," she assured her grandma, feeling a bit stronger again, "my youth has not been wasted."

"Whatever you say," Edna told her, then let the subject drop, for which Rachel was grateful. "Now eat up—we got a long week of apple pickin' ahead." And then Edna started in on how much they needed to get done, by when, to be ready for the apple festival in a few short weeks. After that, she moved onto how much pick-your-own traffic they'd had today, promising that she and Brian had handled it fine.

And Rachel found it all . . . comforting, just as comforting as the chicken and dumplings.

Because it was a nice distraction from the questions weighing on her heart.

What if she couldn't admit she felt something for Mike because . . . to admit that would be to admit her plan wasn't perfect? That she could possibly want something more than she'd always told the whole world she wanted? More than a high-powered career, more than life in the big city? More than being able to take care of herself and her family? The life she'd built made her feel . . . strong, independent, successful. She was proud to never have depended on anyone but herself—financially, or even emotionally—since the day she'd left Destiny in her dust.

And being with Mike at times made her feel . . . too open, too emotional, not nearly as self-reliant as she was used to.

So . . . whether Edna was right or Edna was wrong about her "liking" Mike didn't really matter. What mattered was that—once and for all—she take back control of this situation. If she did feel something for the guy, now was the time to tamp it out, before it got any worse. And besides, she and Mike *did* have a hard time getting along. They truly *didn't* have anything in common besides raging chemistry. They had entirely different lifestyles, values.

So what they shared was heat, desire. And some really phenomenal sex.

That was all.

And if their paths crossed again, well—that would be all she wanted from him. Period.

Early the next morning, Mike sat at his desk at the police station, holding the framed picture of Anna in his hand. Seeing his mom and dad had brought up memories. Of course, the memories never left him—but maybe being with his parents made them stronger.

Whenever he spent time with his parents these days . . . well, no one mentioned Anna because they were all busy trying to be happy—but her missing presence always lingered, hovering in the shadows, hanging over them like a dark cloud. All that loss. It never dissipated. And not just the loss of Anna, but Lucky, too. Despite feeling his mom and dad's love, when Mike saw them, he feared he was a sad reminder that they only had one kid where they were supposed to have three.

He'd sort of lied to Rachel. Well, not lied—but just . . . made things sound better than they were. The truth was, no matter how much Grandma Romo bugged him or his cousins included him in get-togethers, he did miss his parents . . . Lucky . . . Anna. Sometimes he felt like . . . the sole survivor of the shipwreck that was his family. But wait—his parents had survived, too; yet they'd . . . deserted. Jumped ship.

And like he'd told Rachel yesterday, he understood why—he didn't blame them. Yet . . . damn, life had sure turned out different than he'd ever imagined as a kid.

As for Rachel, yesterday had been good—even despite a few bumps along the way. He'd never dreamed he'd see the day Grandma Romo stood around chitchatting with a Farris about things like potato salad and falling leaves. Rachel was . . . a force of nature. A powerhouse in certain ways. Personality. Sexuality.

He'd almost asked to see her again. But then he'd stopped. Because she'd made it so clear she had no interest in romance. And he wasn't exactly real good at that anyway. They'd had a nice day, some moments when . . . hell, when he'd thought he wouldn't mind things going on like that, seeing more of her—yet logic told him if they saw too much of each other, they'd just screw it up and end up back where they'd started. And besides, she'd be leaving before long. And was probably counting the days. He'd believed her when she'd denied thinking she was too good for him, but that didn't change how she felt about the place he called home.

So it had seemed best not to . . . risk getting invested in her. Emotionally. He'd see her when he saw her—they had friends in common, so it would probably happen.

Just then, a tap came on his shoulder and he looked up to see Chief Tolliver. He'd thought he was alone—but it must be time for the busier day shift to start. "Morning, Walter," he said—then set the picture of Anna casually back on his desk, a little embarrassed to be caught holding it in his hand.

"Ain't none of my business, Mike," Walter said, voice low, then he pointed at the frame. "But have ya ever thought about just . . . puttin' that away? For your own peace of mind."

Hell. Until now, he didn't even know Walter had ever noticed the photo. During Mike's interview years ago, they'd talked about what had happened and Mike had been honest about the impact it had had on his life, but they'd never discussed it since. Still, he knew Walter well enough to be honest—so he didn't mince words. "No," he said, not quite able to meet the chief's gaze as he spoke. "Because then I might start to forget about her, and I don't want to do that."

"Believe you me, I can understand *that*," Walter assured him. "Thinkin' about her sorta . . . keeps her alive. I did the same thing with Judy." The chief's late wife, who'd died a long time ago, back when Mike was a teenager. "I kept pictures of her all through the house, in my wallet, everywhere—until I met Anita. Right around then, Jenny helped me see that it wasn't about forgettin'—it was about sayin' goodbye and lettin' yourself move on."

Mike drew in his breath. He remembered when the eight by ten of Judy had disappeared off the chief's desk one day last year—but he hadn't given it much thought. He hadn't even realized until now that it was around the same time Walter had started seeing Anita Garey. And Anna had been gone even longer than Judy.

But in Mike's mind, there was a big difference. Walter knew exactly where Judy was. And he'd gotten to say goodbye to her. With Anna . . . it was all question marks.

Everybody in Destiny assumed she was dead, and Mike had been a cop long enough to know anything else was highly unlikely—but until he got a real *answer, closure,* someday maybe . . . hell, he couldn't say goodbye. He just couldn't.

Finally, he said, "I appreciate your concern, Walter. And I'll try to take your advice to heart."

"Seems hard, I know," Walter said. "Puttin' the pictures away." Pictures, he'd said—plural. It was almost as if he knew Mike had pictures of Anna all over his house, too, despite never having been inside it. "But once you let go, son, it starts gettin' easier."

On Tuesday, a few days after the Romo family party, Rachel sat at Dolly's Café on Main waiting to meet her old group of high school friends for lunch. She'd come early and brought her laptop—after finding out from Amy that, amazingly, Dolly's had WiFi! Destiny *was* changing, and she looked up from her screen from time to time to find herself surprised by the busy lunch crowd and the midday traffic on the streets that circled the town square. An elderly waitress named Mabel had even managed to seat her at one of a few umbrella-covered tables out on the front walk.

Rachel had barely used the laptop—only once at the Destiny library; she'd brought it home forgetting she couldn't access the Internet from Edna's house. Thank God for her Blackberry, which at least allowed her keep up with e-mail—whenever Edna wasn't hiding it from her.

Although she'd discovered, to her surprise, that since getting the Natural Girl account nothing much at Conrad/Phelps had really required her direct attention. But she still wanted to keep an eye on things and she had occasionally chimed in where she'd felt her insights were warranted. And she'd shown up at the café early today with the idea of doing some work.

Opening her e-mail program, she found a message from Chase and quickly double-clicked on it.

Not sure if you're checking e-mail, Rachel—but Stan Harriman from K&K called. As you know, he planned to take their business elsewhere, but has found he isn't as impressed by the larger agencies as he expected to be. He's considering coming back, so I've put your team to work on some new campaigns. A call from you to let him know we're committed to serving them might be a good idea. In other news, we miss you around here. The office is too quiet.

Oh God—K&K! The makers of everything from baby wipes to laundry detergent were up for grabs again? This was big. *Really* big. She hit REPLY.

Great news about Stan. I'll call him this afternoon and work my magic—if I still have magic left to work. ☺

Rachel bit her lip, thinking. About flirting with Chase. It seemed like a good time for that. Since she'd decided, very firmly, that Mike Romo meant nothing to her. Other than great sex, of course—because it would just be silly to deny that part.
But quit thinking about Mike. Flirt with Chase. She started typing.

I miss you guys, too. Mostly you—and your muffins.

Rachel was notorious—back in Chicago anyway—for never eating breakfast, so Chase frequently brought her muffins, surprising her with different flavors. Satisfied, she hit SEND.

A moment later, an IM window appeared—along with a real-time message.

CALEXANDER: Oh, don't worry, you've still got plenty of magic. ☺ How's the apple business?

Rachel sighed. The apple business was actually pretty good. But she didn't really want to discuss it with her boss. Her other boss besides Edna, that is. Still, she decided to be honest.

RFARRIS: The apple business is . . . tiring. But not a bad way to spend pretty fall days. Anything else going on there I need to know about? Like . . . do I still have a job?

CALEXANDER: I'm working on that, singing your praises constantly. No decision yet, but I'm doing what I can for you. You're going to owe me. ☺

Rachel pursed her lips, pleased that Chase was still flirting with her, even from afar. It reminded her there was more to life than Mike Romo. *But quit thinking about him already!*

RFARRIS: What will I owe you exactly?

CALEXANDER: Dinner at the very least. Maybe even a good bottle of wine.

RFARRIS: That can be arranged. Whether or not I keep the job.

CALEXANDER: Hey now, no negative thoughts allowed. But . . . when are you coming home?

Oh crap. She bit her lip.

RFARRIS: Unfortunately, my grandmother still needs my help and I don't feel I can leave her. Can you keep singing my praises a little longer?

CALEXANDER: I'll keep hitting those high notes as long as I can. But get K&K back and it'll make my performance easier.

RFARRIS: Understood. And Chase, thanks. I appreciate your support.

Just then, Sue Ann arrived. "Hey," she said with her typical upbeat smile.

"Fab dress," Rachel said, taking in Sue Ann's cream-colored frock with tiny gold and rust leaves embroidered at the neckline and hem. Then she typed.

RFARRIS: Chase, sorry, I have to run—am meeting friends for lunch and they just showed up.

CALEXANDER: Have fun—and let me know what happens with our man, Stan. And hey, Rach, it was nice chatting with you, even if not in person.

She sighed happily. *Take that, Mike Romo.* Not that she was thinking about him or anything.

RFARRIS: You, too. And I'll be expecting a whole BASKET of exotic muffins upon my return. ☺

Just as Rachel powered down and closed her laptop, Amy and Tessa showed up, Jenny arriving directly behind them.

"This is so great," Amy said, smiling brightly as they settled around the table. "All of us together again! Who'd have believed it could happen?"

Who indeed, Rachel nearly quipped but held her tongue. Frankly, her discussion with Chase had her feeling a little indignant again about being back in Destiny. Her life was in Chicago, and the online chat had been a good reminder.

However, that didn't mean she shouldn't enjoy this time with her girlfriends.

"So what did everyone do over the weekend?" Amy asked after they'd given Mabel their drink orders and gotten menus.

Jenny, looking vibrant in a teal sweater set and coordinating skirt, merrily replied. "Well, Mick finally finished my balcony."

"Your balcony?" Rachel asked, and Jenny explained that her handy bad boy of a husband had built a balcony onto their bedroom, facing Blue Valley Lake.

"For stargazing."

Ah, Rachel remembered Jenny being into astronomy back in high school—apparently it had become a lifelong love.

"And they christened it when it was done," Sue Ann chimed in.

Amy smiled across the table at Jenny. "Oh, so you finally got to check out the stars from your side of the lake?"

"Yeah. Before, pointing the telescope up through all the trees was a lost cause."

"But that's not what I meant by christen," Sue Ann said. "I meant that she also got to check them out while under Mick on a lounge chair."

As Jenny's jaw dropped, she smacked Sue Ann's arm. "Sue Ann! For God's sake."

"Sorry—I just can't help myself sometimes," Sue Ann replied, actually looking remorseful. "Your sex life is too fun not to talk about."

Jenny crossed her arms. "Well, *you* had a good sex life this weekend, too—shall I spew *those* details in the middle of the café?"

Rachel just laughed quietly—she'd forgotten how much she loved Jenny and Sue Ann, best friends to the core even when they bickered like sisters.

"Or I can just do it myself," Sue Ann announced. "Because unlike you, I have no problem talking about sex to my friends." Then she told them that she and Jeff had just had a Grandma weekend, explaining to Rachel that this was when her mom took Sophie for the whole two days. "This time they went to the Bob Evans Farm and Sophie got to pet baby goats. But where was I?"

"Sex," Tessa reminded her.

And Sue Ann smiled. "Ah, yes. We did it all over the house, and in the bathtub, too. And late Saturday night, we did it in the backyard, in Sophie's playhouse."

"That's gross," Amy said.

"Sophie wasn't there at the time," Sue Ann pointed out, defensive. "It was fun—and it felt kind of . . . *risky*, wondering if the neighbors would hear."

Amy made a face, and everyone else laughed, and Jenny clearly thought it was a good time to change the subject. "What did *you* do, Tessa? Anything fun?"

"Well, I did *not* have sex of any kind this weekend— gross, risky, or otherwise, I'm sorry to say. Instead, I went to Amy's for a Jane Austen movie marathon with her and Mr. Knightley."

"And we had a perfectly nice time," Amy added, "even if we don't have any torrid tales to tell."

"We did," Tessa agreed warmly. "I'm glad I have you to hang out with. But sue me if I wish you and I both could find a man."

Rachel continued to feel depressed on Tessa's behalf. With Amy, it was different—she seldom dated, yet it didn't seem to bother her. But Tessa it bothered.

That's when Amy said to Tessa, "What about Adam Becker? For you."

Jenny gave her head a speculative tilt. "I could see that." Jenny and Adam had been a couple in high school, so she should know. "He's handsome, he has his own business, he's a nice guy—the whole package."

"Yeah," Sue Ann agreed, "Adam is pretty prefect."

Yet Tessa didn't look overjoyed. "I know—he's great. But count me out. I'm just not a big fan of the fix-up."

And Amy scowled. "Just because it didn't work out with Logan? I've been known to make at least *some* suggestions that have come to fruition, you know. Cara Collins and Tyler Fleet are going to the homecoming dance together thanks to me. And I also suggested Rachel and Mike would hit it off, and look how *that's* going!"

"Yes," Tessa said, shifting her gaze to Rachel, "how *is* that going?"

Just as Sue Ann screeched, "Rachel and *who*? *Mike*? As in Mike *Romo*?"

"Whoa," Jenny said, lowering her chin—as Rachel kicked Sue Ann lightly under the table and said, "Quiet down. I don't need the whole town to know."

"Yep, Rachel had the most interesting plans of all this weekend," Tessa informed the girls. "She went with Mike to Grandma Romo's birthday party. And I've been dying to hear how it went, but Edna keeps her too busy to chat much these days, so she promised to give me the scoop here at lunch."

Jenny and Sue Ann both appeared stunned. "You and Mike Romo, huh?" Jenny asked, at least keeping her voice appropriately low. "My dad thinks a lot of him—says he's a good cop. But . . . he's so surly."

When Rachel had promised Tessa the scoop, it had been before she knew Sue Ann and Jenny were coming. And she loved them, she really did—but the situation seemed too complex to go into here, now, with all of them. And Sue Ann did have a big mouth. Talk about tongues wagging. So, to keep things simple, she boiled it all down to the main factor of the relationship. "It's about sex," she replied.

"Ah, you want to have it with him," Sue Ann said matter-of-factly. "*That* I get."

"No—she already did," Amy informed them.

After which Sue Ann and Jenny both sat there with their mouths hanging open, Jenny appearing surprised and maybe a little entertained—while Sue Ann merely looked eager for more dirt. And then, like an angel sent from café heaven, Mabel arrived, her fluffy gray hair appearing bluish in the sunlight, to take their orders. Rachel made a note to leave the old woman a big tip.

Of course, as soon as Mabel departed, Sue Ann started her good-natured prying. But Rachel kept it simple, no details. Yes, he was good in bed—not that she'd ever done it with him there, but she didn't mention that part. And yes, it really was just a sex thing—there were no pesky emotions involved. She stayed adamant about that, no matter how much Amy tried to beat her down and insist that surely she felt something more for a guy she'd been intimate with multiple times now.

And it was almost the truth, since anything she *had* felt for him had been . . . brief and temporary. Temporary insanity, she decided.

She'd never been so thankful in her life to see food show up, and was grateful when the girls turned their conversation to things like the café's selection of pie, Sue Ann's next grandma weekend, and Amy's upcoming book club pick.

Yet as much as Rachel wanted not to be thinking about Mike, it gave her thoughts a chance to wander—back to him. Even if her insane little burst of emotions was over, she still felt bad about his past, and the scars he still carried inside—at least according to Amy. And she wished she could forget how strangely well they'd gotten along on the way home the other day. She still couldn't *believe* he'd taken her to see a donkey. And that she'd liked it! Who *was* she? At moments, she almost didn't know anymore.

"What are you smiling about?" Amy asked then—and when no one answered, Rachel realized they were all staring at *her*. And that she hadn't touched her food.

"Sex with Mike Romo, obviously," Sue Ann said in a loud whisper.

No, not just the sex. The other stuff, too.

But she didn't tell them that. Because they'd get the wrong idea, especially Amy. She could have pleasant memories about the guy without it meaning she was all wrapped up in him.

As soon as the checks came, Amy paid hers, announcing she had to get back to the bookstore, so Rachel took the opportunity to leave with her. She would have enjoyed hanging out longer, but explained, "I really need to get back to Edna's." And besides, if she hung around, they'd just keep asking her more about Mike.

She walked back to Under the Covers with Amy since the closest parking spot she'd found was just past the store—fortunately not in front of a fire hydrant. After Amy unlocked the door, Rachel stepped inside—she'd agreed to go with the girls to some softball tournament this weekend at Creekside Park and Amy was going to look up the schedule in the *Destiny Gazette*.

Of course, as soon as she set foot in the store, Shakespeare was rubbing up against her ankles—all gazillion pounds of him. "Annoying cat," she muttered. But she bent down to scratch behind his ears anyway.

Amy glanced up from turning newspaper pages. "That reminds me, did you ever ask Edna about him?"

"Oh, yeah, I did—I forgot to tell you."

"And?"

Rachel hesitated, though, because something about the answer bothered her. Maybe she'd sort of forgotten to tell Amy on purpose. "She said she could take him off your hands as a barn cat."

Amy's eyes brightened. "Great."

"But he would live . . . in the barn. Outdoors. On his own," Rachel explained.

"Yeah," Amy said. "So?"

Damn it, Rachel had been sure Amy would see her point without her actually having to make it. "Well, the thing is . . . what if he's not used to that? He doesn't seem . . . like the outdoorsy type."

Amy shrugged. "Neither do you, but *you're* getting by."

Rachel just sighed. He was so fat. And pushy. Clearly used to getting what he wanted. And at the same time he struck her as sort of . . . innocent in a weird way. Defenseless. "I don't know if it's a good idea." She bent down to heft the humongous cat into her arms, plopping him on the counter. Then she looked into his eyes, which she hated to admit were sort of sweet, and grimaced. "You seem too fat to catch mice anyway. One of them might catch *you*."

Behind the counter, Amy rolled her eyes and let out a huff. "Great. Now *you're* attached to Shakespeare, too. You're supposed to be the unemotional voice of reason here who helps me get rid of him."

"I wouldn't say I'm *attached*," Rachel quickly denied. Although she didn't feel quite like the same unemotional woman who'd come speeding into town a few weeks ago, either. "It's just that he's a big fat blob and I'd worry about him a little. It's . . . stressful being forced into new situations you're not ready for."

Like working in an apple orchard.

Or hearing about your grandmother's sex life.

Or . . . fearing your all-about-sex relationship with a hot cop wasn't really all about sex, no matter how hard you tried to convince yourself. Ugh.

Is love a tender thing? It is too rough,
Too rude, too boist'rous; and it pricks like thorn.

William Shakespeare, *Romeo & Juliet*

Eleven

Half an hour later, Rachel had changed into apple-picking clothes and called Stan Harriman. Since Edna was out picking the first freshly ripened Jonathan apples, her parlor made as good an office for Rachel as anyplace.

Stan had seemed happy to hear from her, and they'd had an encouraging conversation—one that restored Rachel's faith in herself. Not that she'd ever lost it, but . . . maybe knowing Pamela was considered her equal had started to chip away at her professional self-worth a little. Yet talking with Stan had shown her she still had the magic, just as Chase had promised.

Now, sitting on the same sofa where Mike Romo had stroked her to orgasm, she dialed Chase's direct office number. Having enjoyed the flirting around the edges of their conversation at lunch had reassured Rachel that . . . well, maybe she didn't have it as bad for Romo as she'd started to fear in certain fragile moments. Sure, she'd

gotten caught up in thinking about him before lunch—
okay, *and* during lunch—but that didn't mean anything.
And it would be good to hear Chase's voice—a nice reminder that she had plenty of wonderful things awaiting
her back in Chicago.

And then—damn it—she got Chase's voice mail. So
much for hearing his voice—other than the message he
left for callers.

"Hey, it's Rachel," she said, "and I've just had a great
talk with Stan. He's looking forward to seeing what we
come up with and he sounds very positive. If we can
put together a campaign that knocks his socks off, he's
ours."

As Rachel disconnected, she felt energized by today's
work-related happenings. But . . . to her surprise, she realized she was eager to join Edna out in the orchard, too.
The Jonathans and Red Delicious ripened at the same
time, so they'd have their work cut out for them between
now and the festival.

The Jonathan grove rested at the far end of the orchard,
a considerable distance beyond the barn, and Rachel was
glad to see Edna's pickup gone, indicating she'd driven
there rather than walked. Yet since the same bright, warm
weather from the past weekend remained, Rachel didn't
mind the trek herself. And as was so often the case these
days, simply meandering among the billowing trees amid
a light autumn breeze lulled her into a pleasant relaxation.
She remained ready for work, but she felt . . . well, as if
Chicago was a world away. And she guessed it really was.
She'd be back there soon, but she was beginning to see,
despite herself, that this extended trip to Destiny was . . .
refreshing her, reviving her, and forcing her to slow down,
to stop and smell the roses—or maybe the apples—for a
change.

Finally, she came upon a ladder—and two short legs in
cotton pants extending from the greenery above. Just as

she was pondering how to let Edna know she was there without scaring her to death, two words echoed down through the branches. "'Bout time."

Rachel just shook her head, smiling to herself. "Yes, I had a nice lunch with my friends, thanks for asking."

"Well, I had me a nice time with some Jonathan apples, and now you can, too. Second ladder's in the truck."

As Rachel retrieved the easel-style ladder and set it up near Edna's, she said, "So, what happened after Giovanni went back to Italy?"

"Well, that," Edna said with a sigh, "is where things get mighty complicated."

Everything had changed for Edna since Giovanni's departure in August. Everything.

Although she and Giovanni had picked the first ripe apples together before that fated telegram had arrived, the bulk of the autumn harvest had happened after he'd gone—and she, Wally, Dell, and Eddie had handled the whole thing, selling bushel upon bushel to markets and produce stands all over the area. Edna had also spent many an hour sitting out across the bridge, next to the road, selling apples and grapes to folks driving by. The rest of the apples, along with the farm's crops—corn, taters, green beans, peas—they'd stored for winter. It had taken Edna a week to can the beans and peas.

They'd written their parents to explain they couldn't come home yet—and they'd sent money, the better part of their wages. Still, they knew Daddy wasn't happy their absence had stretched beyond summer. He'd counted on their help to get the hay in and do their fall harvest—and it meant the younger children had been put to more work than anyone had counted on.

But all three siblings agreed it was the only thing to do. Giovanni had been good to them, so they could hardly abandon his farm while he was away. Eddie had offered to oversee the place as best he could on his own, yet it was too much for one boy. They didn't tell their folks about Edna's engagement, but both of her brothers knew, and that was another big reason to care for the farm— Giovanni would soon be part of their family.

The good part about sitting out next to the mailbox those fall days had been being there when the mailman arrived. Edna had waited and watched for him to come rolling around the bend, just praying he carried a letter from Giovanni. And he had, three different times.

It had disappointed Edna that the letters were brief— that she'd waited so long to hear from him and yet saw all he had to say to her in only a few seconds. But she could forgive him. According to the letters, his mother's illness was lingering, and he couldn't leave. And in each, he'd told Edna he loved her and would be home to marry her soon. So even though the letters were short, she clung to those words, reading them over and over, even touching her fingertips to the page. It was as close as she could come to touching Giovanni.

Now, though, it was December, and the winter had brought illness—the worst of Edna's life. The doctor feared it was a leftover case of the Asian flu that had come over the ocean and killed so many last winter.

Now Edna floated in and out of her head due to the fever—she'd never felt so lost or helpless. All she wanted was Giovanni, and at moments she grew aware that she was saying his name again and again. And then she would hear Eddie's voice—not one of her brother's, but Eddie's— saying, "He'll be home soon, Edna, but I'm here for ya now. Don't you worry none—you're gonna be right as rain real soon, I promise."

It was hard to understand why Eddie was at her bedside, but he was, almost constantly as far as she could tell. When the fever was especially rough with chills and sweating, there he'd be, stroking her hair, and even sing-

ing to her real quietly—that Everly Brothers song about dreaming. His voice wafted over her, soft and deep.

He brought her what little bit of food she could eat. And he crushed up ice and poured Coke over it, the same way her mama always did, promising it would settle the sickness in her stomach. He delivered cool washcloths, pressing them across her forehead, her neck, gliding them down her arms. Sometimes she'd burst out of some confusing fever-induced vision in the middle of the night, and there Eddie would be, sitting in a chair next to her bed, slumped over asleep.

"Am I gonna die?" she asked him one day. Even in lucid moments, she felt so weak, like she was slipping deeper and deeper into some invisible hole she couldn't crawl out of.

"Shhh—no such thing, Edna. You think I'd let you die? No ma'am."

And she wondered where her family was. The fact that her brothers weren't there, nor her mother, frightened her all the more. "Where's Wally and Dell? I miss 'em."

"Doc told 'em they best stay away, honey, 'til you get over this thing."

It made her all the more confused, because . . . "Well, what about you? Can't you catch it, too?"

He simply shook his head and appeared . . . sure, strong. Stronger than she'd realized Eddie could be. "Not me, no sir. I'm tougher than I look." And then he winked, and she felt it somewhere deep within. She understood he was there, risking himself, for her. And . . . he was the only person in the world at her side right now.

The realization startled her all the more and, in her depleted state, she couldn't hold in her fears. "Don't leave me, Eddie. Don't leave me alone. I'm scared."

And then Eddie squeezed her hand in his and leaned down over her, kissing her on the forehead. "Don't worry, honey. I wouldn't leave you for nothin', and that's a promise."

They were the darkest days of Edna's life. Time moved so slowly and she drifted in and out of sleep, barely able to make sense of what was happening around her. She felt that darkness closing in, stealing more and more of the light inside her, and she knew in her heart she wasn't getting better.

Through tears one day, she asked Eddie, "Is Mama comin'?"

And he said yes. That Dell had driven down to Kentucky through a snowstorm to fetch her folks. And as much as it relieved her to hear her mother was on the way—she also knew she was right; she was dying.

"I don't wanna die, Eddie." She was so young. There was so much in life to see, to do. There was Giovanni. Although, now . . . well, sometimes he seemed almost like no more than a nice dream she'd had. She hadn't seen him in so long.

Eddie just kept telling her she wasn't going to die, that he wouldn't let her.

"Ain't nothin' you can do to stop it if the Lord wills it," she informed him weakly.

But, above her, he shook his head, looking almost angry. "The Lord ain't gonna take you yet, Edna. I won't let Him."

And then . . . Eddie slowly drew back the blanket that covered her. And he gently climbed into bed, stretching out alongside her.

Edna was too ill to even think about how little separated their bodies, just vaguely aware that she wore only a thin white nightgown, damp with sweat. All she knew in those moments was the warmth of another human being. All she knew was the strong arms that wrapped around her, the tender kisses that rained gently across her cheek. All she knew was the sense of being cared for, loved.

And when she awoke the next morning, she felt . . . different. More . . . normal. Eddie was no longer beside her and she wondered if it had been just one more fever dream. Yet what seemed more important just then was that she felt . . . alive. More alive, more in her right mind, than she'd felt for . . . she didn't know how long.

"I feel better," she whispered up into the air, to no one in particular.

But, of course, Eddie was right there with her—as always. A few seconds later, his sweet face smiled down on her. He looked exhausted, wrung out, but happy. "Fever broke," he told her.

Oh, Oh Lord! The fever had broken. She was going to live. She was going to get well. Tears filled her eyes at the news, and when she met Eddie's, his glistened with wetness, too.

"Your mama oughta get here today," he said.

But she couldn't even think about that right now. All she could think about was, "Why?"

"Well, we thought it was best to send for her—but she'll be real relieved you've took a turn for the better."

It required effort, but Edna shook her head softly against her pillow. "No—I mean why . . . did you stay with me? Why did you stay—when no one else would?"

For the first time since she'd gotten ill, Eddie looked a little shy. Yet then his expression changed, into something stronger, more stalwart, and she realized the boy she'd met last summer had somewhere along the way turned into a man. "Dell and Wally were both willin'—but . . . I said I'd do it."

She simply blinked at him, and asked again. "Why?"

"Edna," he said softly, leaning down to cup her cheek in his hand, "I know you love Giovanni . . . and that I don't stand a chance against a fella like him. But I reckon I stayed . . . 'cause I'm in love with you."

"You're stopping *there*?" Rachel asked, gaping at Edna from her ladder.

"Gotta stop somewhere. And besides, you don't pick

apples as fast when I'm tellin' stories." Edna didn't even look over from her work.

"You're evil, old woman."

"And you're impatient."

Well, that much was true—always had been. But as she'd acknowledged to herself earlier, something about picking apples, and just being in the orchard with Edna, did more to relax her than most things. For a moment, she considered telling Edna the good news she'd gotten about her job, simply to make conversation, but just as quickly she decided against it. Since, again, out here in the trees, that stuff didn't seem to matter as much. At least not as much as stories about Edna and Giovanni and Eddie.

And then, like a bolt of lightning, it hit her. "Wait— Eddie's going to turn out to be Grandpa Farris, isn't he?" She'd never heard her late grandfather referred to as Eddie, only Edward—but it only made sense.

In response, though, Edna simply rolled her eyes. "Impatient as the day is long."

So Rachel said nothing more and got back to work. Yet she couldn't quit thinking about the thickening plot of Edna's youth. Was she going to eventually find out Edna had cheated on Giovanni? And maybe this meant Giovanni did come back for Edna as promised? How could she *not* be impatient?

"So about you and Mike," Edna said a few minutes later.

Atop her ladder, Rachel just sighed. Edna and Giovanni seemed like much safer subjects. "What about us?"

"Have ya figured out yet that ya care for that fella?"

This time she let out an irritated huff. "No. In fact, I barely know him."

"Sometimes it don't take long," Edna mused, sounding suddenly light and merry, like a woman with a secret.

"You were right the first time, Edna," Rachel informed

her. "With me and Mike, it's all about sex." There, that should shut her up.

And it did—but it also made her smile.

Mike sat in his cruiser, just off Meadowview Highway, monitoring the road for speeders. It was a quiet afternoon, though—just the way he liked them—so maybe he wouldn't have to pull anybody over.

He'd been thinking a lot about his conversation with Chief Tolliver a couple days ago. Mainly because . . . well, other than with Logan, he guessed he thought he kept his troubles pretty well hidden; he didn't think other people realized he'd never gotten over Anna. It was only a picture on a desk, after all.

But if Walter knew—well, maybe it was more obvious than he thought.

And besides that . . . he knew Walter was right in a lot of ways.

And he knew Anna was dead. Whether she'd drowned or been grabbed by some scumball pedophile—it only made sense that she was dead, that she'd *been* dead for twenty-three years now.

But he'd hit upon another big difference between Walter's situation and his. Besides the fact that Walter knew where Judy was, Walter also knew . . . it wasn't his fault she was gone. Mike didn't have that luxury.

Just as that sobering thought settled around him, he raised his gaze to see—shit—that goddamn purple Mustang racing over the horizon! Just as fast as before. Mike hit the trigger on his radar gun—eighty-eight. Son of a bitch.

But he had a few more seconds' warning this time, so he dropped the gun, flipped on his lights and siren, and hit the gas pedal. He got his cruiser onto the road just after the bastard blew past him.

Feeling less caught off guard this time, Mike floored

it and got on the asshole's bumper. The siren wailed and
there was no way the guy didn't know he was being pursued, yet he didn't slow down a bit—in fact, he picked
up speed! Of course, given that it was likely a stolen car,
what else did Mike expect?

He stayed with him, but driving this fast on winding
country roads was dangerous as hell and took every ounce
of focus—he couldn't even free a hand to call for backup.
When he dropped his gaze to the license plate—shit—it
was mostly obscured with dried mud. Of course, if the
vehicle *was* stolen, the plates had surely been changed or
altered by now anyway. With each curve, Mike's stomach
lurched and his heart beat faster—but he wasn't going to
back down and let this idiot keep terrorizing Destiny's
roads.

Then they hit a straight stretch and—holy shit—Mike
spotted a loaded hay wagon up ahead in the same lane,
undoubtedly pulled by a tractor, just creeping along. It
was a common sight around here, and the tractor couldn't
be going more than fifteen miles an hour—but the Mustang wasn't slowing down. Mike realized the idiot was
planning to pass the tractor—at the precise moment he
spied a car coming in the opposite direction.

When the Mustang gunned into the left lane and
went flying toward the oncoming car, Mike's heart rose
to his throat. It was close—way too fucking close—
and Mike slammed on his brakes, hard, just in time
to watch the Mustang whip back over in front of the
tractor as the other car veered to miss him, two tires
hitting the gravel shoulder. Before Mike knew it, the
oncoming car, a late-model mid-size, was off the road,
careening through a fence into a recently mowed cornfield.

The Mustang was gone—long gone—yet Mike had no
choice but to let it go as he brought his vehicle to a halt
and jumped out. The tractor and wagon in front of him
had stopped, as well. A second later, Johnny Fulks, head

of the Destiny City Council, got out of the damaged car—but he didn't look to be injured, thank God.

"You okay, Johnny?" Mike called as he sprinted toward him.

"I think so. What the hell was *that*?" The middle-aged man appeared understandably ruffled.

"I'm pretty sure it was a stolen car, actually. Going upwards of ninety at times." Mike just shook his head, disgusted.

Johnny peered back at his *own* car. "Looks like I'm gonna have to be towed."

"Well, I'm just glad you're okay."

As Mike reached the other man, Fulks nodded. "You're right—coulda been a lot worse."

But talk about understatements. The Mustang could have easily killed Fulks, or the farmer pulling that hay wagon.

Despite the fact that there was no way to cite the other driver, Johnny filled out an accident report—and Mike hung around until a tow truck arrived and pulled the car from the meadow. Then he set off to the nearest house with the unpleasant task of letting them know about the damage to their fence and cornfield.

By the end of the day, he felt . . . pretty damn inept. He knew it wasn't his fault, but why was he wearing this uniform if not to prevent bad shit from happening? And what the hell was the deal with that stolen Mustang? Mike was convinced, more and more now, that it was indeed the missing car from the northern part of the state. So why was someone in a stolen vehicle using Destiny-area highways for a goddamn racetrack?

Back at the station, Mike checked the database again to see that, sure enough, the hot Mustang was still missing. Of course, few stolen cars were ever recovered—but for him and his gut feeling, it was almost confirmation that the Cleveland car was this one.

Now that the sighting was no longer an isolated, one-time incident, Mike decided to fill Chief Tolliver in on the situation—and even though he knew no one could blame him, as he did so, he somehow felt all the more useless and angry.

And apparently it showed, since Walter said, "You did what you could, Mike. And at least you were there to help Johnny out." Walter then reached up to twist his gray mustache, a gesture he often made when thinking things through. "We'd best alert the police in the surroundin' areas. He might go ninety, but he has to stop sometime, somewhere, and a car like that's bound to stand out."

True, yet it didn't make Mike feel any better.

After some computer work at his desk—including sending out the alerts Walter mentioned—Mike powered down and got ready to head home. And his eyes fell on Anna.

It was a somber end to a shitty day, and the sight of that little white dress reminded him once more: *I can't really save anybody.*

And if he did as Walter suggested, if he slid her picture into his desk drawer, it would only make him feel worse. Because to let go was . . . to give up. To stop hoping anything about her disappearance would ever be discovered.

And he knew that with every damn year that passed, with every damn day, it became less and less likely any new information ever *would* turn up—so a smart man would finally start finding a way to let it go.

But the problem was—Mike never stopped needing to know. Never. He never stopped yearning for answers. He never stopped thinking and wondering and lamenting it all. And he knew he never would—not until his dying day.

Like the last time they'd gone to the park, Tessa and Amy picked Rachel up at Edna's. And again, they had insisted it was a gym shoe sort of day. Except for working out, Rachel didn't really *have* gym shoe days in Chicago, so it was a hard reality to grasp. "But would it *hurt* anybody if I wore some attractive boots?" she'd asked Tessa.

"No, but you might hurt *yourself.* We'll be climbing up metal bleachers and walking around in dirt. Wear the gym shoes, for God's sake."

So she finally had, along with jeans and a fitted bright yellow tee with flowers embroidered on the front. "How's this?" she'd asked the girls. "Casual enough for ya?"

"Perfect," Tessa droned, clearly exasperated, as Amy said, "Who cares—let's go!"

"All right, all right," she replied, adding one of Edna's favorites: "Simmer down."

When they reached the park a few minutes later, the atmosphere was a lot different than their previous visit—the parking lot was filled, and cars lined the road. They got lucky, taking the spot of someone just leaving, near the ball fields.

"So, Sue Ann's husband plays on one of these teams?" Rachel asked as they got out. Sue Ann had mentioned at the café that she and Sophie would be here.

"Yep," Amy said as they started toward the crowd. "Jeff plays with Logan and Adam and Mike."

"*Mike,*" Rachel repeated dryly, then halted in place. "No one could have mentioned to me before now that *Mike* is involved in this?"

"What difference does it make?" Tessa asked, shrugging. "I mean, since it's just sex between you and him, as you keep claiming."

Rachel ignored Tessa's dubious look and glanced back and forth between her friends, feeling uncharacteristically sheepish. "Well, I don't want him to think I'm here . . . because of him."

"You're not," Amy said, looping her arm through Rachel's. "You're here with us. Just three fun chicks hanging out in the sun." Then she motioned around them to the busy park. "And besides, you're not exactly the only person here—he might not even notice you."

But why didn't that prospect make her feel any better, darn it?

"And what if he did think that? Would that be so bad?" Tessa asked. "I mean, you guys have had sex—that kind of proves you don't mind being around him."

True enough. But she still felt weird about him knowing that. Especially after the big "See ya," which she promptly reminded her friends of as they wove through the people standing around the softball diamonds.

"So this is where he 'sees ya,'" Amy said. "No big deal. That's what you keep telling us about you and him, right?"

"Right," Rachel agreed at the reminder, and it was a good point. So why was her stomach churning?

On the opposite side of the fence, guys were cheering each other on, and yelling warnings to be ready on third and stuff like that—when the girls spotted Sue Ann excitedly waving them over to a spot low on the bleachers. "Thank God you guys are here," she said when they reached her. "Sophie and I spread out all our stuff to save you seats, but I think people wanted to kill me."

The three of them sat down and Rachel met Sophie, a pretty little blonde who looked remarkably like Sue Ann had back in the first grade.

And that's when it hit Rachel—she'd known these women *that* long, since the first grade! Who could she say that about in Chicago? Something about it seemed . . . well, it just made her feel like . . . like maybe she belonged here a little more than she'd once thought. And it wasn't a horrible feeling.

Sue Ann instantly began to regale them about the tournament, explaining it was down to four teams and "our guys just need to beat the Crestview Fire Department to play for the championship" of what was—according to the banners across the back of the dugouts—the 7th Annual Destiny Fall Softball Tournament.

"Our guys are in the outfield right now," Sue Ann went on—and that's when Rachel spotted Officer Romeo at shortstop. Not surprisingly, he was yelling at the first baseman, who apparently hadn't done something as well as Mike wanted. He wore long khaki cargo shorts that looked like they'd seen better days, and a red T-shirt with the sleeves cut out and the McMillan's Hardware logo stretching across his chest in white. His thick hair was messy, he hadn't shaved, and the muscles on his arms glistened tan with sweat. And despite all that, damn it, he *still* looked good.

As a player from the other team got up to bat, Mike crouched into position, legs apart, knees bent, and Rachel could almost feel his intensity from her place on the bleachers. She could tell he took this seriously.

Then, with his eyes still on the batter, he yelled, "Becker, guy on second's lookin' to steal—watch your back."

"Becker" was Adam, on the pitcher's mound, also looking shockingly good in old clothes and sweat. For her entire adult life, Rachel had been attracted to men in finely tailored suits, but this was starting to change things. Next, she located Logan on third, and Sue Ann pointed out her handsome husband, Jeff, in right field.

As the game progressed, Mike continued yelling at people—but he seemed skilled at the game, making several impressive stops, throwing a few guys out at first, and even hitting a home run. Rachel discovered, unexpectedly, that she enjoyed watching, and she supposed it shouldn't surprise her to find out Mike Romo was Mr. Competitive.

It was in the sixth of seven innings that he finally caught sight of her in the stands. She knew the second it happened—back in shortstop position, he lifted his gaze from the batter to her, and then his eyes took on that sexy, bedroomy look again. Or at least that's what she *thought*, since he was pretty far away—but something about it tightened her chest and sent a surge of awareness to her panties, just like *every* time he looked at her.

That's when the batter hit a line drive—right past Mike.

She saw more than heard him mutter, "Shit," suddenly drawn back into the game as the center fielder was forced to chase down the ball, the batter running to second while a guy on third scored.

And as everyone around her appeared downcast to see the other team bring in a run that tied the game, Rachel could only smile inside. She'd driven Mike Romo to distraction—and despite herself, she liked it.

The skies were clouding over, a cool breeze blowing in, by the time the team sponsored by McMillan's Hardware beat the Bleachers Sports Bar team in the championship game just after five o'clock. The victory felt particularly sweet to Mike since he knew some of the guys on the other team and they were big trash-talkers. Thank God he'd gotten his game face back on after Rachel had caused him to fuck up—damn, what was it *about* that woman?

"Glad we won, dude," Logan said, dropping his mitt in the dirt near the bleachers, "so you can quit acting like an asshole."

"He's not acting," Rachel called over from where she still sat with her friends—the rest of the crowd was already gone and only the small group of women remained.

Meeting her gaze across the space that separated them, he almost smiled at her silly, smart-ass comment. Jeff had made a beeline for Sue Ann and Sophie, and Adam had joined the group, too—so it only made sense for Mike and Logan to meander that way as well. Especially since Adam kept saying how attractive Rachel was, and something about that got under Mike's skin.

"What's up, Farris?" he asked, approaching.

She shrugged, smiled. "Not much. Amy and Tessa dragged me out here to watch you act like a Neanderthal. But it was refreshing to see that you treat everybody that way and don't reserve it just for me."

"Nope, he's an equal opportunity jerk," Logan said, but Mike let it roll off his back. He knew he was a hard-ass on the softball field and that he pissed off his teammates sometimes—but he got into the game and liked to win.

"A jerk with a big trophy," Mike pointed out. Then he looked back to Rachel and gave her a small grin. "And you know I'm not *always* a jerk. In fact, I'm nicer to you than most people."

"Then I feel bad for most people," she informed him—but she still looked flirtatious. The now absent sun had pinkened her cheeks and he thought her unusually pretty with her hair mussed from a breezy fall day outdoors. "Now I see why you need Edna's floppy hat," he teased, pointing at her face.

"I have very sensitive skin," she replied. Which he already knew. From touching her. A different kind of sensitive than she was talking about, but he couldn't help remembering the way she reacted to just the simplest little touch or kiss.

"Hey," Jeff announced to the small crowd, "we're going to the Whippy Dip if anybody else wants to come. It's their last weekend of the season." The ice cream stand on the edge of town had been a summer hangout in their youth.

"And they have way more than just ice cream now," Sue Ann said to Rachel, assuming—correctly—that she wouldn't know. "They make good burgers and sandwiches, and Sophie loves their chicken fingers."

Tessa shrugged. "Sounds good to me."

"I say we *all* go," Logan suggested. "We champions can celebrate our victory with our adoring fans." He motioned to the girls for the last part with his usual grin.

"All right, Whippy Dip it is," Adam said.

And that's when a loud clap of thunder sounded, the skies opened, and it began to pour.

"Son of a bitch," Mike muttered as he and the guys rushed to grab up the mitts and bats they'd each brought.

Getting drenched in a matter of seconds, the group began to scatter, all headed to their cars. Mike heard Sue Ann yell, "See you all there!" Then he saw Rachel running behind Amy and Tessa toward the parking lot.

And that's when he realized—he couldn't let her go with them.

Because he wanted her with *him*.

Even if it was just for a ride to the Whippy Dip. It had been too long since he'd seen her.

Chasing after her, he soon closed a fist around her wrist, holding her back from following her friends. "Come with me," he murmured, then pulled her toward his pickup, both of them still running to escape the rain.

He opened the driver's side door and helped her hurry in, then threw his bat and glove in the extended cab behind the seat.

Shutting them in a few seconds later—the rain buffeting the truck on all sides—made him feel suddenly secluded with her. And it gave him the fierce urge not to wait a second longer to do what he wanted to do.

His heart still beating fast from the run, he turned, lifted his hand to her wet face, and kissed her with all the passion he'd apparently been holding in all week. It roared through him suddenly now, like some kind of avalanche, needing to get out. He pressed his tongue between her lips, heard her pretty sigh, and went instantly hard.

When the kiss finally ended, their faces remained close, and all was still but for the rain still washing down the windows around them—until she whispered, breathlessly, maybe even a little nervously, "We should, um, probably catch up with the others." A glimpse of the sweet, vulnerable Rachel when he'd least expected it.

"Uh, yeah," he murmured, nodding, brought back to the moment at hand—then he started the truck and turned on the wipers. The rain continued falling in a deluge outside.

And inside . . . damn, he was just beginning to realize her top was entirely soaked and that he could see the lace of her bra, as well as the shadows of pretty, dark pink nipples jutting through. And his chest tightened in a way he was quickly coming to recognize. It was the she-makes-me-crazy way.

By the time they reached the edge of the parking lot, he was throbbing behind his zipper. And he wanted to kiss her some more. Hell, he wanted to do a lot more than kiss her. So when he pulled out onto the road, he turned the wrong way.

"Uh, what about the ice cream?" she asked, looking surprised.

Letting his gaze rake down over her, he drew it back up to her deep blue eyes and said, "I'm in the mood for something else."

Back, foolish tears, back to your native spring.

William Shakespeare, *Romeo & Juliet*

Twelve

Mike's words trickled down Rachel's spine. She was in the mood for something besides ice cream, too. Darn it, she was *always* in the mood whenever she even thought about Mike, and watching him all afternoon had only made it worse. And his kiss just now had turned her completely inside out.

But she still couldn't help feeling a little indignant over the whole "See ya" thing. And despite herself, even if she'd told herself all she wanted from him was sex . . . well, they'd shared enough now that she didn't want him to think she would just be at his beck and call. She hadn't come to the park today expecting to get drawn back into his sexy web. So she heard herself begin to argue with him. "Well, what about the others?"

"They'll figure out we're not coming," he said, eyes on the road. It continued pouring outside.

"Well . . . what if *I'm* in the mood for ice cream?"

"I'll change your mind real fast," he promised.

Hmm. "How?" She crossed her arms, the move shoving her breasts upward.

And even while driving through the torrent, he glanced over at her—and her whole body tingled as his gaze rose from her boobs to her face. His eyes were half shut, and when he spoke, his voice came out raspy. "I still haven't shown you what I can do with my tongue. And I've got far better uses for it than ice cream, honey."

Oh. My. Her inner thighs fluttered, and she bit her lip as he peered back through the windshield to concentrate on driving.

Still, fluttering thighs didn't obliterate the "See ya" incident. "That's . . . intriguing, but you can't just have your way with me any time you please, you know."

Next to her, he only let out an exasperated breath. "Since when? You didn't seem to mind the last two times I had my way with you."

Rachel let out an annoyed breath at his shocking-even-if-typical bluntness. But at the same time, her cheeks warmed— because he made sense. Since when did she play hard to get? Oh hell. Maybe, when all was said and done, the "See ya" thing had just plain hurt her feelings. And maybe she just wanted to feel a little bit . . . valued by him. Whether she liked it or not. "Well, I took your advice and quit overworrying our . . . situation," she lied. "But just because this is a totally casual fling, that doesn't mean I wouldn't enjoy being . . . wined and dined a little. Or something. You know?"

In response, Mike simply shook his head, looking completely bewildered. "Hell, you confound me, woman."

"*Confound?*" Rachel blinked. "Color me surprised—I didn't see a guy like you using the word *confound*."

He kept his eyes on the road, trying to navigate through the heavy rain, as he grumbled, "Well, it's probably a first. And you're damn worthy of it. Because one minute you tell me you can't have sex with me because you hate

Destiny—or something idiotic like that—and the next you decide it's a-okay. Then you say you don't want romance, and now you're telling me you do. Just tell me what the hell it is you want, Farris, and I'll give it to you."

Hmm. What a request. And there were so many ways she could answer—so many different things she desired. She wanted Edna and the orchard. She wanted more of what she'd gotten from Mike after the picnic—that surprising sweetness. She wanted to keep being the tough chick who had it all under control and didn't get attached to men or cats or grandmas or anything else that felt impractical in her life. But right now, her breasts ached, and the juncture of her thighs pulsed madly, and the heat flowing through her body seemed a lot more powerful than any of those vague, useless thoughts. So she drew in her breath, pressed her palm to the wet khaki covering his thigh, then slid her touch upward until it covered his erection. And he *was* definitely—delightfully—erect.

Mike let out a low groan that only fueled her longing. "Giving you *that*, honey," he murmured as he drove on, "will be my pure pleasure."

"Just . . . remember what I said," she told him, her voice coming out breathy as she turned toward him in the truck, getting caught up in her own want, pressing her breasts to his muscular biceps.

"About, uh, wining and dining?" She liked that his words came out strained, too, because she was lightly massaging the column between his legs now. "Not a lot of that going on in Destiny, Farris, but if it's what you want, it's what you'll get."

That's more like it. Not that she was really thinking about wining and dining anymore—she was thinking about the rock-hard length of flesh beneath her hand. She squeezed him more fervently through the shorts, and he muttered, "Jesus, woman, you're gonna cause an accident."

She bit her lip. "Should I stop?"

"Hell no."

Rachel hadn't had a chance to ponder where they were going, but it still surprised her when they pulled up a sloping gravel drive to a large white farmhouse with a black barn and several outbuildings in back. The house possessed simple lines—a full covered porch stretching across the front, one gable in the center with a small diamond-shaped window in the eave, the other gridded windows situated symmetrically. But the thing that surprised her was that it seemed like far too big of a house for only him.

"Your place?" she asked, to make sure. But it came out whispery because she was still stroking him and the small of her back ached deliciously.

"Mmm," he confirmed, low, deep, killing the engine.

Okay, who cared how big his house was—she just wanted to get him naked.

"Ready?" he asked. The rain had slacked off a little, but still fell hard.

"Very."

So Mike threw open his door and together they ran for the porch. Both were freshly soaked by the time he stabbed a key at the front door, then shoved it open.

Dusk and gray skies made the interior dark, but at the moment, Rachel didn't care about seeing it anyway— she'd just become very single-minded. And clearly, Mike felt the same since he didn't bother with lights—he simply tossed his keys on a table with a loud jangle, turned to her in the entryway, lifted his hands back to her face, and gave her a long, heated kiss.

They were both breathless, panting, as Mike reached down to the hem of her drenched top and peeled it over her head—she held her arms up to help him remove it. His eyes dropped to her breasts, so hers did, too—to find that the rain had turned her pink lacy bra completely transparent. Instinctively, she reached behind her back to the hook, letting the wet bra loosen, then fall from her shoulders and off.

"Jesus God," he whispered. Her breasts had never felt more sensitive in her life, more in need of attention.

But the rest of her was in need, too, so she was already moving on, curling her fingers into his tee and vigorously stripping it off him, as well. Then they both kicked off their shoes and worked at each other's zippers, pushing, tugging, wiggling—until finally they stood completely naked together in the shadowy light.

"Damn," Mike said, sounding . . . a little weakened, she thought. Yet he regained his strength to add, "You're beautiful."

Rachel bit her lip, whispering, "You, too." Because he was. All muscle and sinew, his body was . . . flawless. And yes, she'd seen him naked before, in the concession stand, but this was different. Because the terrifying truth was, now it mattered. Because now . . . she cared. Edna was right. Amy was right. She cared, damn it. And she could lie about it, but that didn't change it.

And so it somehow moved her more deeply to study the dark stubble on his jaw, the smattering of hair on his broad chest, his muscled stomach. It somehow moved her more to feast her gaze on his majestically hard erection—because it was for her, just for her; she'd made him that way. She'd made him that way before, of course, but this was the first time she'd really *known* it—that this was more than just chemistry, more than just two bodies lusting.

She bit her lip, met his gaze, and felt far too needy at the moment. Like some other girl. Some . . . softer girl than she'd ever been.

And then they were on each other, kissing again, touching. She looped her arms around his neck—his fell about her waist. That amazingly hard part of him pressed against her where she was the softest. She moaned against his mouth and sank still deeper into him, absorbing his warmth, and the dampness of their skin coming together.

Mike's kisses dropped to her neck, then her chest. Soon, she found herself arching toward him, silently begging him to kiss her breasts. The only time he ever had was in the concession stand, and again, that seemed so long ago now—like another lifetime. Of course, as she'd recognized before in brief honest moments, even then things with him hadn't been . . . normal. Normal for her. Even then she'd cared about his opinion of her, and she'd felt unable to hold back, unable to say no.

When finally his tongue raked across one sensitive nipple, she gasped her pleasure as it rippled all through her. She instinctually rubbed the juncture of her thighs against his hardness. She watched as he took the turgid peak into his mouth, then suckled firmly.

"Oh . . ." she moaned—the sensation shot through her body like a rocket, landing directly between her thighs. And as she moved against him more, more, she felt her own wetness—much slicker than any moisture left from the rain.

Mike's hands slid to her ass as he ground against her, guiding their bodies into a more sensual rhythm. "Oh God," she murmured, because it felt so good, *too* good. Better than she'd known it could. So good that . . . oh Lord, she was going to come this way. Just from this. She bit her lip, let out a ragged breath, closed her eyes. She was getting lost in it, overwhelmed by it—she couldn't stop it.

And then suddenly Mike's palms closed tight over her bottom and he hoisted her slightly upward even as he backed her against the nearest wall. "Wrap your legs around me," he said low in her ear, and she obeyed, locking her ankles in back—just before he thrust himself inside her.

"Oh!" she cried out, slightly shocked—by the entry

itself, and by how incredibly well he filled her. Which edged her cry into more of a moan. "Ohhh . . . oh, Mike."

"Aw, honey, you're so wet for me," he growled in her ear.

And then she resumed the same rhythm as before, her body taking back over, her mind going numb as the sensations swept her away again, that quickly, and she whispered, "I'm gonna come."

She caught her breath over and over as the orgasm rolled through her, sweet and surprisingly long—especially considering that her back was pressed against a hard wall. She shut her eyes and soaked up every hot pulse, riding him, feeling him inside her, aware of every spot where his body touched hers. As the scintillating waves eased, she could smell him, smell the rain on him, the dirt from the softball field, the manly scent of him, and she found herself wrapping her arms tighter around his neck, clinging to him, holding on as if for dear life. And she had no idea why, no idea except . . . *oh God, this must be what it's like to start falling for a guy.*

"You okay, baby?" he whispered deeply in her ear.

Mmm, he'd called her baby. But he was also asking her if she was okay—because she was clutching at him like her very existence depended on it. Yet all she could manage was, "Mmm-hmm."

"Mmm," he purred. "Was that good?"

She nodded against his shoulder. "*Really* good."

"I thought so," he said—surprisingly without a shred of arrogance—as he carried her across the room, still inside her, to lower her onto a couch, on her back. His erection never left her—and thank God, because she loved the way it made her feel so utterly connected to him.

He lay on top of her, their eyes meeting in the darkness, and with his big hands still bracketing her hips, he began to deliver deep, delicious thrusts in a slow rhythm that made her feel thoroughly possessed by him. In a good way.

Oh Lord, she wanted to be possessed? By a man? Who *was* she? But she couldn't think right now—she could only feel, she could only soak each deep plunge into her body, could only drink in the low, sexy groans he emitted with every one.

Soon, she was moaning from the lush sensations—they stretched all through her. And she looked up into his dark eyes the whole time, discovering it was another way to feel connected to him.

She'd never cared so much for a man's pleasure before; she'd never felt so very . . . as if they were in this together, to give pleasure as well as to receive. And she knew it was silly, because surely this was just like the first two times they'd had sex—but the feeling permeated her completely anyway.

She never wanted it to end. She hoped he could see on her face how lost she was to him, to his every touch, his every slow, deep drive. She wanted him to hold her forever. She wanted their arms and legs to be tangled up together for the rest of their lives. In that moment, she wanted *everything* with him, everything in the world there was to have with a man. She begged him, "Kiss me," because she needed that further connection, as well as all the others.

He pushed one hand back through her damp hair, then lowered his mouth to hers. She touched his face, the stubble on his cheek. She lifted to meet his slow, magnificent strokes. She felt—insanely perhaps—like she was floating on a perfect cloud with him, like she'd found true serendipity.

"Aw . . . aw, honey," he growled, and his hips jerked against her—reflexively, she thought, almost beyond his control, and she liked it. "Baby. Baby, I'm gonna come in you. I'm gonna come in you."

Rachel bit her lower lip as his thrusts grew faster, harder—she met each, empowered by knowing she'd taken him here. She wanted it to be the most intense climax of his life.

And then he was growling, calling out, as he drove into her again, again, and she loved knowing he was leaving something of himself inside her there. It was the first time she'd ever felt such an emotion and her whole body went warm as he finally relaxed against her, resting his head alongside hers. The scruff of his beard lightly abraded her shoulder.

"Jesus," he breathed in her ear.

"What?"

"Good," was the only word he got out.

As his eyes fell shut, Rachel lifted her hand to touch his bare shoulder where he lay across her chest; she turned to peer at his face in the semi-darkness. And she suffered the full measure of just how very *joined* she felt to him. It was almost painful. Wrenching. Like if she made love to him day and night for the rest of her life, it would never be enough—she'd always want more. Then her own eyes fell shut—because they kind of ached, felt strange. She clenched her teeth. What was going on here?

And then she realized. She was crying a little.

She hadn't recognized it because she *never* cried. *Ever.* Not since she was a kid.

Damn it—what the hell was *that* about?

Reaching up, she turned her face away from his and quickly wiped the wetness away. How weird. And she was trapped between not being sure she liked it, not at all—and how oddly caught up in the moment she still felt, how strangely consumed by the intimacy. She lay in the darkness, looking into the shadows of the room, of his home, his life, amazed she'd ended up here—naked beneath Mike Romo. Or in Destiny at all, for that matter.

A few minutes later, Mike's weight lifted off her and then a light came on.

When she peeked up, she found him looking down at her from the foot of the couch. He remained beautifully naked, but his eyes clouded over a little. "What's going on? You okay?"

Oh, shit. There was still a pesky tear or two leaking free.

She tried to blink it away, then said, "Just . . . something in my eye."

Mike tilted his head. "Are you serious, Farris— something in your eye? Could that answer be any more lame?"

She let out a sigh, *feeling* pretty lame, and not the least bit surprised her Officer Romeo had called her on it. "Okay, I was just thinking . . . about Edna," she fudged, sitting up a little to prop her head on some throw pillows.

Mike's gaze narrowed in concern. "What about her? She isn't sick or anything?"

"Oh—no, nothing like that." She pursed her lips, pondering it. "It's just . . . I think her knees cause her a lot of pain. And even as sturdy and hardworking as she is, she's . . . getting older, slower—I can see it."

Mike came around the end of the couch and used one hand to lift up her ankles and take a seat beneath them, lowering her feet atop his firm thigh. "Hard to watch them age, isn't it?" he asked.

And she nodded. "There's even a part of me that keeps thinking maybe I should find a way to take over the orchard, just to keep it in the family . . . but I can't. I have a job to go back to. It's not something I could just give up." She shook her head against the pillows and realized as the words spilled from her that they were all true—this was just the first time she'd allowed herself to fully acknowledge the feelings. That if she didn't feel so bound by other commitments, maybe she *would* want the orchard.

"Would it be so horrible," Mike asked, his tone uncharacteristically gentle, "if the orchard ended up with me? I'd take good care of it."

"I know you would," she admitted. "But it would just be . . . the end of an era. It would feel wrong to me for the Farris name to no longer be attached to it. Your grandpa might have built it, but *I* played there, I had holidays and Sunday dinner there, I grew up there. So did all my cousins, and my dad, and my aunts and uncles. It's really . . . home to us." And God, that was when it hit her—she hadn't known she felt that way until right now. Until this moment, her home had been in Chicago—but now, suddenly, home was the orchard. She'd been trying to hate Destiny since she came back, but she just didn't anymore.

"So if you want it so bad," he asked, looking down at her, "why *can't* you give up your job? I know the orchard isn't the most profitable business around, but it *could* be, with a little modernization."

"I know." She nodded. "I think the same thing, but Edna refuses to hear it."

"And I'm betting you have enough money socked away that you wouldn't have to worry about starving in the meantime."

How strange it was to be lying stretched out naked on Mike Romo's couch, chatting with him as easily as if they were dressed. But the topic he'd just broached was . . . complicated at best. And how strange it felt to realize . . . she was going to tell him the truth, the truth even Tessa and Amy didn't know. But for some reason, she needed *him* to know.

"You're right, I'm doing fine on money," she said. "But the rest of my family . . . not so much."

It was an awkward thing to say, and Mike didn't respond, so Rachel tried to go on. Except it was difficult, being the topic she least liked to think about. Finally, she took a deep breath and said, "Some of them have kept it camouflaged, and others haven't, but either way, most Farrises don't handle money well. I became aware of it at an early age, and I've spent my whole life being embarrassed and worried by it."

"Embarrassed?" he asked, looking truly perplexed.

She sighed. "My great aunt Liddie and her famous bad checks?" she reminded him. "My cousin Robby always borrowing money from people he can't pay back? And then there was Uncle Gary's insurance fraud—the time he parked his Trans Am on the railroad tracks because he couldn't make the payments? Do I have to go on?"

He appeared to be making a stab at a sympathetic smile. "Okay, guess I do remember those things."

"And don't forget what you said when we first met—about Farrises not abiding by the law."

He looked slightly remorseful. "I wouldn't have said that if I'd known you and I would ever end up . . . like this." He motioned vaguely to their bodies.

"Well, I'm just saying that when the whole town thinks of your family that way, it's hard. Especially when you're just a kid, growing up."

"So . . . what, then? You've got some phobia about going broke and being forced to put your Beamer in the path of an oncoming train?"

"Well, in a way, maybe. Not the train part, but the going-broke part. I always knew I wanted to leave Destiny and lead a different kind of life—and I guess a lot of that was about money worries. I knew if I didn't get out of this town I'd never be any more than another scrambling-to-make-ends-meet Farris. And I didn't want to live like that. And I guess I also wanted to fix it all somehow, by making them all proud, and . . . maybe even by covering up their shortcomings. So . . . it's not just me I'm worried about."

He narrowed his eyes. "What does *that* mean?"

And Rachel sighed. This part was even harder to confide. She wasn't sure why—maybe because it felt so personal to her, like a scarlet letter she was forced to wear
but kept hidden. Or maybe she feared it was a betrayal to
her parents to talk about this—especially with a Romo.
But she still wanted to tell him. Maybe she wanted to get
it off her chest.

"The money issues," she began again, "stretch into
my immediate family. My parents never let it show, but
they've secretly always been in debt. Even now, they have
a nice house not far from me, in the suburbs, and they
lease a new car every two years—but they're so over-
extended that I get sick just thinking about it. And someday, it's gonna come back to haunt them in a big way." She
sighed. "Or should I say haunt *me*?"

She blinked, still somewhat embarrassed, and wondering if he got the picture yet. "The point is, when my parents or Edna reach some critical point where they really
can't get by anymore, who's gonna be there to keep a roof
over their heads?"

Mike raised his eyebrows. "You, I'm guessing?"

She sighed. "Right."

He knit his brow. "What exactly is it you do in your
job, Farris, that makes you able to provide for the entire
Farris clan?"

"I've told you before, I work at an ad agency."

"Making up slogans and stuff?"

"Not anymore. I started out on the creative end, but
then I was promoted and now I manage a team of people
and bring in new clients and try to keep them convinced
that we're the best place to invest their advertising dollars.
I kind of miss the creative work sometimes, but then . . .
I'm usually so busy that I don't have *time* to miss it."

"So, do you love what you do? Is it important to you?
Satisfying?"

"Yes, yes, and yes. It's . . . it's . . . the life I always dreamed of." But . . . why had that last part come out sounding so halfhearted? It *was* the life she'd dreamed of.

"You know, it's none of my business, but . . ." He trailed off.

"What? Spit it out."

"Well, that's an awful damn big burden to put on yourself. To hold yourself responsible for cleaning up other people's messes. I have a hard enough time just trying to clean up my own."

She wondered if he was talking about the loss of his little sister, but simply pointed out, "Not just *other people*. My *family*. I might be embarrassed by them sometimes, but at the same time, I want . . . to protect them. I wish I could make it so no one would be able to look down on them anymore. I wish I could just . . . restore a little pride to the Farris name." Rachel's last words lingered in the air, then settled around her. Maybe she hadn't quite realized the last part before now, before talking about it, out loud.

"I get it," Mike finally said. "I know about feeling responsible to your family. But . . . still. It's a lot to ask of yourself."

"Well, just so you know, that's not the only reason I can't leave Chicago for the orchard. What I've created there is . . . how I know I've done well in life. It's such a huge part of me that without it . . ."

"Yeah?"

She let out a breath. "There wouldn't be much of me left. Just . . . a little girl who worries about her family's money problems and wants to be strong and independent someday."

Mike's eyes fell half shut as he gazed thoughtfully down on her. "That's not true, honey. Surely you know there's a lot more inside you than that—I've seen it myself."

Oh crap. What had she just said? Way too much, that was for sure. And it made her want to cry all over again.

But it also reminded her—she *was* strong and independent, and it was time to resume acting like it. So she took a deep breath, felt tougher inside—and decided to end this particular conversation. "Listen," she said, "everything I just told you—promise you'll keep it to yourself. Edna would be mortified—we've never even talked about this. And besides, it's just . . . personal, you know?"

"No worries," he replied, caressing her calf. "My Farris grudge only goes so far. And lately, that hasn't been very far at all." He winked, lightening the mood—and she replied with a soft smile.

Then she said, "Got anything to eat? You cheated me out of the Whippy Dip."

Reaching in a drawer, Mike grabbed an old Steelers T-shirt for Rachel to wear, then hopped in the shower. She volunteered to put their clothes in the washer in the meantime—his dirt from the ballfield had managed to get everything a little grimy, including her top and jeans.

When he came out in a clean blue tee and a pair of gray sweats cut off to make shorts, she took his spot in the bathroom and he headed to the kitchen to see what he could find.

"Aha," he whispered, opening the fridge to see some leftover lasagna he'd forgotten about. He'd had dinner at Grandma Romo's with his parents a couple of nights ago, before they'd headed back to Florida, and she'd sent the whole pan home with him.

As he put two slabs on plates, then stuck them in the microwave, he remembered the conversation around his grandma's dinner table. About Rachel.

"I thought she was very nice," his mother had said with a bright smile.

"For a Farris," Grandma Romo had added.

His mother had leaned toward him. "Is it serious?"

"No," he'd quickly answered—then remembered the

whole reason he'd taken her there, to make his parents think he was doing the wife-shopping thing. "Not yet anyway," he'd added on a bit of a cough.

It had felt weird even having the conversation—because Mike had never really *had* a serious girlfriend, except for one back around his police academy days who had been so clingy and hard to break up with that he'd pretty much sworn them off ever since. And it also felt weird because of Mike's . . . feelings for Rachel. She stole his sense of control, which he hated. But he'd liked it a lot when she'd hugged him so tight after she came. And the very scent of her was still enough to excite him. And he couldn't seem to keep his hands off her, no matter *what* he hated or liked about the situation. The whole thing was getting a little scary to contemplate.

He let out a quiet laugh. Mike Romo, scared. Most people wouldn't believe it. Most people thought the losses in his life had turned him tough and mean. But maybe he was tough and mean because . . . he didn't want to lose any *more*. And if you didn't let yourself start caring about people, then you couldn't lose them. A long sigh escaped him.

Then he just shook his head. *Follow your own advice. Don't take things so seriously. Move on here. Have a nice night with her.*

"Good idea," he murmured.

Mike wasn't a big wine drinker, but when he spotted the bottle in the back of his fridge that one of his cousins had given him last Christmas, he grabbed it and dug through a messy drawer for a corkscrew. Then he found the wineglasses his parents had left behind in the house when they moved and washed two of them out.

Next, he looked to his small kitchen table. It was old, walnut, chipped in places, and atop it sat a wicker napkin basket and the little football-shaped salt and pepper shakers his mom had given him a few years ago. It hit him then that, shit, if not for his family, he wouldn't have any-thing in this house, not even food.

Regardless, the table just wasn't cutting it. So he opened a drawer and found a red-and-white-checked tablecloth—something else his parents had left behind, of course, and he was thankful. After trying to shake the fold marks from it, he draped it across the wood and didn't bother putting the salt and pepper shakers back on. He folded a couple of the paper napkins in half and laid forks and knives on them in front of two chairs—and even pulled the additional chairs away, out into the living room.

After pouring the wine and setting the plates and glasses in their respective spots, he looked around and thought, what else? Then he noticed a couple of candles in holders in the living room and went to get them. Find-ing some matches in a drawer, he lit them on the table, then turned out the lights.

Not bad, he thought.

But . . . *What the hell am I doing?*

And then he remembered—Rachel wanted to be wined and dined. And he didn't know much about doing that, actually, but he found himself wanting to . . . try. To show her he respected her and enjoyed being with her. Or maybe he just hoped to somehow compare with guys she knew in the city—he didn't want to come off like some country bumpkin. Hell, he just wanted to give her a nice evening. Or at least as nice as he could, with his limited resources.

When Rachel walked into the kitchen, still wearing only his T-shirt, the glow of candlelight made her skin appear luminescent. When she saw the table, she looked at him with a pretty smile. "What's all this?"

"I'll wine and dine you soon," he said, "but this'll have to do for now."

And when they sat down across from each other, he

thought—*damn, I want her again already*. All he could think about was that she didn't have on any panties.

They made small talk then, about the lasagna from Grandma Romo, about his parents' visit, about his job. About her high rise condo in Chicago, about her memories of growing up in Destiny, about where her various relatives had all moved to upon leaving town. They talked about Rachel's worries over Edna's loneliness, and about the orchard itself. He told her, when she asked about the house, that he'd grown up here and had bought it from his mom and dad when they left.

But the whole time, Mike wanted her, and he stayed aware of the way her nipples jutted against the cotton tee, of how her eyes lit up when she smiled. Even with her hair no longer in its chic style—just shoved back behind her ears after the rain—she looked . . . good enough to eat. Which reminded him of his promise to her.

"Listen," he said, "I'm sorry if I made you feel like I just wanted sex from you. I mean, I do"—he flashed a wicked grin, unable to help it—"but this is nice, too. And, uh, as soon as I can figure out where the hell in Destiny I can properly wine and dine you, I will."

Yet to his surprise, she smiled and told him, "No. No, this, right here, right now, is perfect. It's all the wining and dining I need."

He lowered his chin and cast a doubtful look. "Then you're easier to please than I thought."

She just shrugged flirtatiously. "Maybe I am." But then she grew more serious. "Maybe I . . . didn't really *mean* I wanted to be wined and dined exactly. Maybe I just meant . . . it would be nice to think you didn't mind spending time with me, more than just the time it takes to have sex. Like last week with your family—that was nice."

"I get it," he said. "I thought you didn't want that stuff, but . . . I don't mind that you do." *I'm even glad you do. Because I like it, too, despite my better judg-*

ment. Yet then his gaze dropped back to her chest and his hard-on got even harder. "Damn," he muttered without meaning to.

"What?"

Another wolfish expression escaped him. "Just noticing how much better you make that shirt look than I do."

She lowered her chin, playful and sexy. "Is that so, Officer Romeo?"

"Damn straight, but don't call me Romeo."

"What if I do—*Romeo*? Are you going to punish me?"

He flashed a teasing look of warning. "I might. And you're just askin' for it, Farris."

"Asking for what?"

"Well, Grandma Romo's lasagna was good," he said, lowering his chin, locking his gaze demandingly on hers, "but I'm still kinda hungry. So I think I might just have to make you my dessert." And with that, he stood up, stepped to her chair, and hoisted her onto his shoulder—and with her pretty ass bared toward the ceiling, he headed for the bedroom.

Many a morning hath he there been seen,
With tears augmenting the fresh morning dew.

William Shakespeare, *Romeo & Juliet*

Thirteen

*M*ike tossed her on the bed, towering over her, and said, "Take that shirt off."

"*You* take *your* shirt off," she commanded in return.

They both stripped them off over their heads and tossed them aside. And damn, she was gorgeous. Her taut nipples looked like hard pink beads just begging to be kissed, and her smooth, slender legs stretched forever.

"Shorts, too," she said, pointing, so he gladly dropped them and let her see he was already excited. He went even harder when she glanced between his legs and got that dreamy, ready look on her face.

"Lay back and get comfortable, honey," he said, watching her sprawl prettily across his bed. Then he hit a button on his iHome and Mazzy Star's "Fade into You" filled the room with slow passion.

Next Mike was bending over her, sinking his mouth to one breast, then dipping two fingers between her thighs.

Beneath him, she gasped, whimpered. Within moments, he wondered how he was going to keep from plunging his erection inside her until after he was completely done pleasuring her with his hands and mouth—but he was determined to hold back, because her body was beautiful and needed to be touched and kissed and licked by him, and because her unfettered responses made him wild. He was back to being Tarzan again, but he was damn well done trying to fight it. *Me Tarzan. You Jane. Sex good.*

She lay back into his pillows, arms flung carelessly above her head, eyes shut—yet then she opened them and met his gaze. He could see all the yearning and heat inside her and wondered if his own eyes revealed as much, if his desire was just as transparent.

"Watch me touch you," he said, and they both looked to where he now firmly molded and massaged her breasts; she thrust them upward and, mmm, he loved that—loved when Rachel gave herself to him so willingly.

She was the only woman he'd ever met who could give as good as she got with him, verbally and in other ways, too—but now that they were getting to know each other, he was seeing more and more gentleness inside her, more tenderness, and he realized she was . . . *everything.* She was tough and capable, she was smart and funny, she was feminine and sensual, and she could even be docile and sweet.

After thoroughly caressing her breasts, he slid his palms downward, over her slender torso, then peered down into her eyes and said, "Watch me kiss you."

She bit her lower lip, and again, complied—both of them glanced downward as he rained tiny kisses across her breasts and below, sprinkling them across her sexy stomach, over her navel, across her bare hips. The lower he went, the harder she breathed, and the more he wanted her. All of her. In every way.

And yeah, she was still reckless in his book, but he'd

learned that she wasn't reckless in *every* way—like financially, for instance. And so, when she *was* reckless, maybe it was for a reason. Maybe it was because she was carrying a huge weight on her shoulders—this concern for being able to provide for her family, this need to label her success—and maybe being reckless was her way of letting off steam.

And right now she wasn't reckless at all—right now she was simply . . . his to pleasure.

Finally, he used both hands to slowly re-part her thighs. "Watch me lick you, honey."

The sounds that echoed from her throat were like a hot, erotic symphony, drowning out all other noise—the softly playing music, the steadily falling rain outside. He peered up at her and their eyes met. And . . . damn. His chest constricted. He'd never felt so . . . close to a woman. Simply close. More than just the physical part. His scalp tingled and his hard-on intensified. She was all he knew in that moment. Everything else fell away.

Soon Rachel was biting her lower lip, her eyes falling half shut. Her fingers dug into the bedcovers beside her. Mike watched, his whole body tensed and rippling with as much sensation as if *he* were the one being pleasured. He wanted to make her come. But more than that. In that moment, he wanted to make her feel . . . everything *he* felt. That this was more than just physical, more than just the casual sex they kept discussing, that with every tug of his mouth on her sensitive flesh they were growing closer.

"Oh God!" she cried out, and Mike could have sworn he felt the orgasm pumping through her. When her body went still, her breath remained shaky, heavy, audible.

He slid up to angle his body across hers, cupping the nape of her neck, his fingers threading through her hair. He stayed almost painfully aware of his aching erection, pressed against her thigh now, as he brought their faces close, felt her breath on his lips, let their foreheads touch for a long, lingering moment.

"You were right," she whispered.

"About?"

"What you can do with your tongue." She smiled—soft, sexy.

He returned a small grin, her words sending a hot spasm through his already aching cock.

She touched his hair, looked up into his eyes. "Guess you just showed me outrageous again."

"And I'm not done yet, honey."

With that, he lowered a tender kiss to her still perfectly rigid nipple before he eased himself back between her thighs, upright, on his knees. And then he finally took his *own* pleasure, thrusting deep. She cried out, and he moaned at the warm entry. And he couldn't go slowly.

Closing splayed hands over her hips, he drove into her over and over in powerful strokes he felt at his very core. He clenched his teeth, but his groans leaked through at each warm plunge. The longer they moved together, the faster his strokes became, and she looked almost anguished with pleasure as she met each thrust. His heartbeat pounded in his head, and in his arousal, until . . . "Aw—aw, shit, honey—now."

The climax rushed through every molecule of his body, swallowing him, drenching him in sensation. And when finally it passed . . . damn. Two rounds of sex, after three full ball games—he was exhausted and collapsed gently onto her body.

"Was that outrageous enough for ya?" he rasped near her ear.

Rachel's whole body tingled as she watched him sleeping beside her. But she wasn't tired. She was . . . energized. Somehow the sex with Mike just kept getting better. And it had started off freaking *astounding*.

Glancing to the bedside clock, she could see it was nearly ten. And it had been a long time since she'd had to account to anyone for where she was at night, but it dawned on her that she should call Edna so she wouldn't worry.

She was pretty sure—even if she *hadn't* left her purse in Mike's truck—that there was no cell reception here anyway, and she didn't see a phone in the room, so she decided to ease away from him to go in search of one. Leaving the bed, she quietly snatched up Mike's loaner tee and slid it over her head.

Candles still burned in the kitchen, so she blew them out and switched on an overhead light, soon spotting an old wall phone with an old-fashioned dial. She didn't know anyone even had those anymore except for Edna. She put in Edna's number and waited as it rang.

"Hello?"

"It's me. Did I wake you?"

On the other end of the line, Edna sighed. "I'm old, not dead. It's not even ten o'clock."

Good point. She'd been living with Edna long enough to know her grandmother wasn't in the habit of dropping into bed until after the late news.

"Talk fast," Edna said, "'cause I'm busy watching this here Bret Michaels *Rock of Love* marathon."

Bret Michaels? Oh brother. So it was VH1 instead of MTV—close enough. But Rachel tried not to think about the things Edna was learning from *Rock of Love* and said, "I'm just calling to tell you . . . I don't think I'll be coming home tonight."

"Figured that."

"Why?" She'd stayed out this late with Tessa and Amy before and still come home. And on the night of the donkey ball game, too.

"'Cause why on God's green earth would ya wanna sleep alone when you can sleep with Mike Romo?"

Rachel's jaw dropped. But she decided not to admit to anything just yet. "What makes you think I'm with Mike?"

"'Cause I have caller ID, dummy."

Rachel just sighed. "You shun all other forms of modern technology, but you have caller ID?" Edna's old kitchen phone was the only one Rachel had used, so she'd apparently missed seeing a much newer one.

"Yep. Like to know who's callin' me. Especially when it's my granddaughter thinkin' she's about to put one over on me."

Bret Michaels and caller ID—who'd have thought?

After hanging up with Edna—who'd informed her the commercial was over and she had to go—Rachel moved wet clothes from the washer to the dryer, and experienced an odd thrill that bordered somewhere between erotic and domestic just from handling Mike's clothes. She felt the same way about wearing his T-shirt—it turned her on a little just to think of it being *his*, being close to his skin. *Good God, get hold of yourself, woman.*

Next, she went to the bathroom, and a glance in the mirror revealed . . . crazy hair. Especially now that it had dried while she'd been rolling around on a pillow during sex. She hadn't bothered washing it in the shower, thinking maybe it would retain some of its usual style if she left it alone, but clearly she'd been mistaken. And yet . . . the way Mike had looked at her, she'd have thought she was a beauty queen. She sighed, trying to fluff it a little, but then gave up. Because . . . apparently how her hair looked wasn't important to Mike. She usually paid so much attention to her appearance—only . . . maybe she was learning it didn't matter so much, at least not in Destiny, at least not with a guy who really liked you.

And he did. Like her. She knew that now, for sure. It was sex, but it was . . . more than that, too—whether or not she was mentally equipped to deal with it.

She next went about clearing the kitchen table and recorking the wine bottle, remembering how she'd felt when she'd first walked out to see the makeshift dinner he'd put together. All she'd really wanted was to know this was more than a wham-bam-thank-you-ma'am arrangement—and when she'd seen the candles and table-cloth, her heart had fluttered in her chest and it had been better than any five-star restaurant.

Walking through the living room to see if they'd left any other messes behind, she straightened some throw pillows on the couch, and now that the lights were on—shining in from the kitchen—she looked around the room. It was typical—typical furniture, typical widescreen TV, typical *Sports Illustrated* on the coffee table next to some un-opened mail. But it only took a few seconds before Rachel realized the one thing in the room that really stood out. The pictures.

They were on the mantel, and on bookshelves. They hung on walls. And it wasn't the number of them—maybe a dozen total—that struck her; it was the subject matter. His sister.

She didn't remember what Anna Romo had looked like, but she knew this was her. In some, the little dark-haired girl was alone—in others Rachel got to see Mike and his brother, Lucky, as kids with Anna, and their parents, too. In one, a younger Grandma Romo held Anna on her lap. But there were no *other* pictures. None of, say, Mike in his police officer's uniform, or more recent pictures of Mike or his parents. It was like the room was stuck in time, more than twenty years ago. Stuck in time—and in mourning.

As Rachel walked around studying each picture, her stomach went hollow. Because this was Mike's house. Mike's world. Strong, tough, brusque, capable Mike Romo. And sure, Amy had blamed his personality flaws on his past, but Rachel had just never dreamed he was . . . stuck there.

Padding on bare feet over the hardwood floor, Rachel stopped at the bedroom door and peeked in. Mike still appeared fast asleep. A dim lamp had lit the room during their sex and it still did now. And part of her wanted to turn out that lamp and crawl back into bed next to the man who'd just rocked her body into oblivion . . . but first—she couldn't help it, and she knew it was nosy and he'd probably want to kill her, yet she suffered the urge to look around a little more.

After all, he wasn't exactly a guy who went around pouring his heart out to anyone. If she wanted to know anything about Mike, she'd have to glean it on her own. And she felt she'd learned more about him tonight, since coming into this house, than ever before. Besides the pictures, there was just something about seeing a man's home, how he chose to live. With Mike, tonight, she'd learned that he liked things simple, utilitarian—but clean and even sort of homey. She'd learned he didn't place much stock in changing things. And she'd learned he was still heartbroken over Anna.

And to discover more, she found herself wandering back to the entryway, and glancing up the old, polished wooden stairs that led to the second floor. A wall switch turned on a light that invited her upward, and even though it officially felt like snooping now—something Rachel usually liked to think herself too mature to do—she slowly climbed the steps.

At the top, she found a short, wide hallway with five doors. Three were shut.

Walking to the first open one, to the left of the stairs, she looked in to find a simple bedroom with a double bed, dresser, and chest of drawers—clearly the spare bedroom where Mike had told her his parents sometimes stayed when they came home. He'd mentioned over dinner that it had been *his* room growing up. Now that she was here, she was a little sorry no remnants of

Mike's boyhood remained to give her more insights into her lover.

The other open door, directly across the hall, led to another bathroom.

Which left the closed doors.

And . . . it was *really* snoopy to go through someone's house opening doors, but . . . well, she wasn't planning to steal anything or trying to uncover any big secrets—so she decided to just think of it as self-guided tour.

The first closed door, at one end of the hall, turned out to be a linen closet filled with towels and cleaning supplies. Simple enough.

But when she opened the second closed door, to the right of the stairwell, she flipped on a light—and then let out a sigh. It was . . . Lucky's room. She'd barely known Lucky Romo, even though he'd been only a year ahead of her at Destiny High, yet it was easy to tell. Posters of motorcycles and rock bands and scantily clad girls papered the walls—no one had ever taken them down. Apparently, no one had ever changed *anything*. Atop an old desk in one corner lay a couple of magazines with fast-looking cars on the cover. In front of an old TV rested a black Harley-Davidson beanbag chair.

She was a little afraid to open the last door now. Because she almost knew what she would find. She just didn't want to believe it. She didn't want to believe that Mike's parents, and Mike now, too, had left Anna's room untouched. *Please don't let that be the case*. It had been over twenty years. But after seeing Lucky's room, it seemed inevitable.

Turning off the light in Lucky's bedroom, Rachel closed the door, then moved to the one across the hall, turning the knob and easing it open. She easily located the wall switch, illuminating a perfect little girl's room— decorated from top to bottom in a pink ballerina theme. A fluffy pink canopy covered the white bed. Stuffed animals and brightly colored pillows rested beneath it. A wallpaper border featuring ballet shoes circled the room, at just about the right height for a five-year-old girl to enjoy. And—oh Lord—a little pair of black patent leather shoes still sat on the floor next to a toy box.

Rachel almost couldn't breathe looking at it all. It was too much. And she knew that if she started opening drawers or the closet, she'd likely find little Anna Romo's dresses and play clothes and little socks and underwear. God, no wonder Mike's parents had had to leave—they'd . . . refused to let their daughter die. And they'd refused to accept Lucky's departure, too, apparently.

What she couldn't imagine, though, was being Mike. What had it been like for Mike and Lucky to live up here next to Anna's untouched room—to come home to it every day after school, to wake up to it every morning. And what had it been like for Mike after Lucky had finally left, too—to live up here alone . . . with the ghosts of his brother and sister? No wonder he was haunted by the loss.

As Rachel quietly walked back down the steps and turned out the upstairs light, she remained a little stunned. What she'd seen up there was so . . . horribly sad. It made her feel Mike's loss in a way that . . . possibly nothing else could have.

Catching her breath and feeling glad to be back downstairs, she walked over to a bookshelf and picked up one of the pictures there—this one of Anna and Mike. An adolescent Mike stooped down, putting his arm around her; she wore a Smurfs party hat and held up four fingers, apparently celebrating her birthday. *God, they couldn't have known what was coming. They couldn't have imagined there was anything but good times ahead.* Somehow, having just seen her room made her feel so much more real to Rachel than when she'd looked at the pictures a few minutes ago.

"Hey, Farris—get back here. I'm not done with you yet."

Rachel lifted her head to see Mike, rumpled and sexy as ever, coming from the bedroom, wearing nothing but a playful grin.

But when she looked up—maybe it was something in her eyes—he dropped his gaze to what she held in her hand.

She didn't know what to say. They'd only barely, briefly discussed Anna. And yet here she was, all around them.

All the humor left Mike's expression—suddenly he looked sad, almost childlike, and a little lost. Rachel's heart felt like it would burst as she whispered his name. "Mike . . ." And as she let her gaze sweep over all the many pictures around them. She hadn't quite meant to do that—but it seemed impossible to avoid at this moment.

Mike hadn't thought of this when he'd decided to bring Rachel here—the way his past, Anna, was plastered all over the house. Usually, no one came here except Logan, his parents when they were in town, or occasionally Grandma Romo. It made him feel painfully vulnerable, raw, for her to see just how open his wounds still were after all this time. And there was no way to hide it now, no way to put the lid back on the box that was his life.

"You still miss her," Rachel said.

He nodded. "Yeah." Yet all the pictures—somehow they required he say more. "But it's worse than that."

"Tell me," Rachel whispered, setting the frame she held back on the shelf. And she spoke in such a calm, sure, quiet way that he almost *wanted* to tell her. Everything. The whole story.

Only . . . he never had. He'd never told anyone. Except Logan. And that had been right when it had happened, when it was fresh, when everything was falling apart around him.

No one else had ever asked him for the story. No one else dared, he supposed. There were perks to being a gruff cop no one wanted to piss off.

But when he thought of telling her, his throat began to close up. It became difficult to swallow. Shit. What had he been thinking, bringing her here? He'd just done it . . . naturally. It had seemed easy, and right. He'd forgotten that Anna wallpapered his house almost as much as she wallpapered his heart.

"I . . ." he swallowed again, hard. "I can't, Rachel. I . . . can't get it out." Damn it. He hated how weak he sounded. Like the twelve-year-old kid who'd lost his little sister in the first place.

He realized he was looking down, at the Steelers logo on her shirt, so he made himself meet her gaze. And what he saw there was . . . compassion. True, deep compassion. Something he couldn't have imagined ever getting from Rachel Farris when they'd first met—but things had changed. Her voice came out warm, gentle, as she reached to take his hand. "I want to know the things that hurt you," she whispered.

"Why?" he asked, then found a little room for humor, albeit dark, as he leaned over, letting his forehead touch hers. "To torture us *both*?"

She returned the small smile he'd given her. Then bit her lip and said, "No, because . . . I care. About you. And it's probably good to . . . you know, get things off your chest once in a while."

It was sorely tempting to point out that the things she'd just said completely contradicted all her claims that this was only casual sex. Yet so had *a lot of things* that had happened tonight, and . . . well, he didn't want to argue with her right now, so he let it go. He let it go and he . . . soaked it up. Rachel Farris cared about him. Hearing that made something in his muscles, in his bones, feel stronger somehow.

And he still didn't know if he could get the whole damn story out, but to his surprise, again, he almost . . . wanted to. He didn't want to have to remember it, to relive it in all its painful details, but he . . . wanted her to know. What had happened to him.

"Come lie down with me," he said, low, then took her hand and led her back to bed. Together, they crawled under the sheets, pulled them up to their chests. He lay on his back, staring at the ceiling, listening to the rain. Rachel reached out beneath the covers, pressing her palm to his stomach—like silent encouragement. Or comfort. It gave him both.

"We used to camp a lot when I was a kid. The whole family." He glanced over at her—then stopped, swallowed, letting his mind go back there, *really* back there, to the day Anna disappeared. "We . . . we were camping at Bear Lake. It was just far enough from home to feel like we were someplace else, but not even an hour away. That day, after we set up the tents"—another tough swallow; shit, it was hard to talk about this—"Mom and Dad took the car to go get some ice and other stuff we needed, and they left me there with Lucky and Anna. I was the oldest, twelve—I was in charge of keeping an eye on them."

"Lucky was . . . ten, I guess?"

He nodded.

"And Anna?"

His heart wrenched, the same as if this had happened yesterday. "She'd just turned five."

Rachel propped on her elbow to peer down at him, and he tried to go on. But here was where it got . . . grim.

"We were camping in the woods, right next to a little cove, just off the road that circled the lake. It was hot out, and we were gonna go swimming—we were supposed to change into our bathing suits while Mom and Dad were gone and then wait until they came back before we got in the water."

He tried to glance up at Rachel, but he couldn't meet her eyes now—his chest felt like it was being crushed by some invisible weight. Yet he went on, trying to think

how to say this, trying to explain how it had happened so
fast, before he even knew it.

"After we all changed, Anna was playing around the
edge of the lake, wanting to go in. But I kept telling her
Mom and Dad had said to wait. And then . . ." He had
to stop, take a breath—breathing was challenging right
now. "Then I heard Lucky, off in the brush, away from the
campsite, excited about something, and calling me and
Anna over. So I said, 'Come on, Anna,' and then I went
into the bushes. Lucky had found a turtle."

*This was it. Right now. Crucial seconds passing. While
he looked at a fucking turtle.*

His breath grew labored when he opened his mouth to
continue—and he finally summoned the courage to meet
Rachel's eyes. "That's when I lost her, that's when she
disappeared. When I was in the trees looking at a goddamn turtle."

And after that, he talked a little faster, to get it out, get
through it. "When she didn't follow us, we both yelled
for her—I remember thinking she'd either love the turtle
or be scared of it, but I was surprised she wasn't answering. So I told Lucky we'd better go get her, and I had that
feeling of 'I know everything's fine, but I better check
just to be sure.' And I thought I would walk back into the
campsite and see her still sitting at the edge of the lake
throwing pebbles in the water. But she wasn't there."

He shook his head against the pillow, and his heart
raced, just like that day. "She wasn't there. But we weren't
scared yet—we just figured she'd found somewhere else
to play. So we're calling her name and we're both walking
around the campsite, looking around, looking in the tent.
And soon I'm saying, 'This isn't funny, Anna—you better
come out from wherever you are.' "

He stopped then, remembering the moment—the first
real hints of fear, the first real sense that something was
hideously wrong. "But she didn't come out. We looked

everywhere—all around the edge of the lake and in the trees and bushes. Lucky and I both got all scratched up by thorns because we were only wearing swim trunks and tennis shoes. But no matter where we looked or how many times we called her name, she never came. Ever. She was just . . . gone.

"We never heard a sound, we never saw anything—not a ripple in the water or footsteps in the dirt or any scrap of her bathing suit. It was like she literally vanished, *that fast*." He snapped his fingers.

Above him, Rachel just sighed, looking nearly as lost as he'd felt at the time.

And then he started to feel that angry-at-himself guilt that had been eating him alive all these years. "You know, your parents give you one simple job—watch the other kids for half an hour. But could I do that? Could I actually keep an eye on 'em?"

"It's not your fault," she said, leaning nearer, touching his face with her soft hand. "You were a little boy, and even most *parents* don't watch their kids *that* closely."

"Next to a lake?" he asked skeptically. "I think they do." He'd heard the it's-not-your-fault thing before, and it was nice of people to say—but it *was* his fault.

"That's what you think happened?" she whispered. "You think she wandered into the lake?"

Mike drew in a deep breath. It was the question that haunted him. "It makes sense," he said. "It's the only thing that really does."

"But the water wasn't moving at all when you came back? And it had only been a few minutes, right?"

He nodded. "Believe me, honey—I've thought through this, probably thousands of times now. Hell—maybe *hundreds* of thousands. The water wasn't moving. It didn't even occur to me until later that she might have gone in. Because she was a good little girl. She might complain, but she didn't do things she wasn't supposed to. It was only when Mom and Dad came back, and then later, with the police, that it came up. And it seemed like the most logical answer."

Rachel looked troubled as she asked, "Did they . . . look? In the water?"

He nodded once more. "They dragged the lake the next day. They didn't find anything—but they came across deep pockets of water just beyond our shallow swimming area, and a lot of debris under the surface—chunks of trees and other stuff the rescue workers felt her body could have gotten trapped under. So most people still figured it was likely she drowned."

"I guess," Rachel offered, "if she'd just roamed away, someone would have found her."

"Yeah—and she'd have heard us calling."

"Were there any other theories?"

Mike shrugged against his pillow. "A few minutes after she disappeared, Lucky and I heard a loud, fast car racing by on the road just above the campsite. We never saw it through the woods, and we weren't paying much attention because we were freaking out by then—but I remember thinking, 'What if she wandered up onto the road and that speeding car hit her?' I told the cops that, so they checked the whole area. In fact, people searched the woods all night and into the next day. A lot of people from Destiny even came over to help when they heard.

"Another theory was that somebody snatched her. A lot of that was going on back then—kids being taken from amusement parks and shopping malls. But"—he gave his head another shake—"I never really believed that could've happened, because we were so close. And we never heard *anything*. If somebody took her, they were silent as death and fast as lightning."

"So then, you . . . you personally think she drowned."

Mike stayed quiet. Like he'd told her, he'd turned it all over in his head until he almost couldn't make sense of it anymore. And it never got any easier, or more conclusive. "I don't know *what* I think. Because I was twelve. I'm not sure how good my judgment was, you know?" He glanced up at her. Most people didn't make what turned out to be critical life-or-death decisions at twelve. "So there's a part of me that thinks anything could have happened. She could have walked away and gotten lost. She could have been kidnapped. She could have drowned." He took another deep breath—and then he told Rachel what he'd never told anybody, not even Logan. "But sometimes I . . . take some *peace* in thinking she drowned. Sometimes I hope that's what happened."

Rachel flinched at the words, and he understood—they required explanation.

"Because it's a fairly quick, painless death," he said softly. "If somebody took her . . ." Shit, he *hated* thinking about that, hated the idea that it was even a possibility. "If somebody took her, it was probably much worse." Quick, awful visions flashed through his mind: rape, torture, mutilation. A child's body being dumped somewhere. Mike had to shut his eyes and take a deep, slow breath in order to banish the images. "But if she drowned, it was over fast, and maybe she never even knew it was coming."

When he peered up at Rachel, she looked saddened, nibbling her lip pensively. "You think she wouldn't know, wouldn't realize?"

"*I* almost drowned when I was her age," he volunteered. "In Blue Valley Lake." Mike explained that one of his uncles had owned a house on the water back then, and that the Romo clan had gathered there for the Fourth of July one year. "We were swimming off the dock, then all got out to eat lunch. When I was done, I was so eager to go back in that I slipped away without anybody noticing. I got in the water by myself—and forgot my life jacket."

Rachel gasped, but Mike was so lost in the memory

now, the strangeness of it, that he kept right on talking. "I was swimming around—making the motions anyway—but I was gradually drifting under the water, deeper and deeper. It was . . . the damnedest thing." He shook his head softly. "I wasn't afraid. I wasn't worried. I didn't realize anything bad was happening. I guess I was so little that I just . . . didn't have those kinds of fears yet. I remember opening my eyes underwater and seeing different colors—probably from the sun shining down through it. I was completely at ease.

"I don't know how long I was down there—not too long, I guess, or I'd be dead—but then something bumped my shoulder, and the next thing I knew, one of my aunts hauled me up to the surface. She'd just decided to jump back in, too, and happened to kick me with her foot. The timing was pretty amazing. And then the whole family freaked out and nearly crushed me with hugs—and gave me the scolding of my life.

"But the point is . . . maybe kids that little don't have a fear of drowning yet, and maybe that makes it . . . completely peaceful. They say, even as an adult, that you eventually just shut your eyes and go to sleep. It just sounds like . . . well, not a bad way to go, if you have to go at all. I know I'll never get over losing her, I'll never get over the guilt—but if I knew for sure she died peacefully, it would help."

Next to him, Rachel looked wrung out with emotion—but also suddenly . . . adamant. "No, Mike," she said then, shaking her head, "the point *is* . . . when you went into the water, *they weren't watching you*. Not your parents, not your whole extended family. And it doesn't mean they didn't love you—it just happened. It *happens*. Which means losing Anna wasn't your fault."

Mike let out a long breath. Damn. She was right—no one had been watching him, either. He couldn't believe it, but he'd never thought about that before.

Still . . . "That doesn't absolve me, Rachel. It just means they were guilty for a few minutes, too. And if I *had* drowned, they'd probably feel like *I* feel about Anna."

Above him, she tilted her pretty head. "I'm just saying—it really can happen to anyone. Even the best, most attentive parents can look away for a minute."

He nodded in concession. "You're right. I know, logically, you're right. And believe me, my mom and dad have tried to make me get that, too. In fact, I try like hell not to let them see the way it still bothers me. But what it comes down to is . . ." He stopped, peered up at her. "My whole world changed that day, and nothing has ever felt right, really *right*, since then."

Rachel pursed her lips, looking a little bewildered, then finally she said, "Why didn't you leave, Mike? With your parents? I know you said there was no reason to, but . . . I think there was. Doing what they did, starting over someplace new, could maybe help you . . . distance yourself from it. Even just leaving this house—you know?"

Mike only sighed. He knew good and well why he hadn't left Destiny. He'd seriously considered it, many times—when Lucky took off, when his parents moved, and even a few times since then. But there were . . . things he had to do here.

"I didn't leave," he said, "because . . . I guess I feel responsible for keeping Destiny safe. I couldn't keep Anna safe—but if I can keep other people here safe, it makes me feel like I'm doing something worthwhile. It's like . . ."

"Penance?" she suggested.

But he shook his head. That wasn't it at all. "No, it's like . . . an apology. To Anna. For not protecting her. And . . . and . . ." His chest deflated and he had to shut his eyes, tight, to keep the sudden wetness there from leaking free. There was more truth hiding inside him. The truth he'd never let out. Maybe not even to himself.

"What, Mike?" Rachel whispered, touching his arm.

He shook his head vehemently now against the pillow, feeling too much. To leave Destiny . . . would be to close a very big door. It would be to admit . . . to admit what he knew, what he'd known his whole life—that Anna wasn't coming back. And it was one thing to know it—but another thing to truly accept it deep inside.

"I know she's gone. I know she's dead. I *know* that." He forced his eyes open then, forced himself to meet Rachel's. "But . . . what if I'm wrong? What if . . . what if she came back? What if she came back home and I wasn't here?"

What say you? Can you love the gentleman?

William Shakespeare, *Romeo & Juliet*

Fourteen

Oh, Mike," she whispered. Just that, nothing more.

And he realized he'd just given voice to the most crazy, illogical thought in his head. Jesus Christ. What was he thinking? What had come over him? Since when did he spill his guts—to anybody? Shit—he didn't even know he was capable of that. But apparently he was, and he'd just spilled it all to Rachel Farris.

Damn, a part of him felt so weak, so . . . vulnerable. And he *never* let himself feel that way—*never*.

Except for maybe . . . when he was with Rachel.

This was a whole different kind of vulnerability, but from nearly the moment they'd met, she'd knocked him off balance, taken away his self-control. And now he'd just let her see . . . what no one else saw. That there was some insane part of him that still believed Anna could come home more than twenty years later.

"I know that can't happen," he felt the need to tell her, trying to sound more like his usual gruff, commanding self. "I get that. So don't think I'm some kind of a nut, okay?"

She shook her head, still looking sweet and compassionate. "I don't think you're a nut, Mike."

And he wanted to keep being that tough guy—the guy he usually was, the guy he *really* was—but his voice softened again anyway as he realized, "I guess it's just the twelve-year-old kid in me who keeps thinking some kind of miracle could happen. It makes no fucking sense, I know. It's not even really real—it's just the way I felt that day, running around the lake calling for her. There was still . . . *hope* then. *Hope* that the worst hadn't happened. And if I left Destiny, then I would be . . . sure. Certain. That she could never, ever, ever come back. And I guess my mom and dad reached the point where they were ready to be sure. Deep down inside. But maybe I'm just not quite there yet. Maybe I never *will* be. Maybe I just need that last, stupid, tiny little ounce of hope, you know?"

"I know," she whispered, surprising him. "I get it. I get needing hope."

No more arguments from her suddenly. No more advice about what would be good for him. Just acceptance. And that was all he could ask for.

"Thank you," he murmured softly, then lifted his hand to her face and leaned up to give her a small kiss.

After that, they didn't talk anymore, and Mike was glad. He'd said far too much already. It was much easier to stop thinking now, easier to just concentrate on holding Rachel as she eased snugly into his arms. He let them close warmly around her—then reached up one hand to turn off the bedside lamp, bathing the room in darkness.

There, that was better.

No more bad memories or regrets. No more pictures of Anna keeping his illogical hopes alive at the same time that they broke his heart. No more anything—except for the warmth of a beautiful woman in his arms.

He hadn't thought ahead to this part, that she'd likely be staying the night. But she couldn't exactly leave without a car, could she? And she seemed content enough about it. And to Mike's surprise, so was he.

Rachel awoke the next morning with Mike's body spooning hers, his hand loosely cupping her breast through her T-shirt. Mmm, she liked that—everything about the moment felt warm and cozy, right down to the sound of the rain still falling outside.

Funny, in Chicago, she hated rain. It meant getting soaked on the way to work, hoping it didn't ruin her shoes, fighting with umbrellas on the sidewalk. This was the only time she could ever remember the rain making her feel so . . . warm. Kind of cocooned here with Mike in the house.

Daylight shone through closed shades, and she opened her eyes and glanced around without moving. She didn't particular want to wake him yet. She didn't want him to move his hand.

But then she remembered everything he'd confided in her last night. Oh, what a difference a day made. She knew the deepest pains of Mike's heart now, and her own heart contracted just thinking about it. She'd felt helpless to ease his hurt and had just wished she could somehow take it all away. But she knew, already, instinctively, nothing within her power could ever do that. It ran too deep. He was a man wrought with guilt and regret—all she could do was . . . care about him.

Wow, she'd told him that. That she cared about him. Maybe for some people, that wouldn't be a big deal. But for her, especially with Mike Romo, it was. A few short weeks ago, just being attracted to a guy whose last name was Romo—at one time the worst four-letter word any Farris could utter—had seemed unthinkable. Not to mention having sex with him. And telling herself over and over that it was only physical had somehow helped her accept it.

But now—well, turned out it wasn't so horrible. To care for a guy. To even *admit* caring for him—to him and to herself. In fact, it probably accounted for all the warm fuzzies rippling through her right now. And the more time that passed, the less it mattered that his name was Romo. Even the idea of him buying the orchard someday—while it still stung—no longer held the horror it had only a week or two ago.

"You awake?" Even the raspy, sleepy-sounding voice near her ear made her a little melty inside.

"Mmm-hmm. Sort of." She'd been enjoying that lull of not quite being fully wakeful yet.

"What do you smell like?" he murmured.

She flinched and glanced over her shoulder. "Huh?"

"You always smell good and I've wondered for weeks— what is it?"

Oh. Well, when he put it that way, the question was much more appealing. "Is it my shampoo? Mango?" Despite all her hair had been through since yesterday, maybe the scent had stayed with her.

He snuggled a little tighter against her, burying his face in her tresses. "Hmm. Mango. Yeah. It's nice. You should never wash your hair in anything else, Farris."

For some reason, his words turned her warmer than she already was. "Thanks," she whispered. "I won't." And now, because of this, she really wouldn't.

"You in the mood for pancakes?"

Even though Rachel hadn't wanted to leave the bed just yet, she tilted her head a bit deeper into the pillow, liking the suggestion anyway. "Um . . . yeah, I could go for some pancakes."

Half an hour later, they stood over the griddle on Mike's stove while Jack Johnson's smooth voice echoed softly from the bedroom, accompanying the rain as he sang about banana pancakes. Rachel watched as Mike, looking scrumptious in a pair of boxer briefs, poured four perfect round blobs of batter—and she used a wooden spoon to keep it from dripping from the spouted bowl. After which Mike set down the mixture and drew her into a loose embrace.

Mmm, being held by him was becoming one of her very favorite things. She pressed her palms lightly against his muscled chest and tilted her head up to receive his kiss. His gaze shone all sexy, as usual, and it was all she could do not to moan.

"Um, about last night," he said then.

"What about it?"

"I . . . don't usually tell people that stuff." Oh. Well, she knew that. But the look in his eyes said a lot more. Like *I trusted you completely* and *Please don't tell anyone.*

"Don't worry—I'm not a blabbermouth," she promised. Of course, sometimes she *was* a blabbermouth, particularly with Tessa and Amy. But she wouldn't be—not about this. Just as she hadn't told them about Edna and Giovanni, either.

"And, uh, don't expect me to be all open and talkative like that all the time." He lowered his chin, adding, almost as if to himself, "Maybe never again."

Ah—he was embarrassed. Despite the gravity of what he'd shared with her, his sheepishness was almost cute, especially on such a normally brusque guy. Rachel held back her smile and simply said, "Understood."

"Good." Mike drew his gaze from her then to peer out the window above the sink. "Rain doesn't seem to be stopping."

"Nope," she agreed, arms looped around his neck now.

He brought his focus back to her. "You, uh, have anywhere you need to be today?"

"Well, Sunday is a 'pick your own' day at the orchard, but there won't be any day-trippers out in this weather. And Edna keeps urging me to take weekend days off anyway, probably afraid I'll get apple burnout. Why?"

Giving his head a thoughtful tilt, he replied, "Because I don't, either, so . . . after we eat, maybe we should just go back to bed for a while."

Rachel bit her lip, her inner thighs already aching for him. "To sleep? Or to . . . ?"

The grin he flashed was at once sweet and wicked. "Both."

Mmm. Sounded good to her. So she lifted a quick kiss to his mouth and said, "Hurry up with those pancakes, Romo."

It was late that afternoon before Mike drove Rachel home. Everything outside still glistened and smelled of fresh rain, but the last drizzle had finally stopped, letting the sun burst through the clouds. As they wended their way toward the orchard, Rachel sat up close against him in the truck, a habit she'd picked up that he liked. It was chillier out than yesterday, so he'd given her a big, warm flannel shirt to put over the little yellow top she'd worn to the ball games.

"*Really?*" she'd said, scowling, when he offered it to her a few minutes earlier. "You want me to wear *that*?"

He'd just shaken his head. "Don't worry, Farris, no one will see you."

"*You* will."

"And I'll still think you're sexy as hell. Promise."

"You didn't think I was sexy in Edna's smock," she pointed out.

"Well, that was awful. This isn't so bad. Trust me."

"All right," she'd finally conceded with a sigh, and now he couldn't help thinking she looked pretty cute all wrapped up in his flannel.

He still regretted how open he'd been with her last night, just because . . . he wasn't like that, and he'd never before felt compelled to trust a woman that way. But she'd said no more about it, which he appreciated—and he'd almost forgotten it all when they'd gone back to bed after breakfast, when he'd been moving inside her again, making her moan her pleasure.

When he was thrusting hotly into her warmth, he didn't feel weak *or* vulnerable—no way. Nope, in those moments, he went back to being Tarzan. Funny, when he'd first suffered that overpowering lust for her, the fact that he couldn't restrain it had left him feeling . . . defenseless. Before her, he'd been accustomed to having a firm command over most everything in his life. But once he'd started getting used to it, to *her*, all those negative feelings had finally fled, leaving nothing but good, hot ones behind. Losing control, it turned out, wasn't always such a bad thing. If he hadn't lost control with Rachel in the first place, he wouldn't know how good it felt to be deep, deep inside her.

And he was starting to think he had a pretty damn good thing going with her. It couldn't go much *further*, of course—since she'd be leaving soon—but he planned to enjoy her while he had her.

"Oh, look at the trees," Rachel said as they drove back past Creekside Park. Mike had noticed, too, that the fall colors had deepened, brightened, just over the past couple of days. Autumn was here in earnest now, and winter lay just around the corner.

But it wasn't winter yet—and Rachel still had apples to pick before she could go back to Chicago. So as they drove across Sugar Creek to the orchard, he asked, "If I make plans to see you again, you won't freak out and accuse me of inducing romance or anything, will you?"

"No," she said softly. Just that, nothing more.

Of course, this *was* romance now. But if she still didn't want to acknowledge that, he'd let her have her way.

Pulling the truck up beside her 325i, he said, "Well then, I'm invited to a big bonfire Friday night at the Schusters' pumpkin farm. If you want to go with me. Bob and Mary

Schuster were friends with Logan's family when we were growing up, and I know them pretty well, too. There'll be a hayride, marshmallow roasting, that sort of thing. It's usually a nice night." He turned to peer down at her, his next words half teasing, half serious. "Unless it sounds too boring for a big city girl like you."

Rachel shook her head and smiled. "I'd love to go. And I'm *never* bored with you, Romeo."

As Rachel pulled up outside Under the Covers, her arms ached. And as she got out of the car, the arches of her feet hurt and she suddenly regretted wearing her carmel-colored Prada boots. It was Wednesday night and the last few days had been busy—she'd picked so many apples she was seeing them in her sleep. And when she wasn't picking them, she was wrapping them in newspaper and stacking them in the root cellar.

First thing Monday morning, Edna had informed her it was officially crunch time, so when Amy had called about getting together, Rachel had explained she couldn't take time away for any more lunches—they'd have to do dinner instead. Now, as she pushed through the bookstore's door, making the overhead bell jingle, the muscles in her back complained, too, and she felt happy to get away from apples for a while—but the truth was, despite her aches and pains, she was gratified by the work. By helping Edna. By just *being* with Edna.

"Is that you, Rach? I'm in the back," Amy called.

"Yep, it's me."

"Can you lock the door and turn the Closed sign around in the window?"

"Sure," Rachel said, flipping both the lock and the cheerful sign, decorated with flowers done in felt tip pen. She couldn't help smiling—only Amy would find a way to make being closed look so merry.

"I'm just shelving some new arrivals in the romance section, but I'll be right out. Tessa is meeting us at Dolly's. Sit down and play with Shakespeare or something," she suggested.

As if on cue, that's when her old buddy, Shakespeare, silently appeared from between two bookshelves. The fat cat looked up at her and said, "Meow."

"Hi," she whispered down to him, not particularly wanting Amy to hear her greet the cat. And the second Rachel took a seat in one of the easy chairs near the door, he hopped up into her lap as easily as if he belonged there, as if they did this together all the time. It *was* sort of becoming a habit, though, she supposed. He plopped his wide body down across her denim-covered thighs, paying no attention to the fact that he knocked her purse to the floor.

She simply shook her head at him, stuck somewhere between annoyance and affection, and said, softly, "You're a pushy guy, but I like you."

So . . . *maybe that means I like pushy guys, since I like Mike, too.*

Or maybe I like you because I'm *kind of pushy.*

Whatever. She stopped analyzing it and scratched behind the tabby's ears. She and Mike had pushed each other all the *wrong* ways at first, but now they were definitely pushing each other in the *right* ways.

Four days after her admission that she cared for him, she still felt that way, so strongly that sometimes her chest tightened and her stomach churned. And she was no longer in denial or upset about it, despite it being the first time in her life she'd felt this way. She'd just always been so single-minded about her career that romance hadn't been on her personal radar screen—she'd dated, even had boyfriends, but she'd never fallen for them like her girlfriends had. Until now.

But she'd decided she'd die before admitting this to anyone—like Edna, or the girls. Give them *that* little piece of info and they'd latch onto it and never let go, like a bunch of rabid dogs.

Just then, Amy appeared, pretty and perky in a pumpkin-colored sweater. She instantly bit her lip, looking impatient. "Okay, I know I should wait for Tessa, but I can't. What happened to you and Mike after the softball tournament?"

Rachel just smiled—she couldn't *not* smile. "He didn't want to go to the Whippy Dip."

"Where did he want to go?"

"His place."

Amy's eyebrows lifted. "Where I guess you engaged in wild sex all night long?"

"Something like that," Rachel said, trying to look more turned-on than melty inside. Given that she was currently both, it was just a matter of getting rid of the melty.

"And you're still trying to tell me it's completely meaningless?"

Hmm—she wasn't pulling it off? Could Amy see through her façade? "Of course," she said anyway.

Amy crossed her arms. "I don't believe you. You took too long to answer."

Crap.

But then Rachel remembered who she was. Not this mushy girl who got all gooey over a guy. "Well, believe it. Mike Romo is great in bed and it's the one place where we completely get along. So that's all there is to it, Ames."

Yeah, sure, that was all a lie now—but she really needed to start putting this back in perspective. Not just in her words, but even in her mind. It was a temporary affair—his life was here, and hers wasn't. And besides the fact that she didn't believe in long-distance relationships, it was a leap to even assume he'd be interested in more anyway. Because Mike was like her—he didn't fall in love.

Sex and some really great talks—that's what they'd shared and it was good stuff. *Very* good stuff. And maybe, when it was all over, it would be good to have finally fallen for a guy. She was thirty-two, after all. And this was . . . a life experience, one perhaps every woman should have.

But even as nice as this was becoming, she'd be leaving soon, and then all this caring business would be behind her, and that would *also* be good. Since the truth was, she wasn't quite sure how to be the Rachel Farris she'd always been and care about Mike Romo at the same time.

So she would let herself have this right now, but she'd also be careful not to let herself get sucked in too deep. And the way she felt for Mike would remain her little secret. It would make their time together more special. And it would make the sex even more spectacular. But then she'd put it away, like an old letter or a favorite book, and it would be done. That simple.

When Friday night rolled around, ushering in the last weekend of September, Mike showed up at the orchard in Giovanni's convertible again. As Edna's eyes lit up at the sight of it, Rachel reminded her, "You've got a story to finish, you know." They'd been working so hard, Edna hadn't given her any new installments lately.

"Shush, girl," Edna told her, still spying the car out the window. "I'm busy relivin' my youth."

The warm evening allowed them to leave the top down on the long ride out to the Schusters' place; orange and gold leaves covered the road in spots, swirling around the car as Mike drove through them.

The bonfire was everything Mike had promised. Logan was there, with a girl from Crestview, and Rachel was reintroduced to a few other people she hadn't seen since leaving Destiny. They all asked about her parents, or commented on always getting apples from Edna, and it reminded her how kind people here could be, and how instantly accepting of you when you came back.

Friendly pumpkins sat in large stacks alongside the road and barn at the Schuster farm, so even though they weren't officially open for business during the party, Rachel bought a few for Edna's front porch, stowing them in Mike's trunk. The irony struck her that, fifty years later, she was carrying pumpkins to Edna in Giovanni's car.

The hayride around the farm came with rich autumn colors, even in the dusk, and the crisp smell of fall scented the air. Then hamburgers and hot dogs were grilled, and after dark, late-season fireflies lit up the night. Kids ran around playing, screaming, trying to catch them, as the grown-ups settled in a circle around the large fire Mr. Schuster built.

Rachel hadn't done anything like this since her youth, and yet, for her, the odd part was . . . that it didn't seem odd. Maybe she was getting used to small town life again. She'd even worn gym shoes without anyone telling her to. Although she topped her jeans with a cute short-sleeved sweater, convinced she could be casual and stylish at the same time.

After Mike fashioned marshmallow roasting sticks from branches, they debated the best method for cooking them.

"Oh God, you're one of those people who lets them catch on fire?" Rachel asked, aghast.

"Dude, that's against the fire code," Logan said, straight-faced, then cracked a grin. After which he challenged them to each eat a marshmallow cooked by the other.

So while Mike ate the gooey, lightly browned marshmallow from the end of *her* stick, she was forced to eat the burnt, blackened one *he'd* prepared. Fearing for her taste buds, she waited for it to cool, then held the ruined marshmallow carefully between her fingers and took a small bite. And was horrified to have to admit, "Wow—that's not awful."

Mike gave a triumphant nod, then ate her

marshmallow—which produced a big sneer on his face. "And that was nothing but a glob of goo. A waste of a perfectly good marshmallow, Farris."

She widened her eyes on him. "Marshmallows *are* globs of goo, Romo."

Soon enough, the air turned brisk and people broke out chocolate and graham crackers for s'mores. A friend of the Schusters played a guitar and sang. And when Mike returned from talking with Mr. Schuster, whom he'd seen admiring the Cadillac, he sat down and wrapped his arms around Rachel from behind.

She bit her lip in response—mmm, cozy. She couldn't help turning to look at his handsome face, so close to hers, and in return, he gave her a little kiss.

"You're freezing," he said, rubbing his hands along her lower arms.

She shrugged it off. "Freezing is a strong word. Chilly would be more accurate."

He just gave his head a dubious shake. "What is it with you and clothes, Farris? Why are you never dressed for the weather?"

"I *was* dressed for the weather, last weekend and tonight, too. But then the weather *changed*. And I almost brought my pashmina, but it didn't seem . . . bonfire-ish."

He simply cast an indulgent smile, then leaned back to begin unzipping the navy blue hoody he wore.

It was a sweet, gentlemanly gesture, but Rachel said, "Don't give me your hoody—then *you'll* be cold."

"So?"

"Well, who'll keep *me* warm then?"

Mike ignored her and draped the hoody around her shoulders. "Put this on and zip up," he said. "I wore a warm enough shirt underneath."

True, he had on something made of waffle weave that looked pretty snuggly. "Thanks," she whispered, figuring there was no use in arguing. Then reclined back against him again, happy when his arms folded around her once more.

Although when had she started getting into things that were *cozy*? And how did Mike make hoodies and waffle weave look so completely sexy?

She didn't know the answers—but she forgot about the questions when he pulled her closer, resting his head against hers as they listened to the guitar player sing a romantic old James Taylor song, "Something in the Way She Moves."

As she listened to the lyrics, however, something strange began to happen inside her. She began to feel . . . out of sorts, emotional, and like . . . well, like she could cry.

Again? With the crying? Oh God—what was *that* about?

Since she *didn't* cry, she pushed the unidentified emotions back. But . . . did she want that? Did she want a man to feel about her the way the guy in the song felt? Another question that had no answer.

So she leaned her head back into Mike's shoulder and found herself gazing up at the dark sky—clear tonight, filled with countless twinkling stars. It reminded her once more of her youth here, of being able to look up and see the heavens, since in the city . . . well, she wasn't sure she'd seen many stars in the years since she'd left Destiny. She'd never before appreciated the night sky so much, and maybe she suddenly had some idea why Jenny was so caught up in it.

When the song ended, Mike gently kissed her cheek and she turned to meet his sexy eyes.

"Wanna head home?" he whispered.

"Home?" she asked for clarification.

"*My* home."

She just nodded, feeling strangely dreamy inside and

very ready to be with him—in a way she couldn't be in public.

As they got in the car a few minutes later, Mike started to put the top up, but Rachel stopped him. "Wait. Can we leave it down?"

"We'll freeze to death."

And yes, it was cold now, but . . . "The stars are so bright tonight. Couldn't we just drive slow and look at the sky?"

Mike appeared hesitant, like he thought it was impractical, but finally said, "Okay, honey—if that's what you want."

So they meandered along the twisting, turning roads, and Rachel tipped her head back and took in all the points of light shimmering above them like diamonds. Mike's iPod played Nick Drake's "Pink Moon," and though she'd been wondering for years now what it was about, what the pink moon in the song represented, suddenly she thought she might know. She could scarcely give it a word in her mind, though. It was too scary that she was even *thinking* about that word right now. It was another four-letter one, and it started with L, and, for Rachel, was far worse than Romo.

So she had to change her thoughts, quick.

Smiling up at Mike, she cuddled a little closer. "For a Romo, you have good taste in music." Her own choices had always been just a little left of current pop trends—one more rebellion against small town life, she supposed—and she'd noticed Mike's musical selections were often similar to hers.

"For a Farris," he said, "you have good taste in men."

She cast a playful smirk in reply, but when she saw again how damn sexy he looked and how close he was to her, when she drank in that scent of his that was like a mating call to her, she couldn't help leaning over to kiss him.

He returned it warmly—before grousing, "Are you trying to make me wreck the car?"

"No, I'm trying to make you hurry," she explained, placing a hand on his thigh. Because just that one kiss had lifted the level of her desire from smoldering to blazing.

He sucked in his breath. "What happened to driving slow so we won't freeze?"

Reaching down, she found the heat controls and turned them on high. "There—it won't matter now."

He simply cast her a firm look of warning. "I won't speed, honey—even for sex."

Oh, for crying out loud. Rachel wanted him, suddenly, badly—and he was concerned about a little speeding?

She held in her growl of protest, though, and went straight to the heart of the matter—she moved her touch upward, pressing her palm to the bulge between his legs. Mmm, he was half hard already, and as usual, got harder the second her hand molded to him through his blue jeans.

"Shit," Mike muttered—then pressed down on the gas, gunning the car forward. "Damn it, woman, you're a bad influence on me."

"That's what you get for hanging out with a Farris," she said, then couldn't hold back a victorious little grin. Because she was making Mike Romo break laws again.

By the time they got home, Rachel was nearly feverish with want. Mike had sped, but not by much, and now he was actually taking the time to pull the car slowly into a garage to one side of the house. "Are you kidding me?" she asked, massaging him through his jeans.

His breath came heavy, but he still remained practical Mike Romo. "It's a vintage Cadillac, Rachel. You don't just leave a car like this out in the elements."

"What elements?" She motioned skyward with her free hand. "It's a beautiful night!"

"I'll show you a beautiful night in a minute—if you'll be quiet and let me pull the damn car in."

She bit her lip—both in impatience and to try to shut up. She never liked letting Mike or anyone else boss her around, but she was dying to get him naked, so it inspired her silence.

Within moments, Mike was jabbing the key in the lock and they were nearly falling through the front door. "Finally," she breathed.

And he said, "Shut up and kiss me."

As Mike's arms came around her, Rachel lifted her hands to his stubbled cheeks and met his mouth with hers. They exchanged frantic tongue kisses and she nearly melted to the floor just from having that one small part of him inside her.

They inched their way toward the bedroom as they made out with wild abandon, and the next thing Rachel knew, Mike was shoving his hoody from her shoulders and grabbing at the bottom of her sweater. She lifted her arms, then stopped kissing him just long enough to let him rip it off over her head. He let out a low groan at the sight of her bra—a lacy lavender confection she'd selected with him in mind—then he yanked the straps from her shoulders.

That's when it hit her—a weird, shocking urge. "Wait," she said, pressing her palms to his chest and taking a step back.

"What is it?" he asked, obviously frustrated. "I thought you wanted me to hurry. Now *I* want to hurry, too."

Breathless from the heat between them, Rachel tried to explain herself—even as she attempted to dissect her own feelings. "I just . . ." She shook her head. "I *was* in a hurry to get started, but now that we're here . . ."

"What?" he asked, exasperated.

What it came down to was—a lot of the sex she'd experienced had borne similarities to this. Rushing through the door for a frantic coupling that was over too fast. And sure, that didn't mean there couldn't be a round two, but . . . "I like it most when we go slow, when we take our time." She bit her lip, knowing that the best sex of her life had been slow, steamy sex with Mike. "You do slow *good*," she said, her voice dropping.

In response, Mike let out a breath, but didn't argue. In fact, he said, "You're right. With us, slow *is* good. With us, slow is . . . amazing."

But in the time it had taken to have the conversation, Rachel's body had started going crazy again. Because he wasn't touching her or kissing her anymore. Her breasts burned for his hands, and the spot between her legs pulsed desperately.

Which meant . . . mother of God, what had she been thinking? "Wait, I was wrong. Let's hurry!"

She reached for him again, back to being as eager as when they'd burst through the door—only to have Mike grasp both her wrists, holding her back. "No—you want to take our time, we'll take our time."

Oh brother. "Are you crazy? Since when do you listen to me? I clearly don't know what I'm talking about." And with that, she ripped her arms free and went for his waistband, hurriedly undoing his jeans and lowering the zipper.

But Mike grabbed her arms *again*. "Seriously—slow down, Farris."

"I told you—I changed my mind. We can go slow later. Now I want fast."

Her pleas didn't matter, though—Mike just shook his head and sounded completely sure when he said, "Too late for that."

Rachel drew in an aggravated breath—and ignored him. The second he released her from his grip, she reached for his jeans once more.

Only to have Mike grab back onto her wrists. "Fine," he growled. "I'll *make* you slow down."

Oh yeah? She lifted her gaze to his, feeling challenged,

and this time she couldn't ignore the urge to fight back. "I'd like to see you *make* me do anything."

In response, Mike did what he'd done once before—he picked her up, tossed her over his shoulder, carried her to the bedroom, and dropped her on the bed.

Okay, this was more like it. Now they were going to get down to business.

Breathing heavily, Rachel smiled eagerly up at him, sweet relief mingling with fervent anticipation inside her, until . . . he reached for something near his bedside table, grabbed her wrists yet one more time, pulled them up over her head, and—*click*.

She leaned back and looked up. Son of a bitch. He'd handcuffed her to the bed.

If love be rough with you, be rough with love.

William Shakespeare, *Romeo & Juliet*

Fifteen

*M*ike took in her startled look, watching as it changed into something . . . better.

"Oh. Wow. Kinky," she said.

He grinned. "Just slowing you down, Farris. You wanted to go slow, we're going slow—whether you like it or not."

She tilted her head, casting a saucy look. "Is this what you do to all speeders?"

"Only the hot ones."

After that, Mike shed his thermal pullover and got on the bed.

Damn, she looked so pretty just lying there in her jeans and that sexy bra that cupped her round breasts so perfectly. Of course, she was right, the cuffs turned it kinky, but he'd just found out pretty and kinky could fit together nicely.

And it pleased him to see she looked a little more compliant now. Impatient still, but acceptant that she'd have to let him set the pace, make the decisions. In fact, as Mike unbuttoned her jeans, then slowly eased the zipper down, he realized that . . . this was letting him take back some control. He'd had a great time with her at the bonfire, but he *needed* to get a little control back here—so tonight, he'd control the sex, like this. For a little while anyway.

"Lift up," he told her softly, then tugged the denim to her thighs and off. Underneath, she wore the sexiest little lavender panties he'd ever seen—a combination of lace and silk, they matched the bra and hugged her slender hips. He let out a low groan at the sight. Then he said, "Turn over, honey."

He'd hooked the cuffs around one thin wrought iron bar on his headboard, so she could easily roll. Her eyes looked skeptical, but she wordlessly obeyed his command. He'd wanted to see her panties from the back, and that's when he found out she actually wore a thong. A lavender bow decorated the tiny piece of lingerie, as if tying the scant bits of fabric together. "Damn," he murmured.

"What?" she asked, even though he couldn't see her face.

"Your ass."

In response, she wiggled it.

And he groaned some more. After which he reached down both hands to begin massaging her backside.

He heard her light intake of breath as she instantly arched toward him. "That's nice," she nearly purred.

"See now, aren't you glad I slowed you down?"

"Well . . . I have mixed emotions. Part of me is still frantic inside, but . . . mmm . . ." Though she didn't bother to finish the sentiment, he understood it perfectly. So he molded her gorgeous bottom in his hands for a few long and lingering minutes.

Soon, though, he gently rolled her back over and, lowering a gentle kiss to her belly button, drew those hot little panties down. Then he went to remove her bra, but before he even touched it, they both realized . . . "You can't get it completely off me while I'm cuffed to your bed, can you?" she said mockingly. As if that was really going to ruin his plans for her.

"A minor tactical error," he assured her, then smoothly curled his fingers into both cups of the bra and tugged downward. Her sweet breasts tumbled free as she sucked in her breath. Damn, they were beautiful, her nipples so pink and hard, and Mike instinctively framed them within his hands, then bent to kiss and suckle them. He kept things nice and slow, though—which soon had her begging.

"Please, Mike," she whispered.

"Please what, honey?"

"Please . . . inside me . . . now."

He wanted that, too. He was *dying* for that. So he didn't refuse her anymore. But he also didn't speed up any. He simply rose to his knees and undid his jeans, pushing them down while she watched. Her eyes locked on the erection still hidden in his underwear and her hungry look made him want to explode. "*Please*," she said again.

"Shhhh," he soothed her. "We're getting there."

When his pants and briefs were gone, he slowly parted her legs and positioned himself there, sitting back on his knees. Her breath came rough—and he realized his own breath had grown labored somewhere along the way, too.

Finally, he lifted her to him and slid deep into her warmth. They both let out hot sighs and—hell, his whole body tingled, from his scalp to the tips of his fingers and toes.

This was . . . this was different. He didn't know why, couldn't explain it. But somehow, every time he was with her it grew more powerful. Now, he was inside her, unmoving, their gazes locked, and he felt more contented than ever in his life—but also as if his body might burst apart any minute.

And then he began to thrust. Slow. *Agonizingly* slow. Because Rachel was right—slow was good. Slow was fucking fantastic. He remained upright on the bed—he anchored his hands at her hips as he drove into her moisture, and she let out a low, lingering moan with each steamy stroke.

The problem was—going slow was getting damn hard. He wanted to pound wildly into her soft flesh now. He wanted to make her scream. But going slow was also . . . delicious torture. For both of them. Rachel thrashed against the sheets, teeth clenched. And at some point Mike's body actually began to shudder.

Until finally he said, "Damn it, I can't go slow anymore," and began to plunge into her, harder, faster. She cried out, her eyes dropping shut, and Mike got lost in the pure driving heat as she met each thrust. They moved together that way for a long while before exhaustion eventually gripped him, forcing him to go still. And then he even pulled out, because he didn't want to come yet, and being inside her right now, despite not moving, was threatening to make that happen. Hell, even handcuffed to a bed, this woman managed to steal his self-restraint.

"I want to be uncuffed," Rachel said then. She'd been so docile there for a few minutes that it almost caught him off guard.

"Why should I?" he asked, half teasing, half serious. "I like having you where I want you."

Below him, she sensually bit her lower lip. "Because . . . there are things I want to do to you that I can't like this."

That's when her gaze dropped to his erection. And he knew what she wanted to do. His limbs went weak.

"Oh," he murmured, a little stunned, a lot excited. "Okay." And he tried not to *race* to uncuff her—but still, race he did, moving across the bed to find the key on his police belt hanging over one side of the headboard.

As soon as both her hands were loose, he said, "All right. Feel free to have your way with me."

But she didn't look the least bit playful as she said, "Lie down."

And suddenly Mike didn't feel playful, either. He'd tried to be, just for a minute—yet somehow this had turned . . . intense and serious in a way that had his chest tightening all over again, not to mention other *harder* parts, as he met her sexy gaze. She wanted him to lie down? He'd lie down.

As he reclined next to her, she sat up, her eyes returning to where he remained stiff and ready. She studied him so intently that he had to concentrate on breathing evenly, and it still came out shaky.

Finally, she situated herself the same as he had before, with her—parting his legs, she moved between them. Then she wrapped one firm fist around him—making him shudder again, just briefly—and leaned over to drag her tongue across the tip. He moaned as the pleasure swept through him like a brief but powerful storm. Then he watched as she bent again and this time sank her mouth over him.

He hissed in his breath, then cursed. And as she began to move, he heard himself telling her how beautiful she was, how amazing this felt, what a perfect lover she was. And shit, he was shaking again, damn it, trembling—as her ministrations echoed wildly through his whole body. He lay there basking in it, moaning as it stretched all through him, watching her every move—and as much as he hated to admit it to himself, he had to: Giving up control could be more than good. It could be *astounding*.

After a blissfully long while, she pulled back, releasing him. Her lips looked prettily swollen, and Mike told her exactly what he was thinking. "God, you're good at that."

She offered up a surprisingly timid smile in reply.

And he couldn't resist a teasing look. "If I'd known you were so good at that . . ."

"What?" she asked when he trailed off.

He sat up, cracked a grin. "Maybe I would have been nicer. Sooner."

She gave her head a coquettish tilt. "Lucky for you, you stuck around long enough to earn it."

"How did I earn it?"

She shrugged then, giving him a playful grin of her own. "You gave me a hoody earlier when I was cold."

"That's all it takes? Then I should start carrying hoodies everywhere I go."

She smiled, but as their eyes connected, the smile faded . . . into something more serious, and her voice dropped to a whisper. "That's not all it takes."

Mike's chest constricted as he lifted a hand to her face. "I know," he replied.

She looked a little surprised and said, "*How* do you know?"

"Because you told me the first time we were together that you don't usually have sex that soon. And because this is the first time you've done this. So I know this is . . . special," he finished.

Rachel nearly couldn't breathe. Because of what he'd just said. About what she'd just done being special. Because it really was.

It was hardly the first time she'd done that to a guy, but before now, it had always been like a lot of her sex up to now . . . about expectation, about wanting to be the bold, wild Rachel everyone knew. This was maybe the first time she'd done it when she'd felt the true intimacy of it. The first time she'd done it because she wanted to express her feelings for a guy in some new way she hadn't before. The first time it meant something.

The fact was, sex with a man she cared for was making all other sex pale in comparison. No wonder sex with Mike had been the best of her life from the very start— caring for him had been . . . destiny.

Destiny in Destiny.

Even now, as he kissed her, as their faces lingered together, their cheeks touching, she felt closer to him than she'd known was possible.

"I want back inside you," he rasped in her ear.

The words stretched all through her, igniting her desires anew. "I want that, too."

She wanted it enough that she pushed him back in the bed. Because sometimes she really *was* bold Rachel. And with Mike, well . . . it seemed like she could be whatever she felt like in any given moment.

As she straddled his hips and sank down onto him, it felt like coming home. She rode him that way until she reached a spectacular orgasm, and only seconds later, he came, too—hard, nearly lifting her from the bed.

Destiny in Destiny, she thought again as she slumped against him, tired, replete. In that moment, she was almost sorry she couldn't stay. Almost sorry she couldn't let herself fall completely in love with Mike Romo.

Later, they lay in bed snacking on some Oreos Mike had found in his cabinet after deciding he was hungry. Of course, it left dark crumbs in the bed and Rachel was surprised Officer Romeo would allow it, but he didn't seem to mind. That, plus the fact that he'd technically broken the law to have sex with her a couple of times, made her think maybe hanging out with her was loosening him up—just a little.

On the other hand, now that he was loosening up, she feared she might be . . . well, going in the opposite direction. Because somehow, she was starting to care about things she never had before. "I'm glad you remember," she began, a bit uncertainly, "about my telling you I . . . don't fool around with just every guy. Because despite the impression I've probably given you, I really don't."

Mike stopped eating and met her gaze, his look turning

serious. "You don't need to tell me this, Farris. Because I just told you, I already get that. And . . . I wouldn't judge you on that anyway. I'm not exactly celibate myself."

She knew Mike had been with a lot of girls, and to her surprise, it even made her jealous. And she also knew she didn't have to tell him anything about her sex life, but for some reason, she wanted to. Because she knew her friends saw her as someone who had a lot of casual sex, so she figured Mike did, too. And she'd seldom given a damn about anyone's opinion of her morals—but now, somehow, it mattered to her. Even much more than it had that first night they were together. "I . . . just want to explain that . . . well, I've never had any lengthy relationships, but . . . almost all the guys I've slept with are men who I knew pretty well, from being in the same social circle, having friends in common, that sort of thing."

"And . . . ?"

She shook her head, bit her lip, stared at the sheets around her torso. "I just wanted you to know. I'm not your typical sweet, nice Destiny girl . . . but I'm not a slut, either." She swallowed, saying the word. She'd never defended herself this way before, never even thought in those terms.

And Mike suddenly looked mad. "Who called you a slut?"

Her eyes shot open wide. "Nobody. Calm down. I just . . . don't want *you* to think of me that way." Lord, there, that got to the heart of the matter. She suddenly *did* care what someone thought of her morals, and it was Mike Romo.

Mike lowered his chin, peering intently over at her, looking serious. "Listen," he said, his voice soft, deep, comforting, "I would never think of you that way. I thought I kind of just told you that, before, when we were . . . you know."

She nodded, bit her lip. Now she felt dumb for even

bringing it up, like she'd let him see an insecure side of her, a side she hadn't even known she possessed up until this moment. "I guess it's just the whole small town thing. It's making me care what people think or something."

Mike simply shook his head. "You don't need to worry about that, Farris. Besides—sweet Destiny girls don't really do it for me. Never have." Then he laughed lightly. "They're all afraid of me."

Rachel felt a small smile form on her lips. "Lucky for me, I don't scare easily."

And Mike's mouth quirked into an ironic grin. "Lucky for me, too."

Okay, enough of this girlish worry—*too much* of it, actually. Reassured now, she decided it was a good time to change the subject. And the conversation had provided a perfect segue. "Speaking of . . . Lucky, tell me about him." She was still curious to learn more about Mike's life, which included his family. And the fact that they were all Romos meant less and less to her all the time.

"What do you mean?" he asked, drawing another Double Stuf from the wrapper.

"Well, you told me about Anna, but I don't know anything about Lucky. Except that he left town at some point." And, of course, from back in high school, that he'd always been in trouble—but not in the same way she had. For Rachel, it had been mischief and making out with boys; for Lucky, it had been things more like drugs and alcohol.

Mike looked a little sad as he replied. "We were close as kids, but after Anna disappeared, it all changed. We grew apart—I'm not sure why." He shook his head, then met her gaze. "Lucky became the black sheep of the family, and . . . this'll sound awful, but in a way, it was almost a relief when he was gone. I heard from a guy in Crestview that he'd run into Lucky a few years after he left home—that he'd joined some outlaw biker gang in California." Mike sighed, looking troubled, and maybe a little disgusted. "I still miss him, he's still my brother, but . . . I miss the *old* him, I miss the little kid I played with in the backyard."

She couldn't resist flashing a skeptical look, teasing him. "Yeah, because Officer Romeo is such a fun-loving guy."

He simply raised his eyebrows. "I *can* be. I think you know that."

"At moments," she conceded, biting into a cookie.

Propped up on his elbow, Mike tilted his head and actually looked wistful. "I guess I quit having much fun after Anna, guess it toughened me up. But you have to be tough to be a good cop."

"You were pretty damn mean when you pulled me over," she reminded him.

"You were pretty much of a smart-ass when I pulled you over."

"Fair enough."

Mike dipped his head to lick dark cookie crumbs off her chest, making her shiver slightly, and said, "Besides, you know I hate speeders." The comment reminded her of the car he'd told her he'd heard blasting past the lake when Anna had gone missing—maybe that was why Mike felt so strongly about that particular offense. She listened now as he talked about a couple of high-speed chases he'd engaged in lately, with a souped-up Mustang he thought was stolen.

"There are high-speed chases in Destiny? And stolen cars?" Not only was she surprised, but also a little alarmed. It was one thing for her to go sixty-five in a forty-five, but another altogether for Mike to go *ninety*-five on the same roads. Her heart constricted.

"Not usually. And I hope never again." His jaw set and his teeth began to clench. "Stupid asshole," he muttered.

"Here, have a cookie," she said to lighten the mood,

holding her own up to his mouth. He bit into it and she took it back to eat the rest.

"So, tell me something, Farris," he said then. "Is Chicago really all that great?"

"Of course," she answered automatically. "It's big, and exciting, and there's always something happening." But even to her own ears, the words sounded weirdly . . . hollow. So she added, "And don't forget about my job. Good money, you know."

Mike just shrugged, busy twisting the top off another Oreo. "Yeah, well, it's possible to be happy without a ton of money." Then he scraped the white filling off with his teeth.

"True, but . . ."

"Yeah, yeah, I know—you feel responsible for your whole family."

"Well, as I've told you before, living in the city is also about my sense of success," she argued. "It makes me feel good about myself and the things I've achieved."

"Ya know," he began thoughtfully, "maybe if that's what it takes to make you feel good about yourself, you're trying too hard."

Ouch. And whoa. She'd never thought about it like that before.

So she simply shot him a look yet decided to ignore the remark. "And about my family, maybe it *is* a lot to put on myself, but I think *you* feel responsible for things you shouldn't, too—so do you really want to go there?"

"Good point," he said. "And no."

"That's what I thought. And just so you know, I do get to enjoy my money, too. I get to shop. And travel."

"Where have you gone?" He looked sincerely interested, but somehow Rachel felt . . . a little braggy as she named off places. "New York. Paris. Italy. Spain. Miami." If she was guessing right, Mike probably hadn't traveled much, maybe just to Florida to see his parents. "A lot of that is work-related—but sometimes I take trips with friends from Chicago, too."

"What's your favorite place? Of everywhere you've been."

"Italy," she said without hesitation. "It's amazing."

"I'd like to go there someday," he said. "See where my dad's family came from."

"Of course," she added, a bit glum, "who knows if I'll ever travel anyplace exciting *again*. I might be losing my job soon." She scrunched her nose up as she met his eyes, unsure why she suddenly wanted to confide in him about that. Maybe she'd just gotten used to them sharing stuff with each other—and it seemed strange to realize he didn't know about the big fear in her life right now.

He looked adequately surprised, so she told him all about Pamela. In a way, she didn't like letting him know she was scared, or intimidated by someone younger than her, but he'd revealed a lot to her, too, so telling him felt . . . surprisingly okay.

"I can't believe your bosses would pick anybody over you," he said. "You're smart, determined, gorgeous—what more do they want?"

She smiled, truly flattered. At moments, it was hard to believe this was the same guy who'd pulled her over on her way into town. "Sometimes, when business is bad, *any* business, and the higher-ups are grasping at straws trying to fix whatever's wrong, they seem to think *newer* means *better*. And sometimes they're even right. But I have to hope *my* higher-ups decide to stick with the tried and true."

"What if they don't?" he asked. "What will you do?"

"Get another job, I hope."

The cookie package crinkled as Mike reached back inside. "So . . . you wouldn't decide to buy Edna's orchard and move home?"

She lowered her chin teasingly. "Don't worry—the orchard is still yours to steal from us. Because I love my life the way it is—I really do." Yet just like before, it sounded oddly as if she was trying too hard to convince them both. And *was* it bad if she defined success by her career?

"So when do you leave Destiny?" he asked, sounding nonchalant as he focused on the cookie wrapper.

"The Tuesday after the apple festival."

Was she mistaken or did Mike's jaw clench again—just slightly? "That's coming up quick."

"Yeah," she said quietly, glancing down toward their feet, under the covers. The festival was next weekend, in fact. It had seemed so far in the future the whole time she'd been in town, but now it lay just around the corner. She'd decided staying 'til Tuesday would give her time to help clean up, pack her bags, and spend a little time with her friends before taking off. Feeling awkward, not quite knowing what else to say, she pursed her lips, then let out a sigh.

"So," Mike finally said. "If you're leaving that soon, we should probably, uh, quit wasting time talking and let me show you some more outrageous."

Feeling a familiar tingle race down her spine, and relieved the uncomfortable moment had passed, Rachel gave him her sexiest grin. "I could *go* for some more outrageous."

It was on Monday that Edna informed Rachel, while they picked apples, that they were in trouble. "Remember when Mike said to let him know if I needed anything? Well, I think I'm gonna have to let him know. Because me, you, and Brian—we're not gonna make it."

Rachel practically spun on her ladder to face Edna, stunned. "What do you mean?" They'd been working so hard.

"Four days left, and that's includin' set-up for the festival." She shook her head. "Nope, if we don't call in some extra help, we're gonna have apples go bad in these trees. More than any day-trippers can pick over the next few weeks. And more than I can store, even if we picked 'em afterwards. And bad apples is lost money, somethin' I can't afford. I thought I could make it without the usual hired hands this year, but looks like I thought wrong."

Edna sounded matter-of-fact, like this was an everyday conversation, but her troubled look told Rachel how hard it was for her to break down and ask for Mike's help— since even if she liked him and might consider selling him the orchard, he *was* a Romo. She instinctively understood that, for Edna, asking family for help was one thing, but going *outside* the family was like asking for a handout. It hit Rachel all over again how much Edna really *had* needed her this year—and made her *so* glad she'd come.

And the truth was—Rachel didn't even know how Mike could solve the problem, but she still asked, "Do you want *me* to call him?" thinking that would be easier on Edna.

Edna just nodded.

So that night, Rachel got Mike on his cell. He was on duty, but offered to meet her at Dolly's for a piece of pie.

"I don't know what you can do, if anything, but Edna seemed to think you could help," she said, sitting next to him at one of the small café tables. The place was mostly quiet—it was after dark, considered late by Destiny standards.

"Woulda been nice to know about this a week ago," he said, digging his fork into a piece of pumpkin pie, "before things got this drastic."

She nodded. "I was thinking the same thing. But I had no idea until she told me this afternoon." As for *her* pie, she was just staring at it, fiddling with her fork handle.

He reached out to cover her hand, stilling it on the fork. "You're really worried, aren't you?"

She met his gaze and found herself responding honestly, again no longer concerned with being bold, brave
Rachel with Mike. "I guess I am. I mean, if the apples
go to waste, I can supplement Edna's income through
the winter. But I see that as a last resort. I'm glad I have
the means to help her—but I think she'd hate if it came
to that." Despite Rachel's plans to provide for Edna if
needed, this was the first time she'd thought through it
realistically and factored Edna's pride into the equation.
Some people could accept money graciously and others,
not so much. Suddenly, Rachel was pretty sure Edna fell
into the latter category.

"We'll get the apples harvested," he said. That simple.
Like it was a done deal.

So she just slanted him a doubtful look. "How?"

He squeezed her hand. "You just leave that to me,
Farris," he said, then leaned over and kissed her.

On Thursday morning, Rachel and Edna peeked out the
window to see a line of cars and pickup trucks come driving across the bridge.

"What the hell?" Rachel asked, squinting to see.

But when she realized the last vehicle in the caravan
was Mike's truck, she understood. She simply looked
at Edna. "I believe the cavalry has just arrived." They'd
spent the last two days picking apples like maniacs and
hoping for the best. Rachel hadn't heard from Mike and
had begun to wonder if he would come through, but now
she was sorry she'd doubted him.

Walking out the back door, she found Logan, Adam,
Tessa, Sue Ann, and some other people she didn't even
know, all getting out of their vehicles, all dressed in sweat-
shirts and jeans for the cooler weather that had blown in
this week. She just stared at Mike, mouth gaping.

He slammed his door and came over to lower a small
kiss to her shocked mouth. "Sorry I didn't warn you about

this—there wasn't time. I've been busy rearranging my schedule and everybody else's so we could all get here on the same day. We've got more people coming later— Sue Ann enlisted Jenny and Mick when they both get off work, and Jeff'll be here then, too. Your buddy Amy is gonna close the bookstore early and head over. And those guys"—he pointed to some of the people she didn't recognize—"work for Adam's landscaping company and agreed to help. Between all of us, I figure we can kick some apple-picking ass today."

Rachel just stood there. She couldn't believe it. It was a simple enough solution, she supposed—but it just hadn't occurred to her to go around asking their friends. Yet here they all were, ready and willing to help. If Rachel had been the type of girl to cry, it would have brought tears to her eyes. But since she'd firmly decided her recent tears in front of Mike had to be her last, she instead just threw her arms around his neck and whispered, "Thank you."

Just then, the back screen door slammed and they looked up to see Edna. "Mike, I do believe you're a prince among men, and I officially take back every bad word I ever said about the Romos. Except maybe Giovanni. But otherwise, I take it all back."

"I'd say that's more than fair, Edna," Mike told her with just a hint of a smile.

"Well, you'd best put us to work, Edna," Logan said. "We're burning daylight."

"Damn straight we are," Edna replied, then turned into her drill-sergeant self. "Rachel, you take Sue Ann and Tessa and work on separatin' what we picked yesterday. You know how many to store for winter and the rest are for the festival. I'll take the rest of these fellas out to the far grove and get 'em started. When you girls are done with that chore, we need to go back over the front groves to get the late apples just now turnin'."

After that, they all worked like mad. A couple of the guys had brought boom boxes, which blared out the seventies and eighties hits played by the only radio station Destiny received, and though Rachel normally liked the peacefulness of the orchard, today the music fit the mood and kept them all moving. And the whole time, Rachel's heart filled with the knowledge that it was Mike who had pulled this all together. Five or six weeks ago, she wouldn't have believed it was possible, but maybe this made it official—the Farris/Romo feud was over.

Edna clearly saw her job today as taking care of the troops and providing provisions. At lunchtime, she came out with trays of sandwiches and cans of soda, making sure everyone got fed.

A few hours after that, as promised, more people arrived and Edna set them to work, too—and by late afternoon, everyone was laboring vigorously in the front orchard, finding those just-ripened apples hidden deep within the trees. Even Tessa, who promised Rachel she felt fine today, was enjoying a burst of energy. Jenny's husband, Mick, brought a couple of guys he worked with building homes in a new subdivision across town, and Amy provided a few teenagers she'd recruited from the bookstore after school. Everyone talked and laughed the whole time, and somehow, by the end of the day, Sue Ann even ended up renting Logan a cottage on Blue Valley Lake that had recently been vacated by one of her relatives.

When the sun began to dip slightly toward the horizon, Edna called Rachel inside to help her fry up some chicken and bake a few apple pies for their helpers. She put Rachel to work on mashed potatoes and corn on the cob.

"How about all this!" Edna said, beaming as she quickly crimped the edges on three pies before sliding them into the oven. "Mike really came through, didn't he?"

Rachel returned her grandmother's smile. "He really

did," she admitted as a fresh sense of relief rolled through her. "We're gonna make it. And now we can spend all day tomorrow setting up our booth and getting ready for Saturday."

"Gives ya a good feelin', don't it?"

Rachel gave a sincere and cheerful nod, then refocused on peeling potatoes.

"Goes to show ya—sometimes there's more to life than glitz and excitement. Sometimes it's about the simple things—like a man who'll take care of ya."

At this, though, Rachel stopped peeling and narrowed her gaze on Edna. It didn't take a rocket scientist to get what she was driving at. So she pointed out, "Mike's here for you, not me. Remember, he's a decent guy, just like you told me."

Edna cast a quick sideways glance before returning her gaze to the pies. "If you think Mike's here for me, you think again, Rachel Marie Farris."

Rachel took in the words, the idea, and almost didn't know what to do with it. Was that true? Had Mike organized all this for *her*? And if it *was* true, did it make her happy? Or did it just make her . . . sad to be leaving in a few days?

She didn't know the answer, but she refused to let Edna see any emotion on her face, or to even reply at all. So she kept peeling potatoes, and instead said, "Maybe this would be a good time for more of your story about Giovanni. I still don't know what happened when he came back to Destiny."

Short letters arrived from Giovanni on a regular basis, but the entire winter passed without his coming home. Home, though, Edna had decided, was getting to be a hard thing to define. Giovanni's farm truly felt like her home now—she'd come to love it more and more. Yet was it really Giovanni's home, or was his heart in Italy?

The more time that passed, the more their summer together began to seem like something she'd made up, like a fairytale she'd told herself. It had been so perfect, but ended so abruptly. And though she'd written to tell him about her illness afterward, the fact that he'd entirely missed something so traumatic and frightening in her life made her feel disconnected from him. A simple letter, after all, couldn't express how truly grim her battle with the flu had been. And his return letters merely said things like: So sorry you were ill, my *fiore.*

As the winter months crept by, Edna's energy was slow to return, but she eventually regained her strength as spring approached. Her brothers frowned on how much time she spent with Eddie, even though she explained she felt only friendship toward him. And how could she not feel a certain attachment to the person who, to her way of thinking, had literally saved her life? She reminded Wally and Dell more than once that it had been Eddie who'd stayed by her side in those dark days.

It was a sunny April morning when Eddie invited her on a walk through the apple grove, the orchard suddenly bright white with apple blossoms. They fluttered down like snow when the wind blew and Eddie plucked them from her hair.

She was truly shocked, though, when Eddie grabbed her hand and leaned in to kiss her. So she pulled away, saying, "You know I'm engaged!" Ever since her fever had broken, she'd been sure she'd just imagined Eddie saying he loved her, but now . . . well, maybe she hadn't imagined it at all.

"Yep," Eddie replied boldly, "but he's not here, and I am. *And I believe you care for me, too, Edna. I believe it with my whole heart."*

Oh Lord.

It was in that moment that a dam broke inside her. And she let her soul fill up . . . with Eddie. With his kindness. With his generosity. With his sweet smile and simple good-

ness. With the memory of how he'd been there for her, day
and night, without fail, when she'd needed someone.

Her soul also filled with something else in those
moments—a warm and easy desire. It felt right, natural,
to kiss him back. And maybe it had felt right all winter
long, but she'd been trying so hard to be true to Giovanni
that she'd refused to let herself see it. There was no denying it now, though—now they were wrapping their arms
around each other amid a flurry of blossoms dancing in
the breeze and kissing, again and again. Being in his arms
felt . . . safe.

Of course, she was still promised to Giovanni, and
her feelings for him hadn't suddenly vanished. In fact,
she realized with horror—even as she pressed her body
against Eddie's—that she was in love with two men. One
who was well-off and worldly—and another who was
just as poor as her but who understood her so very well.

She turned that over in her head lying in bed that
night. She compared the two men in other ways, as well.
While Giovanni's kisses were confident, sensual, seductive, Eddie's were sweet, gentle, and loving. Where Giovanni seemed exotic, exciting, Eddie came from simple
beginnings, just like her. And while Giovanni was older
and had always seemed like a commanding, self-assured
man, she'd watched Eddie transform from a friendly boy
to a capable man himself over these past months.

She knew the choice between the two seemed obvious,
but she'd never felt so torn. Other than the fact that they
were both hardworking and knew how to run a farm,
Giovanni and Eddie were as different as night and day—
and both men held their own unique appeal.

Of course, as Eddie had pointed out, Giovanni wasn't
here. Giovanni had been absent from her life now for far
longer than he'd been in it to begin with. And the sad truth
was, if not for a snapshot she'd taken with his camera one
day last summer, she might have a hard time remembering the details of his handsome face now.

It was in May that Edna found herself alone with Eddie again. Wally and Dell had gone to town to buy supplies now that it was time for spring planting. Edna and Eddie had stayed behind to start work on it—the cornfield had been plowed, and last season's crop had provided the seeds.

Edna didn't know much about raising things like apples or grapes, but she knew about common farm crops— she'd been planting her family's garden since she was big enough to walk. The freshly turned soil here was dark and rich, good for growing, and when she knelt down, wearing an old flowered hand-me-down dress from Mama, her knees sank into the soft, cool earth. She dug a small hole with a trowel, dropped a few yellow kernels of corn inside, then used her hands to gather the dirt back over them.

Eddie worked in the next row, facing her, and though they stayed quiet, she sensed him watching her. More than that, she sensed him . . . wanting her. She began to feel too warm for early May and avoided glancing up. Yet a familiar longing clawed at her; it had nagged her for a month now, and it was familiar because she'd felt it for Giovanni, too.

"Edna," Eddie finally said, his voice lower than usual.

She looked up, aware that her hair hung in her face and her cheeks were surely smudged with dirt.

"You're beautiful," he said, and his eyes burned with a stark hunger she'd never before witnessed.

Her heart fluttered nervously in her chest as she said, "Don't be silly, Eddie—I'm a mess from plantin'."

"The most beautiful mess I ever seen," he told her— and then he was crossing the garden row on his knees, lifting his hands to her face, and kissing her.

Just like in the apple grove, Edna couldn't resist. His kisses flowed down inside her like sweet, slow molasses, seeming to trickle through her whole body. The next thing she knew, she was pressed against Eddie from chest to thigh, and they moved together in an intoxicating rhythm that made her crazy with yearning.

Soon his hands were gliding smoothly up her thighs, under her dress. And she felt so very close to floating away, to giving in—especially when he lay her back on the soft dirt, whispering again that he loved her. "If you had died, Edna," he told her, "I'd have died, too."

Her breath came shallow when he ran his palms over her breasts, and then, again, up under her dress. She wanted him just as much as she'd ever wanted Giovanni.

But that's what reminded her—Giovanni! She loved him, and she'd made him a promise. "Eddie, I can't," she said, pushing him firmly away. "I just can't."

"You want to," he breathed, his voice raspy now. She felt his words in her gut.

"That don't make it right." And she knew if she stayed there alone with Eddie for even a minute longer, right wouldn't matter. So she pushed abruptly to her feet and ran from the garden, her toes digging into the dirt with each stride. She stopped at the edge only to snatch up her shoes from the grass.

"Well, I'll be here for ya, Edna, whenever you want me," Eddie called behind her, "whenever you decide it's right. And it is right, Edna. It is right."

"You're stopping?" Rachel snapped.

Edna gave a brusque nod.

"You are . . ." Rachel's frustration ran so deep she could barely find the right word. "Incorrigible," she finally spit out.

"Whatever that means," Edna said, then turned toward the stove. "All I know is I need to concentrate on fryin' this chicken or I'll burn myself." Although she took the time to point a spatula at Rachel. "And you ain't exactly settin' any records with them cobs of corn, neither, so buckle down and get crackin'."

Parting is such sweet sorrow.

William Shakespeare, *Romeo & Juliet*

Sixteen

A celebratory atmosphere filled the air as everyone ate dinner outside, some crowding around the two picnic tables near the barn, others standing up with plates and forks in their hands. Everyone complimented Edna on her chicken, but it was nothing compared to the reaction when the pies came out. As Rachel and Amy cut and scooped slices onto paper plates, Rachel felt weirdly proud that Edna's pie prowess was known far and wide. Maybe she just liked seeing her ornery grandma being appreciated, a real part of her community.

While dessert was being gobbled down, Edna said a few words. "I can't thank ya all enough for pitchin' in and helpin' us out here today. It means a whole lot to me."

"Edna, your pie is more than enough thanks," Logan assured her.

After the dinner mess was cleaned up, people started to leave and Rachel sought out her girlfriends to give them hugs of appreciation. It meant a lot to her, too, that they'd come. Living so far away, she felt she'd done so little for them over the years as a friend—and with Jenny and Sue Ann, well, she hadn't seen them since high school. Yet here they all were.

"How can I thank you guys?" Rachel said, walking along between Tessa and Amy, her arms hooked through theirs.

"Believe it or not," Tessa said, "this was actually fun, so no thanks necessary."

"But if you really want to thank us somehow," Amy said hopefully, "you could . . . stay."

Rachel just sighed, her stomach clenching slightly, as Amy went on.

"I know, I know—you have a great life in the city, blah blah blah, but . . . I'm just gonna miss you so much."

"Well, I'm gonna miss you guys, too," Rachel admitted. "A lot."

After getting Tessa and Amy on their way, Rachel saw Mike talking with Adam, so she walked over to express her gratitude and say goodbye as the crowd quickly thinned.

When Adam's truck crossed the bridge a few minutes later, quiet returned to the orchard, the only sound that of Edna washing up dishes—the light clatter of pots and pans echoed through the open kitchen window. Dusk fell sweet and cool over Destiny as Rachel finally found herself alone with Mike.

She barely knew what to say, but like earlier, just kept it simple as she peered up into his dark, sexy eyes. "Thank you."

He answered by using one bent finger to lift her chin, then giving her a kiss. As always, it moved all through her, and that one kiss turned into another, and another, a soft evening breeze washing over them as Rachel let her body relax against his.

Was Edna right? About why Mike had helped them

today? It made sense he should help *Edna*—he needed to prove to her he'd take care of the place, plus it just made sense to get on her good side. But the warmth of his kisses made Rachel wonder, maybe even believe, it had indeed been for her, too.

She walked into the house tired but happy, gratified by a day spent working with friends and knowing they'd accomplished the task at hand.

"Does he kiss good?" Edna asked.

Rachel looked over at her grandmother, still at the sink. "You were spying on me?"

"Wouldn't call it spyin'. Would call it workin' in front of a window while you stand outside it kissin' Mike Romo."

Rachel just let out an acceptant, forgiving sigh. "Okay, yes, he kisses *very* good. Now do you need my help here or should I go take a bath?"

"Nope, I'm almost done. Head to the tub, darlin', but make it a shorty, 'cause I'll be right behind ya."

Fifteen minutes later, Rachel was in pajamas, fresh and clean, when she noticed her neglected Blackberry on the bedside table in Edna's guestroom. Blegh. She'd been working such long hours this week that she'd barely glanced at it—and had even sort of forgotten it existed the last couple of days. So she grabbed it up and headed for the sofa in the parlor, figuring she'd take a glance at her e-mail while Edna was bathing and couldn't scold her for it.

The first thing that caught her eye was a message from Chase with the subject line: K&K. It felt like being struck by a bolt of lightning—one that gave her back her memory. She suddenly remembered she'd been waiting to hear what happened with the new pitch to Stan. And with her job, too. Her heartbeat went from normal to beating like mad in just a few seconds as she opened the message.

Rachel,

Incredible news! Stan LOVED the new pitch, enough that K&K signed a new contract with us for three years! All thanks to you! Stan actually said it was mostly due to the confidence you instilled in him. So you've definitely still got the magic.

And I hope you're sitting down, because when I told the big boys you were responsible for getting K&K back, they realized it would be foolish to let someone with your great track record and general advertising brilliance go to some other agency.

We haven't broken the news to Pamela yet—we're waiting until you return to the office (soon, please????)—but you've still got your job. Not to mention a healthy raise, given that you'll be the sole Account Director. Your stock is rising, big-time!

And the muffins are gonna flow when you get back, baby!

Chase

Wow. She still had her job. And a raise! The worry that had plagued her for nearly two months now was over, with a happy ending. Just like that, with a mere click of a button.

Strange relief poured through her. Life wasn't going to change. She would still keep doing her fabulous job in fabulous shoes and living her fabulous life. She would travel again. And she would no longer have to worry about her family's financial future.

In short, things would be normal again soon.

Very soon. God, she was leaving on Tuesday. Four short days from now.

When had she lost track of how quickly this "vacation" from her real life was ending? And when had the idea of it ending actually started making her a little . . . sad inside?

That was the strange part about her relief. It was laced with an unexpected melancholy.

Yikes—what was *that* about?

She let out a big breath, trying to think.

Well, you've admitted to yourself you have feelings for Mike, so this is just what happens when you let yourself care. When you let yourself get all gooey over a guy.

And maybe if she'd lost her job, well . . . would she have, could she have . . . considered staying in Destiny? Just for a while? Maybe she'd been *waiting* to lose her job for that thought to surface.

But she *hadn't* lost the job. And as she kept telling herself, she'd get over Mike and any other attachments she'd formed here after she left. Life would go on. It would.

Except . . . well, okay, *one* thing would be different. Sex would never be the same—it would never be as great. It would never make her feel as good in her heart as it made her feel other places. And that was disappointing to contemplate, no two ways about it. .

"You watchin' anything?"

She flinched, then looked up to see Edna wrapped in an old-fashioned quilted robe that that buttoned down the front, pointing at the TV.

"No," Rachel said, shaken from her thoughts—which was probably a good thing.

"Then scoot over. *Rock of Love* is on."

Friday was busy, busy, busy.

First thing in the morning, before Edna and Rachel had even finished eating breakfast, people showed up wanting apples. Most of the locals had picked up their apples for festival events over the preceding couple of weeks, or bought them at the General Mercantile, but Rose Marie Keckley had made a late decision to enter the pie contest, and LeeAnn Turner had just been roped into making apple tartlets for the high school band boosters' booth.

"Good thing you ladies got here bright and early," Edna said, still in her robe, " 'cause in half an hour we'll be long gone, settin' up in town."

After dressing in what had become her usual "work uniform," a fitted tee and jeans—since finally refusing Edna's smocks—Rachel grabbed a hoody to guard against the chilly morning air, then met Edna in the barn. Their first job was to load several painted plywood structures into the back of Edna's truck, along with Edna's toolbox. Once they got to town, the pieces would fit together to make the Farris Family Apple Orchard booth.

As they pulled into the town square, they spied Johnny Fulks and Logan standing on tall ladders, stretching a Destiny Apple Festival banner across the street. Amy stood below, directing them on whether it should be higher or lower.

Early as it was, Rachel practically felt like they were late, given all the action taking place. Many booths were already erected on the streets circling the square—traffic would be limited to one lane today and the area would be closed to vehicles completely tomorrow. On the grassy square itself, guys in DFD T-shirts busily set up tables and chairs, "where folks'll be able to sit and eat or watch the entertainment," Edna explained.

It was noon by the time Rachel and Edna—with Logan's help—got their booth hammered sturdily together. The plywood structure was painted white and a wide board across the top bore the Farris Family Apple Orchard logo with some apples painted at each side. "Paid me an art student at the high school to do that one year," Edna said as they sat in the booth and ate the takeout sandwiches Rachel had grabbed from Dolly's. Tessa wandered over from the bookstore to join them.

When Edna got caught up in talking to Grampy Hoskins from the Mercantile, Rachel took the opportunity to pull Tessa aside. She'd decided to get Mike a fun little gift

as a way of saying thanks for organizing all the help yesterday, but she didn't know where to shop. "I'm thinking
of some sexy undies," she said.

"For you or for him?" Tessa asked.

"For him. *I* have plenty."

Yet Tessa appeared skeptical. "Not that I know him as
well as you do, but that doesn't really sound like the right
gift for Mike Romo."

Rachel just rolled her eyes. "It's in the spirit of fun," she
pointed out. "And I won't get anything *too* out there. Just
something sexy, like I said."

Just then, Sue Ann passed by, hauling some crates, so
Tessa called her over and told her what Rachel was looking for.

Without a second's pause, Sue Ann directed Rachel to a
department store in Crestview. "I've gotten Jeff some cute
stuff there," she promised.

With a *task-accomplished* nod, Tessa said, "I knew if
anyone would know where to find crap like that around
here, it would be Sue Ann."

A few minutes later, Rachel and Edna headed back to
the orchard, after which Rachel set off for Crestview in
her BMW, promising Edna she'd be back soon to help get
the apples and baskets ready for tomorrow.

It was a little over an hour later that she came racing
over the hills, speeding back toward Destiny—only to
hear a siren split the air behind her.

Her jaw simply dropped.

No way.

And when she glanced in her rearview to confirm that,
indeed, Mike was pulling her over *again*, in those silly
mirrored sunglasses of his *again*, she couldn't believe it!

Her mouth still hung open when he approached her window. "You *cannot* be serious, Romo? *Are* you? *Serious*?"

And—oh brother—he even looked *mad*, just like the
Officer Romeo she'd first met. "Damn it, Farris, you

know how I feel about this! If you're gonna speed, I have to give you a ticket."

Rachel sucked in her breath, still not willing to accept it. They were practically a couple! And what cop gave his girlfriend a ticket? She set her jaw. "For your info, I have a good reason for speeding today. I need to get back to the orchard to help Edna finish getting ready for the festival."

He sounded a little less angry when he spoke again—but it didn't change the outcome. "Well, for *your* info, I'm still giving you a ticket, honey. Sorry."

Rachel just scowled. "Clearly, there are no perks for going to bed with Officer Romeo."

Mike lowered his chin and peered at her over those mirrored glasses. "Oh, there are *plenty* of perks, babe—just not *this* kind." With that, he tore the ticket off his pad and shoved it into her hand—then he leaned in the window and kissed her. Without backing away, he brought his mouth to her ear and spoke low. "Listen, I'm gonna make you forget all about this ticket after the festival tomorrow night—promise."

"I thought you worked tomorrow night," she said snippily, still irate.

"I do. But I get a break, and I thought I might take it with *you*."

She crossed her arms. "Well, I hope I'm in the mood to let you. Maybe I *won't* be."

Mike just tilted his head and gave her a *get-serious* look. "Come on, Farris. You can't resist me."

Since she couldn't argue the point, she only responded with another eye roll and said, "By the way, those glasses are stupid."

He simply flashed a grin, somehow *still* sexy behind them, then walked away.

Rachel couldn't believe the crowd at the apple festival! Nor could she believe how many baskets of apples she and

Edna were selling from their booth, which stood between the General Mercantile's, where Grampy sold homemade apple cider and apple juice for the kids, and the PTA booth, which offered brownies, Toll House cookies, and jars of homemade applesauce.

They stayed busy almost constantly, and Rachel found it invigorating. And though when she'd first come back to Destiny she'd often found herself avoiding running into people she used to know, now she enjoyed it, and this was the perfect venue.

"Why, Rachel Farris, I used to have you in my geometry class," a portly older woman said, and then Rachel remembered her.

"Mrs. Cosway?"

"Yes, indeed. And now I have a classroom right next to your old friend Jenny Tolliver—well, Jenny Brody now."

Mrs. Cosway ordered a basket of McIntoshes as the two took a few minutes to catch up.

And for anyone who *didn't* recognize Rachel, Edna was quick to say, "You remember my granddaughter. She lives up in Chicago now, but she's been here helpin' me with the apples this fall," and she'd drag Rachel over to say hello.

Around noon, Edna asked Rachel to venture from the booth to get them something to eat. "But take your time," she said. "Look around, enjoy yourself." So she meandered over to Under the Covers, where Amy and Tessa sat on the front walk behind a table covered with cookbooks featuring apple recipes. Amy had just come back from walking around the festival with Logan for a while, so when Rachel asked for company, it was Tessa's turn.

The fire department was roasting corn on the cob and had a dunking booth set up alongside a bright red fire engine they'd pulled out for kids to look at. Next door, the police department grilled burgers and hotdogs, and Mike was giving safety talks to children. As they approached, Rachel and Tessa hung back, listening, and both were amazed at how . . . *gentle* he sounded talking to the little kids. He seemed to be reviewing stuff he'd already told them.

"When should you get into a car with a stranger?" he asked the group of seven small children gathered around him, among them Sue Ann's little girl, Sophie.

"*Never*," they said in unison.

"What if the stranger tells you your parents sent them to get you?"

The kids all shook their heads, and Sophie said, "Our parents would never send someone we don't know," clearly reciting what she'd learned from Mike.

"That's right. But what if the stranger says he's lost his dog and wants you to help him find it?"

A dark-haired little boy spoke up. "They shouldn't ask a little kid like us for help. They should ask another grown-up."

Just then, she caught Mike's eye and he gave her a quick wink before looking back to the kids and proceeding with his talk.

As she and Tessa continued making the rounds, Rachel discovered that the real estate office where Sue Ann worked part-time had sponsored a booth with face-painting and jars of apple butter for sale. The Destiny High Science Department table was manned by Jenny, who'd made dozens of individual-size apple and peach cobblers. And the Schuster farm sold pumpkins and squash from the back of a pickup truck. Several organizations hosted craft booths, and a stage set up in front of the old Ambassador Theater featured every kind of entertainment, from bluegrass bands to the high school chorus to Sophie's ballet class later, according to Sue Ann.

"At four," Tessa told her, "there's an apple-bobbing contest for kids, then the pie-eating contest, and right after that, the members of the town council will judge the apple pie bake-off. Did Edna enter?"

Rachel shook her head, smiling. "She told me she retired after six consecutive wins—it started pissing people off and no one else would enter."

A few minutes later, Rachel said, "Well, I'd better get a couple of burgers from the police department and get back to work." Then she sniffed the air. "But wait—do I smell funnel cakes?"

Tessa pointed just past the face-painting festivities. "Town council booth."

"Okay, burgers for lunch, a funnel cake for dessert."

Tessa helped her carry the food, and as they walked back toward the orchard's booth, Tessa said, "You know, I don't want to sound like Amy, like I don't get it, but . . . there's *not* any chance you could stay longer, is there?"

Rachel just looked at her, stunned. Unlike Amy, Tessa understood about life outside Destiny, about careers and security.

Before Rachel even opened her mouth to respond, though, Tessa shook her head. "Wait, never mind. Like I said, I get it. I just . . . wanted you to know it's not going to be the same around here without you. And it seems like you and Mike are getting . . . pretty solid. Am I wrong about that?"

Was she? Well, it didn't matter. What mattered was what Rachel told her as they made their way through the crowd. "We have a nice thing going, but . . . we've both known it was temporary, from the start. So the way I'm looking at it is . . . all good things must come to an end."

"Ya done real good today," Edna said as the crowds began to die down.

Rachel laughed, still in good spirits. "Did you expect me to do bad?"

Edna just grinned. "Well, no, of course not. But . . . you seemed like you were actually enjoyin' yourself, and I didn't expect that part."

Rachel gave her head a thoughtful tilt. "Neither did I."

The truth was, she hadn't expected to enjoy *anything* on her trip back to Destiny—but she'd found a *lot* to take joy in. Spending time with Edna, the peace she found in the orchard, her friends, the sense of community . . . and a certain Destiny town cop. And wow, now that she thought about it—she'd even ended a family feud. "It's been a good visit," she went on, then motioned around her to the whole festival. "And I'm impressed as hell that you created this entire event."

Her grandmother just shrugged. "You make your own fortune in life—don't ya think?"

Rachel nodded. "Most of the time, yeah, I do think that."

"Listen," Edna said, "not to get all mushy on ya, but I'm gonna be damn sorry to see ya go. I've had my fair share of children and grandchildren come home to help me out from time to time these past few years, and . . . well, much as I like seein' 'em, turns out I'm usually ready to say *adios* when the time comes, too. But that ain't how I feel this time around."

"Well, not to get all mushy in return, but I kinda feel the same way," Rachel confessed. Then she gave Edna a teasing smile. "Not everybody has a sarcastic, smart-mouthed grandma who tells them all about her torrid affairs."

To her surprise, though, Edna's face took on that now familiar wistful expression. "Maybe I thought if I kept things interestin', you'd stay."

But Rachel just rolled her eyes. "What is it with you people? Everywhere I go now, people ask me to stay when they know good and well I can't."

"There's worse things in life than havin' people care about ya."

"Okay, good point."

"And I'm just sayin', if ya ever wanted to come back here—well, there's always a room for ya under my roof."

They sold every last apple by the time the festival drew to a close near dark. The Schusters' guitar-playing friend

was the last performer on the stage, his quiet music relaxing as the busy day wound down. Tired, Edna headed
home—all the cleanup would take place tomorrow—and
Rachel said she'd catch a ride with Mike later.

Alone, she wandered to the chairs in front of the stage
and took one in the last row, unable to prevent that strange
melancholy from settling back over her. As the festival
ended, she sensed a bigger ending in her own life: the end
of her days in Destiny. She'd done what she'd come here
to do—and now it was time to go home. She'd just never
dreamed she'd feel so conflicted about it.

As the man with the guitar sang that same James
Taylor song as at the bonfire, about a woman helping
a man leave his troubled world behind, Mike settled
quietly next to her and slid his arm around the back of
her chair. Neither spoke, but she felt the song's lyrics
sinking in to her bones somehow, making her sad—even
though the story they told was a happy, moving one. Was
Mike feeling the same way? Feeling the strain of her
impending departure? She didn't know for sure, but she
suspected maybe he did.

When the guitar man finished and said good night,
the remaining crowd gathered their apple products and
children and began to head to their cars, and soon she
and Mike were two of only a few people still lingering in
the square. Booths stood empty all around the perimeter,
along with overflowing trash cans, and the occasional
smashed bit of apple littered the ground. But something
about the solitude made her think of that morning in
Mike's bed when it had been raining outside. She felt the
same way now, like they were in a cocoon here, like they
were the only two people in the world. It dawned on her
then that maybe it wasn't the rain that had made her feel
that way. And maybe it wasn't the empty square now.
Maybe it was just . . . Mike.

"Listen," he said in his deep, sexy voice, "there's something I want to tell you."

She looked over into his eyes, his face illuminated by nearby streetlamps.

"I put away a picture of Anna today."

"Huh?" she asked, not quite understanding.

"I've always kept a picture of her on my desk at the station," he explained, pointing over his shoulder in that general direction. "Chief Tolliver recently suggested I put it away, but I couldn't do it. And then . . . well, I guess you got me thinking—about trying to move forward, at least a little, so that's how I started. Today. I put the picture in a drawer. And I'm a long way from putting them *all* away, but it's a start."

An autumn chill had come on with the fall of night, but Rachel felt warm inside. Because even if it was just in a small way, Mike was telling her that maybe she'd made his life . . . a little clearer, a little better. Given how long she knew he'd been struggling with these demons, at the moment this felt even more important than having helped Edna harvest the apples. In response, she wrapped her arms around his neck and gave him a hug. He hugged her back, and they embraced a long while.

Finally, he pulled back and said, "You wanna go somewhere, get something to eat?"

"I'm stuffed on funnel cakes, but yeah, let's take off—just go for a drive or something."

"I'm in my cruiser," he told her.

"Is that a problem?"

"Not if you won't miss cuddling up against me too much. There's a console."

She bit her lip. "Well, that *is* kind of a bummer, but it'll be better than nothing."

As they walked hand in hand toward the police station, though, Rachel suddenly remembered. "Wait, I have to get something from our booth." She'd brought Mike's gift with her today, knowing she'd see him tonight.

Soon they were driving away from the heart of town in Mike's police car, but after they passed Creekside Park, he put on his signal and turned onto the lane leading to the orchard.

"Am I a bad date?" Rachel asked kiddingly. "I'm boring, so you're bringing me home early?"

He slanted her a look. "Not possible, Farris. I just decided I don't like having a console between us, especially with you leaving in a few days."

She liked that. Because it might be totally high-school-ish, yet she *had* missed pressing up against him from the moment they'd gotten in the car. "But, uh, you know Edna's here, right?"

"Not stopping at the house," he said at the precise moment he drove past it on the gravel drive that led to the barn.

"Oh." She liked that, too.

Though he didn't stop at the barn, either, easing the cruiser onto a path that led behind it, where he finally parked—out of sight of the house.

"This is for you," she said, holding out the little black shopping bag she'd been toting since leaving town.

He looked surprised—apparently, he'd thought it held something she needed to take home, or to Edna. "What is it?"

"A thank you gift for helping us get the apples in on time."

He met her gaze, looking curious, then took the bag and reached inside—to pull out a pair of silk leopard print boxer shorts.

He just blinked at them, repeatedly, like he didn't quite understand what he was seeing. Finally, he said, "You're not serious?"

Rachel just sighed. The big lug. Tessa had been right. "Is that your way of saying thank you? Because if it is, you could do better."

He looked at her, then back at the shorts—which she thought were adorably cute and sexy. "Okay, you're right. Thank you. But I won't wear them."

"Not even for *me*? The way I wear pretty bras and panties for *you*?"

"No." Unequivocally.

"They turn me on," she pointed out.

He only flashed a look of disbelief. "Seriously? These?"

"Yes. I like leopard print and these are totally cute and
hot."

"They're silly," he said simply.

She couldn't help frowning, disappointed her gift had
gone over so badly. "That's why I was speeding back into
town yesterday when you pulled me over, you big jerk-
face. I'd dropped everything to go buy you a present."

His brows knit slightly, and finally, he looked a little
guilty. "That was sweet of you," he admitted.

"I know."

Then he tilted his head, the corners of his mouth turning up in just a hint of a smile. "Who'd have thought?
Rachel Farris, sweet."

"You, on the other hand," she complained, pouting,
"are reverting to form."

"Come on now," he prodded, trying to make up, "don't
be mad." He reached over, took her hand, and pressed it
between his thighs. And—oh my—he was nice and hard
through his police uniform. Despite herself, her whole
body tingled hotly when he said, "All you *really* need to
turn you on is this."

She let out a sexy sigh and her voice came out breathy.
"You know me too well."

Looking back to his gift, he informed her, "I think
I'm gonna pass a law against leopard boxer shorts in this
town." Then he put on his serious cop voice. "In fact,
ma'am, I'm gonna have to ask you to step out of the vehicle."

Ma'am again, huh? Well, now that she'd beat out
Pamela for the job, it didn't feel *quite* as offensive. Especially since she was getting more aroused each second by
whatever little cop game Mike was starting here.

By the time she'd exited the car, he'd walked around to her side. "Assume the position."

"Huh?" She knew the phrase, but wasn't exactly sure what it meant.

"Face the car, hands on the fender, feet apart."

"Oh." And as she did so, she couldn't deny it had the potential to be a very *sexy* position.

It got that way fast when Mike moved behind her and began to pat her down—quickly at first, like they did on TV—but then he slowed down, frisking her in a more leisurely, intimate manner. His hands moved up her sides and onto her breasts, making her let out a light "mmm." Then he eased them back down her body until they curved around her inner thighs.

She sucked in her breath as Mike smoothly undid her jeans and proceeded to tug them down over her ass.

Then she looked over her shoulder, into the game now, to say, "Officer, I'm not sure this is appropriate."

His heated gaze captured hers as his palms closed on her bare hips—and a second later, he was plunging into her. She cried out at the impact, then said breathily, teasingly, "I'm gonna have to report you for police brutality."

As his arms wrapped warm around her waist, up under her top, he leaned close to her ear and whispered. "I think you can take it." And then he began to move in her.

"Oh God, I think I can, too," she murmured as the pleasure spread through her, thick and deep. Mike always filled her perfectly, but standing up, she felt him even more. She instinctively arched her bottom toward him, wanting him deeper—and he gave her what she needed, over and over, in hard, smooth strokes that vibrated through her entire being.

And it all felt very sexy and very fun until . . . it didn't anymore.

At some point his actions slowed, became more sensual. He kissed her neck, drew his teeth down her earlobe.

She felt it everywhere, shut her eyes, and tilted her head so he'd do it some more. The playful cop game was over and now it was just them, him and her, making love, slow and passionate.

As Mike delivered thrust after deep, lingering thrust, she leaned her head back and looked up at the stars. It was another beautifully clear night, and the sky twinkled with light so vibrant it seemed to rain down upon them.

After a while, he drew back from her and said, "Take off your jeans."

She hurried out of them, instructing him, "Take off your shirt."

A minute later, his uniform shirt and badge were on the ground and he was picking her up and pressing her back against the barn. Her legs wrapped around his waist automatically as he re-entered her. This time, they both groaned and he crushed his chest to hers and kissed her, firm and long.

Their gazes met as they rediscovered that slow, sensual rhythm. Oh God, that was one thing she'd never done with a guy before Mike—looked into his eyes while he moved inside her. The stark intimacy, their faces so close right now, made her breath tremble. They said nothing—words felt unnecessary. Their bodies, their eyes, said everything.

This is intense.

This is way more than just sex.

This is spectacular and wondrous and moving.

And this is tragic because it's one of the very last times.

And in the midst of it all, she found herself thinking of Edna and Giovanni, who'd made love all over this orchard. Her grandmother, his grandfather. But they, too, had eventually parted, just like Rachel and Mike would soon. Some things, she supposed, just weren't meant to last. Even without yet knowing exactly how Edna and Giovanni's story ended, this felt—in a strange way—like history repeating itself.

Everything inside Rachel moved in all the right ways as she strained against him, meeting his strokes, seeking her own pleasure. It built inside her, slow and deep, just like their sex itself, and when finally it broke, she screamed it out. She sobbed all through the gloriously extended orgasm, the pleasure buffeting her, owning her, wrenching her in his arms. And when it was done, her whole body trembled now—not just her breath.

Mike held her tight and whispered, "You okay, baby?"

She bit her lip, feeling so connected to him, so safe and warm in his arms, that she could barely fathom it. She could only nod. And then she burst out, "Come in me. I want to make you come in me. Deep, deep inside me."

"Aw Christ, honey, that's all it took," he growled, and as he climaxed, she relished the idea of him leaving a part of himself inside her that way.

A little later, they sat on the back of the cruiser, looking up at the stars.

"You're probably late getting back on duty," she said.

"Yeah. Your fault again, Farris." But he didn't sound as upset as he usually did about such things. Then he said, out of the blue, "If you wanted to stay in town, Rachel . . . if you wanted to take over the orchard . . . I wouldn't even care about not getting it back into my family."

She looked Mike in the eye. This came up over and over again, the idea that she should give up her career and run the orchard. But in this moment, that wasn't the part she was concentrating on. The part that got her was . . . was he asking her to stay? Not for the sake of the orchard, but . . . for him? And if he was, was it that easy? To give up one life for another?

Can I go forward when my heart is here?

William Shakespeare, *Romeo & Juliet*

Seventeen

Rachel took a deep breath, turning the questions over in her mind. And . . .

No. No, she didn't think so. It was the stuff of movies, novels. But in real life, it was one of the hugest changes a person could make.

And yeah, maybe the city didn't hold the same thrill for her it once had; maybe that was a season of her life that had come and gone. And maybe, over time, it had become the power of her job, the success, that she valued more than the work itself, ever since the creative part had been taken away from her. But none of that added up to just abandoning a highly lucrative career and moving back to the place she'd been so eager to leave once upon a time. If she didn't have that job, well . . . again, things might be different. But she *did* have it. She'd worked to get it back and had succeeded.

And as for her and Mike, well . . . neither of them had ever even uttered the word *love*. Which was just as well—

because it was something she knew nothing about. And what about Mike's sexcapades all over Destiny and Crestview? From the start, she'd understood that he was just as big on not getting serious as she was. She cared for him, too much now, and she believed he cared for her as well—but she simply couldn't get caught up in a moment here and believe it was more than it was. The fact was—Mike could move on from her in a heartbeat. The practical woman inside Rachel could easily see herself a few months from now, broke and lonely and stuck at the orchard picking apples for the rest of her days if she made some silly, hasty decision here. That was *not* what she wanted her life to be.

Finally, she said, "I'm gonna miss you, miss *us*, but you know I have to go."

When he began to protest, she touched a finger to his lips, quieting him.

"And it's for more than just my family. It's for me. I have a life somewhere else. It's a good life, Mike, I promise."

"I'm sure it is," he said, but he sounded sullen now, distant.

She drew in a breath, a little hurt by his attitude. So she tried to win him back over, make him celebrate with her a bit. "I forgot to tell you, I get to keep my job. I found out a couple of days ago. I couldn't be more excited."

He met her gaze, but still seemed disgruntled. "Congratulations. I'm happy for you."

She just sighed and tried to go on. "You don't *sound* very happy. But I'm sure you can see it only makes sense. It would be crazy to leave something I've worked so hard for."

"And *you* don't sound very excited. I mean, this job is supposed to mean everything to you, and you're just now remembering to mention it?"

He might have a point there, but she refused to think about that right now. "Are you mad? You seem mad."

"What would I be mad about?" he snapped.

She tried to lighten the mood. "I don't know. Especially since I just told you, again, that you can pretty much have the orchard whenever Edna decides to sell it to you. And she will. And I'll be fine with that now. I'll be happy for you to have it."

He let out a breath—and sounded a little more relaxed when he said, "Sorry if I'm acting like an asshole."

She smiled. "I'm used to it."

And he returned the grin, even if it looked halfhearted. "Listen—I have to work tomorrow night, and I work Monday from noon to eight, but . . . if you don't have plans with Edna or your friends for your last night in town . . ."

"I don't," she assured him. "I think Edna wants to make me a nice home-cooked dinner, but after that, I'm free."

"Then why don't you come over to my place, meet me when I get off work."

"Sounds good," she said—then glanced over at him. "Did you have anything special in mind?"

"Yep," he said. "Taking you to bed. Making you pant and scream. Doing it all night long. Leaving you so limp from orgasm after orgasm that you can barely move."

Rachel simply sucked in her breath. "All righty then. It's a date."

After he got off duty on Sunday night, Mike went home, changed clothes, and headed back out in his truck. It was nearly midnight and he needed to be back on duty tomorrow at noon, but he felt . . . pent up inside. Trying to sleep would be futile.

The road led him to the Dew Drop Inn. Given that most people had work tomorrow morning, it didn't surprise him that only a few cars and pickups dotted the parking lot. So it caught him off guard when he walked in to see Logan sitting at the bar chatting with Anita Garey.

"Dude, you look mad," Logan said as Mike climbed up

on a stool beside him and motioned to Anita for a beer. "What's wrong? Purple Mustang again?"

"No, thank God," he muttered. "What are you doing here at this hour anyway?"

"I went with Sue Ann to look at the cottage on the lake, and we came here afterward to go over the contract—so I just stuck around."

"You're definitely taking it?" Ever since moving out of his parents' house, just up the road from Mike's place, Logan had lived in an apartment in town.

Logan tipped his bottle to his mouth and gave a nod. "It's a nice little house, and I wouldn't mind having a yard."

"Mmm," Mike said—but knew it came out more like a growl. One thing he'd never developed a skill for—hiding his moods. He was only lucky Logan continued to tolerate him.

Anita brought his beer and the two guys sat quietly for a moment, until Logan gave him a speculative look and slowly said, "Ah, I got it now."

"Got *what* now?"

"What your problem is. Rachel leaves in a couple days, doesn't she? Sue Ann mentioned it. That's what's got you back in your usual shitty mood."

Mike considered denying it, but decided not to bother. So he just said, "Whatever," and took a long drink of his beer.

"You should ask her to stay," Logan said. Just like that. They hadn't discussed Rachel all that much, so Mike had no idea how his buddy understood his feelings on this, but he guessed Logan just knew him that well.

"She's not into it," Mike said simply.

"You talked about it?"

"More or less."

"Sorry, dude," Logan said.

Something about that made his stomach pinch—he

hated when people felt sorry for him. "Nothing to be sorry for," he groused. "Life goes on." Then he dug out his wallet, slapped a five on the bar, and stood up.

Logan raised his gaze to Mike's. "You just got here."

"And now I'm leaving."

Logan arched a brow. "Something I said?"

"Just ready to go home now is all."

He *wasn't* particularly, but he'd also just figured out that he wasn't in the mood to be with people right now, either.

Back in his truck, he headed toward home—because apparently there was *no* place he wanted to be right now, nothing that would make him feel better. Ben Harper sang "Show Me a Little Shame" over his iPod as he tried to figure out what the hell was going on inside him. Logan was right—it was about Rachel. But how had he gone from thinking she was nothing but a pretty, smart-ass Farris to feeling miserable at the thought of no longer having her in his life? How had he—who never got hung up on a woman—gotten so damn hung up on a woman?

And then it hit him, plain as day. In Rachel Farris, he'd finally met his match. In fact, the reason they'd butted heads in the beginning was because, unlike most people around here, she didn't put up with his grouchiness and meanness. The fact was, as a cop, he could usually get away with it; most people, he guessed, were afraid they'd get hauled to jail or something if they argued with him. But from the start, she'd clearly had no intention of letting him scare her or push her around.

And he *liked* that. Turned out he liked it far more than he could have imagined.

And maybe he *was* a little mad at her. For not seeing . . . *what*?

How good they were together?

Or maybe he was mad at *himself* for not having the guts to just say what he felt, straight out. That this was bigger

than something that lasted only a few weeks. That he'd
never experienced these kinds of emotions for another
girl. That he'd already lost enough people in his life, and
even though he hadn't known her long, well . . . this was
going to feel like one more person he'd made the mistake
of caring for only to watch them walk away. And hell—
maybe he had no one to blame but himself, since he'd
broken his own rule: He'd let himself care for her.

Or maybe he was mad that when he *tried* to start telling
her some of that stuff, she gave him *nothing*, no encouragement. He didn't know how to say any of it, and every
time he even inched near it, she shut him down. He knew
when he looked into her eyes, when he was inside her, that
she felt something for him, but she obviously didn't feel
the same way *he* did. She'd even admitted she cared for
him that first night he'd taken her home with him—but
she'd never said anything like that again.

Okay, so that was why he was mad. All of that.

And . . . because she was leaving.

And because there was a part of him that had felt *better*
lately—almost actually . . . happy. She'd sort of . . . awak-
ened pieces of him that . . . well, pieces he guessed had
been dead for a very long time. She made him let go of all
the bad stuff long enough to enjoy life for a change.

But maybe when Rachel left, he'd feel worse again.
Empty inside again. Maybe that picture of Anna would
come back out. Maybe he'd turn back into the same hard-
ass jerk most people thought he was.

The truth was, when he'd suggested getting together on
her last night in town, he'd wanted to do way more than
take her to bed. He'd wanted to talk, he'd wanted to maybe
take her out somewhere nice in Crestview—he'd just
wanted to be with her, both *in* bed and *out*. But after their
conversation in the orchard, it had just made more sense
to invite her over for sex. Because when all was said and
done, that was still when they got along the best, wasn't

it? Anything else they could discuss now might just piss him off and ruin the night. Like her leaving. Somehow even getting her blessing to buy the orchard had pissed him off a little. He didn't *want* her to want him to have it—he wanted her to want it for herself. He wanted her to want to be *here*, close to him. He wanted her to see how good it could be. He just wanted her to stay, damn it.

Was that selfish? Maybe. As she kept telling him, she had a life in Chicago. But it had been a long time since she'd convinced him it really made her happy. In the beginning, maybe. Yet this place had changed her, softened her, in a good way, and whenever she talked about Chicago now, it sounded forced, like old words that had lost their meaning. And he'd *seen* her be happy here—with Edna, with her friends, with him.

Just ask her. Ask her to stay, straight out. Could he? Should he?

Hell, *hadn't* he already? And been shot down?

Maybe he was a stubborn SOB, but he didn't think he could put himself out there with her any more than he already had. He'd already given her so much more of himself than he'd ever thought he'd give to *any* woman. He'd told her about Anna, for God's sake. He'd told her about the rest of his family. He'd even taken her to meet them.

To give her any more, when she didn't seem to want it, would just be . . . fucking humiliating. Emasculating.

As he pulled into his driveway, he realized his throat was tight, swollen. His eyes hurt a little. He crushed them shut, trying to hold back his emotions. Throwing the truck into park, he banged his hand on the steering wheel.

There was a part of him that wondered if he should even see her again. If it wouldn't just end up hurting more than it helped. He couldn't imagine *not* seeing her one last time, but . . . hell, he just didn't know the answers with her anymore. Maybe he never had. And maybe that was the problem.

As he unlocked his front door and stepped into the house, he somehow felt way more alone than he ever had before he'd met Rachel Farris.

On Monday, Rachel had lunch with the girls at Dolly's. It was a beautiful, warm, sunny day, and they were able to sit outside. Tessa said she'd heard a cold snap was coming tomorrow and this would probably be the end of nice weather for the year—and Amy had burst into tears.

Everyone had just looked at her, and Jenny had dug in her purse for a tissue, until Amy said, "It's not the weather. It's that Rachel's leaving."

And somehow Rachel had felt like a slug for making her cry.

In the end, hugs were exchanged and *everyone* cried a little—well, everyone except Rachel, since she never cried. Other than that one time with Mike. But she had to bite her lip and sniff a little as she walked to her car afterward.

After that, she went home to pack her suitcases, the sadness sticking with her more than she liked. She realized she'd become accustomed to Edna's clawfoot bathtub and the old porcelain sink. And over time, she'd come to think of the old quilt on the guest bed as quaint and cozy rather than just outdated. She'd found that, for two strong-willed women, she and Edna had shared the little house quite amicably.

Now she'd dressed for her date with Mike in dark jeans and black boots, and a stylish red wraparound blouse. Underneath, she sported a sexy black demi bra and a pair of matching lace panties. And somehow she felt more like her old self—no more T-shirts and gym shoes.

"Come and get it," Edna called from the dining room, and Rachel walked in to see the table covered with food: breaded pork chops, mashed potatoes and gravy, green beans, homemade corn bread, and the last of Edna's apple pies she'd get to eat for awhile.

"This looks great," she said.

Edna sounded a little put out, a little depressed, as she replied, "Well, it's your last meal here. Wanted it to be a good one. God only knows what kind of crap you eat when I'm not around to feed ya."

Rachel tried to smile, but it was difficult. Leaving Edna, it turned out, was going to be harder than she'd thought.

After they'd both filled their plates and Rachel was cutting into her pork chop, she felt like there was an obvious topic to cover, so if her grandmother wasn't going to bring it up, she would. "Well, this is it, Edna. Are you gonna tell me about Giovanni coming back or not?"

It was June, a year after she'd first come to Destiny, that Edna peeked out the window one day to see Giovanni's turquoise Cadillac come rolling across the bridge as cool and leisurely as if he'd left just a few hours ago. Her heart nearly stopped beating. And she realized that somewhere along the way, she'd begun to believe he might really never come back. But suddenly he was here.

Except for those few moments of passion with Eddie, she'd stayed true to Giovanni, no matter how agonizing it was. She'd reminded herself over and over of Giovanni's promises to her, and that she was always his number one. She'd kept her distance from Eddie as much as possible, because being around him without being close to him only tortured them both. But then again, not being around him was just another kind of torture.

Edna took a deep breath, then ran out the door to greet her fiancé. Oh Lord, he was still just as handsome. And his smile just as winning, intoxicating on sight.

"Edna, my fiore," he greeted her as she ran into his embrace. It felt good yet strange to be back in his arms.

Because of all the distance that had stretched between them now for so long—the kind you could measure, but also the kind you couldn't.

Finally, she pulled back and said, "Your mother?"

His smile faded—he looked sad but acceptant. "She is gone."

"I'm sorry."

He nodded somberly, but then his expression brightened. "However, as I had hoped, I convinced the rest of my family to come to America. They will arrive by summer's end."

They talked a few moments more until Giovanni said, "Now, your brothers—are they well? Everything has run smoothly here?"

"Yes, and yes," she assured him. "They're in the back field with Eddie right now, tendin' the cattle."

"And you, my dear—how are you? You have missed me, yes?"

For some reason, Edna's throat nearly closed up at the questions. Both were . . . complicated. "I missed you somethin' awful. And, well . . . you know I was sick in the winter."

He nodded. "You told me in your letters."

"The doctor was afraid I would die," she said.

And it helped a little when Giovanni's handsome face went grim. "Die?" He blinked rapidly, closing his hands over her shoulders. "I . . . did not realize."

The memories still shook her, as well. "It was . . . terrible. And scary. I wished you were here."

Giovanni pulled in his breath. "I am sorry for that, my fiore." Then he smiled. "But you are well now and it is in the past. We can look to our future."

Something in Edna deflated. His concern seemed genuine, but his willingness to brush it aside after just a few seconds made her feel . . . small. Like the darkest time of her life meant nothing to him. He didn't care how she'd suffered. He didn't care how much she'd ached for him to comfort her.

"What is wrong?" he asked.

It was all so confusing now.

She'd had every intention of marrying Giovanni when he came back, every intention of forgetting her feelings for Eddie. But somehow, Giovanni's long absence had made things between them feel . . . empty. And she began to realize that . . . maybe she couldn't forgive him. For not being here when she needed him. Even if it wasn't his fault. He hadn't been here. And Eddie had.

And in her heart, she knew if they stood any chance at all, she couldn't keep secrets from him, like about how hurt she felt right now. And . . . even about Eddie.

She had to tell him—she had to just spit it out and not stop or it would weigh her down and make her even more miserable than she already was. "When I was sick," she began, "Eddie took care of me."

"Eddie, our farmhand?"

She nodded. And then she rushed ahead. With all of it. She laid her soul bare. She told him Eddie had fallen in love with her, and that before it was over, she'd developed feelings for him, too.

By the time she finished, Giovanni looked crestfallen. "You . . . love him?"

She could barely breathe. Just tell him. Be honest. It's all you can do. "I'm afraid I do. But I love you, too—I swear it! And it's tearin' me to pieces."

It was then that Giovanni's face changed—from shock and confusion . . . to something simply sad but resolute. "This . . . is unacceptable."

Edna tried to swallow past the lump in her throat and no words came.

"Did you think it would be? That I would accept this? A woman who loves another?" Then Giovanni pointed toward the bridge, his eyes downcast. "You must go, Edna."

"Go?" She sucked in her breath.

His brow knit and sorrow laced his voice. *"Do you think I am stupid? I have my pride. I will not play the fool to a woman, ever. Pack your things."*

Oh Lord. She shouldn't have told him about Eddie. At least not so soon; she shouldn't have just blurted it out. Yet she'd had to or she would have burst. And she'd known it would hurt him, yet . . . she'd never imagined this. *"But what about . . . us?"*

He drew back as if she were crazy. *"Us? There is no us. You destroyed us. You betrayed me."*

"But Eddie and me, we never . . . we never . . ." She looked down, shamed, yet then lifted her gaze back to his. *"I stayed true to you, Giovanni, 'cause I love you. And maybe I said all this too fast, too soon, but I thought I should be honest. I still wanna marry you."* Or she'd thought she had before he'd ordered her off the farm. She'd felt she should honor her commitment, try to move past the things that had come between them while he was away.

"You would expect me to marry you now?"

She drew in her breath. *"I thought we could . . . work through it. And I thought . . . what with you bein' gone so long and all, that you'd at least try to understand."*

Giovanni looked at her for a long while, his expression still desolate—and still unrelenting. *"You are not the girl I thought you were. Innocent, sweet, obedient. Someone who would stand by me no matter what. I was wrong about all of that. And after I chose* you.*"*

Edna blinked. *"Chose me? What do you mean?"*

It was only now that his eyes turned colder, harder. *"Have you any idea how many women desire me? And I chose* you. *Even back in Italy, there were beautiful women everywhere. And I chose* you. *Even when I found out one of them was carrying my child, I chose* you. *I returned ready to marry you because I loved you above all of them. I was willing to give up my child for you."*

Edna feared she might faint. Was she hearing all this right? "You're sayin' you've . . . been with other girls while you were engaged to me? That you got another girl pregnant *while you were engaged to me?*"

She watched, stunned, as Giovanni raked his hand through the air, as if it were nothing. "The pregnancy, that was a mistake. I was not careful enough."

"That's not the point! You had sex with another girl! Lots *of other girls, it sounds like!*"

But again, he played it off as being trivial. "It is nothing. It is what men do. I did not love them. I always planned to marry *you.*"

Edna had never been more taken aback, or more outraged, in her life. He'd . . . thought she was so *innocent that she'd let him have affairs on the side! She'd been his number one, but not his* only *one.* "You think I'd put up with that? You think I'd wanna marry some two-timin', cheatin' bastard?" *She might love Eddie, but her feelings for Giovanni had been just as strong, and she'd never been more wounded. Her hands curled into fists, which she pounded into his chest, shoving him a step back.* "And to think I pushed Eddie away for you!"

"And now you will go off with your hayseed farmer and live a life of poverty, when you could have had all this, with me." *He motioned around him to the farm, his jaw now set in anger.* "You are a stupid girl. But no matter. Carlotta will be happy to come to Destiny and live the life you could have had, and then you will see how foolish you are."

The man was . . . unbelievable. He belittled her for having feelings for another man, yet he thought it was nothing to sleep with God knew how many other girls!

And then it hit her—the telegram. From Italy. And the note on the back.

And as the next words left her, something deep inside Edna changed, darkened, hardened. She stood up a little straighter. "No. You gave the farm to me. As a promise."

"A promise that I would marry you. Which I was will-
ing to do. Until just a few moments ago."

"You also promised to be faithful to me," she pointed
out, sure, stalwart.

"Well, that silly note is not legal—you must know that,
you foolish country girl."

"Quit calling me foolish," she snapped. "We'll see
who's the foolish one here."

And then Edna silently made a promise—to herself:
that she would never again allow anyone to hurt her,
push her around, or break her heart.

Rachel was aghast. She'd long since forgotten her dinner.
"What then?"

"Well, Giovanni was convinced it wouldn't hold up in
court. And he brought Carlotta over and married her and
moved her into the house here. Dell and Wally went home
to Kentucky, but I stayed with Eddie—I married him, in
fact.

"Only that's when old Giovanni got himself a surprise.
Carlotta's pregnancy *proved* he hadn't been faithful to
me, and what he wrote on the back of that telegram *did*
hold up in the local court. That's right, I pursued it. I took
the orchard from him because he wronged me. Him and
Carlotta bought the farm where she still lives today, but
losin' the orchard left him to start out with nothin'. In the
meantime, your Grandpa Edward and me made a home
here for many a happy year. It was him who decided we
should plant the whole property with apples, in fact. And
that," she said, "is the end of my story."

Rachel just let out a breath. Whoa. "That's some freaking story, Edna."

Edna just gave a succinct nod. "Told ya back when I
started it was a good one."

Rachel's mind swirled. "So this baby Carlotta was

carrying—and that Giovanni was willing to give up— that was Mike's father?" She couldn't help wincing at the last part.

Her grandmother nodded again. "But reckon that's why I don't tell the story. I've held a long grudge against the Romos, but I figured there wasn't no reason to tell anybody about that. It's just too hurtful a thing."

"Indeed," Rachel agreed, horrified.

"Somethin' you should know, though. For what it's worth, I believe Giovanni truly did love me—in his twisted way. Some men, back then, really believed that kinda double standard was okay, a man's right. And I also believe Giovanni really loved Carlotta and their children. As far as I know, he never cheated on her after they married. Fatherhood seemed to settle him down. That's another reason I saw no need to tell folks about his wanderin' eye—and penis."

"You know," Rachel said, unable not to voice the thought, "if you *had* told the whole story, the rest of the Romo clan might have understood why you took the orchard. It might have avoided this whole family feud thing."

Edna just shrugged. "Figured it was easier to let 'em hate me, and for me to just hate 'em back, than to let 'em know what a snake their beloved Giovanni was. Figure it's easier to hate a stranger than to hate your father or your grandpa."

"Wow," Rachel replied, seeing her grandma in a whole new light. "That was . . . big of you, Edna."

But her grandmother only shrugged again. "Maybe, maybe not. Giovanni changed somethin' in me that day he came back. I ain't never been the same since. Lost my innocence, I guess. Believe it or not, I was a shy, sweet girl before that."

They both laughed at the very idea of Edna being sweet, or shy, but Rachel believed it. The old pictures of

Edna on the piano gave away the truth about who she'd once been.

"I'll tell ya one more thing," Edna said, pointing her fork at Rachel before scooping up some potatoes from her plate. "You're makin' a mistake leavin' Mike."

Sheesh—double whoa! "What? First of all, I'm not *leaving* Mike. He and I are just . . . you know, a casual fling, as I've made very clear all along. And besides, you just told me the Romo you once loved *cheated* on you— and you think I should want one of my own?"

Edna merely shook her head. "You're missin' the point, darlin'."

"Then enlighten me."

"The fact is, it's a toss-up whether it was right or wrong of me to keep the orchard—it all depends on how ya look at such things. I was angry and hurt, and when I realized that piece of paper was the only bit of power I might ever have in this world, I used it to strike back at him. But the older I get, the more I think Giovanni's family had a right to their legacy—they shouldn't have lost somethin' just because he was a jackass. And I shouldn't have taught my family to judge all Romos by the actions of one. And I shouldn't have taught you all to look at the whole world in such a harsh way."

Rachel let out an exasperated sigh. Good God, how many times did she have to explain this? "Edna, this has nothing to do with how I look at the world." Or she didn't think it did anyway. "I'm leaving because I have a life somewhere else. And because I'm proud of what I've built. And because . . ."

"Because what?"

Should she tell Edna the rest, which had almost just come spilling out of her? Oh hell, maybe she should just get it on the table once and for all. Given what a staunch believer Edna was in family, maybe she would under-stand and even respect Rachel for it. "Because . . . the truth is, I've just come through a big scare where I almost lost my job due to downsizing. But I just found out I get to keep it, and it's a huge relief because . . . well, you know Mom and Dad and Noah aren't exactly great with money, even when they have some. But I *am*. So if they—or, say, you—ever need it, I'll have it."

Edna just looked at her for a long moment, her face grave. Finally, she said, "Rachel, that ain't your responsibility."

She met Edna's gaze. "But it's my worry." She swallowed, then went on. "I mean, I worry, you know? And you should be glad I do, because to be honest, worry is the only thing that's kept me *here* this long. Worry over your knees and . . . " She looked Edna in the eye and finally just asked her. "Tell me the truth. Did you really hurt your knees? Or was that just a ploy to get me here, to spend time with me?"

Edna made a disgruntled face. "Of course I hurt my dang knees. Ain't you seen the way I been hobblin' around here? You think I move slow as Christmas for fun?"

"Well—there is some belief in the family that you . . . make up stories about your health just to get us to come see you."

Edna gave her head a matter-of-fact tilt. "If it worked out that way a few times, who am I to complain? But yes, darlin', I *really* hurt my knees. Tripped over a dang rake in the yard and they ain't been the same since. And if I'd known about this job scare of yours, I woulda called on somebody else. Figured you'd tell a person if you really couldn't come."

Rachel just sighed. It was true. From the very beginning, she'd had that option and she hadn't taken it. "I guess I have a soft spot for you, old woman."

Edna pursed her lips. "Guess it's perty clear I got the same for you, too." The room went quiet but for the ticking of the old grandfather clock in one corner—until

Edna went on, full steam ahead. "But back to this business about you thinkin' you need to provide for the whole damn Farris clan, well . . . you listen to me, and you listen good. If that's the only reason you're leavin' Mike Romo here, it's a damn foolish one." Then she was back to pointing her fork at Rachel again. "The other point of my story is that a girl's lucky to find a good, honest, lovin' man. By the time my engagement to Giovanni ended, I was hurt more than I knew I *could* be, and I realized exactly how fortunate I was to find such a good man in Edward. And you've found just as good a man, in my opinion, in Mike. And I've seen the way ya look at him, and I know there's more in your heart than you'll admit, even to yourself."

Rachel let out a breath. Then swallowed. She didn't deny anything. Somehow, at the moment, she couldn't. Edna had always been so good at seeing inside her.

But that still didn't change the situation. "Okay, so he's good, and honest. As for loving, though, I don't know. He's never said anything about loving me."

However, at this, Edna just shrugged. Like it was nothing. "Men. They're idiots that way. Don't mean they don't feel it."

"Doesn't mean they do, either."

"Then maybe you oughta tell him first and see what happens."

"Tell him what?" Rachel asked.

"That ya love him, you silly girl."

Rachel just blinked, her stomach churning. "Well—I don't know that I do. I mean, I've never . . . felt that for anyone. And besides, we live seven hours apart and I don't see him moving to Chicago or me moving back to Destiny any time soon."

Edna pinned her in place with a glare. "Are you tellin' me—*truthfully*—you couldn't be happy in this town if Mike wanted to build a life with you here?"

Whoa. *If Mike wanted to build a life with her here?* It

was hard to fathom. Kind of. And she suddenly felt the words in her gut. The possibility. And . . . oh Lord. The shocking truth was—maybe, just maybe, it would change everything inside her if it were really true.

But again—why should she think he wanted that? He'd never said so. Again, if she'd lost her job, maybe she'd be willing to . . . wait, to see what happened with Mike. But it was a hell of a lot to risk on a man who'd plainly told her he didn't fall in love. They'd only known each other for six short weeks.

So she simply replied, "I don't know. It's a complicated question. And, thankfully, one it doesn't look like I'll have to answer since *he's* never asked it."

Looking tired now, Edna just shook her head. "Ya know, you can lead a horse to water, but ya can't make it drink. If you can't see what's starin' you right in the face, then there's nothin' more I can do. I do believe you and Mike might be the two most stubborn people I've ever met."

Rachel sat outside Mike's house in her car, waiting for him to get home. But he was late. And that was giving her too much time to think. The outcome of Edna's story still blew her mind—she'd never once imagined Giovanni was cheating! And it saddened her to realize how deeply the affair with Giovanni had affected Edna, in lifelong ways. But more than that, Rachel's focus wandered to all the stuff Edna had said about her and Mike, like they were some kind of star-crossed lovers or something.

Checking her watch, she saw he was more than twenty minutes late. *Wherefore art thou, Officer Romeo?*

And in the meantime . . . was Edna right? Could she really be in love with Mike? Was he really as good and true as Edna thought? Truer than Giovanni? Was she somehow really meant to stay here, in Destiny?

And could she truly let go of the vow, the capability, to provide for her family if needed? How would it feel to give up her job, the thing that so defined her in her own mind? And would it *be* like that, like giving something up, or might it somehow be . . . maybe *freeing* just to let it all go?

The questions were so big they almost overwhelmed her.

Because . . . maybe, just maybe there was some part of her that . . . wanted that. Every day with Mike. Time with Edna, and the girls. A simpler, quieter life. A life that revolved not around money or working but around . . . love. A whole different kind of security than a person could ever get from a job. And maybe even a type of happiness you couldn't reap from any career.

But as another ten minutes passed, she started to get pissed, thinking more about the fact that he was standing her up than whether she should stay in Destiny. God, *was* he? Standing her up? That wasn't like him, but then . . . Edna had never thought it was like Giovanni to be gallivanting all over Italy, either. And she'd only known Mike a short time, hardly long enough to be certain whether something *was* or *wasn't* like him.

The later the hour grew, the more angry Rachel became. Her stomach churned. How dare he? It was bad enough to be stood up—much worse to be stood up at a guy's *own house*. After all, how hard was it to just come home? Where else did he have to be?

A lump grew in her throat. He really wasn't going to show. Because of the weird tension she'd felt between them the other night? Or just because something better had come up and making her mad didn't matter since she was leaving tomorrow anyway?

Shit, it hurt. She didn't like to admit that—she'd been back to being strong, tough Rachel—but it just plain hurt. Pretty damn bad.

Hell. She didn't have to take this. She didn't have to sit here feeling wounded and disregarded and embarrassed.

And to think, just a little while ago, she'd honestly been wondering if Edna was right and she should say those three little words to Mike. *I love you.* She still didn't feel like an authority on the subject, but the fact was, she'd begun to wonder if it was true, if she'd actually fallen in love with the big lug.

But that didn't matter now. He didn't even care enough about her to show up.

Well, she'd had it with this. Her bags were already packed and sitting by Edna's front door. And she didn't have to wait until tomorrow to leave. She could just leave now. Tonight.

Starting the car, she turned around in Mike's wide gravel driveway, tossing a little of it up when she peeled out onto the road. She was heading back to Edna's to get her bags. And then she was getting the hell out of Destiny once and for all.

Mike drove toward his house, still fighting mixed emotions.

Should he ask her to stay? What would she say? Would she take him seriously or brush it off without really considering the gravity of the question? And hell—was he ready for such a big commitment anyway?

The only thing he knew for sure was that he was running late—because there had been a part of him that, like last night, almost didn't want to see her again. It was hard knowing it would be the last time, and the truth was, he didn't want to say goodbye.

But then he'd pulled himself together and gotten in the car to head home. Because come what may, he *had* to see her again. He *had* to. Because . . . he was pretty damn sure now that he was in love with the woman.

Just then, an Amber Alert came over his radio from dispatch. A little girl with blonde hair and blue eyes had just been abducted from her home north of Chillicothe *in*

a late-model purple Mustang believed to be stolen from a
Cleveland suburb. Holy shit.

The abductor was believed to be Ronald Maitland, who
had recently done repair work at the family's home. He
had two previous convictions for sexual abuse of a minor
and a long record of misdemeanors like petty theft and
various traffic violations. Authorities were uncertain
where Maitland might be heading.

And Mike didn't know where he was heading, either—
but he thought he knew the road the asshole would take
to get there. All his senses went on red alert. The son of
a bitch had been going on practice runs. Down country
roads. To stay off the main roads and interstates.

Mike was already on Meadowview Highway—it led
to his house. And no matter how fast Maitland drove, he
couldn't be here yet. But soon probably.

As Mike found a spot to wait, he called dispatch and told
them what he suspected, instructing them to alert all surrounding municipalities that the car had been seen speeding through this area twice in the past six weeks. He even
asked for a roadblock to be set up at a rural intersection a
few miles down the road, ASAP. He wished he could call
Rachel to let her know he'd be later than he already was,
but there was no signal here, so he'd just have to make her
understand afterward how important this was.

And that's when he spotted it—that damn Mustang!
It was headed right toward him, just like he'd known it
would be the moment he'd heard the Amber Alert. He'd
be damned if Ronald Maitland got away from him this
time.

As usual, the car was flying—so fast that Mike automatically feared for the child's safety above and beyond
the abduction. The second it passed, Mike gave chase,
siren blaring, blue lights cutting through the dusky night
air. He kept up, on every damn twist and turn, cussing the
guy all the way.

And then the unexpected happened. The Mustang started to lose control.

Mike used his brakes to keep from hitting the other car, and he prayed the guy would get command over the vehicle and not kill the little girl. The Mustang slid off the road onto the flat land running alongside this particular stretch, and Maitland struggled to get the car back on the pavement. But he'd been forced to slow down—a lot, so Mike pulled alongside him to prevent him from re-entering the highway. Both cars still went around sixty, but the Mustang would soon have to stop because a large tree grew directly in its path just ahead, and with Mike boxing him in, the landscape prevented driving around it.

Finally, the Mustang braked to a halt. A good twenty yards from the tree—Maitland had seen the inevitable coming, Mike guessed. His heart hammered in his chest as he radioed for backup, bringing his own car to a stop, as well, flanking the Mustang's rear fender. And he would have liked to *wait* for that backup, but he had a feeling if he did, Maitland would get away. And he couldn't have that. He had to act now.

Through a speaker in his cruiser, Mike instructed Maitland, "Stay in your car."

As he cautiously exited his own, gun drawn and tazer at the ready, he spotted the little girl in the backseat crying—and their eyes met through the back window. Oh God, she looked so scared. All he wanted in the world was to save her. All he wanted was to promise her everything would be all right.

And his heart broke as he thought of Anna. Whom he'd failed to save. And the memory stole his thoughts . . . for one crucial heartbeat.

He saw the barrel of the semi-automatic weapon jutting from the driver's side window for only a split second before everything went black.

Give me my Romeo.

William Shakespeare, *Romeo & Juliet*

Eighteen

As Rachel sped around a bend in the road, the blue glow suddenly filtering the dusky air caught her off guard, making her slow down. Squinting to peer up the highway, she realized it was coming from a cop car, stopped up ahead.

She braked further as she approached, and then she saw—oh, dear God—a body in the road. Lying there. Still.

Lord, was that blood? Every muscle in her body tensed as she drew closer, horrified, petrified.

And then . . . oh, shit. Was it—was it . . . ?

God, no—it was Mike!

No! No no no no no.

This couldn't be happening! It couldn't be real! "*Mike!*" she screeched, slamming on her brakes and jumping out of the car.

As she ran to him, she heard herself screaming, "Nooooo!" Her legs went numb beneath her, yet she kept moving, racing toward where he lay stretched out on the pavement, eyes closed, the pool of blood surrounding his head growing, spreading. Oh God! *Oh God!*

Without thinking, she dropped to her knees. Her whole body shook and her heart threatened to crumble in her chest. "Mike! Oh God, Mike!"

She grew vaguely aware of tears streaming down her face as she bent over him, pressing her hands to his chest. *Please don't be dead! Please, please, please.* But—oh! His heart was beating! *Thank you, God!* It was as if the very knowledge breathed fresh life into her.

Only—what now? She already knew her cell phone didn't get a signal here, damn it. Yet—Mike's police radio was right in his car. She was just about to run to it, to try to figure out how to work it, when she heard sirens in the distance, growing rapidly closer.

"Thank God—they're coming," she told him anxiously, even though he was unconscious. "Help's on the way." Her breath ragged with fear, she touched his heart again, just to ensure them both he was still alive. "It's gonna be okay, I promise," she whispered. "Because it has to be."

But God, there was so much blood! Too much! A body shouldn't lose that much blood. What if he . . . what if he . . . ?

Oh God, no. Just . . . no. He couldn't die—he couldn't.

More tears fell—she had to wipe them away to see. She simply kept stroking his chest with her hand, feeling the warmth of his flesh, feeling the very strength of him—praying that strength was enough to carry him through. "Please don't die, Mike," she sobbed. "Please don't die. I love you."

Rachel sat in the hospital room, watching Mike sleep.

He was going to be okay. *Thank you, thank you, thank you, God.* She'd been thanking God for an hour now, every time something went right or she got a piece of good news. In times like these, she figured you couldn't be too thankful.

Logan was outside in the hall making calls—to Mike's parents, to Grandma Romo, to Chief Tolliver—and Edna was with him. But both had left her alone with Mike for now, and the longer she sat there, the more she realized what a blind, in-denial idiot she'd been.

In response to the thought, more tears fell. That had continued happening for the past hour, too—every few minutes she started up again. *Damn it—you managed not to cry for all these years, and now you can't seem to turn it off.*

So it had turned out that Mike was the only thing in the world that could make her cry—whether it was because the sex with him made her feel so complete, or because she was scared to death he was going to die. Or maybe it was also because of the startling revelation consuming her now: He was *the one.* The man for her. The man she couldn't live without. The man she could love forever. She, who'd never even *wanted* that. And now she supposed she was crying because she'd been such a fool, and because she'd been so afraid she would lose him when she'd seen all that blood, and—Lord, it was just a lot to take all at once.

When his eyes fluttered open, she jumped to her feet. "You're awake!" Oh, it was so good to look into those beautiful eyes, still so warm and brown.

"You're here," he said softly.

She stepped up to the bed and took his hand, careful not to jar his IV. "Of course I'm here."

He blinked, looking around a little, seeming to get his bearings. "Did they get the girl back?"

Of all the things he could ask, that was the first question. Edna was right—he was such a good man. "The state police managed to stop him at the roadblock you ordered. The little girl is safe and sound."

He breathed a visible sigh of relief. "Thank God."

"And you're gonna be okay," she informed him. "There was a lot of blood, but turned out the bullet just nicked your shoulder." The memory of that blood made tears well behind her eyes again, but she tried to hold them back. Still, her next words came out between shaky, gaspy sniffles. "You . . . hit . . . your head . . . on the road . . . too . . . but it's only . . . a bump."

"That would explain why it hurts like a son of a bitch," he said. Then he squinted at her, looking confused. "Are you *crying*?"

"No," she lied, despite that she was clearly sniffing back tears.

He tilted his head on the pillow propped beneath it. "Looks like it."

"Well," she said, "it's been an upsetting evening."

Just then, his face took on an odd, troubled expression and he whispered, "Jesus Christ."

"What?" she asked, worried.

"Do I still have on underwear?"

Okay, maybe it was the pain medication making him ask, but Rachel was about to appease him by peeking under the covers to check—when a plump, cheerful nurse in Hello Kitty scrubs hurried in. "You sure do," the nurse said. "All the girls in the ER really enjoyed 'em, too."

"Hell," he muttered, letting his eyes fall shut.

Rachel waited as the nurse checked Mike's vital signs, told him the doctor would be in soon, and bustled right back out. Then she lifted the edge of Mike's sheets to see what the heck was going on, and—oh God. He had on the leopard print boxers. "You wore them? For me?"

Mike just gave her a look. "Don't make a big thing of it."

But it *was* a big thing. For Mike anyway. And though Rachel had planned on waiting until he felt better to tell him this, she couldn't. She'd already waited too long. And she was pretty sure he hadn't heard her at the crime scene. So she just blurted it out. "I love you!"

His jaw dropped and he simply stared at her—but she didn't care. She had to get this off her chest, once and for all. "The moment I saw you lying in that puddle of blood, I realized that if you died, I'd fall apart, I'd never get over it. I've been a fool not to tell you sooner. And I'm scared to death to be telling you right now, but at the same time, it's all right, because . . . I have way more fears than I ever let most people see, and . . . and you're the man who can help me get past them. You're the man who can take them all away." Wow, what a mouthful. But she'd said it. And it was out there now, no taking it back.

Mike just blinked at her a few times, and she couldn't read his face. Her heart felt like it would beat through her chest. But finally, he said, softly, "Give me your hand," so she did.

Then he looked her in the eye. "I don't know how to say stuff like this, and it might come out better if I waited until I wasn't being pumped full of drugs, but . . . I've been feeling . . . the same way. And when I think of you leaving town . . . aw hell, it makes me feel shitty."

Ah, her charming silver-tongued devil. She just smiled. "Are you asking me to stay, Officer Romeo?"

Mike closed his eyes briefly, then let out a breath. "Damn it, woman," he said, "I'm asking you to marry me. Probably not the way you envisioned it, but it's the best I can do right now."

Oh! Oh God! "Yes," she said. She didn't even need to think about it. Her thoughts had scarcely gotten that far, but the second the words left him, she knew that was what she wanted more than anything in the world. More than her job. More than her old life in Chicago, something that, she realized fully now, *had* truly run its course. She wanted it even more than the financial security she'd clung too for so long. "Yes, yes, yes," she repeated.

He actually looked a little surprised. "Really?"

She nodded, squeezing his hand.

"Ow!" he said.

Damn, the IV. "Sorry." She released her grip. Then got back to the point. "I never thought I wanted to marry *anyone*, Mike, but now I do."

A wary expression took over his face. "Not because I'm lying in a hospital bed in leopard underwear looking pathetic? Because if that's why, I take my proposal back."

She tilted her head and gave him an indulgent smile. "That's not why."

"Then . . . why?"

"Because I like to argue with you. And laugh with you. And flirt with you. And because you make me crazy in bed—and wherever else we do it. And because you're a good man." Just like Edna had said. "A *really* good man. Who I want to run the orchard with. And grow old with. And have lots of sex with as soon as you get well."

Somehow her Officer Romeo still managed to look completely arrogant, even now, as he said, "Get in bed with me, Rachel."

Glancing toward the door to make sure a doctor wasn't about to come rushing in, she carefully pulled back the covers and climbed in next to him. Oh God, it felt so good to be near him again, pressed up against his warmth.

Their faces were but an inch apart on the pillow when Mike said, more tenderly than she'd known he could, "For a guy lying in a hospital bed with a gunshot wound and a bump on his head and embarrassing underwear on . . . hell, I think you just made me happier than I've ever been. I love you, honey."

Mmm. The words melted down through her warm and sweet—the best words any man had ever said to her. Pressing her hand gently to his bare chest, she leaned over for a kiss.

They both moaned lightly as their mouths met, and

Rachel felt it in her chest, and she couldn't help kissing him again, and again. Until he shifted, rubbing against her in such a way that she realized he had a hard-on—even now.

"Holy crap," she said.

"That's right, woman. Even in a hospital bed, after being shot, and under the influence of pain medication, I want you. That's how damn crazy you make me."

My man's as true as steel.

William Shakespeare, *Romeo & Juliet*

Epilogue

Rachel stood with Edna in her kitchen, watching her take an apple pie from the oven. As always, even the mere scent filled the little house with deliciousness.

"Do you think if you gave me lessons," Rachel asked, "I could learn to make apple pie as good as yours?"

Edna patted Rachel's hand where it rested on the counter. "I doubt it," Edna said. "We can give it a whirl, but lucky for you I won't be goin' anywhere for a while."

Winter had passed into spring at the orchard that bore a new sign and a new name: the Farris-Romo Family Apple Orchard. Rachel and Mike hadn't gotten married yet, but revising the sign had just seemed like the thing to do, for many reasons. Besides, Mike was there as much as Rachel these days, to keep both women from doing too much heavy labor. Meanwhile, Rachel had put her creative skills to work on a website, and by the time the fall harvest rolled back around, there would be family activities and cider making on weekends and a small store, featuring a display case with Edna's pies, apple butter, apple sauce, and whatever else Rachel could talk her into whipping up. Edna still wasn't crazy about all the changes, but it was a concession she'd been willing to make in exchange for Rachel and Mike becoming her partners.

And it had finally hit Rachel that if she really wanted to restore pride to the Farris name, well, how better to do it than working together with Edna and Mike to make the old orchard thrive in a whole new way?

As for the wedding, they were waiting until they had time to plan something big—for two reasons. Rachel had decided that if she was actually going to get married, she wanted to do it in a fabulous gown, with her close friends at her side. And she and Mike both thought it would be a good idea—even if daring—to force the entire Farris and Romo clans into the Destiny Church of Christ at the same time. And if it turned out to be the biggest brawl Destiny had ever seen, they'd be able to escape on their honeymoon to Italy and forget all about it.

"Rachelllll!" The back screen door of Edna's house slammed as Mike walked in with a scowl on his face. "I found that damn cat of yours helping himself to my breakfast cereal this morning!"

"Well, I guess you shouldn't leave your cereal around where you know there's a pushy cat." They'd adopted Shakespeare at Rachel's urging—Mike had claimed it qualified as the traditional Romo engagement gift—but so far they hadn't broken any of his bad habits. Yet Rachel didn't mind—she'd discovered she liked having the big fat feline curl up next to her on the sofa at night. As for Mike, she was still trying to win him over on that.

"It's one thing to share my house with *you*, another to have to share it with that dumb cat," he griped.

And Rachel said, "Growl, growl, growl." She really thought Mike *needed* a pet. And she thought she and Shakespeare made a pretty good start on replacing the family he'd all but lost. And she'd once seen him scratch the cat behind the ears when he hadn't known she was watching—she'd learned Mike was often more bark than bite.

"I'll leave you two to hash this out," Edna said. "I'm due to take a couple bushels of apples up to the General Mercantile."

"Need help getting them in the truck?" Mike asked.

"Nope—already there, but thanks." And then she was out the door.

"Listen," he said, watching Edna go, then stepping up to slip his arms around Rachel's waist, "I was thinking about how you could make it up to me, about the cat."

She flashed a tolerant grin upward. "This oughta be good."

"I need to haul some fertilizer out to the McIntosh grove, but I was thinking that first, I could have my way with you. So what do you say, Farris? Can I interest you in a little afternoon delight?"

The man was insatiable. But that worked out okay, because when it came to Mike, so was she. Rachel bit her lip. "I really should work on Edna's books—I'm trying to get everything computerized."

Mike just lowered his chin and cast one of his *get-serious* looks, and she let out a breath. "Okay—you talked me into it." Since her breasts were getting a little tingly and the juncture of her thighs already ached.

"It's nice out," he told her, so she let him lead her out into the orchard. The apple trees were in full spring bloom, their white flowers making the whole place appear to be covered in lace. She wasn't sure she'd ever seen anything so lovely—the sight nearly took her breath away every time she saw it, and made her thankful all over again that she'd looked deep inside her heart and made the right decision. Even if it had taken fearing for Mike's life to wake her up.

Turned out that giving up her job had, in the end, felt more liberating than painful. Rachel had finally figured out that sometimes being a strong, responsible woman meant admitting you wanted something different in your life, something new—and now her life was suddenly richer, fuller, than it had ever been. And as for her worries over her family and money . . . well, she still had plenty saved, but if her family ever really needed a lot, they'd be on their own. Edna was right—it wasn't her responsibility—and she finally understood that. Heck, maybe knowing they wouldn't have her to turn to anymore would make them start being a little more careful.

As for Mike, she'd hoped he might be more at peace about Anna by now, especially after saving another little girl. And that victory had helped—but Rachel had come to understand that Mike would *never* be completely at peace about his sister. All she could do was be there for him, and help him deal with the never-ending sense of loss.

"By the way," he said as they walked deeper into the front grove, near Sugar Creek, "I saw you speeding today."

He'd been on duty until just a little while ago. "And you didn't pull me over?" She was truly stunned. After all, he'd given her a ticket as recently as a few months ago— and even by-the-book Chief Tolliver had been shocked that he'd hand out a citation to his own fiancée.

"Well, you don't go as fast as you used to, so I'm trying to show some leniency."

She smiled up at him. "Wow. Now I *really* know how much you love me."

"But slow the hell down, Rachel," he said, casting a look of warning, "or next time . . ."

"Yeah, yeah," she said, pulling him under a flowering apple tree, taking his hands in hers. "I know—you speed, you pay, we don't tolerate speeders in Destiny, and all that. Got it, Officer Romeo. Now shut up and kiss me."

Unforgettable, enthralling love stories,
sparkling with passion and adventure
from Romance's bestselling authors

At Avon Books, we know your passion for romance—once you finish one of our novels, you find yourself wanting more.

May we tempt you with . . .

- **Excerpts** from our upcoming releases.

- Entertaining **extras**, including authors' personal photo albums and book lists.

- Behind-the-scenes **scoop** on your favorite characters and series.

- **Sweepstakes** for the chance to win free books, romantic getaways, and other fun prizes.

- Writing **tips** from our authors and editors.

- **Blog** with our authors and find out why they love to write romance.

- **Exclusive content** that's not contained within the pages of our novels.

Join us at
www.avonbooks.com

OCT -- 2012

An Imprint of HarperCollins*Publishers*
www.avonromance.com